SHE DEMONS

SHE DEMONS

A Mister Jinnah Mystery

Donald J. Hauka

DUNDURN PRESS
TORONTO

Copyright © Donald J. Hauka, 2010

All rights reserved. No part of this publication may be reproduced, stored in a retrieval system, or transmitted in any form or by any means, electronic, mechanical, photocopying, recording, or otherwise (except for brief passages for purposes of review) without the prior permission of Dundurn Press. Permission to photocopy should be requested from Access Copyright.

Copy Editor: Cheryl Hawley
Design: Jennifer Scott
Printer: Marquis

Library and Archives Canada Cataloguing in Publication

Hauka, Donald J.
 She demons : a Mister Jinnah mystery / by Donald J. Hauka.

(A Castle Street mystery)
Also available in electronic format.
ISBN 978-1-55488-763-7

 I. Title. II. Series: Castle Street mystery

PS8565.A774S54 2010   C813'.6   C2010-902314-5

1 2 3 4 5   14 13 12 11 10

We acknowledge the support of the Canada Council for the Arts and the Ontario Arts Council for our publishing program. We also acknowledge the financial support of the Government of Canada through the Canada Book Fund and The Association for the Export of Canadian Books, and the Government of Ontario through the Ontario Book Publishers Tax Credit program, and the Ontario Media Development Corporation.

Care has been taken to trace the ownership of copyright material used in this book. The author and the publisher welcome any information enabling them to rectify any references or credits in subsequent editions.

J. Kirk Howard, President

Printed and bound in Canada.
www.dundurn.com

Dundurn Press	Gazelle Book Services Limited	Dundurn Press
3 Church Street, Suite 500	White Cross Mills	2250 Military Road
Toronto, Ontario, Canada	High Town, Lancaster, England	Tonawanda, NY
M5E 1M2	LA1 4XS	U.S.A. 14150

To Donatella, who believed.
To Nicolas, who listened and laughed.
And to Saleem, who simply is.
My thanks.

Chapter One

It was the time of Diwali, the festival of light and release, but the corner of Main and Terminal was still a prisoner to darkness. The intersection marks the social fault line that divides the city of Vancouver between east and west, poor and rich. A stone's throw west of the corner the futuristic dome of Science World glitters under its metallic, spiderweb frame, studded with glowing, blue gems. Beyond lays False Creek with its sailboats and little docks: a swimming pool for the privileged whose condos line its banks. On this overcast morning, the waters sat still, sullen, barely rippled in the wind — blue grey in the rain.

To the east, achingly close to this beauty, is The Corner: the wine-soaked, refuse-strewn intersection where the street people scrabble for a slow death. They are Leonard Cohen's children, leaning out for love amid the garbage and flowers, looking for their mother in a bottle, their father in a needle, sucking in forgetfulness, transforming a filthy alley or a bus station washroom cubicle into the shores of Lotophagia.

It is the turf of the squeegee kids. "Kids," they call them, although they can be thirty, or forty, even fifty years old, and look as ancient and gnarled as desert trees. Today, as every day, they were up early to greet the rush hour traffic, stiff limbs and aching muscles moving mechanically, like a medieval clock tower's figures, working to the rhythm of the traffic lights. Green. Hustle the westbound lanes, walk between the lines of cars, looking left, looking right, hoping for the nod or smile of agreement. Amber. Wipe the windshield. Quick, quick. Take the money, try to smile. Red. Cut across the four lanes that run like asphalt veins into the city. Face the east and a fitful, rising sun glimpsed through ragged clouds. Green. Walk down the line of cars, looking left, looking right....

On the east side of Main Street, two young people, a boy and a girl, were waiting for the light to change, watching the squeegee kids weaving through the BMWs, SUVs, and compacts. At a glance you could tell they didn't belong — not yet. Their clothes were too clean, too new. Value Village shoppers by choice, not necessity. The boy, Andy, was excited.

"It's going to be so cool," he said for the hundredth time that morning. "The Magus totally rocks."

The girl, Sam, was slightly older. Teenagers, she thought, but not unkindly. Andy had a gleam in his eyes that lit up his brown, lean face. He was, she considered, an ideal candidate for the task ahead of him,

She Demons 9

at least physically. In his late teens, Andy was well-built. But his mind needed training. The camp would see to that. The camp and Arnie, Sam grinned.

"Focus on what we have to do now," she urged him as they crossed the avenue, the sole pedestrians not out hustling for change. "Service before reward."

"Oh yeah, 'course," said Andy. "Present moment."

On the other side of the street they came to the park in front of the bus station. It was dotted by overgrown maples, aged and diseased, losing their leaves in the late autumn, dropping withered limbs that littered the thinning, ragged lawn. Andy glanced over at them and felt his stomach constrict. Ragged bundles like discarded dolls — the junkies, the winos, the insane — were sprawled under every tree. Condos for the crazies. Nothing in Andy's past had prepared him for this and he was still unused to it. He looked up at Sam, guilty, but her hard, blue eyes were staring to the right. She stopped abruptly.

"Thad? Thad?" she called out.

Andy followed her gaze. In the middle of the park, under the lone oak tree that was its centrepiece, a hooded figure, sitting cross-legged, immovable, like Buddha. Sam started across the lawn towards him.

"You're not going to go over there!" cried Andy, unable to hide the disgust in his voice.

"He's a friend!" Sam snapped, looking carefully at the ground in front of her, scanning for used needles, broken glass, the unidentifiable.

Andy started after Sam, trying hard to evoke the compassion that was at the heart of the Magus's teaching. But it was difficult, looking at this dirty young man dressed in a faded grey kangaroo sweater, face hardly visible, to feel pity or remind himself that this figure contained a spark of the divine within. Sam stood behind Thad now, calling to him as Andy approached.

"Thad. You okay?"

Probably on junk, thought Andy. What was Sam doing associating with a junkie? A frown creased her smooth, white face as she knelt down beside the figure.

"Hey, Thad? Thought you kicked. Weren't workin' this scene anymore."

Silence. Andy stood beside Sam. He was about to politely suggest that they were going to be late if they wasted much more time here when Sam made one last attempt to get through to her friend.

"Thad?"

Sam grabbed the figure by the shoulders and gave him a shake. Thad's head emerged from his hood, tumbled neatly off his shoulders, described a slow ellipse, and landed, staring straight up, in his lap. Andy's eyes were wide, involuntarily taking in every detail of Thad's face, from the flat, lifeless look of his eyes to the horrific cuts tracing his cheeks. Sam was still holding Thad's shoulders, looking down, unbelieving, at the familiar face below. For a moment, there was absolute silence filling Andy's ears: no sound of cars or ghetto blasters. The world revolved around the axis of the tree and The Corner fell away, insignificant, meaningless in the face of this obscenity. Then Sam screamed. The world returned: a world full of angry horns and screaming people. And police cars. Andy, obeying his ancient

She Demons   11

instincts, fled, heedless of the perils underfoot, running, running, running, still carrying the horror before him.

"These are not mere playthings we are selling here, my friend. They are a little girl's dreams."

The dream in question sat cradled tenderly in Hakeem Jinnah's slender brown hands. Nearly two feet tall, she wore a beautiful wedding sari and looked remarkably like a Barbie doll, save that her skin was like coffee and there was a chocolate dot on her forehead. Encased in glass, she was gorgeous, a vision. This was lost on the person on the other end of the phone.

"Listen buddy," said Jinnah wriggling his shoulder and chin to get a better grip on the receiver. "These are going to be big sellers, I'm telling you … Okay. Your loss. Sonofabitch!"

Jinnah carefully placed the glass-cased doll back down on his desk so he could slam the phone down with both hands. Around him, the newsroom droned sluggishly, the ambient noise scarcely louder than the fluorescent lighting's incessant hum. It was early yet. Deadline was too far away to give anyone but the editor a sense of urgency. It was the perfect morning to mix a little personal business with the pleasure Jinnah took in his work as crime reporter for the *Vancouver Tribune*. He grabbed his contact book and flipped petulantly through its pages while reaching for his coffee. He sipped. Sickeningly sweet. Four creams and four sugars mixed with just a soupçon of coffee. Perfect.

"What's with the doll?"

Jinnah, nervous by nature, jumped, nearly spilling coffee all over his desk. He spun his chair around to look at the attractive woman in her early twenties standing over him, her red hair glowing faintly like a halo in a stray beam of sunlight that had somehow pierced the gloom. Crystal Wagner, the city desk clerk had, as usual, made her question sound like a derogatory remark. No mere clerk was worthy of giving Jinnah pulmonary embolism. Thanks to Allah, it wasn't anyone important like that asshole editor, Whiteman. Jinnah took a breath, adjusted his glasses and switched gears from affronted malingerer to frustrated philanderer.

"Ah, Mademoiselle," he growled in a voice as dark, low, and sweet as molasses. "You have come to invest, perhaps? Or for something else?"

Crystal kept her cynical expression intact. Jinnah was an "NBT" — Nothing But Talk. Used to Jinnah's routine where he affected a French accent, she kept her face a sardonic study. "Skip the Pepé Le Pew act, Hakeem. You trying to get rich again?"

"Ah, ze lady is playing hard to get," said Jinnah, taking her hand. "Come, be my partner, and with our riches ve will live in Zanzibar, in splendour."

"I thought you were selling little girls' dreams, not adolescent boys' fantasies."

"Let me show you the reality," purred Jinnah, running his hand the length of her arm.

Crystal sighed. If she protested and moved away, Jinnah was likely to start unbuttoning his shirt and show

She Demons   13

her his "African rug." If she didn't, he'd probably do the same thing. She was rescued by an unlikely Lancelot.

"Really, Hakeem. There is such a thing as sexual harassment!"

Jinnah tore his unwilling eyes away from Crystal's fair, freckle-flecked skin and glanced over at the intruder. Ronald Sanderson, his desk mate, was a typical west coaster. Politically correct to a fault. Courteous. Would say "Sorry!" to a mugger. He snorted. "Ronald, Ronald! There is nothing sexual going on here. This is purely platonic harassment."

"You can't just grab your fellow employees and start pawing them," said Sanderson sternly, reminding Jinnah of a particularly prissy private school prefect.

"My arm was possessed by demons — I didn't do it on paw-pose," Jinnah grinned. "Perhaps this is supernatural harassment, hmm?"

"Oh, please," said Crystal, making no effort to extricate her extremities from Jinnah's clutches.

"Look, don't you have any work to do, Hakeem?"

"Oh, ho!" crowed Jinnah. "And just what is your contribution to the Daily Miracle going to be today, hmm? Another gripping tale of death by mould?"

Sanderson flushed red. Jinnah always belittled his stories. It was part of the unending feud between general assignment reporters like Ronald, who had to cover everything and anything under the sun, and beat reporters like Hakeem, who were specialists. Jinnah was referring to Sanderson's front page story, describing how exposure to a rare form of fungus had killed a Vancouver Island man.

"You're just jealous because my fungus victim was the line story," Sanderson said crossly.

"Ronald, Ronald. If only you had listened to my advice, it would have been a much better story."

"Like hell! I will not have you trivializing that poor man's death!"

"You yourself said the victim was full of life and an all around good fellow," Jinnah chided. "Think of the headline: 'Fungi Kills Fun Guy!' You'd be famous by now. But you will never drink at the fountain of fame, for you never take my advice."

Jinnah braced himself for another self-righteous lecture, but Sanderson had abruptly abandoned his attempt to defend his integrity and Crystal's honour. He was now shamelessly ogling a little girl's dreams and his eyes had narrowed in what Jinnah would have considered a shrewd and calculating manner had it been anyone else.

"Nice doll, Jinnah," said Sanderson, trying hard to sound nonchalant. "How much you selling them for?"

Jinnah was so astonished that he released Crystal's hand. This was totally unlike Sanderson. He'd expected a rebuke from him for conducting personal business on company time, not interest in his product line. His inherent instincts tingling, Jinnah grabbed the doll, hugging it protectively. "She's not for sale, Ronald!"

Crystal's laugh was hard, staccato. "Liar! You and your cousin Sanjit have bought over a thousand of these Barbies —"

"Not Barbies, *Babjis*," Jinnah corrected her. "They're for personal use. Not for sale."

She Demons 15

Slightly bewildered, Sanderson looked over to Crystal in a mute appeal for explanation.

She obliged. "He's trying to corner the North American market. Says Indo-girls here haven't had a decent non-white role model since Vanessa Williams —"

"I meant Michelle Obama!" Jinnah cried, hating how Crystal made him look dated.

"But how much?" demanded Sanderson.

"You wanna know the price, go to Jinnah's website. They're about $39.95 — right, Hakeem?"

"In U.S. funds," said Jinnah stiffly, twisting around and placing the Babji doll under his desk. "Sorry, Ronald. No infidels need apply."

Sanderson's egalitarian protests were pre-empted by a bellow from city desk. Sanderson leapt for his desk. Crystal drifted indifferently towards the coffee machine, leaving Jinnah alone to face the considerable wrath of Nicole "Frosty" Frost, senior assistant city editor in charge of poking indolent crime reporters with a sharp stick.

"You are supposed to be making calls, not flogging dolls."

Jinnah looked at Frosty with a perfectly calm, totally professional exterior. His intestinal tract, however, was being savaged by Sanderson's deadly fungi. Frosty was in her fifties and the original tough broad. Before being promoted to middle management she'd worked every beat worth having on the *Trib* while out drinking and out swearing her male colleagues. Now she ran city desk with an iron hand and an enlarged liver, and had everyone's respect or their fear. She had

16 *Donald J. Hauka*

been Jinnah's mentor when he had arrived at the paper and there was a genuine affection between them. But at the moment, Frosty looked like one of those angry prophets in the Old Testament whom she was fond of quoting. Since Jinnah was an Ismaili Muslim he didn't give a moment's thought to whether he was supposed to be Solomon or Rehoboam.

"Frosty. You're looking ravishing this morning! What can I do for you?"

"Some work!" snapped Frosty and winced at her own volume. "You haven't filed a story in two days. Don't make it three."

"It's ridiculously early," protested Jinnah. "I shall rise again on the third day. Don't worry — News God will provide."

Despite her foul mood and her habitual hangover, Frosty almost smiled at this. Jinnah must be really desperate to invoke the name of the fickle deity quietly worshipped by all good news reporters.

"News God helps those who help themselves by doing cop checks," she growled.

Jinnah was about to take a cheap shot, something about scotch and corn flakes, when, as if in answer to the invocation of the Name, his telephone rang. He looked at the call display and smiled. Thanks to Allah. It wasn't that damned doll supplier wondering where his money was. Jinnah snatched up the receiver as Frosty stood, arms crossed, making sure he wasn't freelancing on company time. "Y'ello, Craig."

"Would it hurt you to address me as 'Sergeant Graham, sir,' just once in a while?"

She Demons 17

Sergeant Craig Graham's voice faded and surged over his cellphone. Jinnah grinned. Aside from being in a bad cell zone, Graham was sounding persecuted, and that usually meant he had something good. Graham was the closest thing Jinnah had to a friend on the Vancouver Police force. Frosty, satisfied Jinnah was not persisting in the sin of sloth, returned to her desk.

"Where the hell are you, Sergeant Graham, sir?" Jinnah yelled into his phone. "Outer Mongolia?"

"Close. Corner of Main and Terminal. Get your brown ass down here."

"Is it good?"

"Spec-bloody-tacular."

"Be there in five."

"Bring a barf bag. It's not pretty."

Jinnah hung up. He grabbed his coat, notebook, and microcassette and called out to Frosty at city desk. "I'll be back in a couple of hours with the front page story, Frosty," he said smugly.

"Got a hot one?" chirped Sanderson from his desk.

Jinnah wasn't fooled. Sanderson couldn't get around him by appealing to his massive ego. Well, not all the way around him anyway.

"Yes. And while I'm gone, keep your filthy, white, effeminate hands off my Babjis."

"I had no intentions —" sputtered Sanderson, but Jinnah cut him off.

"Remember, Ronald: News God is watching you."

As he slammed out of the newsroom, Jinnah was delighted when Ronald actually looked involuntarily over his shoulder.

18 *Donald J. Hauka*

* * *

Jinnah walked down to the company parking lot and climbed into his van. His colleagues had dubbed it the "satellite-guided Love Machine" because, in a moment of weakness, Jinnah had tried to convince Crystal Wagner that he had a waterbed in the back. He didn't, really; just a small fridge and a propane stove. He did, however, have a satellite guidance system, which was his prized possession. He loved seeing where he was on the digital map screen, plugging in coordinates, having the computer remind him, "You must turn right at the next intersection to reach your preset destination." His son, Saleem, had helped him alter the system's voice menu and now Jinnah could be prompted to change course by Ensign Sulu's voice. But Jinnah didn't need satellite guidance to reach Main and Terminal. It was all too familiar territory.

"Name of God," Jinnah whistled when he reached The Corner.

Main and Terminal was a three-ring media circus, complete with freak show in the heart of the concrete jungle. A phalanx of TV camera crews, print and radio reporters, and photographers were pressed against the circle of yellow and black crime scene tape that protected the centre of the park from their advance. Wandering around the edge of this massive scrum were the drunks, the deinstitutionalized, and the druggies, displaced from their sleeping quarters, taking the opportunity to tell their life stories to the cameras and

She Demons 19

bum a little change. Their ranks were swollen by the squeegee kids, who had forsaken hustling to take in the spectacle.

But it was the third ring that caught Jinnah's attention. About a dozen clean and sober youths dressed in white bomber jackets marched back and forth, carrying signs bearing slogans like "Repent!" and "Jesus Died for You." All the while they and anyone else who cared to listen were being harangued by a white-haired man in his fifties, who looked like Elijah in a cheap suit, shouting through a megaphone. Jinnah groaned. He always did when the Reverend Peter Hobbes and his God Squad manifested.

Jinnah felt sorry for Graham. Investigating a murder was a tough job at the best of times, but how the hell was he going to work in this kind of zoo? He decided to park in the MacDonald's lot a half block away. It was free, unlike the more secure pay parking at Science World across the street. But unless you had a good car alarm, you could find your tires slashed or your stereo gone if you tarried too long. Fortunately, Jinnah had rigged his alarm to let out an ear-bleeding shriek, followed by the booming voice of Lieutenant Worf crying, "Phasers on kill, Captain! Fire!" It was remarkably effective, in even the toughest neighbourhoods, and Jinnah left his van feeling only slightly uneasy about its well-being.

Crossing the street, he skirted the side of the scrum where Hobbes was berating the crowd. Jinnah had had more than one visit from the Reverend over the years. His very first week at the paper he'd made the mistake of writing an article about Hobbes's unceasing campaign against Lionel Simons, a former shock-rocker turned cult leader. Hobbes claimed that Simons was really a Satanist. Lionel Simons was no saint, but you certainly couldn't prove he was a Satanist. Not with his legal team. Jinnah still winced when he remembered the crawling retraction he'd had to write to avoid a lawsuit. He'd been wary of Hobbes ever since, but the Reverend was nothing if not dogged in his crusade against Simons, aka "The Rock Messiah!"

Jinnah squeezed through the crowd, taking care not to step in anything that would irreparably soil his new Gucci loafers. He peered past the tape into the centre of the crime scene and saw the sad ritual following a violent murder being performed by a full complement of death's acolytes: the CSU guys in their white suits; the coroner, the only guy wearing street clothes besides Graham; uniforms, looking bored and apprehensive, holding the crowd back and taking considerable abuse from the street people. He caught Graham's eye and waved.

Craig walked over to the edge of the tape. "About time, Hakeem."

"Traffic was murder. Pun intended," said Jinnah. "What'cha got, buddy?"

Graham looked pointedly at several street people who were standing against the tape beside Jinnah. "Beat it," he said.

One, a short but muscular, bare-chested young man drinking a beer for his breakfast, glared belligerently. "Free country, man. Make us," he said, mulish.

She Demons 21

"Want me to check and see if there are any outstanding warrants for you and your pals?"

The dissipated muscleman snorted, belched, threw his beer can at Graham's feet, and stalked off with his buddies. Jinnah and Graham had near privacy for their chat. Jinnah took out his notebook and looked at his contact expectantly.

Graham spoke in his clipped, curt manner. "One victim. Male, aged twenty. Name, Thad Golway."

"So? What makes this special? Guys get knifed down here all the time," said Jinnah.

"They don't often get their heads severed, then placed carefully on their shoulders, Hakeem," said Graham, a shade peevishly in Jinnah's opinion.

"You're kidding!"

"No. I figure he was killed somewhere else, cleaned up. Even dressed in fresh clothes. Then placed here, under a tree, with his kangaroo hood pulled over his head."

Jinnah shuddered. His mind instantly tried to reconstruct the crime. He could see a Dark Figure bending over a kneeling Thad, a sword raised over his head. The blade flashed downwards and ... Jinnah's legendary weak stomach skipped the gruesome details. But he did imagine Main and Terminal at night. With everyone asleep or stoned, the Figure, having arranged Thad's body to look as if he was sleeping, would stuff the body bag he'd carried the boy's corpse in back into a knapsack and walk away, unquestioned, into the darkness. It was terrible.

"Sonofabitch," said Jinnah. "Who found him?"

Graham pointed to a young woman sobbing uncontrollably a few metres from the tree, her face obscured by a Victim Services officer trying to calm her down. Good luck, thought Jinnah.

"She says she knows him. But that's all I've been able to get out of her. She was with another kid. An Andy Gill. Know him?"

Jinnah shrugged, irked. "How should I know? There are thousands of Gills in the Indo-community, for God's sake. Even after all these years, you still seem to think I know every damned person with brown skin in B.C."

Before Graham could apologize, a strident, amplified voice suddenly sounded close behind them. Jinnah flinched.

"The wages of sin is death! But the gift of God is eternal life through Christ our Lord!" bawled the Reverend Peter Hobbes.

"Jesus, that guy!" cursed Graham. "I've already got a bastard of a headache!"

Jinnah shifted himself slightly so Graham was between him and Hobbes. The last thing he needed was to have Hobbes make a beeline for him and demand to be interviewed. He need not have worried. Graham grabbed Jinnah's arm and swung him around. He started marching across the park towards the bus station.

"Come on, we need to talk."

"I thought that's what we were doing."

Jinnah allowed himself to be led, a little concerned at Graham's behaviour. He'd never seen him on edge like this before.

She Demons 23

"I just wish that goddamn born-again would let me get on with my job," the sergeant said vehemently.

"He means well," said Jinnah. "He's fought a lonely war on drugs for years —"

"Well, he's losing!"

They stepped over the concrete curbing, which marked the edge of the bus station's parking area, in silence. Jinnah ransacked his memory, trying to guess what was eating his friend. The violence of the murder? He'd seen worse — just. The kid's age? Graham had handled cases involving infants. The macabre nature, maybe? It was, in a way, a ritualistic killing. Maybe that was it. Jinnah suddenly realized he had no idea what religion Graham was, or if indeed he had any. Graham took Jinnah over towards the deserted arrivals area and turned abruptly.

"Look, Jinnah, I gotta tell you something off the record."

"Is that off the record as in, 'Confirm it somewhere else and run with it' off the record or 'If this gets out I'll kill you?' off the record?" asked Jinnah.

"It's 'breathe a damn word and my careers over' off the record."

Jinnah whistled and closed his notebook as a show of good faith. This was serious. "Okay. My lips are sealed. So is my pen. And my keyboard."

"It's like this: Thad Golway was a good kid. He got caught up in the rave scene and started dealing. But he had a change of heart. Remember that bust I engineered down here last month?"

Jinnah nodded. It hadn't been a front page key

story. He'd managed to get a page top on five out of it. Twenty dealers, mostly squeegee kids, busted. More important, their supplier had been nailed and his operation shut down. A rare victory in the war on drugs.

"Well, Thad was one of my informants. He and two of his buddies, they helped me get the warrants."

"Oh, shit," said Jinnah with feeling. "Craig, I'm sorry."

"It gets worse," said Graham. "I wanted to put Thad into Witness Protection. Move him outta town with his two friends, right? Only they wouldn't go. Dropped outta sight on their own. So now …" Graham trailed off.

Jinnah read his thoughts. "Now you have one dead and two missing, both possible targets — or victims. Right?"

Graham forced a wretched smile out of his facial muscles. "Yeah. Jinnah, about the informant angle — how long do you think I can keep it quiet?"

Jinnah did the math instantly in his head. "Think you can catch the killer in three days?"

"Why three days?"

"Simple, my friend. Day one, a brutal and macabre killing. Who would do such a thing, hmm? The standard, 'Why did he have to die?' story."

"You mean user-key one."

Jinnah ignored this slight. It was a standing joke around the cop shop. Jinnah only wrote three kinds of articles and did so with such a consistent formula that they were referred to as "User-key" stories. User-key one, "Why did he/she have to die?" Usually

She Demons 25

guaranteed the front page. And this was definitely front page material.

"Day two," Jinnah continued. "Find the boy's parents. His sweetheart. His high school teacher. Great TV clips. Did his parents know he was working for you, by the way?"

"Nice try, Hakeem," said Graham. "No comment."

"Day three: in the absence of any suspects, hmm? Where were the police while a body was being placed in plain view on one of Vancouver's busiest street corner? One that has a history of drug deals and drug busts. You had to file an affidavit to get the warrant, right?"

"Of course," said Graham. "But the informant's names are severed from the document."

"Won't take long for someone to guess," said Jinnah sadly. "Might even take less time if that bastard in traffic gets wind of it and leaks it to one of his pet reporters."

Graham gave a little, disapproving cough. There was a certain corporal in the traffic section that made it his business to make his life misery. Graham suspected even Jinnah had likely been fed one or two tips by the son of a bitch over the years.

"Three days to catch the perp with dick all to go on. Not bloody likely, Hakeem."

"Then what, Sergeant Graham, sir, do you propose?"

Graham eyed Jinnah warily. He was, he knew, playing with fire. But he had little option. Jinnah's assessment of the media's moods and appetites had been too brutally realistic and had corresponded too closely with his own suspicions.

"Look, if I can feed you stuff, exclusive, so the pack is busy chasing you, it'll take 'em longer to start asking awkward questions, right?"

There was a pleading note in Graham's voice that Jinnah didn't like. It was usually his job to whine about getting an exclusive. He genuinely felt sorry for Craig. But it did not do to accept such a generous offer without a bit of unseemly haggling first. Pride would not allow it.

"I don't know, Craig," said Jinnah, pulling out a pack of cigarettes. "A petty detail here, a petty detail there. That's your usual idea of an exclusive."

"I'm not talking about giving you what kind of clothes the kid was wearing when we found him," said Graham irritably. "I mean good stuff. Juicy stuff."

Jinnah took out his gold lighter and flicked its beautifully crafted wheel. He inhaled deeply. "Front page stuff?" he asked, the words entombed in a shroud of blue smoke.

Graham coughed and waved a hand in front of his face. "Look, Aikens already has the body. Go see him in an hour, give or take. I'll tell him to give you a full briefing for once."

Jinnah's heart soared. A full briefing with Rex "Dr. Death" Aikens could keep him on the front page for a week, easily. Jinnah stuck out his hand. "You got a deal, buddy."

They shook on it. On the walk back to the crime scene, Jinnah was already writing his story out loud,

She Demons

27

bouncing it off Graham. "It's a murder with a message: Beware."

"Yeah," muttered Graham. "But who's the message for?"

"Too bad he wasn't found in a strip club."

"What the hell difference does that make?"

"Craig, Craig — it's one of the greatest headlines in journalism yore. 'Headless Body Found in Topless Club.' Great, hmm?"

"Charming."

"I was thinking of something like: 'Under the spreading oak tree, the village junkie stands — but not on his head.'"

"Real sensitive. His parents will love you."

"They always end up loving Jinnah in the end, my friend...."

They almost made it back safely behind the tape, but just as they were a few metres shy, a TV reporter and her cameraman leaped out from behind a tree and barred their path.

"Sergeant Graham! Have you any suspects yet?"

Oh shit, thought Jinnah. Caitlin Bishop.

"I have no comment."

Graham tried to brush past Caitlin, but she had positioned herself squarely between him and the tape. Jinnah felt a pang of conscience. He had taught Caitlin that trick. It seemed another lifetime ago that Caitlin had been a shy, mousy intern at the *Tribune*, being mentored by the great Jinnah-ji. She had talent and promise — ah, such promise! Jinnah sighed. Then she had thrown it all away for a job in television news. It

28 *Donald J. Hauka*

only pained Jinnah slightly that she now made almost exactly twice as much as he did.

"Was he a dealer or a junkie?" Caitlin asked as Jinnah smiled politely at his former protegé.

"No comment."

"Is this in any way linked to last month's major bust down here?"

To Graham's credit, he didn't miss a beat. His "No comment" was in exactly the same tone as his previous utterances — which was something Jinnah hated. Unlike so many other cops, Graham never gave that dramatic pause that said "yes, but I can't say so," unless he wanted to.

"May I say I find that hard to believe?"

Part of Jinnah admitted that he would have made exactly the same comment. But the rest of him knew this woman was endangering his exclusive. He was about to say something when, fortunately, Graham was rescued by Constable Bains.

"Sergeant, we need you over here."

Bains, one of Vancouver's few Indo-Canadian policemen and built like a brick ashram, had lumbered up behind Caitlin and was politely but firmly leaning against her, prompting her to take a step back. Graham saw the crack of light and dove to safety without answering the last question.

Caitlin pouted for a second then turned her perfectly capped teeth on Jinnah. "Jinnah!" she said in a voice that was a pale imitation of Hakeem's saccharin tones. "What were you and Craig talking about all by yourselves?"

She Demons 29

Jinnah was not fooled by Caitlin's studied coquetry for a moment. "He offered to buy me a one-way bus ticket out of town. Then released me on my own recognizance."

"Very funny. Spill. What do you know?"

"TV has been very bad for your patience level. You know, you used to be so much more polite when you worked in print."

Before Caitlin could reply, Jinnah turned and walked away.

"Hey. Where are you going?" she cried.

"I have a doctor's appointment," said Jinnah, blowing Vancouver's premiere pit bull a kiss.

Rex Aikens had earned the sobriquet "Dr. Death" long before Jack Kevorkian came along, and came by it honestly. There were few ways of shuffling off the mortal coil (or having it shuffled off for you) that Aikens did not know of. His lab was as sterile as a double vasectomy and impeccably neat. But Jinnah always found the wide, white room with the gleaming stainless steel fixtures too cold, as if the Grim Reaper himself was putting a hand on his clammy skin. Nothing seemed to work against the chill; not wearing a sweater under his leather jacket, not even the warmth of Aikens himself, who, despite his profession as Vancouver's top forensic pathologist, was a cheerful fellow.

"This is a day to mark on the calendar," Aikens said, putting down the phone as Jinnah sat shivering on a stool. "I must go out and buy myself a lottery ticket."

Jinnah smiled. He loved Aikens's voice, which retained just a touch of the lilting Irish accent he'd largely left behind along with his youth in Dublin.

"It is indeed a rare day when we can speak frankly without worrying about what Those Who Work Above may hear," agreed Jinnah.

"Those Who Work Above" was the code Jinnah and Aikens used to refer to the police, who worked in the upper storeys of the building where the forensic lab was located. Usually, they frowned on Aikens having these off the records with Jinnah. But Aikens found it useful talking things over with Hakeem. The reporter had a keen eye for detail and good instincts. Pity he was so damned squeamish about autopsy photos.

"Well," said Aikens. "Where do you want me to start? I have but with a cursitory eye o'erglanced the victim."

"Start with the cause of death, Rex."

"Excellent question," Aikens's eyes gleamed behind his thick, black-framed glasses. "Would you believe me if I said beheading?"

"No," said Jinnah. "Not unless the kid was so stoned that he was unconscious when the murderer did him."

"Got it in one, old boy," said Aikens. "Toxicology's not in yet, but the poor lad shows every sign of having a sizable amount of heroin in his bloodstream. I think I should illustrate this over at the light table."

"Oh, for God's sake, Rex!" groaned Jinnah. "I just ate."

She Demons   31

"Come come, Jinnah. I *think* I may have shown you worse."

Jinnah reflected briefly on the lunches he had lost in the line of duty as he followed Aikens over to the light table, where a series of X-rays and photographs were hanging, all neatly marked "Golway, Thaddeus." Jinnah squinted, feeling his stomach rebel at the sight. Aikens pointed to an X-ray of the boy's severed head. Jinnah looked away.

"Now, now, my man," Aikens's triangular eyebrows were knit together in a frown, making them look like two twin, bushy peaks. "Observe and learn."

Jinnah forced his eyes open and immediately regretted it. The sugar and cream-charged coffee churned and curdled in his stomach, desperately trying to escape. But he held it down, trying to focus on the pure mechanics of the murder and not the person. Not yet.

"A single, swift stroke with an extremely sharp, heavy blade. Unless I miss my guess, something akin to an executioner's axe."

"You're kidding!"

Jinnah now had another grisly detail to add to his mental reconstruction. The Dark Figure now clutched a headsman's axe.

"You're saying this was an execution-style killing, Doc?"

"Yes, in a somewhat more medieval manner than we are accustomed to, Jinnah."

Jinnah grunted. At the end of the day, did it matter whether it was by Rambo knife, ceremonial sword, or meat cleaver? A beheading was a beheading.

"Could it be a cult thing, hmm? A ritual slaying?"

Aikens frowned, sending white waves rippling up and across his pale forehead. "I want you to look very carefully at this next photograph. And if you are going to be ill, like the last time, you know where the sterile receptacle is."

Jinnah knew where the stainless steel bucket was — right at the end of the table. He braced himself as Aikens carefully selected one of the photographs on the table's flat surface and placed it on the shining upright wall of light in front of them.

"This is a photograph of the victim's face. It will appear ... reasonably unpleasant at first."

Jinnah opened his eyes as fully as he dared. There were Thad Golway's lifeless eyes, his reddish, matted hair. His mouth, open slightly, showing cracked, nicotine-stained teeth. But it was not these details that Jinnah found disturbing. It was the marks on Thad's cheeks. At first, all he registered were the wounds. Someone had carved the kid's cheeks with a knife. For a moment, he thought he would need the bucket, but he managed to keep his stomach under control.

"You will notice, Mister Jinnah, that the pattern of scarring is quite plainly visible. Which is extremely odd, don't you think?"

Jinnah looked at Aikens, but his pale face gave nothing away. This was one of Aikens's little quizzes. He made Jinnah think for his stories. It irritated him, but it took his mind of the dreadful sight before his eyes.

"Where's the blood, Doc?"

She Demons 33

Aikens smiled, framing his dark eyes with a latticework of wrinkles. "Spot on, my man. There was none. Someone carved the victim's cheeks post mortem, then washed away the blood so his handiwork could be seen."

"Name of God," said Jinnah, sweating and wondering why he never thought to pop a tranquilizer before coming here.

"I used the word 'carved' deliberately, by the way," Aikens continued. "Have you noticed the pattern?"

Jinnah stared as Aikens traced the design on Thad's cheeks with a capped ballpoint pen. A crooked line ran vertically up either side, from chin to the top of the broad cheekbone. Cutting across the axis of these were three, wavy lines. They looked like a series of lopsided Ws: jagged crosses, macabre Christmas trees.

"Identical on both cheeks," said Jinnah.

"Rather like trees, don't you think?" said Aikens, voicing Jinnah's thoughts.

Jinnah's inherent instincts started to tingle. His stomach was forgotten. "Have you ever seen a signature like this before, Doc?"

"Not in my long service here in the first circle of hell, Jinnah," said Aikens, a touch sadly. "It is not any known gang or cult sign that I can identify."

Jinnah took out his notepad and made a sketch of the markings. He knew this was a breach of the usual protocol with Aikens: no attribution and no note taking. It had an immediate effect on Aikens, who began mopping his receding hairline with a linen handkerchief.

34 *Donald J. Hauka*

"Look, my man — do you think that's wise?" he said, a shade nervously.

"Hey! Graham said a full briefing, didn't he?"

"Indeed. Quite right."

"Besides," said Jinnah. "You want to know whose signature this is, hmm? Well, I'm pretty sure I know where to find out."

"You do?" said Aikens querulously. "Pray, where?"

Jinnah snapped his notebook shut. God, he needed a cigarette. "The scene of the crime," he said.

By the time Jinnah returned to Main and Terminal, the circus was breaking up. Most of the media had gone. So, mercifully, had the Reverend Hobbes. The CSU guys were finishing up. But the people who Jinnah wanted to talk to were there, of course. They lived there.

He looked at the small knots of people still hanging around the lawn. One was composed of emerging alcoholics, led by the bare-chested, well-muscled mule man who had challenged Graham. Another of older street people, chatting and leaning over the handles of their shopping carts the way people in the suburbs leaned over their fences to gossip. The third group was mostly younger people in faded and ripped jeans and T-shirts. Several were holding squeegees. Jinnah strolled up to them with what he thought was just the right mixture of casual coolness and understated authority.

"Gentlemen, ladies," he said. "Making much money today?"

She Demons 35

The half-dozen squeegee kids glared at Jinnah and fell silent.

"Did any of you know Thad?" asked Jinnah, keeping a verbal foot in the door.

A scrawny young man of about twenty, wearing a red bandanna that covered most of his long, greasy brown hair, turned to face Jinnah. A spokesman. Good. The rest watched as Red Bandanna challenged Jinnah.

"You a cop?" he demanded.

Jinnah laughed and fished his cigarettes out of his shirt pocket. "Do I look like one?" he said, offering his cigarettes.

Red Bandanna looked at the package suspiciously, hesitating. "These regulars or Mother Nature?"

"Sadly, just tobacco," said Jinnah.

"We live in hope, man."

Red Bandanna took one. So did a very thin, pale young woman who Jinnah took to be his girlfriend. Jinnah lit both their cigarettes.

"Was Thad a squeegee kid?" he asked.

Red Bandanna scowled. "Why you wanna know? You're not a cop. You an undertaker?"

"No, I'm Hakeem Jinnah, crime reporter for the *Tribune*." Jinnah had waved a red flag in front of Red Bandanna, who had his soap box ready.

"Why don't you assholes in the corporate media tell the truth about what's happening down here instead of parroting the fucking fascist cops who are owned and operated by the global money men who are ruining our planet, huh?"

Jinnah kept his face carefully neutral. Just as long as they didn't identify him as the author of last month's piece of fascist police propaganda, he might just get something out of this. Simultaneously, he wondered if he could claim expenses for two cigarettes.

"We can't tell the truth if you don't talk to us, my friend. For instance, I assume most of my colleagues in the corporate media will refer to Thad as a street person or a junkie. Is he either?"

"Labels!" spat Red Bandanna's girlfriend through skinny, magenta lips. "Cut-price tags to put on a person so you can write them off as no loss. What does it mean?"

This was a little too esoteric for Jinnah to follow, so he kept roughly to the subject. "So are you saying you didn't know Thad? That he wasn't a squeegee kid?"

"He'd blown the scene, man," said Red Bandanna. "He wasn't one of us."

"Ah, but he used to be. And was he a dealer or a user?"

"We don't deal, asshole of the corporate media!"

"Look, I don't give a shit if he was either," said Jinnah sharply. "He was a human being and he didn't deserve to end up under a tree with his head cut off."

This took Red Bandanna aback for a second. Girlfriend stepped up to the plate. "He wasn't around much. So don't try and label him."

"I just want to know a little bit about him, as a person," persisted Jinnah. "Was he part of a gang or something?"

She Demons 37

"We don't have gangs, apologist for the state!" Red Bandanna had recovered. "We're like a family down here."

Jinnah found this rich. Well, as long as they pretended to be a nuclear family, he might as well drop the bomb on them. He flipped open his notebook to the sketch of the marks on Thad's cheeks. "So what's this then? The family coat of arms?"

Red Bandanna and Girlfriend could not hide the look of surprise and fear that flickered briefly across their faces and was mirrored in the rest of the gang. They recovered their collective cool quickly, however. "What's that? Your night school art project?"

"It was found on Thad's cheeks. Know whose sign it is?"

"Look, fuck off, media puppet," shouted Girlfriend. "You're scaring away business."

"Yeah. Beat it," added Red Bandanna, flicking Jinnah's cigarette back at him.

Jinnah beat it. He didn't know what he had, but he knew it was hot. Had to be to scare this group. Lines on paper that scared people. That was Jinnah's job, often as not. It was time to put the fear of God into city desk.

"He was marked for death. In an exclusive *Tribune* report, we reveal how a deadly new gang has staked its turf on Vancouver's mean streets by decapitating a young man from a good family."

Jinnah's editor antennae twitched, twisting ever so slightly to catch the subtle signals issuing from Dick Whiteman's mouth; anything in his tone or facial expression that suggested approval or disapproval. It had been so much easier under Whiteman's predecessor, Conway Blacklock, who could not hide the contempt in his voice as he read every story. But at least Connie had given the game away by the degree of derision with which he proofed the promo cards to be dropped into *Tribune* news boxes in advance of an exclusive. Whiteman wasn't like that. He was the king of deadpan, a man who made Buster Keaton look like Jim Carrey. If he hadn't been an editor-in-chief he could have made his fortune as a poker player. At the moment, Jinnah had no idea if the promo he'd filed suited Whiteman or not.

"It's all ours, chief. Exclusive," Jinnah ventured.

Whiteman turned his pale, blue grey eyes on Jinnah and stared right through his imitation silk shirt, past his gold, zodiac medallion (Aries), and even his African rug into a region uncomfortably close to his heart, where Hakeem did some of his finest writing.

"A chilling tale of callous murder almost unparalleled in Vancouver history."

Whiteman's delivery was as deadpan as his face. Since he'd only lived in Vancouver for three months his grasp of local history was somewhat shaky. Jinnah's own history with Whiteman was too hit-and-miss to form a definitive analysis of the situation.

"You know for certain, of course, that this young man was either a dealer or an addict?" said Whiteman, voice still neutral.

She Demons 39

This was a question Jinnah had been anticipating. He had his arguments — and a liberal dose of BS — ready. "The squeegee kids on The Corner said he'd been part of the scene," said Jinnah, antennae shivering. "Plus Aikens said the initial prognosis showed Thad was dosed to the tits — the limit on horse."

Whiteman said nothing. He arched his greying, ginger-flecked eyebrows and looked over to Frosty. "And do we have anyone — anyone at *all* — talking on the record, Ms. Frost?"

Frosty shook her head. "No, but given Jinnah's instincts —"

"We all know about Jinnah's legendary instincts. They have, I understand, cost this newspaper a fair amount of money in the past."

Jinnah opened his mouth to protest, but one look at Frosty's ravaged face silenced him. He ground his teeth, worrying the gold fillings (purchased at the expense of the union dental plan despite his suspicion that the mercury amalgam was slowly poisoning him).

Frosty stepped into the breach. "The kid was decapitated," she said reasonably. "He had an established history on The Corner —"

"And we have the inside track here," Jinnah cut in quickly, regaining the conversational initiative. "The cops are eager to co-operate with us."

Whiteman let this last comment fall into a well of silence, where it rattled around in a hollow of unspoken suspicion. Name of God, thought Jinnah. What's more important to this bastard? Selling newspapers or keeping the legal bill down to a minimum? The answer came a nanosecond later, emptying like a volcanic eruption from the contour map of Whiteman's lined face.

"Proof, Jinnah. We need proof. Not co-operation, not instincts. I can't let this run unless you get more to back it up."

"What do you mean, proof?" Jinnah howled. "You've got the cops, you've got the kids —"

"I need a name," said Whiteman calmly. "That would be a start. I would also like to know how you can say this man came from a good family."

"Because Graham told me so."

"And have you interviewed this good family?"

Jinnah had been hoping Whiteman wouldn't raise that particular point. "Still trying to track them down," he lied.

Whiteman closed his eyes, a sign of editor impatience. "Art?" he said softly. "Do we have any art, other than those long-distance snapshots of a body bag being loaded into an ambulance, which, by the way, seems a bit ludicrous, even given the state of our health care system?"

"I'm in charge of the words, Whiteman, not the visuals," said Jinnah irritably.

Jinnah could tell by the look on Frosty's face that he had gone too far. Certainly Whiteman's visage betrayed nothing new. Well, in for a dinar, he thought.

"Listen, Chief," Jinnah changed his tone to that of the pleading, whining toady. "My instincts tell me that these markings are the signature not just of the murderer, but a sinister new gang. I'm telling you, this will put us ahead of everyone else. They'll be eating our dust."

She Demons 41

"Fine," said Whiteman. "Prove it."

Sonofabitch! It was the legal budget the bastard was worried about after all! Well, Dick Whiteman was about to find out what happened to infidels who crossed Hakeem Jinnah. He grabbed his coat and notebook and started out of the newsroom without a word.

Whiteman called after him. "Jinnah! Where do you think you're going?"

Jinnah paused by the door. He made good and sure everyone in the newsroom was listening as he shouted his reply. "Deepest, darkest gangland, chief."

An hour later Jinnah was still chuckling as he paced up and down the lush lawns in front of the Museum of Anthropology on the grounds of the University of British Columbia. The green campus at the tip of Point Grey, surrounded by sea and mountains, hardly looked like the set of *The Sopranos*, but nevertheless it was there that the very brave and the insatiably curious probed the dark secrets of the new millennium's tribal societies. Jinnah smoked and waited for his gangland connection to appear. He considered the exquisitely carved totem poles standing guard over the museum entrance. The bright, simple colours painted on the wood were reflecting the glorious sun that had burst through the afternoon cloud. Typical west side. Hogging all the sunshine along with all the money. It was hard to believe that such beauty, such tranquility, could exist just a few miles away from the filth and squalor that was Main and Terminal.

The museum was practically deserted and few people were wandering around the grounds. Probably at Wreck Beach, Jinnah thought, and grinned in a slightly lascivious manner. The clothing optional beach was just around the corner from the museum and had once been a favourite site for Lionel Simons to stage mass, nude baptisms for his cult, Millennial Magi. Ah, those had been the days to be a crime reporter. The interviews he had conducted there. But he was looking for something quite different today. He spotted a woman in her early fifties walking towards him, dressed in a cardigan and a long, plaid skirt, and wearing stout, black walking boots. Jinnah quickly ground out his cigarette with his foot and smoothed down his hair. Showtime.

"Ah, Professor Bruce! How are the tribes doing these days?"

Dr. Alexandra Bruce was a plump, pleasant-looking woman with dark hair, dark glasses, and a bright wit. She looked more like a den mother than an expert on the social organization and mating habits of North American gangs. But the looks belied a tough interior and Jinnah always felt slightly guilty in her presence, like a student who had failed to do his homework.

"Jinnah. You said you had something special for me," said Bruce, panting slightly — Jinnah could not tell whether from excitement or overexertion.

"Yes, professor. This." Jinnah opened his notebook and showed Bruce the sketch of the marks on Thad Golway's face. Bruce frowned and pursed her lips, holding the sketch quite close to her thick glasses for a long moment. Everything was riding on her pronouncement.

She Demons 43

Jinnah's insides felt like they were being used to create a particularly elaborate origami sculpture. Sweat covered his face and his breathing came in quick, shallow pants, almost as if he was having a heart attack. It was a sure sign his inherent instincts were right. Or it could be, said his habitual hypochondria, the first symptoms of necrotizing fasciitis.

Finally, Bruce handed Jinnah his notepad back. "Definitely and without a doubt the *Yakshas*," she said, beaming, as if Jinnah had given her a drawing of a particularly rare bird. "And you say this was found on the face of that poor young man they discovered this morning? Well, that is a first!"

Jinnah's symptoms miraculously disappeared as a fierce glow of triumph spread throughout his system. *Goddamn it, I knew I was right!*

"Yakshas? Gesundheit. What the hell are Yakshas?" he asked.

Bruce looked at Jinnah, amused. "Jinnah, you surprise me. They're part of the Hindu pantheon. Forest demons who, disguised as beautiful young women, lure travellers into the woods and to their deaths."

Jinnah sighed. Bruce was an expert at North American gangs and could tell the difference between groups that appeared indistinguishable to most people, but she had a blind spot where Jinnah's heritage was concerned. He put it down to watching too many Peter Sellers movies at an impressionable age.

"Listen, professor, you can't tell me that a bevy of beautiful forest demons have set-up shop at the corner of Main and Terminal."

Bruce laughed. She took an almost perverse joy in her work. "In this particular incarnation, Jinnah, the Yakshas are a U.S. based drug cartel that started off in southern California. Decapitation of victims is a Yaksha hallmark. So is scarring the victim with their logo. The twin trees."

"Holy shit. You're kidding me," said Jinnah, furiously scribbling notes.

"I'm not in the habit of kidding you, Jinnah. They are now so large and well financed that they claim to be a legitimate business organization."

"What? Like the Hells Angels?"

"Yes," nodded Bruce vigorously. "This is the first time I have ever seen this signature north of the border. So be careful what you say. They're quite sensitive about their image."

Sonofabitch. Sensitive, New Age killers who could cut the head of a young man, mutilate him, then scream for their lawyers. Well, they would soon learn that there were things worse than trial by judge and jury.

Jinnah closed his notebook. "To hell with these assholes' image, Professor," he said. "These bastards are about to undergo trial by Jinnah."

"How on earth did you get Bruce to talk on the record?"

Jinnah sat in his chair by city desk like a king surveying a field where he had routed his enemies foot,

She Demons 45

horse, and dragoons. The layout for the front page was on Frosty's Mac. "Beheaded by Demon Gang!" was the main headline. There, at the top of his *Tribune* exclusive story was Jinnah's byline. Not in the size of type that he felt was appropriate, but still, there all the same. It was what Jinnah lived for. The artwork was an illustration of the tree design lifted from Jinnah's notebook. Hakeem had tried to charge the company for a freelance artwork fee, but Whiteman had rejected his claim out of hand.

"She always talks on the record when she has a first," laughed Jinnah, answering Frosty's question. "Then Alexandra Bruce *loves* seeing her name in print."

Frosty, an unlit cigarette hanging from her mouth, ran her cursor up and down the story. For all his outward braggadocio, Jinnah was nervous. This was the crucial moment when an attack of cold feet could sink the whole thing.

"I dunno. Any sick puppy could have carved that design into the kid's cheeks. You sure you want to tangle with a drug cartel that makes the Hells Angels look like choir boys?"

"Like they're going to sue us, Frosty!" Jinnah snorted.

"Their idea of a lawsuit is to fit you with a cement sleeping bag."

Jinnah's congenital cowardice twitched slightly at that. True, gangs sometimes took vengeance on reporters who made their lives difficult. Like Michel Auger from the *Le Journal de Montréal*. But the chances of the Yakshas doing so were very slender.

"Look, they put a giant neon sign on the kid's face saying, 'Here we are! Don't fuck with us!' For God's sake, they *want* their name mentioned."

"In which case, aren't we doing them a favour?"

"I hope not," said Jinnah. "But if it makes you feel better, send them a bill for a full page ad."

Frosty's finger hovered over the send key. Jinnah willed her to punch the button. After a long hesitation, she did so. "Okay, Reilly! You got the front page."

Reilly, the night news editor, adjusted his glasses on his long, Gaelic nose and brought the story up on his terminal. Jinnah's unrestrained smile broke out, cleaving his face in two. God, he was tired. Wearily, he rose to his feet, slinging his black leather jacket over his shoulder.

"Going straight home or do you have time to stop for a quick drink?" asked Frosty.

"Sorry," said Jinnah. "I have a few errands to run first."

At the top of the Jinnah shopping list was the Battery Stop. He had only replaced the alarm system batteries last month, but it paid to be extra cautious in his line of work.

Chapter Two

Jinnah drove home humming a *Bhangra* tune and puffing happily on a smoke. Caitlin Bishop was going to shit herself when she saw the paper. It would have her and the rest of the Vancouver media — no, the international media — trailing in his wake. They'd be busy for days following this one up. Graham would, of course, be pathetically grateful. He wondered what else he might be able to squeeze out the sergeant in exchange for his gratitude. Hmmm …

"You have reached your predetermined destination. Please power down the warp engines and secure the starship before leaving," Ensign Sulu's voice reminded him as he pulled up in front of his house.

Jinnah made sure the car alarm was on and looked at his home. The "Jinnah-mahal," as Sanderson called it, was an aging Vancouver Special with dirty white stucco on the walls and iron bars on the windows.

48 *Donald J. Hauka*

Given the day's events, these precautions seemed somewhat inadequate. Jinnah wondered if he should spring for that perimeter motion detector Sanjit had been pestering him about. Surely that would keep the Yakshas out? He thought of Thad Golway's face and shuddered. Uttering a brief prayer for the poor boy, Jinnah walked down the concrete path to his door. After a hard day of horror at work, it was good to be back in the relative safety of home. Manjit would pour him a scotch, fuss and fret over him, then tell him all about her day at work or Saleem's time at school — the normal, domestic stuff that was a balm to his frayed nerves.

"You are not going and that's final!"

As Jinnah opened the door, his picture of a quiet, family evening collapsed into a heap of ruins. Manjit's voice carried all the way from the kitchen. Jinnah frowned. His wife almost never raised her voice. There was only one thing that could possibly irritate her more than his own behaviour.

"Saleem!" Jinnah roared, striding into the kitchen.

Manjit's dark eyes flashed at him as he entered the room. "Really, Jinnah," she said calmly. "There's no need to bellow like that."

Jinnah flinched as if he'd been slapped. There stood his beautiful wife, dressed in her white health care worker uniform, all five-feet nothing of her. A second ago she had been trembling like a clarinet reed, facing their sixteen-year-old son who was taller by a scruffy, peach-fuzzed head. Having raised her voice only a moment earlier, now she was composed and elegant as Mahal herself.

She Demons   49

"Bellowing? You call that bellowing?" protested Jinnah, trying to control his voice. "If my father were here —"

"But he is not, Hakeem," said Manjit, sweetly but firmly. "Yelling didn't work very well for your father on you, did it?"

"He was a Kenyan police chief! Yelling was one of the perks of the job! And stand up straight, for God's sake!"

Saleem turned his bored, bespectacled, adolescent face on Jinnah and sunk slowly into a chair sideways, dangling one long, skinny leg back and forth. Jinnah fought to control his temper. Saleem was insolent, stubborn, self-possessed. Excellent qualities in a crime reporter but liabilities in a son, as far as Hakeem was concerned.

"What's all the shouting about?" Jinnah demanded.

"Saleem wants to go to a rave tonight."

"The boy's got lips of his own," said Jinnah irritably. "And you might say 'hello' to your father."

"Didn't hear you saying, 'Hi, son' as you blasted in," said Saleem.

Jinnah opened his mouth, his volume cranked up, but Manjit's melodious voice cut him short. "He might say more if you let him get a word in edgewise, Hakeem."

Jinnah closed his eyes. Allah, strength. Dealing with Manjit was frustrating. Under that slender form and angelic face beat the heart of a lioness. She could be maddeningly reasonable. It was like being set upon by an attack sparrow. Conceding the point, Jinnah

50 *Donald J. Hauka*

pulled a chair towards him and sat down on it backwards, his arms folded over the back.

"All right, son," he said, choking only slightly on the words. "Let's rap."

Saleem rolled his eyes. "Dad! That's so retro!"

"I've already told Saleem how dangerous raves can be," chirped Manjit. "Drugs everywhere."

"But mom! It's a legal rave. It's licenced by the city, for God's sake!"

"Don't say 'For God's sake' to your mother," snapped Jinnah.

"Saleem," said Manjit. "I've seen the overdoses. I know what those drugs can do to kids. Besides, the problems aren't on the dance floor. They're around the edges, in the parking lots, the washrooms...."

Jinnah marvelled at how swiftly he'd been cut out of the conversation his wife had urged him to have with his son. Fine. If she wanted it that way, fine. He wouldn't say a thing.

"But Mom! Lionel Simons is playing tonight and everybody knows he's —"

"A fraud!" roared Jinnah, springing out of his chair so fast that it toppled over, beating a drummer's tattoo on the kitchen linoleum.

"— anti-drug," finished Saleem, his voice rising above his father's.

"Hakeem!" said Manjit, warning.

"Don't give me that 'Hakeem' bullshit!" shouted Jinnah. "Lionel Simons is a cult leader and a crook! He works his devotees into a frenzy and then sends them out to beg for cash so he can live in his West Vancouver

She Demons   51

mansion in the lap of bloody luxury!"

"Then how come he tells all his followers not to do drugs?" said Saleem defiantly.

"So there'll be all the more for him! Next thing you'll know you'll be a member of his Millennium Magi gang, singing at the top of your lungs in some posh pit —"

"It's called a mosh pit and they prefer to be called the MiMis," Saleem interjected.

"Whatever! You're not ending up as some screaming MiMi!"

Saleem gave up shouting at his father and appealed to his mother. "But everybody goes to raves, Mom! Like, everybody!"

"Not everybody, Saleem."

"You're going!"

"I have to go. It's my job. Somebody has to hand out the free water and deal with the overdoses."

"I mean all my friends go."

"Name one of your friends who is allowed to go," said Manjit, brightly.

Ahchah! She has him, thought Jinnah as Saleem stared, open-mouthed at his mother. Poor kid's searching his memory banks. There were not many parents in Jinnah's social circle within the Indo-Canadian community who would knowingly let their children go to a rave. If Saleem actually gave a name, he could be sure that Manjit would be on the phone in an instant, checking the veracity of his claim. But Saleem only hesitated for a couple of seconds.

"Andy Gill goes."

52 *Donald J. Hauka*

Jinnah was stunned by this. Surely this couldn't be the same Andy Gill who Graham had mentioned?

But Manjit was already ahead of him. "Andy Gill is two years older than you and his parents wouldn't know what he was up to if he was on the nightly news," said Manjit. "Try again."

"No, wait a minute," said Jinnah, sitting down again, instincts tingling. "This Andy Gill, Saleem? He's about eighteen, right? Just out of high school?"

"Why do you wanna know?" asked Saleem, eyes narrowing with well-founded suspicion.

"Because his reputation precedes him."

Manjit looked at her husband quizzically. "Hakeem, what's this about? You sound like you're interviewing your own son."

"I am," agreed Jinnah. "Look, Saleem, this is more important than any stupid argument we're having. Who is this Andy Gill?"

"If I tell you, can I go?"

"We'll talk about it. I'm offering you a plea bargain. Anything you say will not be held against you."

Saleem studied his father's face in much the same manner that Hakeem had earlier sized Sanderson up. He spoke smoothly, echoing his father's tones. "He's Mr. Puri's nephew. Now can I go?"

Jinnah felt a significant piece of the jigsaw puzzle that was Thad Golway's death go click! Right in his own kitchen. Ram Puri was an *éminence grise* of the Indo-Canadian community and a sort of ethical guidance counsellor for Jinnah. He was now even further ahead of Graham than when he'd left the newsroom.

She Demons 53

"Well? Can I go, Dad?"

Jinnah looked at his son and smiled. Then, Graham's words came back to him. "Thad Golway was a good kid. He got caught up in the rave scene and started dealing." In a flash, Jinnah saw Saleem there on The Corner, squeegee in one hand, nickel bag in the other, being stalked by the Dark Figure with an axe under his overcoat....

"Dad?"

Jinnah snapped back to reality. "I think I'd like to hear more about these raves — and other things, Saleem," he said, rising from his chair.

"Hakeem? Where are you going?"

Jinnah paused in the doorway. "I am going to find Andy Gill and perhaps solve a murder. You, darling, are going to work. And Saleem? You're staying here and doing your homework, hmm?"

And before anyone could contradict him, Jinnah was out of the house.

Within minutes Jinnah was walking down the sidewalk on Main Street. But this was not Main and Terminal. This was well south, near 49th Avenue, an entire world away from where Thad Golway had been found. Jinnah was in the heart of Little India, walking along the several blocks of the Punjabi Market. Here, the windows of the shops were ablaze with lights. Everywhere the *deevas* — little clay lamps — glowed yellow, shimmering like a desert mirage against the glass panes. The light

54 *Donald J. Hauka*

from the flickering flames of the lamps danced on bundles of traditional sweets in red and gold wrappings that were heaped high behind them. Even though Jinnah wasn't a Sikh, he was married to one, and he couldn't help but be swept up in the mood of celebration that swirled through the market. This was one of the highest points in the Sikh calendar: the festival marking the release of the Guru Gobind Singh from captivity and his return home to Amritsar. Everyone seemed happy. Smiles greeted him as he passed friends and neighbours. It was how Sanderson usually described Christmas, only he never saw Sanderson smile at Christmas. He always left his shopping until the last minute and looked so stressed that Jinnah usually offered him one of his many prescription tranquillizers.

Jinnah finally came to the lamp-lit shop where he hoped to find illumination of another sort, the dry goods store of his friend Puri. The door opened with a bright chiming of little bells.

"Ah, Jinnah. How nice to see you." Mr. Puri's smile beamed at Jinnah from behind the counter while the rest of him fussed with merchandise.

"You are stocking up for Diwali, perhaps? I have just the sweets for Manjit."

"Actually, Mr. Puri, I wonder if you can assist me with my inquiries."

Puri closed one dark eye, adding a few more wrinkles to his lined, round face. "Inquiries? Then you had better sit down and have some chai."

Jinnah moved to the back of the store, where a small card table and a couple of battered folding chairs

She Demons 55

sat. This was a tradition. Puri preferred to sip and slurp his hot, fragrant tea while slipping Jinnah the information and advice he needed. Jinnah accepted a small, porcelain cup painted with a bright blue motif of Ganesha, the Hindu elephant god of wisdom. He breathed in the sweet, dark scent of cardamom and cloves mingling with cinnamon and anise.

"Now, how may I help you, Jinnah?"

The steam rising from his cup fogged the bottoms of Puri's glasses, condensing like cataracts.

"You have a nephew, Mr. Puri," Jinnah said, blowing gently into his cup. "Andy Gill."

A shadow passed over Puri's pleasant, clean-shaven face, as if the steam had turned to smoke. Here it comes, thought Jinnah.

"Yes, Andy," Puri sighed. "A most troubled young man. He lives with his father, Sadhu. His mother, my sister, is still in India."

Jinnah nodded. It was an all too common story. Andy was already starting to fit the profile of a street kid.

"They are close, Sadhu and Andy?"

"Is any young man of his age close to his father?" Puri smiled sadly. "That much I can understand. Andy is a difficult boy, but he has a good heart. He wants to do what is right. But his idea of what is proper is not his father's. Sadhu is content to follow the Kirat Karna, earning an honest living like a good Sikh."

Jinnah could not suppress a lopsided grin. He had a good idea what an eighteen-year-old boy let loose in the metropolis of Vancouver after growing up on the farm in the Punjab would think of his father's devotion to hard work. He took a big slurp of chai, the sugary condensed milk leaving a coat on his tongue.

"How does Sadhu earn his living, Mr. Puri?"

"He has two jobs at the moment. I know that he is working on a house as we speak. Consequently, he has a difficult time trying to keep track of Andy's activities. Mostly, they fight."

"Fight?" said Jinnah, leaning forward slightly, instincts tingling. "Over what?"

Mr. Puri paused, cup halfway to his lips, and leaned his head sideways. "You have asked a great many questions about my nephew, Mr. Jinnah. What, may I ask, is your interest?"

Jinnah was ready for this one. He had his cover story courtesy of Saleem. There was no need to trouble Puri with tenuous links to headless bodies.

"My son has informed me that Andy goes to raves — you know, these warehouse concerts. He therefore thinks it is entirely appropriate for him to go, hmm?"

Mr. Puri shook his head and sighed. "Then you know, perhaps, the malady that affects Andy. He is not just rebelling against his father. He is searching for something else. He has a spiritual thirst, which he has tried to quench with materialism. The Western way. But he feels empty and seeks for something more. It's a problem many children in the community face."

Jinnah's solution to the problem of rebellious sons involved a month in boot camp, not a weekend at a temple retreat, but he kept this thought to himself. "There may be something in what you say, Mr. Puri," he muttered into his tea.

She Demons   57

Puri looked especially grave as his put his empty cup down. "Then perhaps you could talk to Andy's father, Sadhu? Give him the benefit of your experience, Jinnah. I'm sure he'll appreciate it."

If Jinnah had not already finished his tea, he would have choked on it. Puri wanted *him* to give parental advice? He must be mad! But unless Puri told him where Sadhu worked, it would be harder than hell to find him in the forest of Gills sprouting in the Vancouver phone book — if, indeed, Sadhu had a phone.

"Of course I will, Mr. Puri," Jinnah promised. "You can depend on me."

It was a long drive to Surrey, south of Vancouver. Jinnah took the Port Mann Bridge across the Fraser River, cursing as he crawled along the slowly curving span. What the hell was all this traffic doing here at this time of night, for God's sake, when he needed to get to his destination ASAP? He also wondered what the hell a construction crew was doing working so late. Whenever he hired workers for a project they arrived at noon and left by three, with a two hour lunch in between. Jinnah was so lost in thought, wondering just how much money one could make in the housing business, that he almost missed the turnoff for Panorama Ridge. The directions Puri had given him were excellent, but finding anything in Surrey was difficult. New subdivisions and streets seem to spring up overnight, and roughly a third of them were not entered in the satellite-guided Love Machine's database.

In the end it was not hard to find the place, a huge monster house that was alive with lights. Nor was it hard to figure out just why Sadhu was still hard at work, along with the rest of the crew visible through the curtainless windows. There were two cars parked bumper to bumper at the head of the driveway — a red Porsche and a black BMW. They were so close together that to Jinnah's eyes they appeared to be trying to mate. He wondered what sort of bastard offspring such a union would create: a PMW? A Borsche? Two expensively dressed men with Bluetooths surgically attached to their ears were pacing beside their respective vehicles as Jinnah approached.

One, a tall man wearing designer glasses and sporting a greying ponytail, was shouting down his mouthpiece as if it was a long, hollow tube. "I said it'll be ready for final inspection tomorrow! Yes, tomorrow!" he hollered. "Of course it'll pass!"

Jinnah put him down as a Type A personality. The other fellow was quite a bit stouter and looked like he had had his suit sprayed onto him. By contrast, he was taking the quiet but deadly approach over his phone. "You told me the moldings would be here this afternoon," he said, voice icy with menace. "I still have a crew waiting to put them on. I don't care if you're closed...."

Jinnah felt a tiny spark of sympathy for the fellow and put his plans to make a fortune in the residential housing market on hold. He was almost past them

She Demons 59

when the tall guy with the ponytail grabbed him by the shoulder.

"Where the hell do you think you're going?" he barked. "The house is sold."

Jinnah found the man crass, presumptuous, and his manners non-existent. He felt no compunction, therefore, to be courteous in return. "I have an urgent message for one of your employees," he said bluntly. "About his son."

The transformation was startling. Ponytail turned from a self-absorbed, driven yuppie into something resembling a human. The look on his face was very close to concern.

"Hey, sorry," he said. "Hope it's not serious."

"That's for his father to decide," said Jinnah, and breezed past him and into the house.

The place was crawling with workers trying to put the finishing touches on the interior without enough time or materials. The foreman, a short, broad Sikh wearing a hairnet under his chin that barely contained his wild beard, hardly looked up when Jinnah asked where Sadhu Gill was. He jabbed an impatient thumb over his shoulder and cursed foully as he tried to get his air nailer unjammed. Sadhu was on his knees when Jinnah found him, fiddling with a corner join in the living room, a chisel in hand. He was a handsome Sikh man in his thirties, his black work turban gilded by sawdust. As he looked up, bright, white teeth shone out, framed by his dark beard.

Jinnah greeted him in Punjabi. "Sadhu Gill? My name is Hakeem Jinnah. It's about Andy."

60 *Donald J. Hauka*

Sadhu's smile disappeared and he looked suddenly older, like a beaten prizefighter struggling up from his knees in the tenth round. His dusted himself off wearily.

"Are you from social services or the police?" Sadhu replied in Punjabi.

Jinnah had thought carefully about how to open this encounter. He assumed Sadhu would be more willing to speak to someone presenting himself as a friend rather than an authority figure. But he had to be careful — not too familiar, not too friendly, or the man would grow suspicious. All Jinnah needed was a few questions answered to make the connection. He wasn't about to blow it by being over-anxious.

"Neither," he replied smoothly. "I'm a friend of Ram Puri's. He thought I should talk to you a bit about the boy. Since my own son wants to emulate his behaviour."

Sadhu looked at Jinnah, face haggard. "Now what has he been up to?" he said, dark clouds swirling about his face.

"I assure you, your son is blameless in this," said Jinnah, trying to keep the man calm. "It's just that my boy Saleem wants to go to a rave tonight. He said Andy goes to them and has told him they are harmless."

"Harmless?" Sadhu cried. "There is no such thing as a harmless rave, Mr. Jinnah."

"There are drugs, hmm?"

"It is not about drugs. It's about the people he has met there. Immoral people. Staying up all night. Dropping out of school. After a few of these raves, he no longer goes to temple."

She Demons   61

Jinnah saw an opening and decided to risk it. "Immoral people, you say?" he said offhandedly. "Tell me, was one of them named Thad Golway, by any chance?"

Jinnah searched Sadhu's face for any sign of suspicion. But the man was too worked up about his son.

"No. I do not talk to him about their names. They are not Sikhs, mostly. Some are Indian, some Asian, a few whites. They do not miss a rave. Not one."

Jinnah cursed inwardly. It didn't rule a connection out, but it did mean more digging. He tried another tack.

"Forgive me, Mr. Gill, but it sounds like you and your son have not been on speaking terms lately. Sometimes it helps if another adult, someone with a different perspective could talk to the boy, hmm? I would be happy to do this for you — for us both."

Jinnah held his breath. For a moment, he thought he had gone too far, for the look of anger in Sadhu's eyes sent a chill through his being. Then the eyes softened from anger to anguish, and tears started around the rims.

"I thank you for your offer, Mr. Jinnah, but it is not possible," said Sadhu, his voice thick, barely controlled. "The boy is gone. He left a week ago with a young woman. I don't know if he's coming back."

The words hit Jinnah square in the forehead, like a cricket ball. A dozen different possibilities sprang to mind. Was Andy one of Thad's missing friends? A young woman? Could that be the one who had found Thad's corpse?

"A young woman, you say, Mr. Gill — his girlfriend?" he asked quickly.

Sadhu shook his head and wiped his eyes with his dirty sleeve. "No. She's older than he — almost like a mother, he says," Sadhu blushed at the words. "Her name I know: Jassy Singh."

That name rang a faint bell in Jinnah's extensive memory bank. Jassy Singh ... where had he heard of her? It was a common enough name in the community. There might be no connection at all. Jinnah realized with a start that Sadhu was looking at him, trembling, eyes wide in appeal.

"I have lost my son, Mr. Jinnah. Help me get him back. Please."

Jinnah didn't know what to say. Of course he wanted to find Sadhu's son. But it had never occurred to him that he would take his offer of being an intermediary seriously. Holy shit! The man's delusional. *Perhaps I should just give him a recording of my latest argument with Saleem. That ought to cure him.* But he found himself shaking Sadhu's hand and clapping him on the shoulder and before he could stop himself, he uttered the words that would send him down the demon path.

"Of course I will, Sadhu. I will do everything I can."

Jinnah kicked himself all the way home from Surrey. How could he be so stupid? What the hell was he — a crime reporter, for God's sake — doing getting mixed up in family counselling? He couldn't even relate to his own son, let alone somebody else's! And he was

She Demons   63

at a dead end. No Andy Gill to question. No definite link to Thad Golway. Sonofabitch. Jinnah glanced at the clock glowing softly blue on the dashboard. Nearly ten o'clock. It was getting late and he was tired. But a plan was slowly forming in his mind, a plan that, when it leapt out at him fully formed, caused him to sail through a red light at First Avenue.

"No, fuck it. I'm going to bed," he growled at the plan.

The plan would not take no for an answer and by the time Jinnah threw open the door to the Jinnah-mahal, his obsessive brain was already laying out the precise timing and cover stories that would be needed to execute it. It took him a moment to register how quiet the house was.

"Saleem! Manjit!" he bellowed.

No answer. Jinnah took the stairs up to Saleem's bedroom two at a time, and immediately regretted it. He paused, wheezing, on the upper landing for a moment. Asthma again. Sonofabitch. He forced himself to wait until his breath returned. He wasn't going to face Saleem without sufficient lung power. A quick blast of medication from his puffer helped and, feeling restored, he entered Saleem's room without knocking.

"Hey!" cried Saleem.

Jinnah paused in the doorway. His son was on his computer, hands covering the screen. Jinnah could see just enough of the display to conclude Saleem was on one of his chat groups. Probably complaining about what a tight-ass his Dad was. Well, he hasn't seen anything yet.

"Your mother's at work already, is she?" Jinnah said, trying to sound pleasant.

"Yeah. Look, Dad, I don't need another lecture —"

"You're not getting one," said Jinnah softly. "Saleem, how well do you know Andy Gill? Think you could pick him out of a crowd, hmm?"

Saleem looked at him suspiciously, like a school boy expecting to take six of the best who sees his headmaster inexplicably put the cane away.

"Yeah. Why?"

Jinnah grabbed Saleem's jacket from off the bed and threw it at him. "Fantastic. Get dressed, son. We're going to a rave."

Chapter Three

It was hard to tell that the sprawling building had once been a church. It looked rather like a community hall; a plain, rectangular box with wooden siding and tall, single-pane windows. But a congregation had once worshipped here, filling the long gone pews that had stretched from the entrance alcove to the raised stage where the pulpit had once stood. That congregation had thrived and prospered even as the neighbourhood around them crumbled into decay. Finally, the worshippers made plans for a new church, raised the money, and had left the building over a decade ago, taking the sacredness with them to the new site and retiring this one in a special ceremony. Now it was used by a variety of temporary tenants: film companies, flea markets, and Lionel Simons, who knew that, deconsecrated or not, holding his rave there would drive the Reverend Peter Hobbes insane with fury.

Jinnah didn't bother to fill Saleem in on that background as they approached the front door. He wanted to keep his son focused on the plan.

"This is gonna be cool!" said Saleem.

"This is gonna be work," Jinnah reminded him. "Remember: you go in there, you look for Andy Gill. You find him, you point me in his direction, hmm? Failing that, drop the name of Thad Golway and see what you can scare up. Understand?"

"I got it," said Saleem, with just the right shade of petulance in his voice.

Jinnah choked down his frustration. His heart was pounding faster than the muffled beat that could be felt emanating from within the abandoned church. He was a mass of anxieties and fears. It was getting on to eleven o'clock. The rave officially ended at 1:00 a.m. Manjit would stay behind to help the rest of the health officials pack up. That gave them less than two hours to get in, get the goods, and get home without Manjit being the wiser.

"And if you should see your mother —" Jinnah began for the tenth time.

"I know, I know," Saleem cut him off. "Lie."

"I am not telling you to lie to your mother," said Jinnah, whining only slightly. "It's called plausible deniability."

"Why don't I get plausible deniability?"

"Because I'm the president of this operation. Just avoid her at all costs and if you get caught, you snuck out of the house while I was out, right?"

"Thanks, Mr. President."

She Demons   67

There were a handful of youths at the doors, smoking. They were from a cross-section of ethnic backgrounds and a wide variety of social circumstances, but had one thing in common: they were all about Saleem's age. Jinnah was easily the oldest person there by two decades. An insolent silence settled over them as Jinnah approached the doorman.

"Two, please."

The doorman was stocky, with a weightlifter's torso and legs that were just a little too short for him. His face was broad, his hair was short, and Jinnah was reminded of the drill sergeant he had been forced to listen to for several weeks while doing his compulsory service back in Kenya. The doorman cleared his throat. "Two? You don't quite fit the demographic, do you, pop?"

His voice was pleasant enough, but Jinnah's hackles went up anyway. "It's my right as a taxpayer to be allowed in!" he thundered. "And as a parent!"

The youths were now staring at them curiously. Saleem looked like he wanted to crawl under the floorboards of the porch. The doorman laughed. "You want to go inside and check things out? Make sure it's safe for your kid?"

"Absolutely," said Jinnah. "Listen, my friend, don't try and stop me —"

"Go right ahead," said the doorman, offering them two tickets. "It's a clean rave, friend. It's about peace and openness, not secrecy and suspicion. That'll be forty bucks."

"Forty bucks!" squealed Jinnah, at which point

Saleem found the courage to elbow him in the ribs, dislodging his wallet and gaining them access to the rave.

Once inside, Jinnah had hoped to give Saleem one last pep talk, but it was useless. The music was so loud, even in the foyer, that he had to shout to hear himself speak. Once they were through the main doors, they were assaulted by a wall of sound. Jinnah felt he was being rocked back and forth by the music. As his eyes adjusted to the gloom, he was startled by the action on the dance floor. Dozens of teens were dancing and writhing, packed in so tightly it was amazing they could move at all. It looked more like a huge rugby scrum than anything else. Jinnah's nose quivered with the warm aroma of human sweat and teen hormones. And the stench of his own fear for his son.

"Live in the present moment. Put peace in this moment. Put love in this moment. Put yourself in the centre. The centre is everywhere...."

Jinnah wrenched his eyes from the floor to the stage. Strobe lights flashed in time to the heartbeat rhythm of the music. There was a lone figure, lit up every half second by the pounding lights: tall, slender, dressed in black silk, his head partly covered by a golden scarf. Lionel Simons, in mid rap homily. Jinnah studied the Rave Messiah's face. He'd never been able to place Simons exactly. He was of mixed race, and could have passed for anything from an Indian yogi to a Tibetan monk. Right now, the former shock-rocker was belting out a gospel rock with a danceable World Beat.

Jinnah felt rather than heard Saleem talking at his side. He turned to see Saleem chatting with a small circle of teens who had surrounded them. Several of them were Indo-Canadians whom Saleem seemed to know. In an instant, they had whisked Saleem onto the dance floor. Jinnah lost sight of them almost immediately. Shit. He moved with difficulty along the wall, pushing past people, trying to catch a glimpse of his son. Just ahead of him, the crowd seemed to thin, promising a vantage point. Jinnah was about to wriggle his way through when he saw a familiar face not ten feet ahead.

Manjit. Handing out water to teenagers.

Jinnah hastily ducked behind a young couple, turned, and headed the other direction. His head was throbbing like the speakers and he was having trouble breathing. He felt claustrophobic, slightly panicked. Head down, he fumbled in his pockets for a couple of tranquilizers, meaning to pop them into his mouth and swallow them without water — definitely without water — and with that he cast a glance back at Manjit. Oh, God, no. She's staring at the dance floor. That's not a look of professional concern on her face either. Jinnah followed her gaze. Well, at least he had found Saleem. The little bastard didn't look like he'd done a lot of talking. Gyrating, yes. He was considering trying to haul Saleem off the dance floor when a new problem presented itself. Manjit was moving in his direction. Keeping one eye on Saleem and another on his wife, Jinnah tried to make good his escape along the wall and ran headlong into a young woman, who doubled over.

"I am sorry!" Jinnah shouted above the din, helping her straighten out.

"S'okay," the woman gasped.

She stood up and looked at Jinnah. In that moment, a spark of recognition leapt between them. Although she was young, she was definitely a little old for this crowd, being in her mid-twenties. Her hair was a long, jet-black mane and her face still had the grace and beauty of a princess carved in the stone temple of Konarak. She was, admittedly, a few pounds heavier than when Jinnah had first seen her, but she was still stunning. He could not help but wonder what she would look like in a sari, but then, even the jeans and white cotton blouse she wore was an improvement over her wardrobe during their first encounter, when she had been totally nude.

"Jassy Singh!" he cried.

It was not until Jassy's tight little mouth set and her soft, brown eyes hardened that Jinnah also recalled that they had not, strictly speaking, parted on the best of terms.

"Jinnah, you son of a bitch!" Jassy screamed above the music. "What the hell do you think you're doing here?"

Jinnah's memory had finally located the file marked "Singh, Jassy." Interview subject eight years previous. Story: Simons's first mass, nude baptism on Wreck Beach. Subject had been eloquent in defence of the MiMis. Wardrobe consisted of flowers in her hair. Had reminded the reporter of a wild pony revelling in new-found freedom. How could she have taken offence at that?

"How have you been, Jassy?" shouted Jinnah. "I must say, you look fantastic."

She Demons 71

"Don't give me that shit!" said Jassy, hands on her hips. "Do you think I've forgotten what you wrote about me?"

Jinnah had, actually. He did remember the photos, of course. Most of which could not be used in a family newspaper like the *Tribune*.

"I'm sure it was nothing but flattery for one so young and beautiful," Jinnah said, resorting to evasive tactics.

"Flattery! You called me a besotted teenage zombie!"

"It was meant in a nice way," Jinnah protested.

"You totally distorted what I said! You completely twisted everything to make me look like I was some ... some *Moonie* or something. And you called us a cult! The MiMis aren't a cult, we're a service organization!"

"I thought I painted a charming portrait of a new generation of flower children," Jinnah riposted, still trying to remember the exact tone of the article.

"Depraved nude revels. Brainwashed automatons cavorting in a public orgy. Charming?!" yelled Jassy, whose memory seemed far more perfect on the subject than Jinnah's. "My parents threw me out of the house! They haven't talked to me in eight years because of the lies you wrote! Maybe if you paid more attention to what I was saying instead of scoping me out —"

By now, several people had gathered around to watch. And the music, which had been at near ear-bleeding level since Jinnah's arrival, had stopped. But Jassy hadn't bothered to lower her voice.

The last thing Jinnah needed here was a scene. He switched desperately from the defensive to the offensive.

"Look, this has nothing to do with your nakedness. Everything I wrote about you and your cult — and it is a cult — was true," Jinnah said, lowering his voice. "Does the naked truth hurt so much?"

"Let me tell you a thing or two about truth —" Jassy started.

"Tell me what you know about Andy Gill."

The question landed like a low blow in a boxing match. Jassy closed her mouth for the first time since she'd bumped into Jinnah. His instincts tingled. Yes. On the right track at last....

"Andy who?" said Jassy fiercely. "I don't know an Andy Gill."

Her eyes cannot meet mine. She's a bad liar, Jinnah thought.

"His family is very anxious over his whereabouts. He left home in your company several weeks ago, according to his father." Jinnah pressed his advantage. "And I have reason to believe he would like to speak to me about — several things."

"I don't know him and I hope I never see your stupid face again!" Jassy stomped off and was swallowed by a crowd of teens, who eyed Jinnah as if he were some lascivious ogre. He turned to find a nice, safe corner to crawl into and ran right into Manjit.

"Manjit, darling! What a surprise!"

"Hakeem. Who was that young woman?"

"A former interview subject who objected to a story I wrote. That's all, my love," said Jinnah, shrugging.

"And do you interview all of your subjects while they are naked?"

She Demons 73

There was no logical response to this question. In fact, Jinnah knew the entire episode was a black pit into which he would be sunk for months, even years. He was about to confess the entire truth when Manjit put up a warning hand.

"Not now, Hakeem. Why have you brought Saleem here?"

"I brought him here to work, not for fun, Manjit. He's on assignment."

"You went against your own word so you could use your son to pursue a news story?"

The words shook Manjit's head for her. They were lost on Jinnah. This was partly due to his ability to hear an ugly truth and have it bounce off his emotional armour, but mainly because his attention was elsewhere. Near the exit, Jassy was pitching into the doorman — likely for letting Jinnah in. It was his subconscious that picked up the urgent tone in Manjit's voice and yanked him back to attention.

"I'm sorry, my love — you were saying?"

"I said don't you think it's about time you took our child labourer son home, Hakeem?"

"Of course, darling. I'll just go get —"

But when Jinnah's eyes finally peeled away from Jassy and the doorman and focused on the dance floor, there was no Saleem. Manjit looked at her husband. Jinnah knew his eyes were twin revelations of guilt behind his tinted glasses. Her words from earlier this evening echoed in his head: "The problems aren't on the dance floor. They're around the edges, in the parking lots, the washrooms...."

74   *Donald J. Hauka*

"Sonofabitch," muttered Jinnah.

Jinnah burst through the crowd at the front door of the building and felt like a drowning man breaking surface. Panting, he put the two Phenobarbitals into his mouth and swallowed them dry. Where the hell was Saleem? He didn't need Manjit's accusing look to know this was his fault. What if he was already shooting up in the parking lot? No, he couldn't be — wouldn't be. Surely he'd raised his son — okay, surely Manjit had raised his son better than that. He found his cellphone in his hand and he almost used the speed-dial to call Graham for help. His finger was on the button when a small circle of teens hanging around the steps broke apart, revealing Saleem at the centre. To Hakeem's immense relief he appeared unharmed and still in his right mind.

Jinnah's heart rate had scarcely begun to slow when he heard a disturbance in the parking lot. Standing at the top of the stairs by the doors, he had a perfect view of its source. A gang of teens was approaching, singing loudly, marching in a tight formation, and sweeping errant ravers before them like a scythe. They were dressed in white bomber jackets bearing logo of the warrior Archangel Michael and his flaming sword. Shit, it's the crusaders. Hobbes's God Squad. Led by the Reverend Hobbes himself. All hell was about to break lose. Without reflecting on the irony of that thought, Jinnah sprinted down the steps and grabbed

She Demons 75

Saleem by the collar. His ring of friends, having spied the God Squad, had already started for the building.

"What —"

"Inside," Jinnah snapped, hauling Saleem up the steps, pushing and shoving against the rest of the teenagers seeking sanctuary inside the abandoned church.

"Fallen, fallen is Babylon the great!" Hobbes roared through his megaphone. "It has become a dwelling place of demons, a haunt of every foul spirit, for all nations drunk the wine of her impure passion...."

The God Squad had made it to the foot of the stairs. Jinnah and Saleem were one step from the top and could go no further. A surge of people trying to get out the door had met the tide of teens trying to get in and become a hopeless whirlpool of pushing, shoving humanity. Hakeem and his son were being squished, elbowed, kicked as young men and women flailed, trying to move. It was like being in the mosh pit without the music.

"What's going on, Dad?" asked Saleem. "What's happening."

"I believe the Christians call this 'tough love,' Saleem," Jinnah gasped as someone trod on his Guccis.

"Repent! Repent! The wages of sin is death!"

Hobbes was standing at the bottom of the stairs, haranguing the crowd, backed up by over a dozen God Squad members. Hadn't anyone thought to call the cops? Jinnah would have done it himself, but his arms were pinned to his side. Where the hell was the doorman when you needed him?

Suddenly, Jinnah became aware of a hush over the crowd. Perhaps a dozen people had entered the old church, but only one person had come out into the cleared space. Standing alone at the top of the stairs, facing down the Reverend Hobbes was Lionel Simons himself, a dark figure facing the forces of white glaring hatefully up at him. Jinnah groaned inwardly. Caught between a rock of ages and a hard place.

"Reverend Hobbes, good evening," said Simons, his voice firm and commanding. "How good of you to come to the party."

"Blasphemer!" roared Hobbes, abandoning his megaphone. "How dare you desecrate this holy ground?"

"I think it was one of your denominations that abandoned this as a place of worship," said Simons, smiling. "It felt lonely. We've restored its sense of purpose."

"Drug dealer!" shouted Hobbes. "Corrupter of youth! How dare you talk of worship! It's the devil you bow to, Simons!"

Simons's smile faded. He walked slowly down the steps. Jinnah found himself among the crowd watching from the front of the porch as the Rave Messiah towered over Hobbes like some dark angel.

"We worship life, we do not deny it, as you do," said Simons calmly. "As you will not listen, you are not welcome to our feast. Go, and take your God Squad with you."

Jinnah found himself holding his breath. He could easily imagine these two men of peace murdering each other. How many years had they been waging a war for the hearts and minds of kids just like Saleem? For a long moment, there was near silence as the two men

She Demons 77

glared at each other. Then, another figure joined them on the stairs. It was the doorman.

"Come on, Magus," he said cheerfully. "Time for your closing set. Unless you want to borrow the Reverend's megaphone and do a little dancing in the streets."

Simons did not take his eyes off Hobbes. "Ray, get inside," he said.

Ray the doorman was nonplussed. "Now, now. Reverend Hobbes, where are your stones, sir? The ones that he who is without sin is allowed to cast?"

"Get thee behind me, Satan!" spat Hobbes. "I know you, Daisley. Servant of the evil one."

"Hey, the evil one pays scale and has a great benefits package. Now if you two want to start a riot, you're both going about it the right way. But despite our differences, we all believe in making love, not splitting skulls, right? Remember the sixties? All you need is love. Incidentally, Reverend, where were you in '62?"

Jinnah looked at Ray Daisley, the doorman, in a new light. He'd looked like a whipped puppy while Jassy was dissing him. Now he stood between these two driven men and tried to kid them out of a potentially violent confrontation. Simons visibly relaxed and even managed a wan smile. "Ray, you're crazy," he said, turning to go.

Hobbes went to lift his megaphone to his mouth, then found Daisley's hand on his arm.

"Enough, Reverend. For the love of the kids, enough."

78 *Donald J. Hauka*

Jinnah was amazed. The words were pleasant enough but carried a distinctly menacing undertone. Suddenly, he realized why Daisley was Simons's gatekeeper.

"Please. I'm asking politely, Reverend. I would add that the police are on their way."

"We answer to a higher authority," said Hobbes.

But Jinnah noted that the Reverend still turned away, waving his megaphone over his head at his God Squad. "The Lord's work has been done here tonight, friends! Let us go and sing His praises in purer air."

Jinnah watched as the God Squad fell in behind Hobbes and marched off singing "Onward Christian Soldiers." Daisley stood still at the foot of the steps, watching them go, grinning. Jinnah looked over at Saleem. Consumed with guilt, he saw the boy's wide eyes watching Hobbes and his crew march off. How could he expose his son to danger like that?

"You okay, son?" he said, voice heavy with concern and conscience.

"Wow! That was wild!" Saleem exclaimed. "Do those guys show up every time?"

Jinnah stared at his son, uncomprehending. "Saleem, I risked my life to save you from being trampled underfoot, lost a pound of heart tissue dragging you to safety, and I have aggravated my meningitis, every symptom of which I am now suffering, and you're telling me you *enjoyed* that?"

It was Saleem's turn to look at a loss. "Does this mean I can't catch the last set?"

To his credit, Jinnah considered it for an instant. Then the image of Manjit swam up before him like a

She Demons 79

Yaksha, a divine demoness who would lure him into the forest, only to slay him.

"Saleem, I gave you a job to do tonight. Did you actually ask anyone about Andy Gill or Thad Golway?"

"I was going to," Saleem whined. "But the music was kinda loud and I was dancing and —"

Jinnah was not angry, just resigned. He had tried to take a shortcut to the truth and in murder cases that seldom worked. One needed to emulate Sadhu's Kirat Karna to solve a slaying. He put an arm around his son's shoulders and steered him towards the stairs.

"Consider the ride home your severance package, son," he said.

Chapter Four

"Y'know, I can count the number of reporters who come in here in a year on one hand," said the police clerk.

Caitlin Bishop smiled her best cream-fed smile. In front of her was the holy grail of cop reporters: the filing cabinet that held all of the affidavits supporting search warrants. It was public knowledge, but only to the few initiates on the beat who knew of its existence, safe behind the counter in the records room, the domain of the police clerk, who seemed almost grateful for the attention. He hovered close — too close — by her shoulder.

"Y'need a hand or anything?" he asked.

Caitlin's smile was considerably cooler as she assured the police clerk she knew her way around the filing system. Jinnah himself had taught her. The police clerk muttered something about being only too willing to help if she needed anything and subsided into

She Demons 81

his chair. Caitlin made sure he was at least pretending to work before turning her attention to the information before her. What did she expect to find? She didn't know exactly, but if it helped her get ahead of Jinnah it was worth it. Her wake-up call that morning had come courtesy of her producer, Ian, screaming about Hakeem's exclusive plastered on the front page of the *Tribune*. Caitlin hated getting beat. She especially hated getting beat by Jinnah.

Her fingers flipped through files; two weeks, three weeks; four weeks ... here. She kept her face carefully neutral as she scanned the document. Affidavit supporting an application for a search warrant. Sponsoring officer: Sergeant C. Graham. Certain activities known to me, occurring at public property adjacent to the intersection of Main and Terminal Streets, city of Vancouver....

"Holy shit!" Caitlin's eyes bulged out as she read the bottom of the document. She glanced nervously back at the police clerk, but he was, thankfully, on the phone and hadn't heard her astonished oath. She composed herself and pulled the file out of the cabinet, laying it in front of the police clerk.

"Do you think you could copy this for me, please?" she asked in a voice as saccharin as Jinnah's coffee.

The clerk put his hand over the phone, solicitous. "Find what y'needed?" he said, taking the file from her.

Caitlin Bishop smiled her best 18 percent milk fat smile.

* * *

It was a short walk from the records room to the main lobby. The brief wait for the elevator to the third floor seemed to take an eternity, so did the momentary hesitation shown by the clerk behind the Major Crime counter. But it was actually a very, very short time before Caitlin Bishop found herself sitting across from Graham, studying the policeman's face as he opened the file she had handed him, waiting for his reaction when he flipped to the final page. He didn't disappoint her. It wasn't much, just a slight raising of the eyebrows, but that was worth a thousand screams of anguish and denial from other interview subjects. Graham's face, however, was a cipher as he turned his eyes on Caitlin.

"So what do you want from me?" he asked, voice neutral.

"You could start by explaining how Thad Golway's name got onto the affidavits supporting the warrant."

"Judges kinda like to know who's swearing out the affidavit. They're picky that way."

"The names are supposed to be deleted from the document once they're put in the public files. To protect the informants."

That hit a bit close to home. Graham simply nodded as he tried to calculate the damage to the case, the department, to himself.

Caitlin fired another shot into the silence. "If Thad was working for you, what was he doing on the street? And who else might have been looking through these papers and found the same information?"

"You can check with records — they keep a list."

She Demons 83

"And they could guarantee that no one even slightly pissed off they'd been ratted on didn't go in there or send someone a little more respectable looking to have a glance at the public record?"

Graham couldn't, but he certainly wasn't going to admit it. It had been a bastard of a morning, what with Jinnah's bloody Yakshas story and Superintendent Butcher reaming him out for being so stupid as to try to manipulate the media. Now this. How hard could it be, to sever a name from a document?

"Extremely unlikely," he lied. "It's just a clerical error, that's all. It's been known to happen."

"Why was Thad back on the street? Was that a clerical error too?"

Caitlin was vaguely disappointed when she saw the look of desperation fleet across Graham's face. He was usually made of sterner stuff. There could be no mistaking the plea contained in his reply.

"Ms. Bishop, all I can tell you is this line of questioning is not helpful to the investigation."

Despite her surprise at having won quite so easily, Caitlin Bishop managed to keep her smile in place as she retrieved the copied affidavit from Graham.

"I'll be doing a stand-up on The Corner at noon," she said, pausing by the door. "It's up to you if you want to go on live with me or not."

"Insurance, Craig. Or home renovation. That's the ticket. Do you think Transport Canada really inspects these things or does the operator just print up a label on his computer, hmm?"

Normally, Graham would have appreciated Jinnah's attempt at humour, but not today. His stomach was in knots and the rocking motion of the Aquabus wasn't helping. The tiny passenger ferry that crossed False Creek was their special meeting place, used only when they had urgent matters to discuss. For Graham, things weren't just urgent: they were desperate.

"When I asked for advice, Hakeem, I didn't mean career counselling," he said peevishly. "I gotta find some way to muzzle Caitlin Bishop."

Jinnah took a drag of his cigarette and considered his friend's face. Was it possible for a man to age so much in twenty-four hours? His hair looked greyer around the temples, there were lines that hadn't been there just a day ago. But then, white guys were like that, he reflected. Like bananas: perfectly ripe one minute, gone off the next.

"You could always send Animal Enforcement down to her station — remind them that pit bulls in the city of Vancouver are supposed to be muzzled."

"You're a great help."

Graham slumped against the fiberglass hull of the ferry. They were sitting in the stern, well out of earshot of the ferryman, the only other person on the vessel as it threaded is way through the yachts, sailboats, and power craft that poured through the narrow waterway as ceaselessly as the tide. Jinnah felt sorry for the policeman, truly, but what did Craig expect him to do about it? He tried summing up the situation.

She Demons 85

"Caitlin Bishop has your balls in a vice, your super wants your head on a platter, and your career dangles by a thread. A very sorry state of affairs, my friend. I don't see what I can do about it."

"You could talk to her, Hakeem."

Oh ho! Things must be worse than he'd thought. Jinnah's inherent instincts, the ones that ensured his professional survival, quivered ominously.

"And just what do you expect me to tell her, Craig? 'Listen, Caitlin, I want you to forget everything I've ever taught you about news? Just be nice to the policeman, darling, and the policeman will be nice to you?' Sonofabitch —"

"You could tell her that there are some things more important than a scoop."

"Aside from vast personal wealth, what would those be?"

"Like the greater good. Like catching Thad Golway's killer."

"My inherent instincts tell me that somehow she has already heard this speech."

"She might listen to it, coming from you. She respects you, Hakeem."

"And I want to keep that respect. In a purely professional manner, you understand."

"I'm just asking you to ask her to hold off for a couple of days."

"You're asking me to help you censor the news."

They were nearing the dock at Granville Island. Graham only had a minute left to convince Jinnah to help him.

He gave it one last try. "Listen, Jinnah, I don't give a shit about what happens to me. If my career's over, fine. I screwed up and I'll take the consequences. But before I'm done, I want to nail the bastard who killed that kid and left him carved like a Thanksgiving turkey in a shop window. You know and I know that if Caitlin runs with her angle, it'll only make it that much harder to catch the murderer. You are the only reporter in Canada who she'll listen to. What's more important, a two-minute piece at the top of the news, or bringing a killer to justice? You tell me."

Not bad, Jinnah grunted to himself. A cross between Sam Spade and Jack Lord. He didn't want to admit to himself how profound an effect this direct emotional appeal had had on him. It reminded him of arguments he'd had with his own father, the police chief. Somewhere, deep underneath the layers of emotional armour and professional pride, the tiny, blackened cinder that was Jinnah's conscience stirred. He cursed his fondness for B movies and old cop shows.

"All right, for God's sake — stop whining like whipped puppy. I'll talk to her. As much good as it will do...."

As they stepped out onto the dock, Graham shook Jinnah's hand and thanked him profusely. Jinnah waited until the policeman had reached the top of the ramp leading up the public market before flicking his cigarette into the water. It annoyed him when he agreed to do the right thing, especially when there was no tangible payoff. The whole thing was beginning to remind him of his Indo-Barbies business.

She Demons 87

"Sonofabitch," he muttered, and started up the ramp.

The cafeteria in Vancouver Police HQ was, thankfully, nearly empty, so there were few witnesses to Jinnah's humiliation. It started badly and went downhill from there. Not even the six sugars and four creams could take the bitter edge from the coffee Hakeem unenthusiastically sipped.

"All I'm asking you is: do you really think the public needs to know this ugly truth right now, hmm?" he tried, sallying forth one last time.

Caitlin fixed him with her coolest ice maiden look. "Aren't you the one who taught me that an ugly truth always looks beautiful in print with your byline above it?" Her tone could have put the lie to global warming.

It wasn't so much the Antarctic disdain with which Caitlin had met his suggestion that she think about the "greater good" that hurt Jinnah: he would have been disappointed with any other reaction. Nor was it any flaw in her logic, which was, of course, impeccable: cops like Graham take advantage of street kids like Thad and his friends all the time. When the cops screw up, kids end up getting killed. Graham had screwed up. Now Thad was dead. The greater good demanded some sort of accountability, didn't it? No, what really cut Jinnah to the quick was the sense he got that Caitlin thought he was past it — was acting out of weakness. In short, had finally been captured by the cops. He kicked himself. He

88 *Donald J. Hauka*

should never have tried appealing to her better nature: Caitlin Bishop didn't have one. Desperate, he changed strategies in midstream, appealing to something far more abundant in her character: vanity.

"Well, you can go with that angle if you like, sweetheart," he said, leaning back in his chair and stirring the syrupy fluid in his cup. "I won't be chasing it."

Caitlin's manner, which made the Ross Ice Shelf seem warm and inviting, grew even more frigid. "I'm not falling for that one, Jinnah. You couldn't possibly have anything better than this."

"No, of course not," purred Jinnah, leaning across the table and reaching for her hand. "Just because you were eating my dust all day today and the fact that I have, as usual, an inside track into the investigation, does not mean a thing, hmm? What could I, a mere crime reporter, one who has covered every aspect of human depravity, whose prose has been ripped and read aloud by more TV and radio stations than any other, despite suffering from the lingering effects of pellagra, hmm? Possibly have up my sleeve?"

"At the moment, my hand," said Caitlin, with just a hint of a thaw in her voice. "Stop giving me your Kenyan Tiger imitation and tell me what you're working on."

"Aside from your hormones?" asked Jinnah, stroking her fingers with his own, which were only slightly sticky from his coffee concoction. "I am working day and night to solve this murder. There is another of your street kids who may know something — a missing kid."

She Demons   89

Caitlin stopped trying to extricate her digits from Jinnah's grasp. The ice maiden look was gone and Jinnah was gratified to see the calculating look of the professional trying to determine whether he was bluffing or not.

"Missing kid? What missing kid?" she asked. "Where?"

Jinnah spent less than a nanosecond congratulating himself on still having the royal reporter jelly. He stopped molesting Caitlin's fingers and put his hands behind his head, leaning back in his chair.

"Somewhere out there." Jinnah smiled sadly. "Lost in the wilderness."

Out in the wilderness, Andy Gill was about to hit The Wall.

The Wall was sheer, carved out of the Coast Mountains that surrounded Andy and a dozen other kids, young men and women roughly his age and from a mix of ethnic backgrounds: all of them disciples. He glanced furtively at their faces, looking for signs of emotion. But they all kept their expressions blank. They had developed the habit quite quickly after arriving in the camp. To the untrained eye, it looked like any other outdoors school. Plain, unadorned log barracks and mess hall, cedar outhouses, and, of course, the training equipment. The Wall was part of that, used to teach mountaineering skills. Andy tried to suppress an involuntary shudder. He didn't like the idea of scaling The Wall. But he liked the idea of displeasing Arnie even less.

"I want you to look at this wall — really look at it!"

Arnie Krootz's voice was just like the rest of him: huge. Unlike his mostly brown and yellow-skinned disciples, he was a classic Aryan, complete with blonde hair and coconut-crushing biceps. Arnie ran the camp with a mix of rigid discipline and compassion that Andy found reassuring after his sudden flight from Vancouver. Arnie was, in his own way, a lot like Jassy. Certainly their messages were identical.

"There are many ways to look at this wall," Arnie boomed. "If you see it as an obstacle, it will defeat you. If you see it as an 'other' of any kind, you will not be able to climb it. But you will climb it, all of you. Not because you want to conquer or vanquish it: that is not the true path. You will climb it because you are disciples. The most promising members of Millennial Magi. You have been brought here to be trained in the way of the mountains and the wilderness. To reach a higher level in the service of the organization. Once you complete this training, you will become prophets and be able to pass your knowledge on to those who will follow in your footsteps."

Andy didn't have to glance around to see the looks of acceptance and anticipation on the faces of his fellow disciples. He could feel it, even as he could feel the fierce desire to prove himself worthy of that acceptance. Then, unbidden, Sadhu's face flashed in his mind and his heart felt a pang. But Arnie's voice steadied him.

She Demons   91

"Your first lesson is the contemplation of this wall and its true nature," Arnie continued. "The truth is, The Wall and you are one, even as you and I are one. There are no 'others' among us. Your future is with us. You belong here. We're your family now."

We are your family now. Andy's face, mirroring his heart, hardened. It was time to start climbing.

The following morning found Jinnah at his desk enjoying a rare moment of peaceful contemplation. It was too early for Frosty to be in and tormenting him, Sanderson was out covering some sort of vegan "Don't be Cruel to Vegetables" rally, and Crystal was busy on the phone further complicating her social life. With his feet firmly planted on the corner of the desk, Hakeem was stretched out, sipping his sickly sweet coffee with his eyes closed, mind floating above the sea of troubles. It was true, there were whitecaps beneath his higher consciousness: Craig's predicament rippled as a constant undercurrent of concern. True, he had persuaded Caitlin to hold off on running her story, but how long would that last? Another foam-tipped thought flickering just above the surface concerned his own situation. He had rested on his laurels all day yesterday and produced nothing that had really advanced the story. He'd been certain that the exclusive on the Yakshas would shake something loose, but the news had met with stony silence. No one was talking about it — no one. That made Jinnah nervous. There was no use being at the head of the pack if the rest of the media curs refused to follow. Why was no one else picking up on the story? Was he losing his touch? He was certainly losing his hair. A mental image of his physically small but emotionally vast bald spot shot to the surface of his consciousness like a water spout. He shouldn't be losing his hair, not at his age. Perhaps he did have pellagra after all, damn it —

The phone, when it broke in on this flow of thought, so startled Jinnah that he leapt to his feet, spilling coffee all over his desk, his pants, and the industrial grade carpet that covered the newsroom floor.

Cursing fluently in Urdu, he grabbed the phone and snapped into it. "Newsroom. Jinnah. What is it?"

The voice on the other end was pleasant, but there was just enough of a hint of steel beneath it to send a shiver down Jinnah's spine. The introduction was brief, the demand for a meeting curt. "We read your article and we want to clarify a few points," the voice said in a tone that didn't invite argument.

Jinnah's congenital cowardice briefly urged him to decline and damn the consequences — and while Hakeem was at it, he could follow his own advice and quit reporting and go into something safe, like disarming unexploded land mines. But the image of Thad's scarred cheek on his decapitated head steadied him, and he found himself saying: "All right, we'll meet. But on neutral ground, hmm? Not on your turf."

The voice agreed and set a time and place. Jinnah hung up, thinking furiously, his damp and sticky clothing forgotten. He toyed briefly with the idea of

She Demons 93

calling Graham then dismissed the thought as unworthy. Better to simply make sure his will was in order and leave a note for Crystal with explicit instructions that Sanderson was, under no conditions, to inherit either his desk or his Indo-Barbies. Grabbing his coat, notepad, and microcassette, he headed for the door.

The sudden movement caught the corner of Crystal's eye. She put her hand over the receiver, cutting off an ardent suitor in mid-plea. "Hey, where do you think you're going?" she demanded.

Jinnah assumed what he knew was a nonchalant air — as nonchalant as a man who looks like he suffers from incontinence can muster. "If anyone asks, I am on my way to meet with the Yakshas Organization. In person. I may be some time."

The Peace Arch border crossing south of Vancouver is set on the sea in the midst of a large park. Straddling the forty-ninth parallel, a large, white arch, sporting Canadian and U.S. flags, proclaimed: "Children of a Common Mother." On this day, this portion of the world's longest undefended border saw the children of the common mother doing their best to keep each other out of their respective territories. There were long lines of sports cars, SUVs, trucks, and vehicles of all other makes and models waiting for entry on either side of the theoretical line. Jinnah noted the increased police presence at both Canada and U.S. Customs, not to mention the antics of the border vigilantes on the American side, backing up the small military presence that made the land of the free safe from would-be smugglers of cheese, fruit, and other agricultural goods, but of no use at all against human smugglers or drug dealers.

"I wonder which side Mom likes best?" Jinnah mused as he walked towards the group of picnic tables on the Canadian side, his bag slung over his shoulder. To his left, the waters of Boundary Bay were grey and flecked with whitecaps despite the autumn sun. The drive from the office to the border had given Jinnah an opportunity to calm himself down and work himself into that frame of mind, known to his colleagues as the "Jinnahad" — the determination to not merely to survive the encounter but to profit by it for the sake of the victim. However, his conviction that he was doing the just and brave thing was still doing battle with his congenital cowardice when he spotted his quarry. The woman was a dark brunette with skin pulling towards black. Jinnah wondered if she had, perhaps, a few Algerian genes beneath her power suit. The eyes behind the designer glasses were undeniably almond and dark; her mouth just a shade wide. Her consort was about as large as Jinnah had imagined him — the sort who had settled his business disputes with cement-filled sleeping bags and was quite capable of hefting several sacks at once. Jinnah instantly named him "Quickset" and was just wondering what sort of tattoos he sported under the Pierre Cardin suit when he gave a mental start at such unwholesome

She Demons

thoughts. With his dark glasses and cellphone earpiece, Quickset could have been mistaken for a CIA wannabe and Hakeem wondered what the legion of camera-toting, image-snapping, shotgun-mic-recording operatives on either side of the border — official or otherwise — were making of their little tête-à-tête. For his part, he was grateful for their undoubted presence — at least there would be a few witnesses to his sleeping bag fitting.

"Mary Demolay," said the dark woman, offering a perfunctory hand. "Director of public relations, Yakshas Importing International."

Jinnah shook her hand and just had time enough to take in the curious design on the silver ring on her index finger before Quickset demanded his attention.

"Chas Kali, senior partner," he said in a *basso profundo* while simultaneously crunching Jinnah's hand in a massive paw that Hakeem swore bore traces of concrete dust.

"Hakeem Jinnah, crime reporter, *Vancouver Tribune*," Jinnah managed to gasp, extricating his fractured fingers from Kali's atom-smashing grip.

The pleasantries over, they seated themselves at one of the picnic tables. The park was otherwise nearly deserted, a few ragged characters combing the trash cans for bottles and other potential treasures were their only obvious companions. Demolay spread out the front page of the *Tribune* on the table. Jinnah noted the red ink circling what were considered the most offensive passages in his story. He was gratified to see so many circles and underlined paragraphs.

"A very thorough reading, Ms. Demolay," said Jinnah smoothly. "Would you like me to autograph it as well?"

Demolay was not charmed and Jinnah made a mental note to dispense with any attempts at mental seduction.

"Our organization is not responsible for this outrageous act," said Demolay, perfectly manicured fingers tapping the paper on the table. "Articles like yours grossly misrepresent the character of our firm, which is a legitimate business enterprise. We want a front page retraction. We are considering legal action in any event."

Jinnah was hardly surprised. He'd heard worse threats from far less attractive opponents.

"Perhaps, Ms. Demolay, you'd care to explain how your symbol came to be carved on the cheeks of Thad Golway — the first time your firm's logo has been seen north of the border, hmm?"

Demolay reached into her briefcase and pulled out a stack of legal documents. She spread them out in a fan on the table in front of Jinnah.

"You'll find the legal record is quite clear. Our organization has never been convicted of a felony. You can see the judgments in several libel actions awarding us substantial damages. Letters of apology from numerous journalists and politicians."

Jinnah was prepared for this. He slowly and deliberately withdrew his cigarettes from his shirt pocket and went through the ritual movements of selecting, tapping, and lighting while keeping up his offensive.

She Demons   97

"All very fascinating, madam, but if you don't operate on this side of the border, then it is quite irrelevant, is it not? Besides, we all know that Canadian courts are not nearly as generous as those in the United States. Plus, we have somewhat higher standards of evidence. And I have some documentation of my own...."

Jinnah hauled out a file folder and flipped it neatly open under Demolay's eyes. He watched as the attorney gingerly picked through the pile of clippings inside.

"A very nice distinction, that between your organization and individual Yaksha members, hmm? Several of whom have been convicted of everything from trafficking to murder. In the murder cases, the victims were decapitated and your logo carved on their cheeks. So even if you were to launch a slap suit against me, I wonder how you would establish damages, Ms. Demolay. It seems your members have done far more harm to your organization than I ever could."

Demolay closed the folder, carefully running her fingers along the spine to ensure it didn't pop open. Her manner changed subtly, from a prosecuting attorney to a defence lawyer. "We cannot be held responsible for the actions of individual members. But let's think this thing through. Your article accuses us of committing this crime to establish our presence in Vancouver. To what end? Why would we declare ourselves in such a manner, even if we are as unsavoury an organization as you claim? We are in the import-export business, Mr. Jinnah. Things are tough enough these days, given the current climate."

Demolay gestured towards the guardsmen at the border. Jinnah took the point.

98 *Donald J. Hauka*

"You're probably dealing with some kind of sick copycat. I reiterate — I can swear to the fact that no one, I repeat, no one in our organization had anything to do with Thad Golway's death."

"A rather extraordinary claim, given your previous statements about the activities of your individual members," said Jinnah, pressing his advantage. "How can you possibly rule out —"

Jinnah stopped in mid-sentence as his antennae picked up a series of rapid, subtle movements from Quickset Kali, who had leaned forward just enough to loom onto Hakeem's threat radar. Kali had also placed a hand on Demolay's shoulder.

"Interview over," he said in a voice as hard as a slab of Joseph Aspdin's finest Portland product.

Jinnah was furious, his inherent instincts for a moment overriding his congenital cowardice. But Kali's tone brooked no argument and he found Demolay politely handing him his clipping file back. He smiled as graciously as he could. "I must say, Ms. Demolay, it is a very unusual choice of name for a business, hmm? I mean, why did you choose Yakshas? Why name your firm after a pack of homicidal female forest demons?"

Demolay could not hide a look that straddled the line between amused and annoyed. She was piling her legal documents into a neat stack as she replied. "I see that you have only read the traditional, misogynist version of the legend. Seen from another point of view, the Yakshas are merely metaphors for the feminine energy of passion and desire within all of us. If someone, male or female, is lured into the dark wood of

She Demons 99

the unconscious and doesn't return, it's not the fault of the Yakshas. It's up to the individual's response to the energy."

"If I'm luring a beautiful female demon into my unconscious, why should I not be able to come out alive, hmm?"

"It all depends on what was lurking in your unconscious in the first place. There are many unknown perils in our psyches."

Jinnah refused to concede the point: his perils were very real to him and, mentally speaking, obviously the work of an outside agency. He set that to one side, however, for he felt he had sufficiently softened Demolay up for the sucker punch.

"Tell me about the disappearance of Andy Gill."

Kali took a step forward, looming over the picnic table. Demolay did not colour, did not pause, did not miss a beat in putting her papers back in her briefcase. "Andy who? What are you talking about?"

"Around the same time that Thad Golway was murdered, Andy Gill went missing. The police have reason to believe the two cases are related. What do you say to that?"

Jinnah was sweating now. First, he knew he was stretching a point, that the police didn't even know of Andy Gill's disappearance, but he had no doubt they'd see a connection if he ever told them about it, and besides, if the Yakshas could be described as feminist redeemers rather than bloodthirsty dreamers, it wasn't that much of a stretch. Quickset looked like he was sizing him for a sleeping bag and Demolay had that carefully blank expression that suggests a conscious effort to control facial expressions.

She betrayed not the slightest glimmer of recognition or agitation as she relayed in perfect lawyer speak, "We have never heard of Thad Golway or Andy Gill before. This is a matter we are totally unconnected with. I suggest, Mr. Jinnah, that you conduct a thorough search of your own backwoods. You may find some true demons lurking there. Good day."

With that, Demolay snapped the fasteners on her briefcase shut, held out her hand for a perfunctory farewell handshake, and turned smartly on her low heels toward her side of the border. Quickset, as far as Jinnah could tell, was looking right past him, as if he'd ceased to exist. He too whirled about and followed Demolay south toward U.S. Customs. Jinnah picked up his clip file along with his courage and headed slowly back to the parking lot and the satellite-guided Love Machine. He was feeling only slightly slighted by Kali's blank, which was perhaps a blessing. He wondered briefly if Demolay was a lesbian and then decided not — more likely an omnivorous predator.

If experience had taught Jinnah one thing, it was to trust his gut instincts. Right now, however, his guts were a quivering mass of semi-liquid relief at still being alive and the dread of being hauled into Whiteman's office to explain Demolay's lawyer letter, which was certain to beat him to the *Tribune*. He had gained precious little, save the unpleasant prospect of having become entangled in the web of a female legal demon who was going to be devilishly difficult to defeat.

She Demons 101

Jinnah was in no way out of the woods, either figuratively or literally, and he hated it. Whatever sin he had committed to anger News God, it must have been a mortal one for the wrathful reporter's god was manifesting himself in his most wrathful aspect.

"Son of a bitch," he muttered as he revved the engine.

If Graham hadn't known better he'd have sworn Giovanni Dosanjh had priors. He talked like a con trying to sell a lame alibi as he led Graham and Constable Bains around the back of his East Vancouver rental house. Dosanjh was a mixed bag: mixed parentage (Italian and Punjabi), mixed income (contractor and slum landlord), and obviously mixed feelings about the police. He had all the hand-waving, hand-wringing excitability of a Latin, and an obsequious, bowing and scraping posture that would have made an extra in *The Jewel in the Crown* wince. His accent was an odd amalgam — part singsong, part fireworks. Graham didn't particularly like it.

"I'm so embarrassed, Sergeant Graham, sah," Dosanjh half shouted as they manoeuvred down the sidewalk cluttered by garbage, debris, and unidentifiable jetsam. "These tenants, they have no pride, no dignity."

Graham had to agree. The place was a typical eastside dump. The ubiquitous car up on blocks sans wheels and engine graced the front lawn, which was also littered with the battered, broken bits of baby toys — plastic cars that mimicked the real thing, broken jolly jumpers, a midden of McDonald's Happy Meal junk, and a cracked (and, mercifully, overturned) plastic potty. All of it barely visible, sticking out of the patches of unkempt grass or peeping out of the soiled gravel on either side of the dog run like exposed fossils in the dirt. The path they took at the side of the house, which was moderately clean and unobstructed, came as something of a relief. Graham glanced at the boarded windows at ground level. Dosanjh followed his glance.

"Goddamn kids, Sergeant Graham, sah! Bastards break 'em as soon as I replace 'em! What's the sense of wasting more glass?"

"Just stow it, okay?"

Dosanjh stowed it. Graham's tone was vicious. He'd just come from interviewing Thad Golway's parents and he was in a foul mood. They had not taken the news that their son had been a police informant particularly well and he was not at all sure they would follow his advice to not speak to the media. At the moment, the Golways were in shock. How deep would the anger be when it arose? Enough for them to go public? Enough for them to file a lawsuit? Enough to end his career? It wasn't a pleasant thing to contemplate, so Graham focused on the present. At the very least, he'd obtained Thad's last known address from his parents. He wasn't expecting to find much — Thad had lived mostly on the street, but hope, that most elusive of qualities, still had a small space in Graham's heart.

The basement entrance was, frankly, sickening. It was flanked by uneven columns of empty pizza boxes,

She Demons

like some collapsed Greek temple. There was something underneath the usual stench of rotting garbage and the reek of sewage that made the smell at Main and Terminal seem almost pleasant in comparison. On The Corner, people were honestly dying. Here, they pretended to be living. The odour also played around the edges of Graham's consciousness, setting off vague alarm bells. The lock, like all locks, was tricky. Dosanjh alternately cursed and whined while he fiddled with it.

"They never took care of the place. Pretty sure they've skipped — never paid their rent, either. They're all on welfare and they get a shelter allowance, but can you get the goddamn government make 'em use it to pay rent? Like hell you can! Ever tried evicting one of these bastards? Impossible! Why I'm in the business in the first place...."

Graham checked the impulse to observe that according to his records Mr. Dosanjh was one of the biggest slum landlords in the city and he must be making money somehow, else how could he possibly afford to maintain some thirty rental properties worth, on paper, some $10 million?

The lock was finally persuaded to click, the door to open, and Graham braced himself for the stench of all the filth within. But as they entered the small foyer, a very different scent reached his nostrils along with the wave of moist, hot air. The smell was rancid, skunklike, and unmistakable.

"I haven't inspected the place in months — who has time? And they always put you off —"

104 *Donald J. Hauka*

Graham glanced at Bains, who grabbed Dosanjh and threw him into the corner by the door, then leaned on him. Dosanjh squealed — until Bains whispered something to him in Punjabi that Graham assumed was laced with the rich vernacular of Amritsar. He drew his gun and cautiously peaked into the main suite beyond. No sign of anyone. But it didn't pay to just walk into this kind of terrain. Graham rolled into the room and landed in the crouch position, gun ready in both hands, and shouted: "Police!"

The basement was deserted and Graham's shouts echoed dimly against the fungi-covered walls and mould-encrusted ceiling. The air, like a foul steam bath, hung heavy and sullen. Graham stood up to take in the sight of the long lines of tables, the battered light fixtures, still glowing, and the general state of decay that suggested Mr. Dosanjh's tenants had run up one hell of an electricity bill.

"Bains!" he barked. "Bring Mr. Dosanjh in here, please."

Bains dragged the reluctant landlord in. He made a decent show of being shocked — shocked! — by what he saw.

"What have they done? My God, what have they done? Maria and Maya!"

Graham said nothing and Dosanjh sputtered into silence. The policeman walked slowly to the far end of the room, taking in every detail of the room. He addressed the ceiling as he moved back towards Bains and his unwilling charge. "Room for about two hundred plants. Of course, the utilities were in their name

She Demons

and they never paid, so you're off the hook, right? By the amount of water damage, I'd say they weren't the first operators through here."

For once, Dosanjh had nothing to say. Smart move. Graham walked past him.

"Bains," he called over his shoulder. "I'd like you to escort Mr. Dosanjh to the car. We're going to visit every property he owns. Oh, and pull the B.C. Hydro records on all of them when we get back to the station —"

"I had no idea!"

Graham turned to see Dosanjh wringing his hands.

"I didn't know what was going on in here, Sergeant Graham, sah! I got rights! You wanna inspect my properties, you gotta have the warrants...."

Again, Graham simply stared straight into Dosanjh's eyes. The feral look in the policeman's gaze silenced the landlord. For a moment there was silence, broken only by the steady drip of condensation on the floor and the horrid hum of an aging fluorescent lamp. Finally, Dosanjh dropped his act. "Okay, what do you want?" he said, matter of fact.

"I want the names and references and anything else you got on the person or persons who last rented this shithole. Presumably you met with them at least once to get their damage deposit before they plugged in the grow lights."

Dosanjh's eyes narrowed, calculating — just like he calculated everything. He did his math and decided playing ball was cheaper in the short-term, even if it was bad for business. "Place was rented by an East

Indian girl. Had good references. I got her name and everything at the office."

Graham refused to crack the smile that was spreading in his soul. A name. References. His own instincts told him he was finally onto something. "We're going to the car now and straight to your office. And you're going to sign an affidavit saying you're voluntarily cooperating with the police."

For a moment, Dosanjh looked like he wanted to squawk again — not happy about forfeiting his right to sue for police persecution, harassment, whatever. Graham took Dosanjh's arm, hard, but not too hard. He knew the fine line between amiability and assault.

"Otherwise, we're going on the grow op flophouse tour. Then straight to city hall's licensing office. Got it?"

Dosanjh got it and allowed himself to be steered out of the basement suite and into the light of day. Goddamn tenants. Goddamn East Indians — they were nothing but trouble!

"You're kidding me."

Jinnah was stalling for time and it showed. Seated across from Graham in the sergeant's office, he felt weak and desperately in need of a cigarette. The exchange of information had not gone well. His description of his meeting with the Yakshas had not impressed Graham (although Demolay's legal letter had made quite an impression on Whiteman, who had ordered Jinnah to find something — anything — to

She Demons 107

back up the gang connection or write his own retraction story). Craig, on the other hand, had presented Jinnah with a wealth of data that was making his delicate position even more uncomfortable.

"No, I'm not kidding you, my friend," said Graham impatiently. "The grow op that was Thad Golway's last known address was rented by a Jassy Singh. What makes this so unbelievable?"

Jinnah was frantically trying to think. It didn't make any sense to him — it was too fantastic. Jassy Singh tied up with Thad Golway? The implications were all too unpleasant to contemplate — especially as they tended to exonerate the Yakshas. But his gut told him the demon gang was responsible and he clung stubbornly to his theory.

"Craig, I'm telling you — Jassy Singh is not tied up in this. I am convinced — convinced! — that the Yakshas are responsible."

"How can you be so sure?" demanded Graham. "Even if they wanted to expand north of the border, would they really announce their arrival by killing a small-time dealer? It doesn't make sense."

"Jassy Singh is tangential."

Graham's eyes narrowed into twin slits of suspicion. "Do you know this woman, Hakeem?"

Jinnah was forced to admit his nodding acquaintance with the former Wreck Beach beauty, her involvement in the MiMis and his own efforts to find Andy Gill, thus retroactively satisfying any slight qualms left by his truth-stretching at the border meeting with Demolay. Graham looked peeved.

108 *Donald J. Hauka*

"Y'know, Jinnah, I seem to recall a deal — one where I gave you unfettered access to this investigation in return for information. So far, you've given me bupkis and now I find out you've been withholding evidence —"

"I am not withholding evidence!" cried Jinnah, offended. "There was nothing to withhold until now. No connection. And there still isn't any. It's got to be a coincidence. What we need is a good, strong working theory, hmm? For both our sakes."

Tired, burnt-out, and weary as Graham was, he couldn't help but raise a dark eyebrow and grin at such audacity. "Both our sakes? C'mon, Hakeem."

"Truly, my friend. Caitlin Bishop is going live tonight at six o'clock unless I have something to give her that's better. Without something's that's real dynamite, your career is in peril."

"Then give her Jassy Singh."

"Before you even get her in for questioning? Is that wise, Craig?"

Jinnah squirmed inwardly as Graham considered him for a long moment. *He knows that I am keeping something from him. Probably calculating on just how much I want to help him — the limits of my grace.* Graham was, in fact, toying briefly with the idea of going live on-air with Caitlin from The Corner to tell all and denounce the inadequacies of the Witness Protection Program, to go out in a blaze of glory. But prudence, forbearance, and that tiny flame of hope called Jassy Singh combined to banish the thought. He needed to find useful employment for Jinnah, which

She Demons   109

would give him time to track down Jassy. He swiftly changed gears.

"Hakeem, you know the drill — we gotta find the connecting threads. Otherwise —"

"Otherwise all you have is a coincidence. How do you know, for instance, that Thad simply gave that address so he could pick up a welfare cheque? I wouldn't put it past Dosanjh — he seems to have been a flag of convenience for more than one criminal activity, eh?"

"On the other hand, Thad could'a been part of a substantial grow operation, one that the Yakshas wanted to take over and he was the first casualty in the hostile takeover bid. You can't disprove that."

"But if I prove there's no connection, hmm? Sever your golden thread, Craig? Then you'll have to reassess your theory."

At that, Graham's stomach, which had been knotting and unknotting steadily, slowly stopped its spasms and relaxed. He had Jinnah in the box at last. He leaned forward and slapped the lid on.

"Well, there's one obvious place to start cutting, isn't there, Hakeem?"

Jinnah cursed foully in Parsee. He'd been so preoccupied by the Yakshas and Whiteman that he'd walked blindly into Graham's trap.

"Listen, my friend, I know exactly where you're headed. I'm not going to do your legwork for you, conduct your investigation on the cheap —"

"Funny, I distinctly remember something about your editor wanting you to talk to Thad's parents. And didn't you say something just the other day about the parents always loving you in the end, no matter what you write about their kids?"

Allah, the compassionate — bookended! Jinnah knew Graham was right. He knew he should have doorstepped the Golways yesterday and had only been spared because the rest of the media pack had failed to locate them. If Caitlin went live tonight, the floodgates would open, a media circus would spring up outside the Golway's home, and Jinnah's name would be an abomination in the sight of Whiteman. The thought that she might have already interviewed them made him sick to his stomach. He knew exactly what he had to do and yet — and yet....

"Listen, Craig, what makes you think the Golways will talk to me?" he asked in a tone verging on the famous Jinnah whine. "After what I wrote about Thad in the newspaper —"

"Don't worry, Hakeem," said Graham brightening (Jinnah whining was a sure sign of victory). "First of all, I know for a fact that Ms. Bishop hasn't talked to them yet, so that helps. Second, when I told them about Thad being an informant, I gave them the usual 'don't talk to the media' bullshit, but they were in shock. By now, they might just be mad enough to speak up. And finally, most importantly, they're subscribers to the *Daily Clarion*, not the *Tribune*. The field is clear, my friend."

Graham stood up, ending the off the record chat. He felt better than he had in some time, which was more than could be said for Jinnah, who was trying to see how many languages he could mutter "sonofa-bitch" in as he stalked out.

She Demons   111

* * *

The Golway's home in Riley Park, a working-class neighbourhood on Vancouver's east side, was an unassuming postwar bungalow covered in green stucco flecked with brown glass highlights and a sensible duroid shingle roof. Like all the houses along this street, it had a traditional low, white picket fence at the front — a relic of happier, more innocent times that posed no barrier at all to B&E artists, home invaders, or doorstepping reporters. Jinnah surveyed the domestic terrain one last time from the safety of the SGLM. No sign of a dog (that didn't mean much — they might have an indoor Rottweiler). One source of comfort: the plastic newspaper box on the front porch for the competing *Daily Clarion*. No sign of other cars, which meant the friends and relations were respecting the Golway's wish to be left alone — assuming there were any friends or relations. Jinnah had been to many a sad scene where the bereaved had been left to mourn in isolation by a complete lack of family or friend support. Those were, in many ways, the hardest interviews. Not that any of them were easy, for Jinnah was about to undertake one of the most difficult and unpleasant tasks that was the lot of a cop reporter: interviewing the parents of a murder victim.

Fortunately, Jinnah had steeled himself for the ordeal by popping two Phenobarbitals and washing them down with coffee. He was waiting for them to reach maximum effect before sallying forth. It wasn't enough to impair his judgment but it would take some of the edge off the waves of shock, anger, and grief he was about to be subjected to. With a brief prayer for mercy to News God, he launched himself from the SGLM and walked down the sidewalk, opened the gate, and strolled up the curving brick pathway to the Golway's stoop with as much nonchalance as a man whose stomach had turned into a sea of acid could muster. He paused at the door and ran a last mental checklist. Microcassette in left hand, already on record and rolling at maximum volume, check. Face fixed with a look of mingled compassion and professional detachment, check. Steel-toed boots on, tied and ready for action, check. He was about to knock when the door itself grabbed his semi-sedated attention. Like the rest of the house, it was green, but painted on it at letter-slot height, in a beautiful script, was the verse: "Be kind to strangers, and welcome them, for some thereby have entertained angels without knowing it." Above the inscription, the black metal door grill featured a Celtic cross. Jinnah wondered what sort of angel he could possibly be mistaken for, other than perhaps the angel of death. The thought made him shiver slightly as he rang the doorbell. Perhaps he had caught something virulent down on The Corner? He was just making a mental note to have himself tested for tuberculosis when the door opened.

"Can I help you?"

The sliver of open door framed a pale, thin face that featured large, dark eyes magnified by larger glasses. Cutting across the pointed chin was the door

She Demons 113

chain, which was firmly in place. Jinnah took in the details in a flash — Caucasian male, mid-fifties, average height, thinning brown hair, eyes red and swollen.

"Mr. Golway, my name is Hakeem Jinnah —"

"If you're a real estate agent you're wasting your time —"

Well, at least he hadn't been mistaken for the angel of death.

"— and I'm with the *Tribune* newspaper —"

The tired, raw eyes grew slightly wider and receded in the sliver of doorway. Jinnah's left foot twitched, ready for action.

"Ah, we're not giving any interviews, thank you —"

Mr. Golway was already in the motion of closing the door as he spoke and Jinnah's expertly trained toes were wedged into that triangle of hope, the holy slice of daylight between the door and the jam, slicing across the hypotenuse and forming an immoveable cosign at its base. The portal shuddered and bounced slightly off Jinnah's steel-toed boots before Mr. Golway reasserted his slender strength.

"Mr. Golway, I know this is a difficult time for you and your wife —"

"We've nothing to say, I told you!"

"— and you have my deepest condolences on the death of your son —"

"Get out or I'll be after calling the police!"

"— but I think I can tell you who killed Thad."

The pressure — surprisingly intense pressure that had tested Jinnah's Kodiaks to the maximum of their endurance — slackened. The sliver of door widened

114   *Donald J. Hauka*

again, like an opening in an ice floe. Mr. Golway looked slightly bewildered.

"You can do that, then?" he said softly.

Jinnah nodded and removed his foot from the doorjamb. He almost hated himself as the door slowly closed and he heard the chain unlatched. It was at best a half-truth — indeed, if Graham was right, it might be an outright fabrication. But that didn't matter right now. All that mattered was he was in. He gave a silent word of thanks to News God as he stepped over the threshold.

"This is Thad's graduation photo — he was the valedictorian, you know, Mr. Jinnah."

As usual, Jinnah was torn between his personal feelings of compassion for the Golways' loss and his professional instincts, which were calculating the odds of getting the parents to part with their photo album — any one of the pictures of a younger, happier Thadeus Patrick Golway would certainly grace the front page of the *Tribune*. He tried to focus on what Mrs. Golway, a rather handsome woman with steel-grey hair and immense natural gentleness, was saying, looking for that natural opening into the interview proper.

"A good-looking boy, Mrs. Golway," he managed to croak. "Such a tragedy."

"Yes, yes," murmured the mother in a detached manner that made Jinnah wonder if she had heard a word he said.

She Demons 115

The Golways were seated in their living room on an aged, plaid chesterfield whose pattern had been preserved by a thick, crinkly plastic cover that was starting to yellow with age. Behind them was the mantelpiece, covered by photographs, cards of condolence, and the smaller of the dozen flower arrangements. At least the Golways were not short in the friends and relations department. Jinnah was seated on a matching armchair, notebook on his lap, politely sipping the lukewarm, half-strength tea that no amount of sugar — let alone two scantly lumps — could make entirely acceptable to his palate.

"He was a fine boy — a fine young man," Mr. Golway spoke into the uncomfortable silence. "Even when he was taking the drugs, he was always worried about his friends, forever bringing someone worse off than him home, always thinking of others more than himself. Maybe that was the problem, who knows?"

To Jinnah, there was something decidedly odd about the Golway's manner. They were so calm, so composed. Jinnah, an expert in medications of all kinds, could tell that it was not a drug-induced state. He glanced around, but there was a lack of religious iconography, which tended to discount spiritual mania as an alternative. The shock alone? Perhaps. Jinnah was so preoccupied with the question that he almost missed the opening provided by Mr. Golway.

"You mentioned, Mr. Jinnah, that you might know just who killed our son."

As far as opening went, it was about as wide as the Grand Canyon. It was also the moment of truth.

Jinnah gave thanks for the potency of his prescription tranquillizers and launched into his carefully prepared speech. It would either open the floodgates of information or burn the bridges of confidence with the efficiency of a small thermonuclear device. Because Jinnah knew that the Golways were expecting a name, a single suspect, some drug dealer or crack addict. That he could not provide. But he had the next best thing and he prayed that this bit of information (or, to be more precise, informed speculation) would suffice. He put down his tea, picked up his notepad, and estimated the distance between himself and the door.

"Mr. Golway," said Jinnah in an even, deadly serious tone. "I am convinced that Thad was murdered by members of a gang called the Yakshas. They're a California-based drug cartel. These are the earliest signs of them expanding their operations into Canada. I regret to say that your son appears to have been their first victim."

The Golways said nothing. Jinnah studied their faces. What was behind their eyes? Resignation? Certainly great weariness. Jinnah braced himself for angry denials, disbelief — to be shot as the messenger. He was completely unprepared for Mrs. Golway's calm acceptance.

"It's a great shame, Mr. Jinnah," she sighed. "The Lord moves in mysterious ways His wonders to perform."

Phenobarbital or no, Jinnah's eyes bugged out at this. Holy shit! He'd just told a mother her son had been decapitated by a drug gang, likely the first

She Demons 117

of many such victims, and her voice didn't even tremble. He looked over to Mr. Golway in search of enlightenment.

"A shame, Mr. Jinnah, because Thad was finally putting his life back together. He had beaten the drugs, you see. Even found religion of a kind. We didn't real approve of it — we're hopeless Catholics — but anything that could get Thad off the drugs and living the good life, well, that was better than nothing."

If Jinnah's inherent instincts hadn't been numbed by tranquillizers, the sensation they sent would have been akin to a jolt from a cattle prod. He knew exactly what Mrs. Golway was about to say — exactly — before the words issued from her lips.

"It was more a cult than a religion. Run by that singer. Perhaps you've heard of Millennium Magic, Mr. Jinnah?"

Jinnah was torn between joy and despair, fear and desire. For a second, he was at the axis of the great story, and all possibilities unfolded before him with absolute clarity. He had to ask the obvious question. But he already knew the answer.

"Did Thad ever mention a Jassy Singh, Mrs. Golway?"

The serene mother nodded. "Yes, yes — many a time. She was the one who introduced Thad to the others, you see."

Jinnah had found Graham's thread — the link between Jassy Singh and Thad Golway. For a moment, it appeared more like a steel cable strangling his Yakshas theory. But then he remembered that Lionel

118   *Donald J. Hauka*

Simmons too was caught up in the web, and Jinnah's heart, despite his loss, was full of a sudden, fierce joy.

"C'mon gorgeous. I'll buy ya a beer."

Caitlin Bishop ground her capped teeth. She was supposed to be going live in ten minutes and she didn't need the amorous advances of Muscle T-shirt, who had been asking her for a date, a cigarette, a lasting relationship, or just "the most deeply religious experience of your life" for the past half hour. She looked over to her oversized cameraman, Kevin, for assistance. But he simply shrugged.

"You insist on going live from The Corner, you gotta put up with this kinda crap," he said. "I'd have told Ian he was obliged under the contract to provide you with security, given the nature of the assignment."

Caitlin's mouth was a compressed line of fury and anxiety. Kevin was right. But then, she had not dared ask Ian Hadley, senior producer for the station, for additional security after having begged him for the satellite truck to make the live hit from this location. She had guaranteed him an exclusive — a bombshell — in return. And it didn't pay to disappoint Hadley.

"Hey, baby! I got some supreme weed here. Let's smoke a fatty together."

Obviously, Muscle T-shirt, who was performing for the benefit of his friends just a few metres away, wasn't going to give up. Caitlin gave Kevin her best "don't fuck with me" look.

She Demons 119

"Kevin. Do something. Now."

Kevin stopped pretending to fiddle with the audio, walked up to the Don Marijuana and assumed his most intimidating stance inches from Muscle T-shirt's face.

"Beat it," he said.

"Free country, man! I got rights! I got friends —"

"I got pepper spray and a taser." Kevin put a hand on his utility belt. "And a direct line to the cops. Now git."

"Fuck off, agent of oppression!"

Despite the verbal defiance, Muscle T-shirt moved off, rejoining his friends. Caitlin was somewhat relieved as Kevin fired her a "Don't say I never do nothin' for you" look. She flashed him a grateful smile and tried to go over her script one last time. Thad Golway, victim of gang violence or police incompetence? An exclusive report....

"Now what the hell are you doing?" Caitlin had, out of the corner of her eye, caught a glimpse of Muscle T-shirt's latest antics. He was now performing one-handed push-ups within feet of her. His friends hooted and hollered encouragement.

"Look, buddy, if you don't leave right now —"

"Ten … eleven … twelve …"

"— I'll call the cops —"

"Fifteen … switch hands — uh! One …"

Caitlin was frozen, watching the spectacle, Kevin was reaching for his phone and Muscle T-shirt had reached ten pushups with his left arm when Jinnah walked up. For Vancouver's premiere pit bull, this was the last straw.

120   *Donald J. Hauka*

"Not now, Jinnah!" she cried. "I'm going live in eight minutes —"

"We have to talk about that —"

"— and I have a situation here."

Jinnah glanced at Muscle T-shirt and snorted. "You're having trouble with him? Hey, my friend!" he called to Caitlin's tormentor. "Get lost."

Muscle T-shirt looked at Jinnah and froze for a fraction of a second. He glanced over at his friends, but they had already discovered that an argument between two Dumpster divers over by the bus station was infinitely more entertaining than being in close proximity to someone who waved gangster graphics under their noses. Without a word, the sinewy seducer jumped to his feet, gave Jinnah the finger, and moved off to join the fun. Kevin raised his eyebrows, Caitlin's jaw dropped.

"How did you do that?" she demanded. "It would have taken an entire ER team to take that guy down!"

"You just have to know how to charm them," said Jinnah smoothly. "Now, about this alleged live hit — you will have to cancel it."

"Like hell I will! Don't give me your police apologist B.S., Jinnah —"

"I make no apologies," said Jinnah. "But I would hate you to go on-air with a story that completely misses the mark."

"And I suppose you've got something better?"

"I have the bull's eye — no B.S. You want to go live and trumpet the fact that Thad was a police informer, fine, but you'll be eating my dust tomorrow morning."

She Demons 121

Caitlin's cellphone rang at that critical moment when she was beginning to have doubts. It was Ian Hadley. "Lovey, are we all set? You're at the top of the first package —"

"Ian, I'm putting you on hold for a sec — got a new source."

"Caitlin —"

Caitlin snapped her phone shut and glared at Jinnah. "You have thirty seconds," she said. "Spill."

Ah, that was the Caitlin Bishop the great Jinnah-ji had mentored as a budding young journalism student all those years ago — news instincts almost as good as his.

"Just ask yourself one question: how does a young man who belonged to a local cult that was virulently anti-drug end up the victim of a drug-related slaying? Or in a position to have helped the police as an informant in the first place? Hmm?"

"What cult?"

"Millennial Magic. The creation of our very own Lionel Simons, the Rave Messiah."

Caitlin instantly assessed the information, saw its implications, and weighed the potential gain of following it up against the loss of Ian Hadley's good graces. He would be furious if she cancelled now — five minutes before showtime? It was ridiculous. Irresponsible. He'd make her do *Breakfast Television* for the rest of her life. Until she smiled sweetly at him, bought him coffee, and told him how much she admired him as a journalist, of course.

"Names, contact information, and your word of

honour you're not screwing me around for Graham's sake," she snapped.

Jinnah managed to keep a straight face as he gave her the Golway's address and phone number, then swore by News God, the hair on his son's head, the money in his bank account, and, most telling, the keys to the satellite-guided Love Machine that it was not only tomorrow's line story, but it happened to be truth.

"Okay, deal," said Caitlin. "Hey, where are you going?"

Jinnah was already on his way back to the McDonald's lot and his van. He blew her a farewell kiss. "I have a story to write, mademoiselle. Give my regards to Mr. Hadley. Tell him I think his accent's a fake."

Ian! Shit! Caitlin pulled out her cellphone. "Ian? Look, change of plans —"

Kevin could hear the screams of the enraged Brit from his position six feet away. With a sigh, he started packing up. If anyone else had tried to pull such a stunt with two minutes to airtime, they'd be toast. But Vancouver's premiere pit bull was apparently part cat.

The outreach office for Millennial Magic was, as Lionel Simons liked to boast, right in the neighbourhood that needed it most. It was only a few blocks from The Corner, down one of those streets used by the wealthy to race between the suburbs and the city core. It was the poorest neighbourhood in Vancouver — one of the poorest in the country — and its residents, the

She Demons 123

dispossessed, the damaged, the soon to be deported, were crammed into crumbling, low-rise apartments, rooming houses, seedy hotels, and houses that had been converted into a dozen postage stamp-sized suites. As Jinnah looked in vain for a semi-safe place to park the satellite-guided Love Machine, he dismissed Simons's claim to compassion. Obviously, his choice had far more to do with cheap rent than philanthropy. Finally, he wheeled into a spot right across the street from the MiMi's office, reasoning that at least he'd be able to witness his beloved van being stripped and vandalized.

The office was in a typical, two-storey block of what had been a thriving, working-class commercial development. That had been fifty years ago, during the postwar boom. The only sign of that long-vanished prosperity was the name of building itself: "The Normandy," which bore, curiously enough, the insignia of the Canadian Paratroop Division carved in splintering, oft-painted wood above the main entrance. This minute reminder of past military glory was dwarfed by the sign proclaiming "Millennial Magic Community Outreach Office." Jinnah sniffed at the New Age symbols and psychedelic colours decorating the door. He recognized a stylized Hindu mandala and what could have been an artist's rendering of the Jain hand emblem. Only in North America, he reflected, could the appropriation of ancient religious iconography be termed "New."

The inside of the office met Jinnah's expectations. It smelled of zealous sweat, patchouli, and painted-over decay; it was noisy, crowded, warm, and well-designed. Straight ahead a reasonably secure entranceway featured a high counter to discourage all but the most athletic panhandler or smash-and-grab artist. Behind it he glimpsed the glassed-in offices from which Simon's lieutenants ran this small portion of his empire. To the left anyone could walk into the open concept interior, where the real work was done by the cult volunteers — ergonomically correct, environmentally sustainable work stations, posters decrying drugs and encouraging devotees to "Get High on Each Other" lined the far wall. On a couch that looked like it might have been woven out of yogourt, or perhaps hemp, two MiMis were tending to a teenager who was strung out on something. But the largest portion of the office was devoted to what looked like a cafeteria — three or four long tables, lots of folding chairs, with a dozen street people slowly and with obvious effort eating soup or gnawing on bread. The whole thing was a cross between a welfare office and a soup kitchen.

Behind the serving counter, Jinnah saw a pleasant-looking young woman (surprisingly professionally attired in a sky blue food server's uniform, blonde hair visible under the mandatory hairnet) dishing up for the walk-ins. Well, since no one was questioning his presence, he bellied up to the bar.

"Lentil or beef barley, sir?" asked the server automatically, stirring one of the steam-heated cauldrons with her ladle.

Closer scrutiny proved her to be pale and slightly shaken looking. For an instant, Jinnah resented being called "sir" by such a lovely creature — coming from

one so young, "sir" was a barely disguised "old man."
Nevertheless, he fixed her with his most casually
charming smile.

"Neither, thanks," said Jinnah, his voice as mel-
low as a third glass of white wine on a sun drenched
restaurant patio. "The nourishment I seek is for the
soul, not the body. I'm looking for a friend of mine."

The server looked up and took in Jinnah's appear-
ance for the first time. He certainly didn't look like
one of the usual clients and even the ambient odour of
the office couldn't mask the waft of cologne emanating from his skin ("Indian Tiger," one of his favourite
scents, calculated to excite female hormones at fifty
metres).

"Oh? What's this friend's name?"

The voice was less friendly, more guarded, the eyes
narrowing. Bad signs. Jinnah switched to rapid-fire
mode to keep her off balance.

"Jassy Singh."

"Jassy?"

Surprise, but no denial. Probably thinks I'm her
uncle — Jinnah flattered himself that he could not yet
be possibly mistaken for her father.

"She's a friend of a friend's, actually. But I was dis-
cussing your organization's fine community work just
the other day."

The searching eyes lowered, looking for courage
in the lentil soup while churning its depths with the
encrusted ladle.

"She's not here. She's at a meeting."

"In the back?"

126 *Donald J. Hauka*

"No, on the Hill. That's the Magus's place."

The eyes met his again, flashing now. Tone a tad sharp. Touched a nerve with Jassy's name? Press a little and see what comes out.

"Not here, eh? I guess she's out of the office a lot — community visits, that sort of thing."

"She's not around a lot, yeah. Are you are relative of hers or what?"

"Definitely or what. My name's Hakeem. What's yours?"

A momentary hesitation.

"Sam. Listen, Hakeem, I got work to do —"

Trying to shut me down. Hit her harder.

"Then maybe my other friend is around. You must know Thad Golway."

Sam's eyes were as wide as one of her soup cauldrons now. She fumbled with the ladle and pretended to be busy cleaning the counter to cover her shock.

"Thad is — he didn't hang around here much," she stammered. "He was with a different program. Higher up than anyone here."

Jinnah refrained from observing just how much above them all Thad now was. He pressed ahead, relentless. "Another program? Which one?"

"The prophets. Don't know much about their ... their work. I'm really sorry, I —"

Jinnah risked a quick glance around. The other office worker bees were stirring to life. He had to use his tongue to see if Graham's thread between Jassy and Thad was substantial or circumstantial. Would he use it as a pair of scissors or a sewing needle?

She Demons 127

"Jassy knew Thad pretty well, I believe — out of the office at the same times, hmm?"

Now Sam's eyes flashed — anger? Jealousy?

"They were pretty tight." Sam's tone had, for a moment, betrayed a rich mix of emotions, but now she was under control and struggling to find a polite way to get Jinnah to leave. "You should really talk to Jassy about all this. I have work to do here — the people need me —"

"This guy bothering you, Sam?"

A very large MiMi with a shaved head and a variety of tattoos and body piercings materialized beside them: obviously the office security. Jinnah made a mental note that, whatever his other sins, you couldn't fault Simons for failing to protect his devotees.

"No, Jordan, it's okay —"

"I was just leaving," said Jinnah. "Next time you see Jassy, be sure to tell her I said hi, okay?"

Sam didn't reply and Jinnah was far too conscious of Jordan's presence right behind him — not so close that he could actually be accused of escorting Jinnah to the door, but close enough to ensure he entertained no thoughts of turning around. Within seconds, Jinnah was out the door and headed for the relative safety of the SGLM. To his immense relief, it was still there, intact, and without even a parking ticket on its windshield. Clearly there were some advantages to parking where meter maids feared to tread.

Jinnah pulled away from the curb, merged smoothly into the light traffic, and lit a cigarette. He'd gained much food for thought from his visit. He had independent

128   *Donald J. Hauka*

corroboration that Thad Golway was a member of the MiMis — indeed, was pretty high up in the organization. He'd established that Thad and Jassy knew each other and, judging from Sam's reaction, might even have been an item. Both had worked outside the office, which would've given Jassy ample time to oversee the grow op and Thad —

Jinnah frowned and exhaled a cloud of thick blue smoke. It didn't fit. If Thad had been involved with the grow op, why didn't he tell Graham about it when he agreed to co-operate during the big bust on The Corner? If he and Jassy had been that close, surely Thad would have known something about it. He was more convinced than ever that Thad had never set foot in Dosanjh's hellhole. But had Jassy seen it with its grow lights on? And where in all of this was Andy Gill? Jinnah kicked himself — in his pursuit of Jassy he had completely forgotten to ask about Mr. Puri's nephew. There had been no sign of him at the office, true, but that didn't mean he wasn't in one of those glassed-in cubicles behind the counter. The more he pondered, the more Jinnah realized he didn't yet have the real goods. The answers lay inside Simons's mansion on the Hill. He glanced at his watch, executed a perfect, illegal left-hand turn, earning angry horn blasts and expletives from a suit in a Saab. He hit a button on his GPS console. Ensign Sulu's voice sounded. "Coordinates, Captain?"

"Set a course for West Vancouver, Mr. Sulu. In this case, the Mohammedan must go to the mountain."

* * *

She Demons　　　　129

As far as mansions go, Simons's was modest, especially by neighbourhood standards. West Vancouver boasts the wealthiest postal code in B.C. and one of the richest in all of Canada. The most ostentatious displays of wealth are found on the waterfront — by far the priciest real estate in the province. The Magus had an estate on a steep slope overlooking the sea with all the mandatory components, but they were not on the same scale as some of his neighbours. The mansion itself was large, but hardly sprawling. The swimming pool was not Olympic-sized, but was still big enough for a substantial party. The speedboat docked at the end of the unassuming private wharf was substantial, but certainly not in the mini-cruise ship class of yacht that his fellow West Van tycoons preferred. Inside, the meeting of the senior management team of Millennial Magic was wrapping up.

"The family is as one soul, united in our belief and our mission. We cannot come to the garden without suffering the same trials as those who journeyed there before us. If we believe in each other, there is nothing we cannot achieve…."

The Magus was on today. Jassy, eyes closed, let his words wash over her. His calm, strong, rhythmic voice was both soothing and inspiring. Along with the rest of the senior staff of Millennial Magic, Jassy was rapt as Simons chanted.

"The spirit kingdom is spread out upon the earth, but the people do not see it. We are their eyes. We will show them the kingdom."

Jassy was seated on the floor in a circle of young people like herself; the sole exception being Daisley, who was on her left. In the middle of the ring was Simons, dressed in ceremonial, white cotton caftans, looking serene and untroubled as he brought them out of their meditation.

"We let it be," Simons chanted.

"We let it be," the circle answered.

Jassy opened her eyes. The world slowly returned. They were in the massive living room: a huge space with high, white walls that Simons had sparingly decorated with an eclectic mix of religious artifacts. Normally it was a seductive mix of austerity and sensuousness. Today nothing, not even the words of the Magus, could completely calm her heart. The business part of the meeting was over and the crowd around the Magus would be thick unless she moved fast. He was already talking with a devotee by the time she made it to his side, gently squeezing his arm.

"Magus, a word, please?" she whispered.

Simons smiled and nodded. He dismissed the devotee with a word and allowed Jassy to guide him to a quiet corner. His smile was relaxed, open. "What's the problem? You're upset."

The Magus could tell — he could always tell. There was no sense hiding anything from him. Jassy felt better about telling him everything now: he'd find out somehow anyway and was better coming from her directly.

"I received a call from some crazy landlord who claims we rented his house as a shelter, Magus. He accused me and the organization of the most outrageous things."

She Demons 131

Simons's smile became lopsided — a goofy grin. He wasn't taking this seriously.

"We can't be responsible for everyone's supposed sanity, Jassy. I don't see the problem."

"The problem is this landlord claims we were running a grow op in his basement. The problem is the police paid him a visit. He claims that we — I — was the person who rented it. That's got to be a problem."

The smile slowly straightened. "Don't worry. I'll take care of it. Give me his name and number."

Jassy searched the Magus's face, but it was a maddeningly calm mask. The more serene he was, the more she felt panic welling up inside her.

"You must understand, Magus — someone has taken advantage of your trust. How can the organization spread our message if someone within it is growing dope on the side, under our name?"

"It's all a simple misunderstanding, Jass," Simons insisted softly. "Trust me, it'll blow away. I'll —"

"I'm sorry to interrupt, Magus, but that reporter is at the door asking to see you." Ray Daisley's face was just as calm and devoid of emotion as Simons'. But there was a look in his eyes that mirrored some of Jassy's concern.

"Jinnah?" she cried. "Magus, you mustn't speak with him —"

"Hey, hey, Jassy — Jinnah and I go way back. He's almost like a friend."

"He prints lies!"

"He can't see the kingdom before his eyes — yet. I don't despair of him seeing it one day, though. Did he say what it's about, Ray?"

"Something about Jassy. Something vitally important," said Daisley, staring at Jassy with eyes suddenly devoid of anxiety — or affection.

Jassy felt a shiver run through her. She had never liked Daisley. It didn't feel good to know he didn't like her either.

"Better go out the back way, Jass," said Simons. "Take tonight to calm yourself. I'll deal with the persistent Jinnah."

Daisley put his arm around Jassy's shoulders and gently steered her towards the rear of the mansion. If she had felt a shiver before now her stomach was an icy ball of fear, despite the return of warmth and kindness to Ray's eyes.

"I'll make sure you don't get lost," he said, adding, almost tenderly: "We don't want to lose you now, do we?"

Jinnah had to grudgingly admit that Simons did possess a certain understated class. It was reflected in the style and décor of the vestibule where God's gift to tabloid journalism impatiently awaited audience with the Magus. Mirroring the motif in the living room, it was full of eclectic religious imagery. Jinnah was especially impressed by the Tibetan tapestry depicting the Buddhist "Hungry Souls" — gateway guardians barring the door of the believer to eternal bliss. He snorted: he didn't want eternal bliss, five minutes with Simons would do

She Demons 133

just fine, likely, and if the Magus didn't show up in sixty seconds, it was going to take more than a tapestry to stop this reporter from entering the inner sanctum. Daisley, on the other hand, was a far more effective gate-keeper, and Jinnah was just wondering how he would get around the bastard when Simons appeared.

"Salaam alikoom," he said. "What's up?"

This was typical of Simons; one minute the mystic, the next just another overgrown teenage pop idol. Jinnah didn't mind — he was about to rock the rapper's world.

"A very nice place you have here, Mr. Simons. I wonder how you can afford it."

"Paid for by my royalties," said Simons pleasantly, his smile slowly becoming lopsided and, to Jinnah's eye, self-satisfied. "And donations from my followers."

"Or some other source of revenue, hmm? You weren't that big a star, Lionel."

Simons laughed. "Who cares? It's all an empty skandha, Hakeem. Now just what, exactly, do you want to talk about?"

"About your other address, actually. About a grow op, Jassy Singh, and Thad Golway — two devotees who doubtless helped pay for all this."

Simons's smile remained, but there was no warmth left in it. "Yeah. Let's go out to the pool and talk about that, okay? I think you'll find the water calming."

Jinnah followed Simons out to the heated pool. Like every other part of the mansion, it had its complement of religious symbols. Marble Buddhas mingled with Oriental deities, some recognizable, most obscure to Hakeem's scanty knowledge of comparative religion. At the far end was an elegant looking patio set. Simons motioned to Jinnah to have a seat. As he did, he took out his notebook and microcassette. The preliminary sparring was over and the Magus was now on notice that everything he said would be on the record.

Jinnah came right to the point — there was no telling how many (or few) questions he'd get in. "How is it that Thad Golway, a member of your cult, ends up the victim of a drug-related slaying, Mr. Simons?"

"We're not a cult," Simons said automatically. "And I couldn't say if Thad Golway was a member of our organization or not. I don't claim to know every devotee, although I'd like to — we're just too large."

"Don't know him?" said Jinnah. "But he was high up in your organization. A member of the prophets, hmm? You must have known him."

The slightest furrow of the brow betrayed — what? Doubt? Uncertainty? Guilt?

"I'm sorry, Hakeem. I can't confirm that for you. I can check and get back to you, if you like —"

"He also lived in one of you rental properties," Jinnah cut in, knowing just how worthless Simons's promise to get back to him was. "A place in Surrey, owned by a Mr. Dosanjh."

"You must be mistaken there. We don't rent properties. We own all our buildings outright; the outreach centre, the youth hostel, the homeless shelter —"

"Are you saying," Jinnah said, lacing his voice with just the right amount of incredulity. "That you

She Demons   135

have no knowledge of your organization having rented Dosanjh's house?"

"I thought I was being pretty clear, Hakeem. You like having me repeat stuff over and over — maybe it's your inner rapper. I'll be specific — we don't rent houses and we didn't rent any place owned by a Mister whoever. Yo-yo-yo-yo."

Simons was grinning as he made gangster rapper hand signals to underline his joke. Well, signal this, pal....

"Then how do you explain Jassy Singh's signature on the rental agreement? You do know Jassy, don't you?"

"Jassy's a valued member of our team," Simons nodded. "But if she rents a house she does it on her own, not on behalf of the organization. I'm not responsible for the private lives of my devotees, Hakeem, even though I hope they make the right choices."

This little speech reminded Jinnah of his conversation with Demolay and the Yakshas. What was it with cult leaders today? No sense of personal responsibility or ability to micromanage. He put it down to the general devolution of state power and Western individualism and pressed on.

"At the risk of being accused of indulging my inner rapper, you acknowledge that Jassy Singh is a senior member of your organization and, indirectly, that you know she rented a house in which a grow op has been found. Would it surprise you to know that this house was the last known address for Thad Golway?"

"Since I never met Thad and since, as I've said twice, we don't rent buildings, I think it's pretty obvious that

I'd be quite surprised, yeah," said Simons, the slightest note of music star peevishness creeping into his voice. "I'm pretty good at finding hidden meanings in difficult questions, Jinnah, but I have to confess, man, I don't see the point to all this."

"The point is, Mr. Simons," said Jinnah, waxing righteous, "the point is, your organization is avowedly anti-drug. And yet two of your members — one of them a very senior one, hmm? — have been directly connected to drug and gang activity. One has paid with his life in the most horrific manner. All you have to do is connect the dots."

He had fired both barrels at close range. Simons sat easily in his chair, the sun shining off his caftan, reflecting the brilliant white of the garment. There was no smile, no goofiness now. He was at his most serene and mystic, which just told Jinnah that he'd made a direct hit.

"We're all connected by dots, as you call them, Hakeem. How many dots does it take to link us together? We're all part of the great web of life. Our separation is an illusion. Underneath it all, we are all one. I grieve for Thad's death because I know he was a part of me. I care for Jassy because she's woven into my soul. I and my family are one, Hakeem, and even you are part of us, if you would only see that truth."

"How about connecting me with Jassy, then?" Jinnah pressed. "So she can tell her side of the story?"

"I'm afraid she's not here at the moment. Her work keeps her in the field a lot. But I'll give her your message."

She Demons 137

Simons rose, indicating that the audience was over. Jinnah stood up and closed his notebook, but kept his microcassette rolling — just in case.

"I thank you for you time, Mr. Simons."

"For you, Hakeem, anything," grinned the Magus. "Ray will show you the way out."

Jinnah whirled about to discover Daisley standing by his elbow. Name of God, how had the man snuck up on him like that? He clicked the cassette off and followed Ray to the door. He knew better than to try to engage the gateway guardian in conversation. Bastard never even said goodbye as he closed the door behind him.

Still, Jinnah was almost content as he launched himself into the SGLM and started the engine. He glanced at his watch. Sonofabitch! It was closing in on 8:00 p.m. He had just enough time to get back to the *Tribune*. Frosty would scold him for pushing deadline. Whiteman would lecture him on keeping in contact with city desk. Hakeem didn't care. News God, that most fickle of deities, had smiled on him and he had enough to blow the competition out of the water. Surely even Whiteman would be able to see that.

"What do you mean it needs to be lawyered?"

Jinnah's howl was one of rage mingled with fear. Whiteman, standing behind Hakeem and Frosty at city desk, was unmoved.

"You're making some very serious allegations about a public figure who has a litigious nature," said

Whiteman. "You're quoting some very questionable sources —"

"Including the litigious public figure! I have it straight from the Magus's mouth, Whiteman!"

"— and I just want to be sure we haven't left ourselves open to unnecessary and expensive legal action."

"You have my word as a seasoned professional, chief."

"That would be a great comfort if your word had the letters 'QC' after it, Jinnah."

"Look, I'm telling you —"

"I am reminded that some of your other words about Mr. Simons have cost us a great deal in legal fees —"

"A drop in the bucket compared to the sales revenue the story generated —"

"— not to mention several front page apologies —"

"Which were completely unwarranted in my opinion."

"The only opinion that is going to get this story on the front page is a legal one, Jinnah, and that's final. Ms. Frost, if you would be so kind as to call Butler and Partners?"

"Not that asshole!" Jinnah wailed. "If you say it was a sunny day she wants a quote from Environment Canada to back it up!"

"You have exactly thirty-five minutes to get this off city desk. One minute longer and we plug the front page with wire. Clear?"

"Clear, chief," said Frosty.

Jinnah's mouth was open and a stream of choice

She Demons 139

invective from the many and varied tongues of the Indian subcontinent was busy working its way from his synapses to his vocal chords, but a ferocious glare from Frosty dried up the torrent before it could burst forth. Whiteman took one last, significant look at the clock and walked calmly back to his office.

"Lawyered in a half hour? You're kidding me! It'll never happen."

"It certainly won't unless you calm down and prepare to give Harriet Butler your smoothest French skunk act," said Frosty, reaching for the phone. "What are you prepared to live without and what's the hill you wanna die on? Chose now."

"That's like asking which of my children I prefer to have slaughtered."

"It's not as if you're new to infanticide, Hakeem. The newsroom floor is littered with the corpses of your prose progeny."

"Sacrifices to News God," Jinnah grunted. "Look —"

At that moment Jinnah's cellphone rang, jangling his already shattered nerves. Cursing, he fumbled to answer it. "This had better be bloody important!" he snapped, a fraction of a second before his brain processed the number on call display — it was Manjit.

"It is important, Hakeem," said his wife, her normally patient voice taut and anxious. "It's about Saleem —"

"Are you crazy, Manjit?" cried Jinnah. "I'm on deadline! My story's being lawyered —"

"Hakeem, he wants to go to a drop-in centre —"

"I don't care if he wants to go to a needle exchange centre — I don't have time for this right now!

"Hakeem —"

Jinnah hung up. Further conversation was pointless and a waste of precious time. And Saleem wanting to go to a bloody drop-in centre could wait for thirty minutes. He glanced over at Frosty, who was staring placidly at her screen, going over his story, pretending not to have heard.

"How can he be so maddeningly calm all the time?" Jinnah whined, changing the unspoken topic. "Having an argument with Whiteman is like quarrelling with a pig. You can't get a straight answer and after a while you realize the pig is enjoying it."

"Hello, Julie? Frosty at the *Trib*. Get me Harriet, stat. Staring at deadline."

"I'm not feeling well. I think I caught something at that damned outreach centre —"

"Fine, go home. Harriet and I will sort it out —"

Jinnah, who had been slumping in his chair and massaging his throbbing temples, sat bolt upright. "Over my dead, brown body! If my untimely death is the cost of printing the truth, then it's a price I'm willing to pay!"

"The price, Hakeem, is going to be roughly five hundred bucks an hour, plus expenses. Hang on. Harriet? I have Jinnah with me. I'm just putting you on speaker phone."

Jinnah's insides slowly writhed, an elastic, spastic mass of fluids. Frosty shot him a smile and said, with her hand over the mouthpiece, "Welcome to hell, Hakeem."

She Demons 141

"Huh!" Jinnah snorted. "This is merely torture. Hell is what I have waiting for me at home."

"It's where all the kids I met at the rave hang out —"

"I know this centre — it's run by Simons's cult —"

"— and he's supposed to be helping me and Poonum with Diwali preparations —"

"— and they're totally cool and non-judgmental —"

"— brainwashed zombies, who graduate to the MiMi soup kitchen —"

"— and it's not helpful when you don't have two minutes to speak with your own wife about something as urgent as this —"

"— besides, I might be able to find out about Andy Gill —"

"— if you insist on calling on deadline what do you expect? 'Hi, darling, how are you doing? Why don't you spend a half an hour telling me your inner-most thoughts?' —"

"— you have to decide where your priorities lie, Hakeem —"

"— and they've got a sound system down there that's the bomb —"

"Enough! What is this? A family discussion or an Italian aria?"

Jinnah had expected to find hell when he finally arrived home, but even for Iblis, this was ridiculous. He'd already been through the wringer over the exact meaning and import of just six hundred words with

142 *Donald J. Hauka*

Harriet Butler and Frosty, and had made deadline by thirty seconds at the cost of about a pound of heart tissue, two rolls of Rolaids, and the likely recurrence of his seasonal malaria. The last thing he needed was a three-part cacophony of conflicting agendas to further vex his limited patience.

"It is quite simple, Hakeem," said Manjit patiently. "Saleem made a commitment to his family and family comes first."

Jinnah knew she was right, but his inherent instincts were tingling, awoken by Saleem's last strangled protest. "Sometimes, Manjit, we must think of our extended family, hmm? Is not Mr. Puri like an uncle to me?"

"Saleem did quite enough undercover work for you at the rave, thank you very much, and I don't want him consorting with the former Miss Nude Wreck Beach."

"Do I get a say in this?" Saleem whined.

"I think you've said quite enough —"

"Manjit," said Jinnah. "If Saleem actually spots either Andy Gill or Jassy Singh, he'll win the news tip of the year and be able to assist the police with their investigation —"

"Hakeem, you can't be serious!"

"I can be on occasion and this is one of them," said Jinnah. "He might find out something useful."

"He might also run into Reverend Hobbes and his friends."

"Unlikely — it's a drop-in centre in a good neighbourhood, not a rave. It ought to be safe."

"So I can go?"

She Demons 143

"Hakeem." Manjit had her hands on her hips and her eyes were blazing. She rarely got mad, but this was obviously her hill to die on.

Jinnah's brain, already throbbing, tried to find the way out. Sanderson, faced with a similar situation, would have asked: "What would Confucius do?" To hell with Confucius, Jinnah thought — he never had to track down someone like Jassy Singh who, his inherent instincts told him with utter certainty, held the key not only to Andy Gill's disappearance, but to Thad Golway's death. This wasn't a question of respect to elders or of a man's *ren* — it was one of a higher good, and if that good could be served by ordering his son to disobey his mother, then that's what had to be done. He looked at Manjit and Saleem, who were expecting his final judgment, and was suddenly at a loss for words. He shook his aching head instead.

"Listen, I haven't got time for this — you two work it out." He turned on his heel and nearly sprinted out of the house before either wife or son could utter a sound.

"I can't believe it. After all these years of devotion to the cause."

"It's probably all a big misunderstanding, Magus."

"She's like a — a little sister to me, y'know. I rescued her, took her in —"

"She's still a hard worker and a valuable member of the team."

"Something's gotta be done, Ray. This isn't good for the movement."

"Don't worry, I'll look after it. Come on, enough of the red wine — there's a limit to the good it'll do your heart."

At Simons's mansion the afternoon's austerity had vanished and the Rave Messiah, wearing a hand-spun, raw cotton bathrobe and swimming trunks, was pacing unsteadily in the vestibule of his master bedroom, spilling local, organic merlot all over the white shag carpeting. Daisley had been enduring his boss's ravings about Jassy Singh for the better part of a bottle and a half and had decided the Magus had vented enough for one night. He needed to forget about these minor annoyances. He took the wineglass gently from Simons's hand and led the former rapper over to the oversized dressing table.

"Lemme handle it — there's likely a simple solution."

"Dunno, Ray, dunno — smells bad, feels bad. Just the sort of crappy karma that gives Jinnah plenty of ammo to fire at us."

"I'll handle it."

"You sure?"

"Handled all your other problems, haven't I? Now take your medication. You're gonna need to be calm tonight."

Simons stared bleary-eyed at the tray of alternative sedatives in front of him. His stomach did backflips at the sight.

"Ah, man, do I have to? This stuff gives me a headache."

She Demons 145

"Talk to your naturopath, not me. I just dish the stuff out. Come on —"

Simons swallowed the array of pills, capsules, and caplets with the aid of the last of his red wine, chugged straight from the bottle. He sprawled in the chair, spent. "Man, I'm wiped. What a day."

"Then you're ready for some relaxation. Come on, upsa-daisy —"

"No, Ray, come on, gimme a break —" Simons protested weakly as Daisley half-carried him towards the doors to the inner bedroom.

"What night is it, Magus? Devotee appreciation night. Now get in there and show 'em how much you love 'em, big guy."

The music, which had been making the closed doors vibrate, burst forth at full volume as Daisley flung the bedroom open. It was some of Lionel Simons's greatest hits. Inside, the party was already in full swing. About a dozen of the younger devotees (equally balanced in terms of gender and ethnic origin) were dancing and cavorting on or around the gigantic waterbed under the strobe lights. Daisley noted that most were still at least half-clothed. Uptight group. But the Magus would change all that. He guided Simons to the bed that was being used as a mosh pit.

"C'mon, Ray — I'm whacked," Simons hissed in Daisley's ear.

"It's not as if you have any heavy lifting to do, Magus," Ray whispered back cheerfully. "Do you good. Now exercise your root chakra, man."

Whatever feeble protest Simons might have muttered was lost under the wave of bodies that drowned the Rave Messiah. Daisley smiled with the satisfaction of a job well done. His eye lit upon a young devotee timidly approaching the writhing mass of bodies. He smiled and pulled her aside.

"It's Lindsay, isn't it?"

Lindsay, unable to speak or make eye contact, merely nodded.

"I'm Ray, remember? Listen Lindsay, would you mind doing me a favour?"

Lindsay managed to raise her head and dart a swift look at Daisley while unconsciously adjusting her half-open robe.

"Okay," she said in a small voice.

"I have some stuff to do — boring office stuff. It's important that someone let me know if the Magus leaves the bedroom. Can you be that someone? There's a cellphone on the dressing table out in the vestibule. All you have to do is hit the send button and it dials my number. You'll let me know, in case the Magus needs anything, okay?"

"Okay, Ray."

The voice was less small, less timid, and Daisley knew Lindsay would not fail him. He gave her a friendly pat on the back and flashed his warmest smile.

"Welcome to Millennial Magic, Lindsay. You'll do just fine."

Lindsay smiled shyly and made her way to the bed. Daisley watched her merge with the writhing mass and, satisfied the Magus was busy bonding with

She Demons 147

his devotees, closed the doors quietly behind him. The party would go on until dawn, most likely, but Simons would not remember much after about another five minutes, when the drugs took effect. If Lindsay was faithful to her duty, Daisley would have lots of time to work undisturbed on fixing the little problem facing his boss. If Jassy Singh had become a liability to Lionel Simons, then she had to be dealt with. He was already working on a solution as he headed out the door and made his way towards his car.

"We are going to get so totally busted."

"Then split. I'll do this myself."

"Then give me keys."

"I need the keys."

"Then I'm staying."

"Then shut up."

"Like, keep your voice down!"

"Shhh!"

Jassy wished she hadn't had to ask Sam for her help in breaking into the MiMi outreach centre, but she was the only one she could really trust (or order around) and she had the master keys that had gained them access to the inner sanctum — Ray Daisley's office. Jassy had been quarrelling with her sometime friend since they'd entered, disabled the alarm system, and started moving stealthily through the darkened centre with the aid of a pair of penlights. Sam's agitation had increased with every step and now that Jassy was rifling through Daisley's filing cabinet, she was starting to freak out entirely. If she could keep her fellow MiMi from totally spazzing for another two minutes, she might find what she was looking for.

"Look, the Magus himself said it was all a big misunderstanding and there was nothing to worry about," hissed Jassy, her pronounciation somewhat hampered by the penlight in her mouth.

"Then why was that reporter dude nosing around asking questions? Why are you here after hours?"

"You know how trusting the Magus is — can't see the bad in anyone. Not even the reporter dude, whose real name is — holy shit!"

"What? What is it?"

"It" was a thick file marked "Rentals." Inside, Jassy had found the rental agreement for Dosanjh's house with her name on it. And about twenty others just like it, making her the tenant of houses scattered all over the city.

"It's something the Magus needs to see, like, yesterday," said Jassy, lifting the file out of the drawer and tucking it into her bag.

"You can't take Ray's files!"

"I'll put it back before he notices. He'll never find out."

"He'll catch you!"

"How, exactly?"

Jassy's defiant question was answered by a noise in the outer office. Both young women froze.

"If that's Ray, we are so dead!" hissed Sam.

"Then let's get outta here, now," whispered Jassy. "Come on."

She Demons 149

The only way out led past the outer office, but if they crept down below the counter height no one would see them. Jassy's heart pounded despite her silent chanting: "We let it be, we let it be...." Sam was whimpering.

"Sam, it'll be okay." Jassy practically breathed the words into the young devotee's ear. "We are all one, there is no fear...."

Jassy dared to glance over her shoulder and into the outer office. All was quiet. Had they been hearing things? And what would Daisley be doing in the office at this time of night anyway? It was absurd. Jassy was almost relaxed when a voice cutting through the shadows gave her a heart attack.

"Jassy Singh!"

The lights snapped on. Jassy and Sam were caught, totally busted, trying to crawl out of their own outreach centre in the possession of Daisley's files. The fight-or-flight response grabbed Jassy and it took a moment for her to recognize both the voice and the face of her tormentor.

"Jinnah!"

Jinnah closed the door and gave Jassy a baleful look from across the counter. "The door was unlocked," he chided Jassy gently. "Anyone might have come in."

Sam, sufficiently recovered from her shock to recognize Jinnah, muttered a breathless "Omigod!" and bolted towards the back door.

"Sam!"

But Sam was gone, leaving Jassy to face Jinnah alone. She stood up slowly and crossed her arms.

"You're trespassing on Millennial Magic property. Get out of here before I call the cops."

Jinnah chuckled, took out a pack of cigarettes and, to Jassy's horror, lit up.

"You can't smoke in here!" she gasped.

"Why? You gonna call the cops about that too?" Jinnah laughed. "They'll be delighted to hear from you. They're looking for you, you know."

"Big deal. They persecute us all the time. Now butt out and get out."

Jinnah took in a deep drag and let out an immense cloud of fragrant blue smoke. He looked at it, smiling, as it slowly spread throughout the office.

"Have it your way, Jassy. But this isn't about some two-bit grow op. You're now officially a murder suspect."

Jinnah was gratified by the reaction, one that not even years of meditation and MiMi training could disguise. Jassy actually swayed for a moment and had to hold onto the counter for support.

"Murder? Whose murder?" she managed to croak.

"Come on, Jassy — you know. Just like you knew Thad Golway. Were you lovers, by the way? Not that it matters, really. Not to me. But to the police — well, the court is sometime lenient when it comes to crimes of passion —"

"Crimes of passion?"

"— but even they draw the line at ritual decapitation. Although you never know with some of these post-Charter of Rights judges —"

"I didn't murder Thad!"

She Demons 151

Jinnah refrained from pointing out that Jassy had just confirmed she knew the victim and pressed on. They were short on time and they had a lot to accomplish before Graham caught up with her.

"And you know Andy Gill, too. Is he next? Just how do you select your victims, Jassy?"

"Andy's safe!" Jassy spat the words out, barely containing herself.

"Is he really? You rather like Andy, I believe. He's like you. Knows what it's like to straddle two cultures. Looking for comfort, acceptance, community. Thinks he's found it in the MiMis. How long will it last, do you think? How long has it taken you to lose your faith? Five years? Six?"

"I have not lost faith in the Magus." Jassy's voice shook.

"Then why are you here, hmm? One former devotee dead, one prospective devotee missing, and then there's the matter of this grow op. How much does it take, Jassy?"

Jassy looked down, conscious of the weight of Daisley's file in her bag. She was trying to think clearly, but there were so many conflicting emotions and notions in her mind that she had no clear idea what to do.

Jinnah, who had been blowing smoke rings, decided to give her a hand. "Are you ready to help me find Andy yet, Jassy?"

Jassy weighed the possibilities. She had what Jinnah wanted. Would he be willing to make a deal? Almost certainly....

152   *Donald J. Hauka*

"Not yet," she said. "Hang on a minute — I'll be right back."

Jinnah almost leapt over the counter after Jassy as she headed for the back door, but something about her manner stopped him. Besides, jumping counters was bad for his knees, which still had not recovered from that bout of rheumatic fever. His legendary laziness was rewarded when she returned seconds later, opened the counter's swinging door and closed it firmly behind her. Sam's keys jangled in her hand as she motioned Jinnah towards the front door.

"First we have another mystery to solve," she said. "You got wheels?"

Jinnah threw down his cigarette and took an indecent amount of delight in grinding it into the centre's worn linoleum. She has spirit, this one — is she a Yaksha, perhaps? For a fleeting moment, Jinnah allowed himself to fantasize about Jassy leading him into the deep woods, but it lasted only a second. In this case, the fantasy was too close to reality for comfort.

"Lead on, Jassy Singh," he said. "And don't forget to turn off the lights."

"Movement."

    "How many?"

    "Two. Landlady and Kenyan Tiger."

    "Direction?"

    "Headed for the shaggin' wagon."

    "Be there in a minute. Out."

She Demons 153

Graham slid his mini walkie-talkie back into its case on his belt with a satisfying snap and headed down the alley. It had been a rewarding stakeout, Bains covering the front, him at the rear. He'd been thrilled to hear Bains's description of Jassy and Sam entering the outreach centre and had cursed viciously when informed of Jinnah's presence. He'd decided to ignore Sam when she bolted out of the back door and into the night. The real target was coming out the main entrance. Upon reflection his annoyance with Jinnah had disappeared and he was almost cheerful as he climbed into the ghost car beside Bains.

"Wanna pull 'em over now?" asked Bains, starting the engine.

"No. Let's see where they lead us. Unless it's back to the *Tribune* building — then you hit the lights and siren. I don't want Jassy Singh all over the front page before I even get to question her."

Bains nodded and pulled away from the curb smoothly. It took no time at all for him to catch up with the satellite-guided Love Machine.

"Not too close," Graham warned his wheelman. "Jinnah can tell when he's being followed."

Bains allowed himself a quiet smile. He had a zero-tolerance policy where Jinnah was concerned. Being an Indo-Canadian himself, he thought the sensationalist scribe brought little credit to the community.

"Don't worry, boss — he won't know what hit him."

Graham stared straight ahead, furiously chewing his gum and silently praying that Bains was right.

154   *Donald J. Hauka*

* * *

It took Jinnah less than twenty minutes to navigate the SGLM from the outreach centre to the address Jassy gave him — the first rental house in Ray Daisley's files. It was in a semi-respectable neighbourhood around Nanaimo Heights on Kesselring Street. An older Vancouver Special, it looked well-maintained and occupied, right down to the neatly mown lawn and the relatively recent gold paint on the manes of the cement lions guarding the entrance.

"You're sure this is the place?" said Jinnah doubtfully, turning off the ignition and pulling the parking brake.

"This is the right address, that's all I know," replied Jassy.

"Well, you are the tenant here, aren't you?"

"I've known about this place and the other houses on this list for about as long as you have, Jinnah. It's not as if I've been here before."

Jinnah locked and alarmed his beloved van and followed Jassy as she strode determinedly towards the front gate. She didn't hesitate while opening the metal flip latch, nor did she falter on the march up the sidewalk to the front door.

"Are you sure this is wise?" said Jinnah, his congenital cowardice asserting itself. "What if this one's occupied?"

"Then we'll have someone to talk to," said Jassy, ringing the doorbell.

She Demons

"And what will we ask them?" demanded Jinnah. "Excuse me, Mister Grow Operator, we're from the Department of Agriculture — mind if we inspect the B.C. bud in your basement?"

"I'll claim I'm answering the 'for rent' ad in the *Tribune*," said Jassy with an icy calmness that alarmed Jinnah. "Besides, I doubt there's anybody in there."

"And if there is, how am I to explain my presence, hmm?" demanded Jinnah.

"I'll say you're my dad, Hakeem."

"You really know how to hurt a guy," said Jinnah, genuinely stung.

There was no answer and Jinnah was spared the mortification of having his true age confirmed. Jassy went around the side and Hakeem had little choice but to follow. The windows to the basement were large and at ground level. They were covered by heavy wooden shutters. Jassy swung them open and peered inside. There was too much condensation on the windows to see inside, but Jinnah could already smell the telltale scent emanating from the basement.

"Locked," Jassy grunted. "Hmmm...."

She cast about for a moment before spying a suitably hefty rock and wrapping it in her scarf before fitting it to her hand.

"What are you doing?" demanded Jinnah.

"Unscheduled suite inspection," she replied, breaking the window almost noiselessly and, to Jinnah's trained eye, almost professionally.

The waft of warm, moist air and a wave of unadulterated skunk smell confirmed Jinnah's earlier analysis

156   *Donald J. Hauka*

that they were two for two in the grow op sweepstakes. Jassy reached in and opened the window.

"Are you crazy?" hissed Jinnah. "For all you know there's a biker gang inside there!"

"So not Ray's style," she said brightly. "Coming?"

Jinnah watched, mute, as the former Wreck Beach beauty queen climbed fearlessly into the basement and dropped out of sight. His congenital cowardice fought briefly with his inherent instincts. Jassy was clearly insane, suffering a psychotic break with reality — possibly due to a drug overdose or prescription drug abuse. She was guilty of breaking and entering and, if the grow op was guarded, was walking into a potentially lethal situation. It was clearly his duty to follow her, protect her, and ensure she came to no harm (at least, not until she told him where Andy Gill was). On the other hand, the moisture and broken glass would almost certainly ruin his Gucci loafers and aggravate his Persian gout.

"Holy shit!"

There was no fear, only amazement in Jassy's disembodied voice, but it was enough to launch Jinnah through the window, glass or no glass, and he landed awkwardly on the basement floor, wondering if he could be accused of breaking and entering after the fact. He rose and, after checking his shoes, dusted the shards and other debris from off his leather jacket. Could he expense the cleaning bill?

"Look at them! I've never seen plants this size before!"

It was only now that Jinnah looked up to see Jassy standing in a forest of marijuana plants. The plants

She Demons 157

were the size of Christmas trees — a crop worth a fortune. For a moment, he saw Jassy as a Yaksha standing
in the middle of the forest, beckoning him to go deeper
into the dark wood. But it would take a considerably
more seductive houri to lure Hakeem Jinnah any further into this labyrinth. He was wondering if it would
be undignified to ask to Jassy give him a boost so he
could clamber out of the window when she started
heading upstairs.

"Jassy! For God's sake, stop tempting fate!"

"You're beginning to remind me of Sam," said
Jassy, disappearing up the steps. "Do you think you
shall enter the garden without suffering the trials of
those who came before you?"

"That's from the Qur'an, you know!"

Jinnah huffed and puffed as he hastened up the
stairs to the main floor. For a moment, he considered
taking his inhaler out for a few quick puffs of hydrocortisone, but decided he'd already shown enough
unmanly weakness in front of this she-devil. He found
Jassy standing in a barren living room. There wasn't so
much as a milk carton to indicate occupancy.

"Seen enough?" Jinnah wheezed.

"Nope. Let's roll."

"Roll?" cried Jinnah, incredulous. "Roll where?
Listen, lady, I'm getting a little tired of having to
answer all the questions around here."

"All you've done is *ask* questions, like 'What do
you think you're doing?' and 'You're not going in
there, are you?' Let's get going."

"Going? Going where?"

158   *Donald J. Hauka*

"Again with the questions. We have eighteen more houses to check out."

"I am not going to check out all twenty grow ops in your empire!"

"Then I'll go by myself!"

Jassy flung open the door, gave Jinnah one last meaningful look, and walked out of the house.

And right into the arms of Sergeant Craig Graham and Constable Harpreet Bains.

"It's not safe for young ladies like yourself to be out so late in such a rough neighbourhood, is it?" said Graham.

Shit, thought Jinnah. Whiteman will never spring for my bail....

"Jassy Singh, I'm arresting you for breaking and entering."

Bains already had Jassy in cuffs and was hustling her towards the front gate.

"Graham, you're making a big mistake —"

"I could have sworn I heard a voice," Graham rode right over Jinnah's protest, but kept his eyes fixed on Jassy. "Lucky thing there's nobody there or else I might have to arrest them as an accomplice."

"Jinnah is my accomplice!" shouted Jassy, struggling feebly. "We planned it together —"

"Now wait a minute —"

"— and he's my lover!"

"In my — in *your* dreams —"

"I'm sure if Jinnah were here he'd deny that," said Graham, maintaining his stony cop face with some difficulty. "And I find it hard to believe, considering he's

She Demons 159

been helping me with this investigation from day one."

Oh Allah, the compassionate, the merciful. The B.C. bud was in the fire now. Jassy stopped struggling and concentrated all her strength and will on twisting her head just enough to meet Jinnah's sheepish gaze as he stood rooted to the top steps.

"Helping you from day one?"

"I'm sure if Jinnah were here he would deny that!" cried Hakeem.

Jinnah stood by the gate while Graham, still pretending the reporter didn't exist, climbed into the ghost car. Shit, shit, shit, shit, shit! I should have taken her straight to the *Trib* office, or a shelter, or a safe house, or my house — well, maybe not my house, unless Manjit has already left me over this drop-in centre nonsense....

"Jassy! Where is Andy Gill?" Jinnah called as Bains stuffed her into the back of the car.

Jassy looked at Jinnah with a cool, haughty pride that would have done Lakshmibai herself justice. "Get me out of this and I'll tell you," she said as the door closed.

Jinnah was so gobsmacked that he said nothing as the car roared away into the night. He remained there, motionless, until the sound of distant sirens reached his ears a moment later. Police sirens. Unless he got the hell out of there fast, he'd be caught in one of the single biggest grow op hauls in Vancouver history.

"Son of a bitch!" he muttered, although the phrase was totally inadequate to sum up the situation. He was going to have to get a better mantra.

Chapter Five

The art of interrogation is not so much to catch your subject out in a lie or trip them up with logical inconsistencies. Those play a part, of course, but the true art is in knowing how to break your prisoner's resolve: what buttons to push, what weaknesses in character or relationship are the decisive ones in the battle of wills. Graham had interviewed some very sick puppies in his time — psychos, killers without conscience, hard cases with emotional armour a foot thick and a mile wide — but they'd been pushovers compared to Jassy Singh. He was getting absolutely nowhere with the MiMi acolyte. In her hour of need all that training and meditation was paying off. It was strange, even as her cult was helping her endure, Jassy was having severe doubts about Millennial Magic. What she clung stubbornly to was her conviction that she was absolutely innocent of the crime

She Demons 161

Graham had accused her of. They'd been going at it for three hours now.

Graham took another slug of coffee and renewed his frontal assault. "We have you dead to rights in one grow op, Jassy. The other one in Dosanjh's basement was in your name. Tomorrow morning City Hall will confirm that the other one was rented out to you as well. Am I painting a clear enough picture for you?"

"It's a very sparse canvas, Sergeant Graham," said Jassy coolly. "I could have rented a dozen houses that happen to have grow ops in them. It proves nothing other than I have bad taste in friends. You have nothing on me. You're hallucinating."

"Really? How about breaking and entering? How about being prime suspect in Thad Golway's murder? See, the picture I'm looking at is pretty complete. You and Thad are tight, in business together. You find out he's working for the police, so you kill him — or have him killed. And what about Thad's two friends? They're still missing. Did you have them whacked too, Jassy?"

"You make me sound like some sort of drug dragon queen, sergeant," smiled Jassy. "A real evil mastermind ruling a vast grow op empire."

"That's what you are, isn't it?"

"What kind of evil mastermind has to break into her own drug empire?"

Graham had thought of this hole in his argument and was ready for it. "One who knows she's being watched by the police. One who's clever enough to drag a reporter with her so he can tell her side of the story —"

Jassy laughed out loud at this. "Now you really *are* hallucinating! The day Jinnah prints my side of the story, hell will freeze over."

"You're going down, Jassy," insisted Graham. "And you're taking your cult with you."

Jassy had no worries on that score. "Police persecution and false prosecution do nothing but strengthen Millennial Magic, sergeant. Every time you have your pet media like Jinnah print lies about us, our numbers grow. The people know the truth. Put me in prison and throw away the key. Millennial Magic will survive."

Graham didn't know just how close he'd come to finding Jassy's weak spot. To his tired and over-stressed brain it sounded like she had a severe case of martyr complex. Had he known that it had taken every ounce of Jassy's remaining strength to give that sermon, that it was only by holding the image of Lionel Simons in her mind and forgetting about Daisley and Sam and the others that she had managed to sound so convincing, then he might have pressed her on it, broken through, won. As it was, he finished his cold coffee and stood up.

"Just hold that thought," he growled and stalked out, leaving Jassy, exhausted but elated, alone in the room.

"She's a tough nut to crack."

Jinnah shook his head sadly. Craig Graham was a fine man, but his experience with the Indo-Canadian community was limited and his knowledge of its history

She Demons 163

scanty. He looked at Jassy through the two-way mirror, her fine, angular face worthy of a carving in the Malabar Temples.

"Craig, Craig, she's a Sikh — a warrior princess whose middle name is 'Kaur,' the lioness. Add to that her current infatuation with the MiMis and Lionel Simons. Her ancestors are used to being tortured, burnt at the stake, and leading armies to battle. She's ready to die for what she believes. How's a slap on the wrist for breaking and entering going to scare her?"

"Breaking and entering is a serious offence!"

"And when the Harriet Butlers of the world point out to the judge that the house was rented in her name and that she was, technically, the resident, how long do you think it will take him to throw it out of court like a rotten chapatti?"

"What about the grow op in the basement?"

"When was the last time you convicted anyone of operating without direct, hard evidence? Catching them in the act? Besides, I will testify that she only just found out about that house late last night."

"Why the hell would you do that?"

"Because, sadly, it's the truth. Listen, my friend, there is only one thing to do here: let her walk."

Graham, who had been up for three days straight and was watching his one golden thread in an otherwise dead-end investigation unravel before his eyes, lost it. "Let her walk? What the hell are you talking about? Jesus Christ almighty, Jinnah! I have enough circumstantial evidence against her to charge her right now! Let her walk?"

164 *Donald J. Hauka*

Jinnah was as unmoved as Jassy had been. "Believe me, Craig, it's what Confucius would do."

"What the hell has Confucius got to do with this?" hollered Graham.

Jinnah let his friend hyperventilate for a moment, calculating just the right interval for the threat of imminent stroke to subside before continuing. "Does she look like a killer? I mean, the one who actually wielded the axe?"

"You just said she was a warrior princess."

"Princesses rarely do the dirty deed themselves, Craig. If she is guilty of having Thad Golway murdered, then she had to have had help, hmm? Let her walk and she'll lead you to the others."

"No way!"

Jinnah sighed and took out a cigarette. "My friend, look through this mirror. You see some sort of criminal mastermind. I see an angry, scared young woman. Not scared of you, of course — why would she be, inside the safety of an interrogation room? But she is scared of someone outside that room and when we find out who that is, we will have her."

Graham hesitated. Part of him was reluctantly coming to the conclusion that Jinnah was right. The majority opinion, however, was still recommending to the Crown that charges be laid and giving Caitlin Bishop some of those *Tribune* photos taken on Wreck Beach for the top of the six o'clock news.

"No deal. I get charges laid against her and go in again, she'll crack."

Jinnah fiddled with his cigarette, going through the

She Demons 165

mime motions of lighting it, pretending to smoke it. He knew it drove Graham crazy. Time to stop pussyfooting about and give the policeman the straight goods. "Funny, I seem to recall me saving your ass tonight and convincing Caitlin Bishop not to go live from The Corner, Craig...."

Jinnah let the comment sink slowly to the bottom of the well of silence that had swallowed the conversation. He was certain that he had won — Graham knew that with a single word from the mighty Jinnah-ji, Caitlin would be unleashed and his career would not outlast her noon news stand-up. Nevertheless, Craig could be bullheaded and Jinnah was relieved when Graham shrugged, trying to put the best possible face on his defeat.

"It's your ass if she slips the net," he said. "I mean that, Jinnah — accessory to a B&E, the whole book I can throw at you."

"I love you too, Craig," said Jinnah. "Give us a kiss, you smelly old asshole."

Graham shook Jinnah's arm off his shoulders and called to Bains. "We're letting her go for now, Harpreet. Give her the 'don't leave town' speech."

Jinnah forced himself to suppress the smile that was spreading inside his soul. Now he had a second chance — a shot at redemption. That didn't happen often in this business. He made a mental note to give an appropriate offering to News God. Unless he smartened up in a hurry, it would be his son.

* * *

166 *Donald J. Hauka*

It was teetering on the border between being very late at night and very early in the morning when Jinnah and Jassy walked out of Vancouver Police Headquarters on Cambie Street and moved awkwardly along the sidewalk, almost like two teenagers who had been out on a very intense first date and had yet to kiss. They stared at their shoes, they looked at the Canada Line construction catastrophe across the street — anywhere but at each other. Jinnah contented himself with lighting his battered and fondled cigarette. They had reached the corner where three ill-lit streets converged, forming a dark fan, when Jassy finally made the first move.

"Thanks, Jinnah, I owe you."

"It's nothing," said Jinnah modestly, exhaling his smoke with real pleasure.

"I can't thank you enough."

Jassy's manner was shy, deferential. Now this was more like it. Jinnah was feeling almost magnanimous — almost.

"I know of several ways you could show your gratitude, but let's start with you keeping your word and telling me where Andy Gill is."

"Yeah, you're right, I oughtta come clean. Andy is — omigod! Are they towing your van?"

"What?"

Jinnah threw his cigarette down and whirled about in the direction Jassy was pointing. He was tired and it took him a second to locate his van parked quite legally on Second Avenue. It took another fraction of a second for him to register that metered parking didn't take effect until 6:30 a.m. and another instant

She Demons 167

to suspect the worst. In the nanosecond it took him to turn around, Jassy was gone, vanished into the darkness. She could be headed down any one of the three streets or, more likely, over any one of the fences or cutting through one of the parking lots in this semi-residential, light industrial neighbourhood. Jinnah cursed half-heartedly. He'd fallen for a diversion that wouldn't have fooled a simpleton. He discounted testosterone overload as the likely cause and put it down to nicotine withdrawal. There was only one thing left to do — go home. He would have to endure a lecture from Manjit, certainly, but at least after that brief moment of eternity, he would be able to go to sleep and put to bed this endless, awful day.

"What do you mean Saleem isn't home yet?"

Jinnah wasn't sure which was worse: the calm, dignified manner in which his wife had delivered this news or the faint suggestion of red, irritated skin around her eyes that told him she had been crying. Probably the latter, although upon reflection he realized that she had let him give his detailed excuse for being so late (and in the unchaperoned company of Jassy Singh) at length and without interruption before giving him the glad news.

"As I have said, Hakeem, we made a deal: I dropped Saleem off at this drop-in centre in South Vancouver after he promised to meet me at Poonum's house at ten. At 10:30, he called to say he'd be late. I haven't been able to reach him since."

"Then he's still there? Why didn't you go pick him up, for God's sake?"

"Because I don't know what to do anymore, Hakeem. I used to know what is right, but now I wonder. I tell Saleem one thing, you tell him another. I try to teach him morals, you talk about the greater good. The greater good seems to be whatever story you happen to be chasing at the moment. The right thing should not change from moment to moment. It should be something lasting. Eternal."

Tempted as he was to observe that his wife was starting to sound like Confucius, Jinnah kept his mouth shut. He grabbed his battered jacket wearily and headed for the door.

"If you want a glimpse of eternity, Manjit, just look at the day we've had. I'm going to pick up Saleem."

And with that, Jinnah went out into the unending night.

"Hey, it's tough to fit into the New World when you're a visible minority. Your family may love you, but they don't always understand. They're stuck in the Old World. We can help you find a place. We're your New Future, your happiness."

Saleem listened like a puppy while Lahki spoke. He and a half dozen other teens were sitting around the MiMi devotee in a semicircle on the floor, hugging their cushions, disdaining the battered couches and comfy chairs grouped around the perimeter of the open plan

She Demons 169

room or even the state of the art computer stations and other features of the centre. The South Vancouver facility was about as far removed from the MiMi's outreach office as you could get; right in the middle of the affluent Southlands neighbourhood, especially designed to appeal to the children of reasonably affluent families like Saleem. It had worked its charms on Hakeem Jinnah's son — or rather, Lahki had. Saleem thought her the most beautiful young woman he had ever seen and this conviction was powerful enough to make him forget that he had been born and raised in Canada, that his parents were about as North American as a Big Mac, and his difficulty in straddling culture was largely confined to the adolescent mysteries of the opposite sex. Lahki was so spellbinding that he didn't even notice his father making his entrance.

Jinnah had moved into the centre like a thundercloud, ready to smite anyone who stood in the way of him claiming his son and, if necessary, smiting Saleem himself to get him back home. He tried to ignore the ugly fact that he had sent his son here in the first place. But Manjit's gentle and anguished words had been working on him during the drive from the Jinnah-mahal to the drop-in and it gave him pause. What was the right thing? How much could he compromise in pursuit of what he considered justice? Where did a husband — a parent — draw the line? As he looked at his son, rapt with attention, his own argument with Graham outside the interview room came back to him. The Great Jinnah-ji, high priest of the Sacred Order of News God, saw a disciple, his own son no less, shirking

170 *Donald J. Hauka*

his duty, disobeying his mother, and consorting with the enemy. Hakeem Jinnah, father of a loving son, son of a loving father, saw Saleem surrounded by teens from a rainbow of ethnic backgrounds, looking happy, the boy's smile mirrored in yellow, brown, black, red, and white faces. Hakeem suddenly felt a calmness and compassion that was, for once, not drug induced.

"Hey, Saleem," he called cheerfully. "Your ride's here when you're ready."

Saleem started guiltily, his brain trying to reconcile the image of his father standing there to take him home (which made sense) and the smile lighting his face (which was incomprehensible). He glanced over at Lahki, but the devotee was looking at Jinnah with a warm, welcoming smile of her own that Hakeem recognized as the signal for "shields up!"

"You must be Saleem's dad — why don't you join us and talk for a while?"

Jinnah knew this game. Lahki was expecting him to throw a fit, demand Saleem come with him, like now, and justify every lie and half-truth she had been filling these kids' heads with. But she had never dealt with the great Jinnah-ji before.

"Sure thing, man," he said, advancing towards the semicircle. "Let's rap."

Saleem stood upright as if he'd sat on a cattle prod. "No, that's okay, Dad, I'm ready to go."

Jinnah affected a stricken look. "Are you sure, son? I'm ready to talk all night if you like. Let's relate —"

Saleem was already moving towards the door. "Thanks, Lahki!" called over his shoulder.

She Demons 171

Jinnah gave the startled devotee a wink. "Nice talking with you, miss," he said and followed his son out of the drop-in centre.

Paperboys, real paperboys, were a thing of the distant past in Vancouver. The multi-channelled cable universe and the Internet had pushed deadlines earlier and earlier, as had suburban sprawl and the need to get the first edition of the paper on the last ferry leaving for Vancouver Island. Gone were the days when kids could deliver papers in a small, confined neighbourhood either before or after school. The *Tribune*, along with its competitor, the *Clarion*, had long ago contracted out its morning delivery to Porpoise Trucking, whose mostly middle-aged drivers started hurling papers onto the doorsteps of their vast routes as early as one o'clock in the morning. The *Tribune* was waiting on Jinnah's doorstep when he arrived back home with Saleem in tow, but he didn't bother to pick it up. He already knew what was on the front page and he would wait until he'd had a good night's sleep before reading his prose with his usual delight, over a leisurely breakfast.

It came as a considerable shock, therefore, when just before noon, he was awoken by Manjit, who was holding the cordless phone under his nose and informing his groggy brain that it was Frosty from the office insisting on speaking with him, like, right now.

"You had better get your brown ass in here stat, Hakeem."

"Good morning to you too, Frosty. Why?"

"Because Whiteman wants to nail it to his office wall. He's furious with you."

"What for? I wrote the line story for him, for God's sake —"

"Have you even looked at the paper this morning?"

"No, I haven't seen the paper yet —"

Manjit thrust the *Tribune* under Jinnah's nose. Even without his glasses, he could tell that his carefully lawyered story about the connection between Lionel Simons and Thad Golway's murder had not graced page one. Instead, there was a wire story about some marijuana bust in Vancouver.

"Why in the name of all that is holy is this on page one?" howled Jinnah, now fully awake.

"Because the cops called every media outlet in town with the tip except us, that's why. Including Caitlin Bishop, who went live from the grow op house itself. Single biggest bust in one house in history. And we didn't have a word on it — had to scalp something from the *Clarion*. Whiteman wants to know why his ace crime reporter missed the biggest story of the day."

If Whiteman ever found out the real reason, Jinnah would be writing obituaries or editing the six point box scores in sports for the rest of his career. He didn't feel well at all. Perhaps he should call in sick?

"A grow op bust, no matter how big, is nothing compared to a new gang moving into our city and the connections between it and one of our most notorious cults, Frosty!" Jinnah said peevishly, trying desperately

She Demons   173

to remember if he's already used his allotment of sick days for the year.

"I know that, you know that. But you didn't see the great footage Caitlin had of the cops hauling all the plants out. You shoulda seen 'em, Hakeem! They were —"

"The size of Christmas trees?"

"How did you know that?"

"A common exaggeration of the Sixth Estate," said Jinnah smoothly, covering his slip. "The real story now hinges on the link between Thad and the MiMis — Jassy Singh."

"Have you been able to find or interview her?"

"Not yet," said Jinnah, retroactively referring to the time period between about three in the morning when Jassy had given him the slip and the present moment, to ease his conscience. "But it's only a matter of time."

"There's no time like the present, Hakeem. You better get in here and start working the phone or Whiteman will have you doing dog stories for a year."

"I'm on my way," Jinnah lied.

He clicked the phone off and handed it to Manjit, who was looking at him with her head tilted to one side, a look of deep suspicion on her face.

"Jinnah, is this not the house that you and Jassy Singh broke into last night?"

"Indeed, my love, it is the same."

"Then why didn't you file a story for the paper?"

"I was busy, Manjit," said Jinnah, hopping out of bed and wrestling himself into his clothes as quickly as possible.

174 *Donald J. Hauka*

"Busy doing what, exactly?"

"Trying to keep Jassy out of jail — look, could you get me some coffee?"

"But surely, Hakeem, one phone call to the paper — you had all that time to kill while your friend Sergeant Graham was interviewing this Gassy woman —"

"It's Jassy and where the hell are my socks?"

"Or is there some other reason you didn't want the other media finding out about this alleged drug house?"

"What are you on about, Manjit?" demanded Jinnah, pulling on his pants.

"I am just trying to determine whether this was a grow op or a love nest."

"If you want proof, go watch the noon news — there'll be plenty of tape. Is that coffee ready yet?"

"Still, it does seem odd, Hakeem —"

"Are you my wife or my editor? I have an ironclad alibi and the police themselves for witnesses, for God's sake. What's gotten into you?"

"Nothing, except you seem to spend more time with this Sassy woman than with your own wife, that is all."

"Manjit," said Jinnah softly, moving over to his wife and gathering her up in his arms. "She means absolutely nothing to me."

"You're lying," said Manjit, writhing to break free — but not too hard.

"You're right — she does mean the front page and perhaps the Webster Award. Other than that, nothing."

"Nothing?" asked Manjit.

She Demons   175

Jinnah answered with a kiss and they fell, as if by magic, onto the bed. After a while, Manjit gasped: "I thought you were in a hurry to get to work."

"I do some of my best thinking this way."

That spoiled it for Manjit, who threw his pants at him before storming downstairs to make the coffee. Jinnah smiled as he pulled his tight, black slacks back on. At least his wife now knew just how much Jassy Singh really meant to him.

"You mean the world to the Magus, to me, to the whole organization, Jassy. But I think this is for the best."

Jassy, operating on no sleep, no food, and still wearing the same clothes she'd had on yesterday, was still in shock. She was seated in Daisley's office, acutely aware of the manner in which she had entered it the previous evening, but what little sense of guilt she'd had over her clandestine visit and theft had vanished about two minutes into their conversation. That was the point when Ray had spread out Jinnah's story (banished to page five, but in print none the less) on his desk for her to read. While she was trying to process Jinnah's prose, Ray told her about the phone call he'd received from Graham that morning asking for the organization's rental records, which he had to admit appeared to be missing.

"So you're firing me?"

"It's just an extended stress leave," insisted Daisley in a maddeningly comforting tone. "What with everything going on in you life now — being questioned by the police about Thad's murder, all these houses registered in your name. We think it would be best for you and for the organization."

It was too much — much too much. She was being hung out to dry, and for what purpose? She'd given up everything for the movement, for the Magus. It couldn't end this way.

"Ray, you know damn well I know nothing about those houses. You're the one who rented them and used my name. I can prove it!"

"I think you need some time to rest and reflect, Jass —"

"Fuck you, Ray! Fuck you! If you're screwing me, I swear to God I'll get you for it! I'll tell the cops! I'll tell the Magus —"

"The Magus is your father, Jassy, and the organization is your family. We're only trying to protect you. You can see that, can't you?"

Jassy looked at Ray, but she could see nothing at all, just the black hole of his eyes sucking the life and joy out of her. Daisley leaned forward and, with an air of the utmost tenderness and concern, said, "I'll have to ask you for your keys."

"Son of a bitch!"

Jinnah slammed down the phone, fuming. Nothing was going right today. The morning interview with Whiteman had not gone well. He had expected the old

She Demons 177

"where were you when the police called?" line of questioning and was ready for it. But the new editor had hardly even mentioned his failure to file on the greatest grow op bust in Vancouver history. The new boss was a big picture man and the portrait he painted of Jinnah was epic in scale and tawdry in nature. Hakeem had had to sit there, sweating bullets, as Whiteman paced back and forth, tossing an old baseball up and down like an athletic abacus, totalling his sins.

"Sensationalizing stories. Frequent absences. Failing to file routine police briefs. Abusive behaviour in the newsroom. Language bordering on sexual harassment ..."

The litany went on and on. Jinnah was beginning to feel like poor old Rubashov from Arthur Koestler's novel. In this case, darkness was not at noon but 10:00 a.m. After about thirty minutes, Jinnah was finally moved to defend himself.

"Look, do I need a shop steward, Whiteman?"

The editor-in-chief paused a moment and considered the baseball's worn, stitched surface. The presence of a shop steward would make this a formal disciplinary hearing and Whiteman loathed going through official channels in these cases: especially when he had far more effective means of punishing his errant scribes.

"No," he said, returning to his desk and placing the ball carefully beside the phone. "No, Jinnah, I don't think we need to go to that extent. Let's settle this between ourselves, shall we?"

Jinnah breathed an inward sigh of relief and made to stand up. Too late, he noticed that Whiteman had

opened a desk drawer and was pulling something out
of it. He had just enough time to wonder if it was a
ceremonial axe before realizing that it was something
worse — far worse. An instrument of torture that
struck true terror into his heart.

"That isn't what I think it is — is it?" he said,
voice flat, unbelieving, as Whiteman placed a parcel
the size of a shoebox on his desk.

"Welcome to the age of convergence, Mr. Jinnah.
This is your new video camera."

Jinnah stared at the thing as if it were a rabid pit
bull. "You're kidding."

"We live in a streaming video clip age, Jinnah. We
must move with the times —"

"You're kidding me?"

"All reporters will be issued one — they're as simple to use as a tape recorder. You did get the e-memo
about how we are moving to a multi-platform configu-
ration, didn't you?"

Jinnah had and had thought Whiteman was raving
about an elaborate timeshare or condominium complex and promptly deleted it. Now he found himself
holding something that Caitlin Bishop's cameramen
hefted. The weapon of the enemy.

"I can't be expected to learn how to use this at my
age!" he howled.

"My twelve-year-old can work this very model,
Jinnah."

"My point exactly! My neural synapses were
formed when there was still lead type to be set! In fact,
I am suffering from overexposure and have advanced

She Demons 179

lead poisoning. I need extended sick leave —"

"Jinnah," said Whiteman quietly. "You will learn how to use this and how to file clips to our webpage. It is a condition of employment."

Jinnah sprang to his feet. "We'll see what the union has to say about this, buddy!"

"The union has already agreed under our tech-change clause. That was in the latest guild bulletin. You did read it, of course?"

The last time Jinnah had read the Guild Bulletin was when it had carried the news of the failed decerti-fication bid (a bid Jinnah had almost single-handedly supported) on its front page.

He tried another tack. "Come on, Whiteman! You used to be a reporter. Remember the thrill of being able to file as long as you had a notebook and a phone? Of being able to beat all those TV hacks because their technology was so cumbersome and we moved light and fast? Hmm?"

"Jinnah, it may have escaped your notice, but the *Tribune* is the last major metropolitan daily newspa-per not to be owned by a media conglomerate that has in its portfolio newspapers, television stations, radio stations, and various web platforms. Even the *Clarion* is now owned by such a consortium. We must evolve or perish."

"Define perish, exactly," whined Jinnah, not liking the way the interview had turned at all.

"Perish, in your case, will mean the night desk in sports doing six point box scores — until I can find some lead type for you to set. Is that clear?"

Jinnah nodded weakly and stumbled from the room clutching the video camera like it was a live grenade. As it was, something explosive was happening in his bowels and it was some time before he made it back to his desk. It had proved no safe haven, however, for within seconds his phone had rung and his supplier had called. How was he going to get any work done with creditors harassing him on the job? It didn't help to have Sanderson at the next desk, smirking and pretending to read the paper while overhearing every word.

"Have you tried getting a business loan from the bank, Hakeem? Or maybe Payday Loans — they might be able to offer you bridge financing."

"Ronald, Ronald — the man is being unreasonable. How can he expect me to pay him before I have sold a single doll, hmm?"

"You're not taking the right approach, Jinnah. You're not selling dolls, you're selling details."

Jinnah looked at Sanderson with disbelief. He had known this man for nearly two decades, most of their professional working life, and yet here was an aspect of Ronald's character emerging that he had never seen before.

"What is it with you and Barbies anyway, Ronald? I hope this isn't some sort of fetish thing, hmm?"

"Of course not!"

Jinnah was gratified to see his desk mate blush. "Then what is it? If you're a cross-dresser, don't be embarrassed — some of my closest friends are transvestites."

She Demons 181

"Oh, for God's sake, Jinnah! It's perfectly simple —"

"These things usually are, my friend, and can be treated with a little therapy. Have you tried the company counselling plan?"

"Jinnah, let me tell you something —"

"If it's about your sex life with dolls, I don't want to hear —"

As usual, the entire newsroom was listening to the daily Jinnah-Sanderson tilt. Bets on who would win were quietly being made and despite a big paper and an early deadline, work had ground to a halt. For once, however, Sanderson was totally unfazed by Jinnah's baiting.

"When I was a kid, I had four older sisters. They all had Barbies. They all outgrew them. I started collecting them as a hobby. Pretty soon, once they reached a certain age, they started wanting them back. But I knew just how much each one of them cost, because each one of them was different, just like each make and year of a car is different. That gives them value. They were surprised to find out just how valuable their old playthings were. Pretty soon, we had a sort of family business going in rare, collectible Barbies. Now, Hakeem, I hate to say it, but I don't think your market is the Indo-Canadian community. I think it's people like me and my sisters."

Jinnah was flabbergasted. He looked around the sides of Sanderson's desk, then over to the reception area, where Crystal was watching, amused. "Okay, buddy — who are you and what have you done with the real Ronald Sanderson?"

"It's the truth, Hakeem," Ronald insisted. "If you'd sell me just one of those dolls, my sisters would treat me like a god."

"Like a god?" said Jinnah.

"It's a cult thing," confessed Sanderson.

"Listen, my friend, the only cult I'm worried about right now is Millennial Magic. Did they kill Thad Golway? Or was it one of the cult's enemies?"

"Lionel Simons doesn't have a whole bunch of enemies. Getting back to the dolls —"

"How about the Reverend Hobbes and his God Squad?"

"The Jesus freaks? They're into peace and love, surely. I mean, a Christian minister wouldn't commit such a gruesome crime, would he?"

"Ever heard of the Crusades, buddy?"

"Point taken. But that was the Middle Ages. This is a whole new millennium and nuts like Hobbes are about publicity, not murder."

"Ronald, Ronald, you have to picture the scene —"

"Oh, here we go again —"

"Stop interrupting. There is Thad Golway, having been given a massive dose of heroin, he is comatose, helpless, stretched out upon an executioner's block —"

"Did this murder take place in the Tower of London or in Vancouver?"

"— a Shadowy Figure stands over him, wielding an axe. Now, who is the murderer? Is it Lionel Simons? Ray Daisley? Peter Hobbes? Jassy Singh —"

"How about this Andy Gill kid? Have you ruled him out?"

She Demons 183

"Not yet, but he's a long shot," admitted Jinnah. "And I would put Mary Demolay and Chas 'Quickset' Kali at the top of the list."

"Maybe they all did it, like the murder on the Orient Express."

"Stick to writing about deadly fungus and let us crime reporters solve the murders, hmm?"

Jinnah's phone rang, and the various oddsmakers had to admit that Sanderson had come out ahead for a change. Jinnah wouldn't have cared even if he had known how much money had changed hands: he had just hit the jackpot.

"Jinnah, it's Jassy. I'm ready to talk."

"Really? Where and when?"

Jassy gave Jinnah the rendezvous point, extorted a promise that he wouldn't tell a soul where she was — especially the police — and demanded he come now, like, right now! Hakeem grabbed his notebook, micro-cassette, and jacket and headed out without a word.

"Hakeem, where are you going?" demanded Sanderson. "What about the dolls?"

"I have a living doll to play with right now, Ronald," Jinnah called over his shoulder. "You should try it for a change. And you're right — what she's selling is all about the details."

Without further illumination, he was gone.

The Sun Yat Sen Gardens are an oasis of peace and beauty in the bustle of Vancouver's Chinatown. Its ponds and gardens are just a few blocks from The Corner and the outreach office of Millennial Magic. Inside its walls, visitors can easily forget the crowds, the traffic, the junkies wandering around Pigeon Park a stone's throw away. Jinnah found Jassy in a quiet corner by the little bridge across the muddy, brown waters, contemplating the koi that drifted slowly among the lily pads. From the moment she looked up at him without her customary hostile coolness, Hakeem knew she was not bullshitting him — something had scared her sufficiently to give him the straight goods. His inherent instincts were tingling. It was all systems go. He slid onto the stone bench next to her.

"Are you okay?" he asked.

"I'm being set-up for Thad Golway's murder. Does that sound okay to you?"

Oh, ho! Jinnah's brain kicked into overdrive. What had happened in the few hours since she had given him the slip outside the cop shop? Half a dozen scenarios raced through his mind at once.

"Just who is setting you up, Jassy?"

"I'm not sure who. And I have no idea why."

"What makes you so sure you're being set up?"

Jassy briefly recapped her interview with Daisley. The information fit at least one of Jinnah's possible scenarios and had the ring of truth about it. But it didn't go far enough in explaining Jassy's loquaciousness.

"So Daisley covered his ass by making you the front for his grow op business. Very sensible from his point of view, but I still don't see how Thad's involved in all this."

She Demons 185

"Neither do I. I just know the two things are connected."

Jinnah was torn. On the one hand, he admired Jassy's instincts — they matched his precisely. On the other, he knew she wasn't telling him absolutely everything she knew. He had two options: press her hard right now and see what spilled out, or try to gain her trust. He'd already seen just how far Graham had got when pressing her. No, this warrior princess required a gentle touch — for the moment.

"So you want me to help you connect the dots and save your ass, hmm?"

Jassy nodded. "Look, I know I shouldn't have taken off on you — that was a shitty thing to do —"

"Especially since I'd already sprung you from jail —"

"— but maybe we can make a new deal?"

She is desperate. She is scared. And now I know who she is scared of — Ray Daisley. If nothing else, Jinnah had to admire Jassy's taste in enemies.

"Okay, here's the deal: you have to help me get inside the MiMis — be my guide. In return, I'll find out just who is setting you up. And you have to lead me to Andy Gill."

Jassy stared at the brown, still water for a long moment. Jinnah had asked for a lot, but it was the bottom line from which he would not budge. Would she agree? It depended on just how scared she was.

"Okay," she said at last. "But the way things are right now, it would be safer for Andy if you didn't know where he is —"

186 *Donald J. Hauka*

"Now wait a minute —"

"Once we get enough evidence to nail Daisley, it will be safe for Andy to come home."

"Nail Daisley? What about Lionel Simons?"

"The Magus is not tied up in this."

"Like hell!"

"Take it or leave it, Jinnah."

"I don't think you're in a position to dictate terms here, young lady!"

"No? You owe me, Jinnah," said Jassy, some of her swagger returning. "You're the reason why I can't run home to my parents or to my community for help —"

"Now wait a minute —"

"You killed me in their eyes. This is the least you can do."

Jinnah's righteous indignation was only moderately troubled by the embryonic sense of guilt he felt over Jassy's parental troubles. What really cinched the deal was the time — nearly three o'clock in the afternoon and Whiteman was waiting for him back at the office. At least this way he had a shot at filing something better than a follow to the grow op bust, which would have presented all sorts of moral and ethical challenges to the ethically challenged Jinnah.

"All right," he grunted. "Deal. But when we're in public, you never refer to me as your dad, got it?"

Jassy, despite everything, found the strength to grin at this. "C'mon, Jinnah — what else could you be? No one would ever believe we were an item."

"You haven't met my wife," grumbled Jinnah.

"What's the trouble — she doesn't understand you?"

She Demons

"No — she understands me too well. Not let's get the hell out of here."

"I don't care, Cameron — she's going to do *Breakfast Television* for the rest of her short career. Weather girl is too good for her, really. Don't you think?"

Cameron Watermann tried to possess himself with patience, but it was hard when dealing with Ian Hadley. As executive producer, Watermann was Hadley's boss, but Ian had friends high up in the network and he had to treat the insufferable Brit with kid gloves. They were in Hadley's office, where the artwork consisted entirely of Ian posing with famous personalities and grinning inanely. But there were also several major awards breaking the celebrity monotony. Hadley might be vain, shallow, and egotistical, but he could make great television when he was on his game. Then again, so could Caitlin Bishop. Watermann had hired Caitlin and felt he needed to go to bat for his protegé.

"Ian, you know as well as I do that all Caitlin has to do is come in here bearing a café latte, flash her perfectly tinted baby blue contacts at you, flirt harmlessly for about ten minutes while stroking your enlarged ego, and you'll forgive her everything."

"Nonsense! When have I ever been so shallow?"

"Four weeks ago when she completely missed the angle on the biker war — the one Jinnah had all over the front of the *Tribune*? You threatened to send her to *Book Television*."

"Don't mention that buffoon Jinnah! Really, Cameron, think about it — if anyone else had pulled a farrago like that so close to air time —"

"She dug up the grow op bust last night, didn't she?"

"Had it handed to her on a platter, you mean. I'd like to know what she promised the cop who gave it to her —"

"Which just shows she has good contacts in the VPD. Give her another chance."

"Are you ordering me to, Cameron?"

Before Watermann could answer this delicate question, one calculated to get him into trouble with the senior execs who thought the sun shone out of Hadley's ass, they were interrupted by a waifish, twenty-something woman with mousy brown hair and glasses. From her lack of makeup and slacker wardrobe, Watermann took her to be a script girl. So did Hadley, who waved her away.

"Not now, lovey, not now — Ian is busy. Take it to the line up editor, that's a good girl."

"I thought the news producer had to okay proposals for undercover assignments, Ian."

The voice was familiar, but it did not match the image in front of him. It was only after registering the name on the top of the proposal that Hadley managed to utter a strangled "Caitlin?"

It was an effort to keep a straight face, but Watermann had made a career of keeping his countenance an expressionless mask while his bosses floated the most absurd story ideas and series concepts past him.

She Demons　　　　189

Still, the look on Hadley's mug required extra effort not to bust a gut.

"Like it?" asked Caitlin, doing a slow turn for their benefit. "This is me before the TV makeover. I looked a lot like this when I was an intern at the *Tribune*."

Watermann watched as Hadley sputtered for a few seconds, his gaze torn between the transformed Caitlin Bishop and the proposal slowly crumpling in his hand. Finally, the Brit exploded.

"What the hell do you think you're on about?" he shouted, waving Caitlin's paperwork over his head. "First you bail out on a story five minutes before airtime and now you look like the kids who pester me for spare change and you have the cheek — the unmitigated cheek! — to ask for a special assignment?"

Caitlin looked so dweeby, so wet, that Watermann half expected her to wilt. But under that slacker exterior beat the heart of a pit bull.

"Thad Golway, police informant, is only half the story, Ian. The other half involves much bigger fish. That's why I have to go undercover. I need to get to the heart of the story and that means infiltrating the MiMis."

Hadley looked at Caitlin, then at Watermann. "Cameron, a little guidance here, please."

"Oh, I don't want to be ordering you around, Ian," said the executive producer. "Use your best judgment. However, I do have to compliment you on your makeover, Caitlin. Fooled me. Fooled Ian too. I'm sure it will fool Simons and his zombies."

"Thanks, Cam," said Caitlin sweetly.

190   *Donald J. Hauka*

Watermann could tell Hadley was still hesitating, so he gave him a gentle prod. "Y'know, if Ian doesn't want your piece, I can always have a word with Clive. I'm sure he'd love it for the news magazine —"

"Clive? You're joking," cried Hadley. "I refuse to let something this good, this important, fall into the hands of a man whose news judgment and social skills are so ... so ... jejune!"

Clive was a fellow Brit and had gone to a different public school and college than Ian. Watermann allowed himself the smallest of smiles.

Caitlin hugged Hadley and gave him a chaste peck on the cheek. "Thanks, Ian! I won't let you down."

"You'd better not, lovey," growled Hadley. "Or your next assignment will be the morning traffic report."

Watermann choked down the laughter bubbling in his throat. Later on, after the news had aired and he was safely holding court at the Media Club, he would relate this story to his trusted cronies and describe how it was Ian Hadley who looked like he'd been run over by a truck named Caitlin Bishop.

"This had better not be another one of your grow ops, Jassy. That would be monotonous."

"Don't worry, Jinnah — this one isn't on Daisley's list."

Jinnah and Jassy were in the SGLM, parked out front of a large, older house in East Vancouver. To Jinnah, it appeared an ideal candidate for grow op

She Demons   191

number three. Although he did have to admit there
was a slightly more lived-in look to the two-storey,
wood-sided structure than the Vancouver Special
they'd broken into the previous evening. There were
plants that did not belong to the genus cannabis in the
window, there was a small but well-kept garden, and
other signs that suggested there were actual tenants.
That didn't rule out an operation in the basement, of
course, but as they made their way up the walk Jinnah
noted that there were no heavy coverings like plywood
or cardboard on the ground-level windows. All of
which begged an important question.

"Why the hell are we here then?" Jinnah demanded.

"You want information? Go to the source."

Jinnah was still chewing over this enigmatic
response as Jassy rang the bell. Its meaning became
clear when Sam answered the door.

"Hey, Sam. We gotta talk."

Jassy used the moment of shock that had immo-
bilized Sam to push right past her and into the house.
Jinnah admired her style and followed suit. He found
himself in a wide hallway, almost like a reception
room, with a stairwell at the far end. The walls were
festooned with MiMi posters, artwork, and a picture
of Lionel Simons.

"We'll use your room, okay?"

Jassy was already on the first riser by the time
Sam closed the door and locked it. Jinnah hurried
after his guide.

"Are you sure this house isn't a Ray Daisley
Special?" he whispered.

192 *Donald J. Hauka*

"This isn't a rental, Jinnah: we own this house. It's for staff."

"Oh? And what other hidden assets have the MiMis got floating under the Revenue Canada radar?"

"It's all legit, Jinnah. Do you know how many times we've been audited?"

Jinnah was almost impressed — he'd been audited himself and hadn't liked the experience at all. Then again, Revenue Canada, as thorough as they were, was not infallible. He made a mental note to check on how much the property tax alone for the cult communal house must cost Simons in a year as he followed Jassy into Sam's room.

It was small. There was barely room enough for the three of them. Sparsely decorated, it reminded Jinnah of any number of student residences he'd seen. But instead of posters about the class struggle or arts or business, Sam had adorned her walls with a few choice sayings of Lionel Simons. The most prominent of these was one Jinnah had seen many times in many different formats over his years of covering the MiMis: "The Spirit Kingdom is spread out upon the Earth, but the people do not see it. Be their eyes." A small desk and a wooden chair by the window completed the furnishings. Jassy sat on Sam's bed and motioned Jinnah to sit beside her. She looked expectantly at Sam, still standing by the door, her hand on the doorknob, unwilling to take her seat on the wooden chair.

"What's he doing here?"

"Jinnah's helping me."

She Demons 193

"Like, I don't see how that's possible —"

"We're all going to need help soon, Sam. Serious shit's going down."

Sam took a step back. She was perfectly framed by the doorway. Jinnah knew what she was thinking: do I call for help, or can I handle this myself?

"Jass, I heard you were on stress leave —"

Ah. Handling it herself. Good....

"Word travels fast. Did Daisley send out an email or just post it on the bulletin board?"

"He called an emergency staff meeting. Said you had some issues to work out."

"And did he tell you I'm now the prime suspect in Thad's murder?"

From Sam's reaction it was obvious Daisley had not. She slammed the door shut, leapt onto the chair, and leaned so far forward that she was just inches from Jassy's face. Jinnah was now genuinely impressed — he couldn't have done it better himself.

"No shit! Really? Like, do the police know about you and Thad?"

Jinnah raised his eyebrows and silently turned on the microcassette in his pocket. No one had said anything about off the record, and they wouldn't as long as he kept the record discreetly tucked away.

"There was no 'Thad and me,' so don't give me that shit," said Jassy sharply.

"Maybe not in your mind, but Thad sure thought so!"

Jinnah observed the same flash of anger that Sam had shown in the outreach office. He glanced over at

Jassy to watch her reaction and decided that for such a pretty face, she had a very ugly scowl.

"It doesn't matter what Thad thought. I wasn't interested!"

"I didn't mean, 'Do the cops know you were lovers.' I meant, 'Do they know you hated him?' 'Cos you sure treated him like shit, Jass. I can see why they think you did him."

This was new information that, if correct, would play right into Graham's hands. Jinnah felt sick to his stomach. He closed his eyes. Mount Jassy is about to erupt, he thought. This is what I get for having chosen a murderess as my guide —

"Yeah, I can see your point."

Jinnah's eyes flashed open. There was no clandestine sideways glance here — he turned and stared quite openly at Jassy. Holy shit! If I'd just been basically called a murderer by a friend, I'd go ballistic. But Jassy's tone had been quiet, gentle, almost resigned. How many different personas were hiding in this one woman?

"But just because I didn't date him, and just because I made his life hard because he wouldn't give up, doesn't mean I hated him. And it doesn't mean I would kill him."

"Yeah, right — whatever —"

"You want the truth, Sam? One of the biggest reasons I didn't hook up with Thad? I knew how much you loved him. I didn't want to hurt you. I guess I hurt Thad all the more because of that."

Sam's lips began to tremble and Jinnah was now certain he was trapped in the middle of one of those

She Demons   195

female bonding moments that might last for hours. All the same, he was relieved when Sam burst into tears and Jassy held her as she sobbed. Was it the first time she'd cried since she'd heard of Thad's murder? How much of it was mourning the relationship she would now never have, and how much was she weeping for the loss of Jassy's friendship? Jinnah shoved down to the end of the bed to give the two young women more room. They had their arms around each other now and Sam was trying to talk through ragged gasps and sobs that marked the intervals between uncontrolled weeping.

"I told him not to do it ... begged him! I thought I'd convinced him but he must have gone behind my back...."

"What did he do, Sam?" asked Jassy softly.

"Thad was dealing ... dealing for someone inside ... part of the family. It was stupid, he knew it was stupid. And now...."

Name of God, how much moisture can one tie-dye T-shirt absorb? thought Jinnah. Each fresh eruption was soaking Jassy's front. Any suspicion Hakeem might have had that this had been a set-up vanished. This was the real thing. His inherent instincts were sending shivers up and down his back. Drug dealing inside the MiMis. Here was his proof....

"Who was Thad dealing for, Sam?"

"I swear, Jass, I don't know. If I knew I'd kill the bastard! But that wasn't it ... it was ... it was ... oh, God!"

Slowly, agonizingly, everything Sam knew came out. How Thad had finally kicked, how he had refused to deal for the MiMi insider. But then two of his buddies had come to him with this whack idea to smuggle a shipment of B.C. bud across the border. Thad had agreed — it was a score too good to pass up. He'd have enough cash to get the hell out of Vancouver and start fresh somewhere else. But Sam had, for once, managed to change his mind. He decided it smelled funny and even tried to convince his two friends not to go. But they'd gone anyway and hadn't been heard from since. As far as revelations went, this was fantastic. But what Sam blurted out next went beyond even Hakeem's wildest fantasies.

"The night Thad was killed he was at the Magus's mansion on the Hill. I saw him come in and go into the Magus's private office."

News God, take me now! A direct link between Simons and Thad Golway. And on the night of the poor boy's murder too....

"What was he doing there?"

"I — I didn't get a chance to talk to him, Jass. He was angry, upset. I could tell. He left before I could talk to him and the next time I saw him...."

It was only after some time and a display of immense anguish that moved even Jinnah to the verge of tears that Sam somehow managed to describe how it had been she who had discovered Thad in the park — she and Andy Gill. This was a piece of information that Jinnah could not ignore.

"Where were you taking Andy, Sam?" he asked.

Sam stared at Jinnah is if she had just noticed his presence in the room. She looked over at Jassy, asking with her eyes for permission to speak.

She Demons 197

It was Jassy who answered. "Somewhere safe, Jinnah."

News God giveth and News God taketh away. Jinnah was sorely tempted to call Jassy on this strange usage of the word "safe" that he had not come across before, but decided to bite his tongue. There would be plenty of time for to have it out with his unpredictable guide.

The Café Ovaltine is a fixture on Hastings Street. It used to be a typical diner where people could have a cheap, filling breakfast before going to Woodward's to shop, or a hearty lunch after strolling along the lines of shops on either side of what had been Vancouver's largest department store. Now its clientele was somewhat different. Woodward's had long since closed and the shops in either direction, such as they were, tended to sell hemp products, drug paraphernalia, or sport "vacant" signs on plywood-clad windows. Customers tended to linger for hours over their coffees, waiting, waiting, waiting. Sometimes they waited for a friend, sometimes a connection, often just for that third Wednesday of the month, Welfare Wednesday (referred to as "Mardi Gras" on the street, even though it's not a Tuesday), when they would, briefly, have money burning a hole in their pockets.

On the whole, the crowd in the café kept to themselves, making the Ovaltine a perfect place for Jinnah to have it out with Jassy after they left the MiMi co-op house. Still, they were on Jassy's turf, and Hakeem needed to find some way to discomfort her, knock her off balance — get at the truth. He decided the best way was to go back to Jassy's roots.

"Why do you keep lying to me, Jaswinder Kaur Singh, hmm?" he asked in Punjabi

Jassy bristled at the use of her full name and her parent's mother tongue. Jinnah was gratified to see her stir her coffee savagely.

"Speak English!" she said.

Ah, a soft spot in that formidable mental armour. Jinnah filed it away for future exploitation and switched to the language of Shakespeare, Joyce, and Spillane.

"I don't care what language you answer in. Just tell me why."

"I didn't lie. I just didn't clarify."

"It amounts to the same thing and you know it. By not coming clean about the true nature of your relationship with Thad — and how he felt about you — you come off as someone hiding the truth. It's a short step from being considered an unreliable witness to someone who is guilty."

"I didn't tell you because I *felt* guilty — that's not the same as *being* guilty, Jinnah. How do you think I feel? Don't you think that I feel a bit responsible for Thad's murder? If I'd given him a break, been nicer to him, let him into my confidence — maybe I could have made a difference."

"Making a difference. That's what it's about, isn't it? Okay, you hid the facts about Thad and yourself — what else are you hiding, besides the whereabouts of Andy Gill?"

She Demons 199

"Nothing, Jinnah, I swear."

"Indeed? Then why are you protecting Lionel Simons?"

"The Magus knows nothing about this!"

"Then I'm Michael Bublé. Sam's testimony puts Thad in Simons's office the night he was murdered. He was upset, they quarrelled — probably over the proceeds of the drug shipment —"

"Sam said Thad changed his mind!"

"Then they fought over who in the MiMis was dealing drugs. What does it matter? A couple of hours later Thad was dead. Jassy, we're after the truth here! You say Simons is innocent? Then find me his killer. Hold your Magus to the highest standards, put him under the microscope. If he's half the Rave Messiah he claims to be, he ought to be able to come out smelling like a rose."

Jassy watched her spoon create little whirlpools in her coffee. The oil slick of fat from the three creams she'd put into the cup formed small eddies in the changing current, swirling and twirling, always eluding the undertow created by the implement. Jinnah had been strangely pleased when she had put in three sugars as well.

"Okay," she said at length. "Here's the bottom line: I don't believe the Magus would ever kill or have anyone killed. Especially over a drug shipment. And I find it really hard to believe anyone in the family is capable of such a thing. But I accept your challenge. I'll help you find the truth, I won't hold anything back. Deal?"

"I recall having a deal just a few hours ago."

"This is a new deal."

"Are you Franklin Roosevelt or something?"

"What?"

"Never mind — before your time," said Jinnah, inwardly sighing at the state of the history curriculum in B.C.'s high schools. "Deal. Now, where do we start? Sam's information is one thing, but we need this from a source higher up in the organization. Who will believe a lowly devotee, hmm?"

"Daisley," said Jassy firmly. "He's a wuss, but he's tight with the Magus."

"And he has something to hide — all those rental grow ops."

"Yeah. Let's go."

"Where?"

"The outreach office. They should still be serving lunch right about now and Ray loves to play big shot as the newbies feed the poor."

"Fantastic!" said Jinnah, sliding out of the booth. "Ray Daisley is in for the surprise of his life. For there is trial by judge, trial by jury —"

"Hey! Who's paying for this?" demanded the waitress.

Jinnah was not happy to have one of his great lines — trial by Jinnah — interrupted for such a trifling cause. He was even less pleased when he saw the bill. Three dollars for two cups of brown water with black grit? Never mind. It would be worth it simply to see the look on Daisley's face.

* * *

She Demons 201

In any event, it was Jinnah who got the shock of his life when he strolled into the MiMi outreach office like he owned the joint. The soup kitchen portion of the centre was crowded with street people and Daisley was there, front and centre, making sure everyone knew he was the boss, just as Jassy had predicted (Jassy herself had opted to stay in the SGLM, claiming her presence might cause a disturbance). But the former Miss Wreck Beach would have had to have psychic powers to predict what Jinnah discovered among the customers from The Corner. At first, his eye had passed over the new devotee wearing the sky blue server's uniform with matching hairnet, doling out stew to the wretched. Then he did whiplash-inducing double take. Name of God! It couldn't be....

"Saleem!" Jinnah roared. "What the hell do you think you're doing here?"

Saleem looked up, deerlike eyes magnified by his glasses. Jinnah's bellow had cast a pall of silence over the entire centre and everyone heard Saleem's reply. "It's lunch hour, dad," he said quickly, trying to dole out another helping of stew onto an already full plate, the client rooted to the spot by the spectacle.

"It's one thirty in the bloody afternoon!"

"I have a study period," Saleem lied quickly.

"Then let me provide the lesson!"

Jinnah advanced towards his son. Gone was the cool demeanor of the previous evening, the patient understanding, the creative solution to gathering Saleem in. Jinnah's wrath knew no bounds: if he could have thunderbolts like Indra, he would have. He was nearly upon his thunderstruck teenager before Daisley recovered his aplomb and stepped between father and son.

"Jinnah, Saleem was kind enough to volunteer his time to help serve the less fortunate —"

"No one here is less fortunate than Saleem right now!" bellowed Jinnah. "And his time is not his own to volunteer!"

"He's not some sort of slave, Jinnah —"

"Are you kidding me, Ray? His ass is owned by the Vancouver School District until he graduates or I send him to Marine boot camp. Get out of my way —"

"Come on, Dad — there's no need to blow a gasket —"

"You mean a casket, which you deserve to be fitted for right now. Now stop hiding behind that ladle —"

Saleem was clutching his ladle in his right hand, holding it out like some sort of cross or ankh to abjure this paternal demon who had manifested so unexpectedly. The devotees were gathering around, trying to block Jinnah's path to his son, and Daisley was trying to manoeuvre him to one side — the side by the door. Still, it would have taken an entire garlic field and a magazine of silver bullets to prevent Hakeem from grabbing his errant child by the scruff of the neck and dragging him bodily home, and he was near success when the MiMi's muscle arrived.

"What the hell is going on here?" demanded Jordan, tattoos rippling as he hurried into the fray, muscling his way to the front to stand glowering beside Saleem.

Shit! Busted by the cult's vampire slayer. The initial rush of fury was over and Jinnah was already kicking

She Demons 203

himself for losing his cool. But he couldn't back down, not now....

"What's going on here is none of your damned business," said Jinnah as pleasantly as he could. "Now kindly get out of my way and let me take my son home."

"Saleem, do you want to go home with your father?"

It was hard for the casual observer to judge who Saleem appeared more terrified of: Jordan or Jinnah. His mind was on fire, the implications of his answer looming as large as an endless void at the edge of his known universe. He didn't know it, but he was in the same place that Jassy Singh had been when a similar question had been put to her years earlier. Fortunately, he was spared his moment of truth by shouting, screaming, and the blare of a megaphone outside.

"Repent, sinners! The day of judgment is at hand!"

All eyes turned to the large, plate glass windows at the front of the centre. A placard-waving crowd filled the frames — many of them wearing white bomber jackets.

Ray Daisley closed his eyes briefly then turned to his staff. "Okay, people. The Reverend Hobbes and his God Squad are here. Places."

Apparently, demos by Hobbes and his fanatics were fairly common, but there was something about the hesitancy, the lack of immediate jump, that told Jinnah this was special. His instincts were almost immediately rewarded by an undisciplined curse.

"Man. Never seen so many of the mothers," said Jordan. "Musta hired some rent a ranters."

Jinnah was gratified to see Daisley annoyed. And Saleem terrified.

"Jordan, secure the door! You others, you know the drill! Everyone keep calm —"

Jinnah saw that he had seconds to grab Saleem and get out before the lockdown trapped them inside. As Jordan moved and the various acolytes rushed to their positions, he leaned across the serving table and looked his son squarely in the eye.

"Time to go, Saleem."

To his immense relief, Saleem dropped his ladle and moved around the serving table to his side in the vacuum left by the scrambling MiMi staff. Jinnah now had his entire focus on the door, which stood ajar just a few metres away. But Jordan was already moving fast towards the one escape route, fairly throwing devotees aside, and Hakeem could see it would be a near run thing. Fortunately, he was not above creating bit of pandemonium to win the day.

"Repent! The kingdom of heaven is at hand! A plague of low-cal yogourt shall rain down upon thy heads! Thy first-born shall be forced to eat non-organic mutton and thy daughters shall be drowned in macro-biotic sprouts!"

It was gibberish, but it was shouted in the loudest, most articulate Pushtu and to the ears of the unini-tiated devotees, sounded like the very voice of the apocalypse. The effect could not have been better if Hobbes and his God Squad had managed to make it into the office. The MiMis had been near panicked before — now people ran hither and thither, even the experienced poor, who had only come here for a free meal, thank you, not the end of the world. Daisley was

She Demons 205

carried to the far end of the room in the melee. Jinnah, speaking in tongues, saw a space open up before him as if he had an invisible force field clearing his path. He made it to the end of the serving table and grasped Saleem by his collar. He turned towards the door to see Jordan knifing through the chaos a step ahead of him. Jinnah raised his voice to its uppermost reaches and used his free hand to propel unfortunate devotees in the muscleman's direction.

"The quick brown fox jumped over the lazy dog! A stitch in time saves nine! My uncle has a red pencil box!" he howled in Urdu.

Through all this, Jinnah was successfully negotiating a path to the doorway, step for step with Jordan, but burdened by Saleem. He saw that he was about to lose the race to the tattooed enforcer. It was all down to geometry now — Jinnah hurling himself and Saleem towards the narrow wedge of open door, Jordan throwing his massive weight against it, the leading edge of the frame trying to close the life-giving wedge of freedom into an imprisoning plane....

At the last possible second, Jinnah knifed his abused and battered steel-toed boot into the tiny triangle of clear air. The door shook with a resounding rebound. Jordan stood right beside him, breath foul with lentils, body odour rank with natural deodorant. Hakeem took the millisecond of time between the door coming to rest on his foot and its recoil to grab the top of the portal and give it a shove with his free hand. The resulting collision saw a number of Jordan's facial piercings bite deeper into his flesh. With a yelp, he

reeled back, the door opened wide and Jinnah dragged
Saleem out of the frying pan of cultism and into the fire
of fundamentalism.

"Repent! This is the devil's own kitchen! Sup not
at Lucifer's trough! Taste the true bread of life in Our
Redeemer...."

As they struggled through the thick press of protesters outside the MiMi office, even Jinnah was
impressed by the sheer numbers Hobbes had managed to muster to the cause. The core of God Squad
members had been reinforced by clean-cut looking
young people (who Hakeem took to be Bible college
students), neat, middle-aged professional born-agains
(sacrificing their lunch hour for Christ), and a contin-
gent of aging but hardly frail senior citizens, most of
them women — one of them was busily trying to chain
herself to the office door with a bicycle lock. Jinnah
recognized her from the abortion clinic battles of over
a decade ago and he almost felt sorry for Jordan, who
was having enormous difficulty preventing her from
closing the ring of kryptonite around her neck without
using excessive force. Name of God, how can people
stand to have those things around their necks, con-
stricting their breathing — Jinnah felt short of breath
just looking at her —

"Dad! Lemme go! I can't breathe!"

Jinnah realized with a start that he'd been convul-
sively clutching Saleem so tightly by the collar that he
was slowly strangling his first and only son. He let go
as they reached the edge of the melee and Saleem, oxygen deprived and obsessed with checking for potential

She Demons 207

scar tissue around his neck (or perhaps a fracture in his collar bone — he was, after all, Jinnah's son), stumbled sideways into a very tall, very hefty protester. Jinnah at once pegged the Aryan-looking Goliath as some sort of lay minister, likely from Abbotsford, the buckle on B.C.'s Fraser Valley Bible Belt. He was waving the Good Book above his head and had that ecstatic, religious joy that Hakeem had seen in some of the Sufis he had met.

"Sorry, sir," Saleem mumbled, his forward progress brought to a sudden and potentially fatal halt.

"Have you accepted Jesus as your personal saviour, boy?" bellowed the Aryan.

Jinnah grabbed Saleem — frozen like a pillar of salt, or perhaps raw sugar — by his arm and hauled him around the rock of religious radicalism.

"He's already got a personal saviour, my friend," said Hakeem. "Let us get behind thee."

Before the Bible-thumping Goliath could process that they were past him and crossing the street. Traffic was already starting to slow and horns were starting to honk. Jinnah knew they had a matter of moments to get the hell out of there before gridlock set in. Within seconds, they were safely inside the SGLM, doors locked, Saleem seated sullenly in the passenger seat, and Jinnah fumbling to get the keys into the ignition despite suffering from a racing pulse, a pounding headache, and a wave of nausea, now that the adrenaline rush was subsiding. He was trying to take a deep breath when an object flashed in front of his eyes and a voice boomed from the seat behind him.

"Guess what this is?"

208 *Donald J. Hauka*

To Jinnah, it was a heart attack on a string, dangling in front of eyes that were about to burst with apoplexy. There was no doubt about it — he was having a major infarction of every vital artery, a stroke, and enduring the sensation of having jumped straight out of his brown hide and collapsing into a pile of shattered nerves on the driver's seat. He cursed with a near religious fervour in Punjabi. Saleem's eyes, already wide, grew wider.

"Get a grip, Dad," he muttered.

"Such language in front of your son!" Jassy chided him in the same tongue, moving her head forward beside Jinnah's throbbing temples. "Guess what this is?"

"It had better be instructions on how to give an emergency heart bypass with a penknife!" gasped Jinnah, reaching for his atomizer. "That or an angioplasty in a bag! What the hell do you think you're doing scaring me like that?"

"Scare the devil out of you? Or something else?" laughed Jassy, switching to English. "And you haven't answered my question. Nor have you introduced me to your charming son."

Jinnah was busy fumbling his puffer into his mouth and giving his lungs a good dose of hydrocortisone. Saleem, with the amnesia for recent trauma that is one of the great strengths of youth, managed his most winning smile and very nearly forgot all about the beautiful Lahki from the drop-in centre.

"I'm Saleem. You're Jassy, right?"

There was something about Saleem's warmth and manner in dealing with the former Miss Wreck Beach

She Demons 209

that engaged the portion of Jinnah's mind not totally preoccupied with self-pity and the certainty that he was about to expire of congestive heart failure. He snapped to attention, grabbing the dully gleaming, rectangular object dancing in front of his face, and examined it.

"It's a five gigabyte JetFlash and if you paid more than twenty bucks for it, you got robbed," he snorted.

"Wrong," smiled Jassy. "This is proof."

"Proof? Proof of what?"

"Hadn't we better be making tracks?"

Jinnah's eyes darted to the street, where the abortion clinic veteran had managed to win her struggle with Jordan and was now fused with the office doorway. Traffic in the far lane was already at a crawl, and unless they left now they'd be trapped. Jinnah gunned the engine, took no more than a cursory glance in the rearview mirror, and veered erratically into the road. As he did, he nearly nailed the Aryan Bible-thumper and was delighted to see the Goliath give him the finger as the SGLM roared away from the scene of the crime.

"So what you're telling me is Lionel Simons is some sort of Pablo Escobar of the north. Is that it?"

"Really, Frosty — that's so dated. I prefer the Cannabis King of Cultism."

"We both know the lawyers will cut it out and we have about five minutes before Whiteman comes out here and demands this one be lawyered too. As it is, I'm having trouble with your theory."

Jinnah rubbed his temples. After the day he'd had, he didn't need this kind of treatment. He'd been through the belly of the beast of cultism, religious fanaticism, and a near-death experience in his own van. He'd had to drop Saleem off at home and endure the scandalized expression on Manjit's face as he roared off with Jassy still in the van. Then there had been the small matter of going over Jassy's "proof." It had all taken a toll and the last thing he had expected after strolling into the newsroom to casually announce that he had the front page story, thank you very much, and that Sanderson should immediately get down to the MiMi outreach office to cover the demonstration ("I am giving you the sidebar, my friend! Think of the shared glory you will bask in...."), was this obstinacy from Frosty. He put it down to some sort of female conspiracy, probably hormonal in nature, and tried one more time.

"Frosty, the MiMi's own financial records clearly show the cult is in a loss position. They don't take in enough to cover their expenses and Simon's royalties can't possibly make up the difference."

"Explain to me again how we happened to get our hands on this plain brown envelope?"

Jinnah nearly quipped that it had been a decorated, burgundy JetFlash, thank you very much, not an envelope, but bit his tongue. He wanted to protect Jassy at all costs and if Frosty found out how the suspended MiMi manager had slipped into Daisley's office during the scene with Saleem at the outreach office, copied all his files on the flash drive, and then slid out undetected to give him a heart attack in the

She Demons 211

SGLM, then she would start asking all sorts of awkward questions about "drinking from poisoned wells" and the like — questions he didn't want to answer this close to deadline.

"I told you — from a usually reliable source," he said smoothly. "And ask yourself: how does Simons afford his mansion on the hill, hmm? This explains why they've turned to grow op houses and drug dealing. Simons is at the heart of the operation."

"Except," said Frosty with dangerous patience, repeating herself for the third time. "The alleged grow op houses are all in Jassy Singh's name, not Simons's —"

"Jassy knew nothing of that."

"So she says."

"And then there is Thad Golway. He was last seen alive going into Simons's office."

"Except Thad had already left the cult."

"I'm telling you, Simons is a drug lord, and drug lords are not above murder."

"You have one report of Thad being in the mansion from an unnamed devotee — hardly the stuff of Perry Mason —"

"Frosty, quit dating yourself."

"— or that Harriet Butler is going to find convincing. There's no firm link between Thad and Simons."

"Then why was he at the mansion the night he was murdered?"

Frosty had reached the end of her tether. She hit the send key, bouncing Jinnah's prose back to his queue.

"Maybe," she said in her best senior assistant city editor "don't mess with me" voice. "Maybe you had better find that out, Hakeem. And leave before Whiteman gets out of the four o'clock meeting and starts giving you a shopping list of dumb-ass questions that the department heads who all hate your guts dreamed up and floated past him during the yackfest, okay?"

Every god has their oracle. Apollo had the Pythia of Delphi. News God had Nicole "Frosty" Frost and, unlike the Pythia, her utterances were neither obscure nor hard to interpret. Wearily, Jinnah stood up and headed for the door, his mission clear.

"Better find something to plug the front for first edition, Frosty," he called over his shoulder. "I'll be filing for the one star."

The one star was the late paper and city desk could conceivably get copy in on a chase up until one in the morning. Generally, the paper was wrapped by 10:30 p.m. and Frosty was in the Press Club by 10:35 p.m. The prospect of waiting around the office for Jinnah to file — *if* Jinnah filed — was hardly a pleasant one.

"Where the hell do you think you're going?" she demanded.

Jinnah paused by the door, shot Crystal a look, and called back in his best, melodramatic baritone. "To Bedlam and back. To find a motive for murder. Wait right there for me, darling."

And before Frosty could decide if she was furious, annoyed, or amused, he was gone.

Chapter Six

"I knew I should have brought earplugs. Do you think the vibrations might rupture your brain casing? Seriously — a man could have a stroke...."

Graham, standing beside Jinnah in the wing of the stage that had been set-up in the cavernous warehouse, saw the reporter's mouth move but the words were lost in the ear-bleeding sonic assault being mounted by Simons and his band. There was much he wanted to say to Jinnah right now — like how he had better be damn sure this wasn't a waste of his valuable time and yet another excuse for Simons to file a lawsuit alleging police harassment, not to mention the sneaking suspicion that Hakeem had only insisted on his presence at the Rave Messiah's latest gig so he could use that magic phrase "cult leader questioned by cops" in his story. Given the volume level, he saved his breath. Instead, he scanned what he could of the crowd near the front, swaying like zombies, all under the spell of Lionel Simons. He looked right through a waifish concertgoer and missed clocking Caitlin Bishop, "disguised" as her old self, blending into the rave culture. Further ruminations over the usefulness of this strictly unofficial visit were lost in the explosion of pyrotechnics signalling the end of the first set. Graham noted that Jinnah was holding his hands over his ears. Now that the music was over, the cheering was almost as deafening.

"Look sharp, Hakeem — it's showtime."

Simons bounded into the wings, soaked with sweat and looking pumped. He even seemed glad to see Graham and Jinnah waiting for him.

"Hey, I knew you two would see the light sooner or later," he said, slightly too loud for polite conversation, the amplifiers still ringing in his ears. "Enjoying the show?"

"You do have a permit, right?"

"Of course, sergeant — all our events are licensed by the City of Vancouver."

"Mr. Simons, what were you talking to Thad Golway about at your home on the night he was murdered?"

Simons slowly turned his head towards Jinnah, smiling fading. "Y'know, this line of work has affected my hearing, Hakeem. I thought I heard you say something about Thad being in my home. I've never met him."

"Then I'll shout," said Jinnah, raising his voice. "Witnesses have placed him there just hours before he was killed —"

She Demons   215

"Keep your voice down!" Simons made shooshing motions with his hands. "Your witnesses are wrong."

"Really?" said Graham. "So you deny it?"

"Absolutely," said Simons, taking a towel from one of his roadies and mopping his sopping brow.

"Then how do you account for the sighting?"

"This is the sort of fantasy Jinnah dreams up to make his stories better, sergeant. But he's wrong. Thad Golway was not at my house. Excuse me — gotta get rehydrated."

Simons slipped past them and disappeared into the rear of the stage area. The stage crew was already rearranging equipment, replacing the pyrotechnics, and using yards and yards of duct tape for obscure purposes.

The towel-carrying roadie stared at the policeman and the reporter meaningfully. "You've had your two minutes — I gotta ask you to get off stage, man."

"Our thanks, young man," said Jinnah. "Remember: don't do drugs."

The roadie gave Jinnah a "whatever" look and went about his business. The cop and the hack slowly turned and wearily made their way off stage. Neither had had a particularly great day. Their way towards the exit was barred by a wall of fans, barely contained by a line of MiMi muscle. Jinnah was relieved to see that Jordan was not among them. Beyond the barricade a churning sea of kids dressed in black, white petal faces with eyes closed and mouths open, were chanting: "Magus! Magus! Magus!" Graham took in the sight with a disgusted look.

216 *Donald J. Hauka*

"Thanks, Hakeem. I coulda been doing something useful with my time, like booking Jassy Singh."

"Come on, Craig! It was worth a shot! Besides, now I can say in my story —"

"That Lionel Simons was questioned by police? Forget it. It was strictly off the record."

"What do you mean, off the record?" howled Jinnah. "There must be a couple thousand witnesses!"

"Like I give a rat's ass! Don't say it."

"But you're a policeman and you asked him a question —"

"You used that trick about six months ago and Butcher gave me supreme mondo caca, buddy —"

"Oh, for God's sake, Graham!"

"I got work to do, Jinnah."

Graham, still hemmed in by the seething crowd, reached into his jacket pocket and pulled out his badge. "Police!" he shouted. "Move it or I give you the full body cavity search right here and now!"

Graham cut a swath through the delirious fans with his upheld shield. Jinnah was about to follow in his wake when a hand on his shoulder caused him to whirl around.

"Mr. Jinnah? Can I have a word?"

Jinnah was stunned to see the grave and concerned face of Ray Daisley staring at him. What the hell did he want? Oh, Name of God! Probably wants to give me shit over what happened at the outreach office....

"I'm kind of busy, Ray," said Jinnah, his con-genital cowardice rising to the fore. "Got a cop to catch —"

She Demons 217

Jinnah became aware of three large forms behind him — MiMi devotees who looked like their choice of drugs were of the steroid variety. They were blocking his path towards the fast-vanishing Graham and the scant protection he offered. Craning around, Jinnah registered Jordan's face with a sickening start. It had a long, narrow bruise down the left side — doorlike in shape.

"It's rather important, Jinnah. You don't mind, do you?"

Mind? Jinnah thought. I'm about to be dragged into the private confines of an abandoned warehouse by three burly devotees of a cult I strongly suspect of drug dealing and ritual murder — one of whom I have recently facially disfigured — and the only other person on the planet who knows I am here is heading in the wrong direction, out of earshot, and would in all likelihood cheer them on as they pummel me, given his present, pleasant mood. And I have perhaps thirty minutes before drop dead time at the paper, but before that I am likely about to drop dead of a heart attack or, perhaps, a massive embolism.

"What's to mind, Ray?" said Jinnah, slapping Daisley on the back with a completely counterfeit bonhomie. "Am I allowed to smoke in here?"

Jinnah found himself sitting on a camp stool next to Daisley, in a small room in the maze of black canvas tenting that made up Simons's private complex in the warehouse. From the first aid kits and water bottles scattered about he guessed it was the medical room. "Scribe Found Dead in Dressing Station," he thought.

Hmm ... not the best headline. Perhaps they would leave his mutilated (and decapitated) body naked? "Journo Undressed to Kill." Much better....

Jinnah was so busy sweating, dying for a cigarette, and composing his own obituary that he hardly noticed Daisley's opening words — or the fact that Jordan and his crew had disappeared. He thought he heard the sentence correctly, but the words didn't make sense.

"Would you please repeat that, Ray?"

"I said," Daisley's voice was low, confidential, reluctant. "That the Magus has a few of his facts wrong."

Sonofabitch. Those damned amplifiers had affected the lining of his brain.

"Which facts are those?"

"It's not that he's lying, exactly," Daisley said quickly. "He probably doesn't even remember."

Jinnah was in that tricky transitional phase where his congenital cowardice was being overpowered by his inherent instincts. What was Daisley trying to say? Should he tell the man to simply spit it out? If he did, would he clam up? Then he realized the role he was supposed to play: confessor. Instantly, he adopted his most sympathetic tone.

"I'm sure you're right, Ray. Lionel would never knowingly lie...."

The confessional canard had a gratifying effect. Daisley stopped squirming and came to the point. "Thank goodness you understand! The truth is, Thad *was* at the mansion the night he died."

It took every ounce of Jinnah's remaining mental reserves to keep his face neutral, his voice calm,

She Demons 219

and his pulse under two hundred beats a minute. He scarcely entertained the immediate thought of "Why in the Name of News God is he telling me this?" There would be plenty of time for that later. The important thing was to keep Daisley talking.

"Really? What about?"

"He wanted to see the Magus about something important. He wouldn't say exactly what. I showed him into the office. From what I heard, they had quite the argument. Very unlike the Magus — lost his temper."

"What was this argument about?"

"That I can't tell you," said Daisley, the reluctant, hesitant tone creeping back into his voice. "Y'see, neither of them were making much sense."

"Why not?"

"Well, Thad was high on something and the Magus ... he's fond of red wine...."

"You're telling me that Thad Golway was in Lionel Simons's office, high as a kite, and the Magus drunk, hmm? Just hours before the kids was brutally murdered. Correct?"

Daisley nodded, looking miserable. To hell with it — Jinnah had to ask, even if it was likely a conversation killer.

"Why are you telling me this, Ray? Are you trying to implicate your boss or what?"

"You gotta be kidding!" said Daisley. "No, it's just — see, I offered to give Thad a ride home. He didn't know what he was doing. 'You just never know what's out there,' I told him. But he took off. I wish I'd followed him. I wish I'd insisted. He might still be alive."

Jinnah's bullshit detector was beeping at full volume. He switched effortlessly from friendly confessor to hostile inquisitor in a heartbeat. "It seems a bit far-fetched, Ray."

"I swear, Jinnah, it's the truth."

"Really? How much of the truth? The whole truth? Or a half-truth to protect somebody?"

"The whole truth and yes, frankly, I am protecting someone, Jinnah. I'm trying to protect the Magus. Either you or the police are going to confirm that Thad was at the mansion sooner or later. I wanted you to know what really happened. We have nothing to hide. I didn't want there to be any accusations of lying or cover-ups."

"Then you won't mind me quoting you?"

"I'm not authorized to speak on behalf of the organization," said Daisley, rising. "But try putting the question to the Magus tomorrow. He may have a somewhat clearer recollection of the evening's events by then."

Magically, silently, Jordan and his fellow bouncers appeared in the flapping doorway. Jinnah stood up, eyeing the room for alternative exits. There were none.

"Hey, Jordan. Hakeem here needs a little help getting through the crowd to his car. Can you make sure he gets there without any difficulties? Thanks, man."

"Glad to be of service," said Jordan.

It wasn't the worst escorted walk out of a building where he wasn't wanted that Jinnah had ever experienced. To his credit, Jordan didn't lay a finger on Hakeem. He confined his vengeance to "accidentally"

She Demons 221

stepping on the reporter's heels; more with the idea of ruining the expensive Gucci loafers than any intent to injure, Jinnah decided. He even managed to shake his gargantuan guardian at the door.

"I can manage it from here, thanks," he said stiffly.

"Be careful. Lots of crazies out there," said Jordan. "Never know who might be lurking around the next corner in this hood. Maybe friends of mine."

"Good night Jordan — I love you."

Jinnah was a good ten feet away from the massive MiMi when he blew him the kiss, but it didn't provoke the anger he'd hoped for, nor did the show of bravado make him feel any safer as he made his way through the dark, ill-lit industrial area to where he had parked the SGLM, several blocks away. There was no sign of Graham, who was long gone. Jinnah was alone in the night, wondering as he walked if Jordan would be stupid enough to have a few of his friends hiding in a nearby alleyway to rough him up, or worse, try to convert him to the cult. "You just never know what's out there." Daisley's words and Jordan's features flitted through his brain on a continuous feed loop. It was enough to drive a man to smoke and Jinnah lit up with trembling fingers. What the hell was Daisley up to? If he was playing spin doctor, he was doing a piss poor job of it. Was he trying to finger Simons? Or really help him? Was he naïve, stupid, or some sort of Machiavellian genius so subtle that even News God's gift to journalism couldn't figure out his true motives? Jinnah sniffed at the last thought — in the end, no one outwitted Hakeem Jinnah.

222 *Donald J. Hauka*

So preoccupied was he that Jinnah didn't hear the faint "flick" of a lighter, nor did he see the red-yellow flame leap into the darkness. His senses full of the soothing aroma of his own cigarette, he didn't scent the smoke from its distant relation just a few metres behind him as it left a slender trail. Had he glanced around, he would have seen the slim figure following him. His head was full of possibilities, scenarios, and conjecture. He'd reached the SGLM and was fumbling in his pockets for his keys when he saw the glow of the cigarette reflected in his van's window. Sonofabitch! Someone was right behind him!

In the instant it took Jinnah to spin around many thoughts flashed through his mind, most of them about his stalker's identity and the likelihood of his immediate (Allah, may it be swift and painless!) demise. The most absurd of these was the thread of reasoning that it could not possibly be Jordan or his friends because he could distinctly smell tobacco, not hemp. His hands flew out, brandishing his car key as a weapon.

"Back off!" he shouted. "I'm packing heat!"

The light laughter took him totally off guard as the silhouetted figure moved out of the shadows towards him. So did the identity of his pursuer.

"The only thing you're packing is an atomizer and a deck of Rothmans. Now, where's that retraction we were talking about?"

Had he not been reduced to his constituent atoms in a liquid state, Jinnah might have been capable of a witty retort. As it was, his reply came out as a sort

She Demons 223

of anguished wheeze. "Jesus Christ! Couldn't you just have phoned?"

Mary Demolay took another drag of her cigarette and walked right up to Jinnah, putting her hand on his upraised keys and slowly lowering them to crotch level.

"I left messages. I paged you. I emailed. I went in person to your newsroom. You really ought to have a personal alarm in your line of work."

Jinnah declined to tell the Yakshas PR person he had several, but had left all of them at home that morning in his haste to get to the office.

"I'm not writing any damned retraction! I am writing a front page story."

Demolay moved uncomfortably close to Jinnah and visions of a shadowy forest with a delightful sunny glen beyond flitted through his brain. He could smell the cigarette mingling with her perfume (his trained nose detected, appropriately enough, Poison) and feel the warmth of her body.

"Are you sure you don't want to reconsider?" she smiled.

Far below, in his root chakra, retraction was the last thing on Jinnah's mind.

"Not unless you have something better to give me," Jinnah said, wondering if Demolay would take this as a single entendre.

"How's this for a front page story: Rave Messiah Guilty of Murder. Oh, and a drug lord, if that's still a crime up here in Canada."

A part — a very small part — of Jinnah's brain was tempted to chide Demolay for her atrocious headline writing, but both the root chakra and his inherent instincts — which had finally risen to the challenge — won the day.

"Prove it," he snapped.

"We will, eventually. I have my sources."

"What sources?" Jinnah asked, suddenly conscious of Demolay's hand on his.

"You'd be surprised at the number of people I know," said Demolay. "They tell me the proof is in Simons's mansion, not his office. Perhaps your police friend should be looking there?"

Jinnah was about to tell Demolay that he had already go his thrill on Simons's hill when she abruptly dropped her cigarette, ground it under her high heels, and released his hand.

"Don't forget my retraction, Hakeem," she smiled sweetly.

Jinnah was speechless as he watched her disappear into the night. He realized he was leaning up against the SGLM, panting for breath, as if he hadn't inhaled for an eternity. Oh, steady now, lungs. Deep breaths. Live long enough to write Mary Demolay's obituary. Maybe even Jordan's. That's it....

Oxygen was finally returning to Jinnah's constricted air passages and his heart was just slowing down when his cellphone rang. How many times must a man's heart fail before you can call him a corpse?

"Name of God, Frosty, not now!" he shouted into the phone. "I've just had that bitch Demolay in an alleyway —"

"Who is this Miss Demolay, Hakeem?" asked

She Demons 225

Manjit's voice. "And just what do you mean you've had her in an alleyway?"

There are perhaps ten thousand different words for idiot in the rich languages of the Indian subcontinent — at least a hundred more in the Swahili Jinnah had learned back in Tanzania. All of them seemed perfectly inadequate at the moment as self describers.

"Manjit, my love, I am so sorry —"

"Hakeem, it is about Saleem —"

Jinnah closed his eyes. Not now. Not this close to deadline....

"What about him?"

"I want you to meet me at the drop-in centre. It's important."

Jinnah looked at his watch. If he hurried, he would be able to make it back to the office on time to file for the one star. He might even avoid having to have the piece lawyered, if Whiteman had neglected to leave strict instructions with the night desk. All he would have to do was sweet talk Frosty ... and explain to his wife who Mary Demolay was and how they had smoked together in a secluded alleyway after he had attended a rave.

"I'll be right there, Manjit," he said.

"Sonofabitch," he added, addressing himself to the night.

"The computer stations were donated by MegaSurf — they're big fans of the Magus. They maintain our website too...."

226 *Donald J. Hauka*

It was hard for Jinnah to focus on what the lovely Lahki was saying. The MiMi drop-in centre staffer was their guide to what he considered the underworld of cultism, despite its ergonomically designed workstations, marmoleum flooring, and carbon neutral lighting fixtures. Despite Manjit's presence at his side, Hakeem found himself imitating his son and simply staring at the lovely creature, who glowed with a kind of religious zeal quite different from the born-agains enlisted by Hobbes. This, he reflected, is probably why Dante had an old dead guy in a toga as his guide through the Inferno — less distracting. If Lahki had shown him around, Signor Alighieri probably would have bought a time-share in the second circle. He was startled back to the present by his wife's elbow in his ribs.

"Hakeem, are you listening?"

"Why? Is there going to be a test afterwards?"

"I can't tell you how much it means to me to have Saleem's parents here and interested in our work," said Lahki. "Millennial Magic is a family organization, you know."

"So is the Mafia," mumbled Jinnah.

"What was that, Hakeem?"

"Are you going to show us the raffia? You do crafts here, don't you?"

Lahki smiled, puzzled, and Jinnah's ribs felt another sharp stab of elbow.

"If you have any other questions, I'll be with the kids," said Lahki, salaaming. "Namaste."

Manjit returned the gesture with a smile. Jinnah reluctantly tore his eyes off Lahki and focused on

She Demons 227

the group of teens in the middle of the room. Among them was Saleem, looking none the worse for wear for his brush with the born-agains. They were playing some sort of word game with complex rules and Saleem had been elected "Dictator of the Universe," no less.

"Well Hakeem — what do you think?"

"She wears too much makeup," said Jinnah defensively. "And she's a bit young to be a supervisor, don't you think?"

"I meant about our son."

"Ahchah. Well, he seems happy enough."

"Hakeem, I don't want you to take this the wrong way —"

"That is usually the prelude to a lecture on what I'm doing wrong."

"Then let me tell you about Saleem."

"I know about Saleem —"

"No, you do not, Hakeem. At least, you think you know, but if you did, you would act differently."

"For the love of God, Manjit —"

"It's true," Manjit insisted, softly. "You must think about where he is, not where you were at his age."

"I know where he is. He has it made in the shade. When I was his age —"

"But he's not. Think of it: he's in adolescence, Indo-Canada, Canada-Canada. And just being your son. That's several hard places to be all at once."

Jinnah mentally conceded the point to his wife — especially the part about being his son. It must be hell having a legend for a father....

"You have to spend more time with him, Hakeem. Listening to him. Not lecturing him."

"I'm a bit short of time at the moment, Manjit —"

"You're always a bit short of time, Hakeem. There's always some story you're chasing after. Right now, you're even chasing after someone else's son. Look at all the young people here tonight — what are their parents chasing? Why do you think Lionel Simons is so popular? Kids want a father on earth, not one in heaven."

Jinnah looked at his son's face and saw his own reflected in it. Then Saleem smiled, and Hakeem saw Manjit's toothy grin. My God, could the boy already be a teenager? He thought about all the battles he'd had with his offspring, how Saleem was increasingly independent — bordering on defiant. How was a young man to find his way in this world of so much uncertainty and, as Jinnah could attest, random evil? Would his son end up like Andy Gill? Or Thad Golway? The thought made him shudder.

He turned to Manjit. "Darling, I am about to break the male code of honour and behaviour. I admit I'm lost. I need some guidance. I'm asking you for directions."

Manjit took Jinnah's hand and squeezed it. "I know how much that took, Hakeem. I will help. Poor Mr. Puri's nephew may be lost, but Saleem can find his way with a little help."

Jinnah nodded. Saleem would be okay. But his conscience was uneasy. Andy Gill was still lost in the wilderness — alone and without a guide. He would resume the hunt tomorrow morning. He hoped he wasn't already too late.

She Demons   229

* * *

But Jinnah was, on a literal level, wrong. Andy had an experienced guide watching over him as dawn crept agonizingly over the dark, jagged fence of the Cascade Mountains, a couple of hundred kilometres east of Vancouver. The Wilderness Master could see the keenness, the strength in the boy as he led the pack of disciples up the steep ravine carved out of the living rock by the stream roaring down the slope and towards the Pacific. But keenness was not the only factor he was looking for — there was care as well.

"C'mon! Pick 'em up! Let's move to the far bank!"

Andy and his fellow disciples gave that extra effort that made their huge packs wobble wildly from side to side, testing their balance and endurance as they humped their cargo up and up the loose, slippery rock, slashing their ankles and, in some cases, their wrists on the encroaching bush and stinging nettles before plunging into the knee-deep, bone-chilling water of the stream. A final lunge and Andy was the first across and at the top. It was all the Wilderness Master could do to keep up with him and he wasn't carrying the massive backpack that Andy had hefted all the way up the slope.

"Okay, let's lay 'em down and open 'em up for inspection. Come on, make a line!"

One by one, the dozen youths lugged their loads to the summit and dropped them in a ragged line along the crest. Below them to the south lay the Skagit Valley, the unguarded gateway to the United States, with its

230 *Donald J. Hauka*

hundreds of kilometres of backcountry trails and access points. The group had done well in terms of time. It was time to see if they had paid attention to the details. The Wilderness Master looked at the disciples, a mix of experienced packers and rookies like Andy, standing in front of their open packs, some slouched and panting with exhaustion, others upright, eager, almost bored. He chose Andy as his first target. The other newbies liked him, he showed promise, and so he must be the example.

"Good job. Let's see if the cargo is dry, Gill."

Andy looked anxious, trying to breathe easily, his lungs constricted both by his recent exertions and his anxiety. The Wilderness Master was rummaging through his pack. He pulled out a brick-like package wrapped in plastic and held it aloft. Sand was dribbling from it — damp sand.

"This disciple has a leaky package. What's his reward, veterans?"

Andy was astonished to see the experienced packers frown as they shouted: "Toast!"

In an instant, the Wilderness Master was in his face. "Toast! There is no water of life inside your backpack, Gill! You get the real goods wet and it will cost you your life."

Andy, sleep deprived, exhausted, confused, was still naïve enough to stand up to the Wilderness Master. "What's the big deal? A little water can't hurt the bud — probably do it good."

The older disciples laughed at this. Now Andy was really worried. And for the first time since he had joined the MiMis, scared.

She Demons 231

"The bud, no. But once you've dropped your loads south of the line, you'll be bringing a more delicate cargo home — heroin. Get that wet and it's useless, understand?"

Scared didn't come close to the complex mix of emotions Andy was feeling now. "Heroin? Hard drugs? But —"

"There's no buts, Gill! Heroin is the lifeblood of the organization. It finances the outreach centre and other good works of the Magus. Everyone is free to make their own choice. We serve a higher cause, a greater good."

"But —"

"What did I say about buts?" roared the Wilderness Master. "You swore to serve without question! If you don't like it, you'll end up under a tree at Main and Terminal. Now, move out! Let's go!"

Andy was in shock as he zipped up his pack and turned for the arduous trip back down the mountain. Around him, he could see the old hands grinning at him. Poor bastard, they were thinking. But he'll get the hang of it. Everyone did, once they'd been given the straight goods by Ray Daisley, Wilderness Master.

"A judge is gonna want more evidence than some second-hand rumour that Simons deals drugs out of his mansion, Hakeem."

"Then you phone Mary Demolay and get her to swear out an affidavit!"

232   *Donald J. Hauka*

"Thanks, but I'll pass on that. And there's no need to be so surly."

"You'd be surly too if you'd been called first thing in the morning by Whiteman demanding to know why you hadn't filed a promised front page story."

"Considering Butcher chews my ass out every couple of hours threatening to hang me out to dry unless I charge somebody with Thad's murder and fast, I think I'd be able to let it slide."

Jinnah was in a foul mood as the Aquabus chugged its way across False Creek. It was a cloudy morning and the water was slate grey, with just enough chop to make his delicate stomach queasy. He'd been trying to convince Craig to raid Simons's mansion since they'd boarded at the Vancouver Aquatic Centre and he was running out of time and patience.

"Demolay has a source in the MiMis. I'm telling you, Craig, get a warrant! Raid the mansion and see what shakes loose."

"It'll be my head that shakes loose unless there're some real goods, Hakeem. And why is this Demolay woman passing you information anyway?"

"She wants to clear her organization of Thad's murder, of course. A murder they committed, I'm convinced."

"So why would I raid Lionel Simons's mansion?"

"To find evidence of his drug empire, of course."

"Jesus, Hakeem! I'm trying to find Thad Golway's murderer, not settle your petty grudge against Simons."

"The two are linked somehow, Craig. What was that you said about finding threads?"

She Demons 233

Graham merely grunted at this. They were approaching the wharf on Granville Island. A half dozen passengers waiting to get on were huddled on the dock, looking miserable, matching Jinnah's mood. He made one last pitch. "Craig, you're thinking too much. You have to follow your instincts — trust your gut. It's the only way you can look yourself in the mirror if you're wrong."

"If *I'm* wrong?" Graham, despite everything, smiled.

Jinnah beamed. He slapped Graham on the back as they rose to disembark, knees slightly bent in anticipation of the gentle bump against the dock. His inherent instincts told him he had won. "Call me on my cell before you move in."

"Don't mess this up for me, Hakeem. And you'd better be right."

"I'd stake my career on it, buddy!"

"You mean my ass."

"Have it your way. Just call. Deal?"

Graham waited until he was halfway up the ramp before calling out over his shoulder to Jinnah, rooted to the dock below. "Deal."

Jinnah's heart soared. Now they were getting somewhere.

"It's about purity of spirit. About getting underneath appearances and finding the true self. Most of our devotees start out a little younger than you are, but I sense you have a youthful spirit, Beth."

Caitlin Bishop didn't know whether to be flattered or insulted by this last remark by the Magus. She was in full "waif mode," looking as mousy as possible to avoid being recognized during her Millennial Magic orientation session, having given the name of Beth Billingsgate. Otherwise, she had to admit that he was good — very good — at inspiring new cult members while subtly leching after them. They were in the living room and Simons was wearing his white robes, sitting uncomfortably close to her on a cushion while she clutched her handbag like a defensive shield in her lap.

"I just want to make a difference, that's all," she said, fiddling with the bag, turning it at an odd angle.

Simons frowned very slightly. "Relax," he said, leaning forward. "You're having a hard time letting go."

With that, the Magus gently took hold of Caitlin's bag. Vancouver's premiere pit bull fought hard to check her immediate impulse to slap her new-found guru.

"Oh, it's okay. I just need this —"

Simons tugged at the sequined, hand-woven, specially tailored hemp bag with an easy but firm insistence. Inside the hidden pocket, Caitlin's mini digital camcorder had a magnificent, wide-angle view of a white sleeve covering its tiny lens.

"Let go of your possessions," said Simons. "All you really need is love."

Caitlin did a swift mental calculation — what were the chances that Simons would actually search her bag? A lot higher unless she let go now. If he did anyway? Would he find the hidden pocket? Notice the

She Demons   235

camouflaged lens portal? Only if he looked very, very carefully. Reluctantly, she let Simons take her bag away.

"That's better," he smiled. "We don't want any distractions between us, do we?"

Caitlin was wondering if he would suggest a back-rub or maybe a fingertip meditation session next when Sam walked in, looking nervous.

"Magus, I'm sorry to interrupt, but it's urgent."

Simons was at his most serene as he stood, still holding Caitlin's bag. Which led Caitlin to believe the Magus would have gone straight to the backrub.

"Let's use the office. I'm sorry, Beth. Wait here and meditate. I won't be long."

Caitlin nodded, looking down and closing her eyes as Simons and Sam exited the living room. Her meditations revolved around the chance that her camcorder would be fortunate enough to be placed in such a manner that she'd have some visuals from Simons's office. Otherwise, she hoped that Kevin could at least still hear her over her wireless mic pin from the satellite truck parked a discreet distance from the mansion.

"Om mani padme om," Caitlin chanted quietly. "Hope you're getting all this, Kevin. Oh, Manny, get me outta here with a story, om...."

Staying alive and out of professional trouble was Jinnah's key objective as he drove slowly through Stanley Park, just a couple of kilometres from the Lions Gate Bridge, to the North Shore where Simons had his mansion. He'd chosen this midpoint with some care, for it was also only a few minutes drive from the Granville Street Bridge to the south, the fastest route to the *Tribune* offices. Not that Jinnah had any intentions of walking into the newsroom any time soon — certainly not until he had the goods on both Lionel Simons and the Yakshas. He wheeled the SGLM into the parking lot overlooking Second Beach. It was still hazy and the container ships waiting in the outer harbour were ghostly images on the steely water. He flipped open his cellphone and hit the speed-dial.

Sanderson answered on the first ring. "Jinnah! What are you doing awake so early? It's not even noon."

"Are you kidding me, Ronald? Whiteman called me at six this morning asking me if I knew this was a daily newspaper and I was expected to file each day, not when I bloody well felt like it, and similar motivational phrases."

"So you're coming in early to work yourself back into his good books?"

"Ronald, how many years have we known each other?"

"Oh, Hakeem! Not again!"

"I haven't even asked you yet —"

"I am not doing your cop checks for you!"

"Ronald, Ronald — it's a small sacrifice!"

"For you, maybe. I have my own work to do, y'know."

"And I am sure your two-phone call story will, with care, take you the rest of the day. All I'm asking is for you to cover for me until I get there."

She Demons   237

"Which will be when, exactly?"

"If I knew that, would I be phoning you?"

"Jinnah —"

"Thank you, my friend. I might be very late."

Jinnah flipped the phone closed on Sanderson's high-pitched protestations. Ronald might squawk for form's sake, but he would conscientiously perform the early police checks, grumbling all the while. There was a small risk that the cop telegraph would start humming, that his absence would be noticed by the law enforcement community and a network warning that Jinnah was up to something would go out, but he doubted it. His absences were just as easily explained by his habitual hypochondria and chronic tardiness. He lit up a cigarette and stared out at the water. Why had Mary Demolay given him the tip about Simons? Merely to divert him? Did she really have a mole inside the MiMis? Was the whole thing bullshit? He checked his inherent instincts. There was the faintest tingle, nothing definite. He was still lost in speculation when his cellphone buzzed. His heart leapt as he saw the number on call display. It was Graham.

"I will probably go to hell for lying to a judge, but I got the warrant and we will be searching Simons's house within an hour."

"Fantastic, Craig! I'll be there."

"No, you won't! You wait until I'm nearly done. Don't mess this up, Hakeem."

"All right, all right! I will follow the path you blaze."

"You'd better be right."

"Trust your gut, Craig."

238   *Donald J. Hauka*

"I already quoted my intestines as a source — how the hell do you think I got the warrant?"

The phone went dead. Jinnah gunned the SGLM's engine to life.

"Ensign Sulu," he cried. "Lay in a course for Simons's mansion!"

"Warp factor ten, Captain," replied Sulu.

Caitlin's meditative state was less than nirvanic. What the hell was taking Simons? Had he found the camera? What was so bloody important that he and Sam had been gone for so long? She opened her eyes and looked around. There was nobody about. Simons had told her to wait in the living room but it took more than a mere admonition to keep Caitlin Bishop sitting on her butt in the lotus position. She quietly crossed the room to the hallway leading to the Magus's inner sanctum. She was just in time to see Simons emerge with Sam, lock the door, and head out towards his deck. There was no sign of her bag, which she assumed was still inside the office.

Caitlin beat a hasty retreat and was back in position on the rug by the time Sam came into the living room.

"I'm really sorry, but the Magus has some urgent business to attend to. He asked me to finish up your orientation session."

Urgent business? She had to know what that was about. Caitlin went fishing. "Wow. Nothing too heavy, I hope," she said, feigning concern.

She Demons 239

"Sort of," said Sam. "You find out about the Reverend Peter Hobbes pretty fast after you join the organization. He's this crazed born-again who has a hate on for us. He's staging another one of his little demonstrations here today."

Caitlin knew all about the Reverend Peter Hobbes. She'd read Sanderson's piece on the demo in front of the outreach centre. If Simons called in the MiMi muscle, things might get interesting — perhaps even violent? For two groups advocating universal peace, that would be about par. But it would also be news.

Caitlin let out a little more line. "What's the Magus gonna do? Does the organization have its own security?"

Sam had a curious, conflicted look on her face. She stood awkwardly, all her weight balanced on one leg, as if she were about to topple over. "Well, sorta, but the Magus has a different strategy in mind."

Caitlin's reel was running out of play. She could tell she was pressing her luck. But a statement like that invited a response. "Call the cops?" she guessed.

Sam shook her head, eyes downcast. "Nope. He's gonna make peace with them."

Peace? Caitlin's visions of sign-swinging protesters and head-bashing MiMis vanished. It was ridiculous, it was unbelievable — worse, it was bad television. But it was just like Lionel Simons.... She had played Sam long enough. It was time to fish or cut bait.

"Look," said Caitlin, losing a considerable amount of her waifish air. "I really need to get into the office. You've got keys, right?"

240   *Donald J. Hauka*

The "Omigod!" look on Sam's face told Caitlin she'd gone a bit too far. She didn't care. Sam could think what she wanted; she needed her goddamn bag back. Sam was slowly backing out of the living room.

"Who are you really and what do you want?" she said.

Before Caitlin could reply they were both distracted by a commotion at the front of the house. Caitlin seized the moment, or, more accurately, Sam's forearm, and dragged her towards the doors to the office.

"Come on, homegirl, let's get my bag outta hawk."

And Sam, as she had for most of her life, allowed herself to be led.

"A search warrant? For my house? You're kidding, right?"

Graham hadn't been sure what to expect when he arrived at the mansion with only Bains for backup. He somehow had pictured Simons as being grafted to his entourage of disciples, legal experts, and handlers. To find him virtually alone in his house without a lawyer in sight was a blessing. Perhaps his luck was starting to change. But Lionel Simons had spent enough time in a courtroom or in legal difficulty to know a thing or two about process.

"You won't mind if I have a careful look at the warrant, sergeant? Just to check it for typos."

Bullshit, Graham thought as he handed the document over. Simons was checking out the scope of the

She Demons 241

warrant, its limitations, and looking for a loophole. It was pretty broad. Judge Davies was a good old-fashioned pre-Charter of Rights bencher who liked to give the police a free hand.

"I see you obtained this with the help of an affidavit, sergeant Graham. Now I wonder how well-informed your source could be, since he or she couldn't possibly belong to my organization."

"Well-informed enough for the judge, Simons. Now —"

"Oh, God...."

Graham noted that Bains was looking down the driveway (framed by the mountains opposite the water) at the rapidly approaching form of Hakeem Jinnah.

Simons smiled. "I see you've brought your public relations department with you."

"If you think Jinnah takes direction from me, you're sadly mistaken," said Graham, quite sincerely. "Now, may I suggest we step inside? Unless you wanna hold an impromptu press conference."

Simons stepped aside and let Graham and Bains in, just as Jinnah leapt up the stone steps. "Mr. Simons, a word, please —"

"The word is goodbye, Hakeem."

Simons had the delicious satisfaction of closing the door in Jinnah's face. The reporter's steel-toed boots were just a fraction too slow. Hakeem wasn't too upset. He hadn't expected to get anything pre-search. He just wanted to establish a presence and he had done so. Graham and the cops liked to go about their business quietly, out of the media spotlight. But Jinnah knew the value of a little press pressure on a suspect. Lionel Simons one-on-one with the police was one kind of character. The MiMi Magus having to answer awkward questions about why his mansion was being raided by police was another. Hopefully, the stress and anxiety would cause the sonofabitch to let something useful slip. Who wouldn't be a basket case with Hakeem Jinnah camped on their front doorstep? He looked about, noting the discreet surveillance camera that blended in tastefully with the porch decor. He also noted the complete absence of any no smoking signs and lit up. He remembered the look on Simons's face when he saw him coming up the steps and chuckled. First the cops, then Jinnah. Bad things usually happened in threes. He prayed to News God the third piece of bad news for the Magus would give him the front page.

The third unwelcome surprise of the morning was waiting for Lionel Simons in his office in the form of Sam and "Beth Billingsgate." Caitlin had only just managed to retrieve her purse by the time the Magus had arrived with the police in tow.

"Oh, sorry —"

Sam's frightened look was totally lost on Graham, who had simply skipped over "Beth" to take in the room's features. But in an instant, he did a neck-wrenching double take. Taken by surprise, Caitlin had accidentally made eye contact and now the policeman recognized his nemesis.

She Demons

243

The look of recognition was not lost on Simons. "Do you two know each other?" he said.

"Yeah," said Graham casually, thinking fast. "This young lady is what you might call 'known to the police.' How you doing?"

Graham had kept the end of his sentence deliberately open so that Caitlin, should she so choose, could play along and supply her own name.

No less mentally nimble, Caitlin gratefully accepted the offer of anonymity. "Beth," she replied, casting her eyes down and looking guilty (which wasn't hard, given the circumstances). "Surprised you remember me."

"Oh, I never forget a collar," said Graham. "Is this your idea of straightening out your life?"

Simons studied both Graham's stern, set features and Caitlin's downcast visage. Graham had to admire the Magus in that moment — he would have made a fortune as a poker player. He gave away nothing.

"We accept anyone who comes looking for enlightenment, sergeant," he said after a tense moment. "There is no past — it's an artificial construct. There is only now, and in the now, Beth is ready to search for the light. Sam, would you take our new devotee out to the deck while I chat with the sergeant and the constable?"

Sam nodded vigorously, gratefully. "No worries, Magus."

Caitlin was just congratulating herself and making a note to take Graham up on that offer of an after-work drink when Simons's hand shot out and grabbed her bag.

"I'll just hang onto this, if you don't mind," he said, enfolding the handbag in his arms. "Is this covered by your warrant, sergeant?"

Graham, making a conscious effort not to look at Caitlin, shrugged. "C'mon, Lionel. Let's get on with this, okay?"

And so Sam led Caitlin out of the office with Simons still in possession of her bag, the camera now recording a dark blank that further illumination would have revealed to be the Rave Messiah's stomach.

Simons turned to Graham, a curiously serene look on his face. "Okay, sergeant. Let's get on with it."

The deck on the ocean side of the house gave them a splendid view of the water, the dock below, and Stanley Park, tantalizingly close on the other side of the narrow mouth of the Burrard Inlet. Amid the stationary freighters waiting for access to the port, powerboats, sailboats, and other pleasure craft weaved and darted on the sparkling surface. Sam stared at the trees, the water, the seagulls — anywhere but Caitlin's face.

"Look," said Caitlin, "I know what you think."

"I, like, doubt that."

"Seriously. I saw the look on your face when the cops came in and recognized me. I'm not an undercover cop."

"Then who are you?" demanded Sam, whirling around, inches from her face, trembling. "What the fuck are you doing here?"

She Demons   245

"I'm a reporter," Caitlin confessed. "I'm investigating the death of Thad Golway."

Caitlin was surprised at Sam's reaction. But then, she had never met the young woman and didn't know about her history with the slain young man.

"Jesus! Jesus! Why can't you just leave us alone?"

Sam buried her head in her arms, stretched along the railing, and burst into tears. In an instant, Caitlin made the connection. If not lovers, then close friends. She assumed her most sympathetic girlfriend mode. "I'm so sorry, Sam. I didn't know, honest...."

Grief is a mysterious thing. Some people need to close in, hide it. Others need to talk, to weep, to work it through. They will do this, surprisingly enough, with a stranger — especially if the stranger is a reporter. It is their chance to state their case to the world at large, as if they know this is their fifteen minutes of fame, even if it was purchased at the ultimate price. Sam was of the latter category and in five minutes Caitlin had the whole story that had taken Jinnah days to piece together. It was dynamite stuff. Dynamite stuff that cried out for an on-camera interview.

"Sam," Caitlin said gently as Sam's sobs subsided. "I really, really need your help to get my bag back. It's got a camera in it."

Through her pain and her tears, Sam looked up, confused. "A camera?" she asked.

"If the Magus or anyone in the organization were to open it, there'd be problems. It'd be best if I just took it away quietly, okay?"

Sam, conflicted once again, turned her red, raw

246 *Donald J. Hauka*

eyes painfully toward the water. A large powerboat was roaring up to the dock below them. She recognized the figure that pulled back on the throttle, idled, and jumped onto the dock with a bowline.

"That's Ray," she said, pointing down at Daisley as he made the boat fast to the dock. "He'll help. Ray always knows what to do."

Jinnah was bored. The thrill and excitement of the search, of lighting up on Simons's own front porch, had faded. No one had come to challenge him or demand he butt out and, of course, there was no sign of Graham or Bains. All he had to stare at from this angle was the wooded drive up to the road. Boring stuff. He cast about. There was no one to stop him from checking out the rest of Lionel Simons's mansion, so he ground his cigarette slowly and deliberately into the porch and made his way down the steps and around the side of the house. The space was quite narrow, the cedar fence unusually high and topped by blue clematis that still sported a few, faded flowers this late in the fall. The windows at ground floor level were made of glass brick, obscuring any view inside, the upper stories were covered by blinds. Jinnah reflected that the only difference between operations like Dosanjh's and Simons's was the quality of the screening they used to hide the true nature of their operations. With that happy thought, he came around the corner to the water side of the house. The light was quite intense,

She Demons   247

reflecting off the waves, and it took Jinnah's myopic eyes a second to adjust. In a sweep, he took in the massive back door area, sheltered by a huge overhang, the suggestion of a deck above it —

— and Ray Daisley headed up the dock towards the house. Jinnah took a last glance up at the deck and registered Sam waving at Ray. She was beside a mousy-looking brunette who seemed vaguely familiar. But Jinnah didn't have time to place her — he had to make tracks. It would not do for him to be caught snooping at the back door by Daisley — not that the giant wuss would do anything about it except give him a lecture on how he could come inside anytime, as long as he was prepared to give up the darkness and look for the light....

Jinnah, who had made it to the drive in front of the house, was so preoccupied with his imaginary sermon from Daisley that he nearly missed the very real presence of a large van that came within a hair of running him over. He leapt aside at the last possible moment as the vehicle, its brakes screeching, lurched to an awkward halt.

In an instant, Jinnah was at the drivers' window. "You stupid, blind sonofabitch!" he screamed. "Why don't you look where you're going?"

Jinnah was searching his brain for some choice in invective, one worthy of a near-death experience, and wondering if this brush with mortality would be the last straw in the long string of shocks that would end in the final, fatal embolism, when the window rolled down and Kevin stuck his face out of the frame. "I'm

248 *Donald J. Hauka*

drivin' blind in more ways than one, Jinnah. You'd better step inside and listen to this."

Jinnah was taken aback at the cameraman's urgency — his near panic. He'd never seen the cool, calm, and collected Kevin so worked up. He was about to ask where Caitlin was when he suddenly remembered where he'd seen the mousy devotee's hairstyle before.

"Sonofabitch," he muttered, and climbed into the van's side door.

"Sam, be reasonable. It's got my ID and everything in it. How would that look if the cops find it? Do you want to get the Magus onto more trouble?"

"Ray will be here in a minute. He'll know what to do."

"Ray will just tell you that you should find some excuse to get my bag outta the office so we can split...."

The sound quality, Jinnah had to admit, was superb. It was tragedy for Caitlin that all her camera was recording was blackness. He also had to admire Caitlin's line of reasoning with Sam: I am your friend, just trying to help you — even though I snuck in here under false pretenses and will fry your Magus's ass given half a chance. That was the Caitlin he had mentored. He slipped one of the earphones off his head and turned to Kevin, standing anxiously over his shoulder.

"Okay, so what's the problem? Can I smoke in here?"

She Demons 249

"No, you can't!" snapped Kevin. "Look, Caitlin —"

"You mean Beth Billingsgate. A lame alias, if you ask me —"

"Caitlin's stuck there with Ray Daisley about to appear and Simons being questioned by the cops!"

Jinnah stared blankly at Kevin, uncomprehending. "That's not a problem — that's a reporter's dream."

"Not every reporter is like you, Jinnah. Listen to Caitlin's voice. Come on —"

Jinnah listened. And for the first time, noted the high tone, the tight breath. That was definitely not the intern he'd mentored, one who had always impressed him with her coolness.

"She's scared, Jinnah — I can tell. When you're scared, you make mistakes. One mistake could end Caitlin's career right now. We gotta help her."

Jinnah was conflicted. Caitlin in trouble was not his problem. In fact, it was a boon. Graham wouldn't have to worry, the pressure would be off, and he could concentrate on solving this bloody murder instead of bailing his friends out every time they got their nose dirty. On the other hand, Caitlin unveiled would be a triumph for Simons, would blow the entire search, would scream media-police collusion (which he knew, thanks to that tiny part of him called his conscience, that he had already helped to establish by his mere presence). Besides, he couldn't just leave Caitlin hanging like this. And if he did manage to get her out, she would owe him massively.

"Does Beth have a cellphone on her, Kevin?"

"Yeah. Here's the number...."

Jinnah dialed, praying that he was doing the right thing. Caitlin was on a professional ledge. He hoped he could talk her down.

"No financing on the house, Lionel? That's odd."

"Paid for in cash, sergeant. Debt makes you beholden to the banks, limits your freedom. And it was a good year."

Graham felt his facial features twitch involuntarily. He had to agree with Simons. His own credit problems were a constant concern. That wasn't all — to his untrained eye, none of the financial statements appeared fishy. Save for the cash purchase of the mansion, everything appeared in order. Then again, maybe the forensic auditors could find something....

"Still, five mill cash is a lot to plop down all at once, Lionel."

"You can see clearly in the revenue column it was my highest-earning year, sergeant. And you can cross-reference that with my record label if you like —"

Simons's smooth and entirely sincere explanation was interrupted by the generic ring of a cellphone that didn't have its own ringtone. Graham, Bains, and Simons all simultaneously reached for their phones, grinned sheepishly, and listened. The muffled ring was coming from a woman's handbag on the table. Caitlin's bag. Simons opened it, reached inside, and answered.

"Wassup?" he said.

She Demons   251

Poker player though he was, Simons could not control the expression on his face for a fraction of a second, and Graham noted the look of surprise, consternation even. But the mask was back in place in a moment.

"You want to talk to Beth Billingsgate? I'm afraid she's busy at the moment. May I take a message?"

Graham's stomach did backflips. Shit. The phone belonged to Caitlin. Who had phoned? Her boyfriend? Her producer? Not — oh, shit! Not Jinnah, please....

"Are you sure?" asked the Magus. After a second he said, "It would be my pleasure."

In the news van, Jinnah hung up.

"Well?" demanded Kevin.

"Simons answered. I think he recognized my voice."

"Shit, Jinnah!"

"How was I to know the phone was in her bag?" protested Jinnah.

"Simons recognized your voice?"

"That is hardly surprising, my friend. Not only have we known each other for years, Jinnah has the most distinctive — and pleasing — voice in the news business. I really ought to be in radio —"

"For fuck's sake, Jinnah! What about Caitlin?"

Jinnah wondered if radio would be an alternative for Caitlin once Simons marched up and unmasked her. Which, of course, might result in him having to work in sports for the rest of his so-called career. But what would happen to him if he were caught trespassing in

252   *Donald J. Hauka*

the Magus's mansion? Especially if Jordan's well-fed frame was lurking inside. It was not inconceivable that Simons had his own torture chamber in the basement....

"It's a delicate situation, Kevin — let's not be too hasty," said Jinnah, beads of sweat forming on his forehead. "Perhaps if we give her a few minutes —"

"Jinnah!"

"Don't yell, my friend," Jinnah winced. "It's bad for my meningitis."

But Kevin had already reached over and opened the door on Jinnah's side. "Get yer ass outta here and give Caitlin a hand."

Jinnah didn't need the shove the cameraman gave him to slide out of the van and onto the tarmac. But it helped. He assumed his most dignified and heroic air. "Okay, Kevin, lemme see what I can do."

"Is there something I can help with, Magus?"

Simons was just pocketing Caitlin's cellphone when Daisley entered, silent and unobtrusive as ever. The Rave Messiah was already in a bad mood and Ray's habit of popping out of thin air freaked him at the best of times. "Don't ask me — ask him!" Simons said curtly.

Daisley turned his best compassionate face to Graham. "I trust you found everything in order, sergeant?"

To Graham's eyes far too much was in order. Bains was burdened with printouts and computer discs documenting what looked like a pretty well-run little

She Demons 253

organization. But then, that's what forensic account-
ants were for. He gave a grudging nod. "Yeah, I think
we have everything we need, Ray — for now."

"That's great. Look, I don't want to rush you, but
the Magus has a few important appointments to attend
to, business matters to discuss."

Subtle, thought Graham. He glanced over at
Caitlin. He wished he had a warrant to find out what
the hell she thought she was doing there. Then again,
maybe he didn't need one. And given the circumstances,
maybe she wouldn't mind getting the hell outta here.
"We're on our way, Ray. Thanks Lionel."

"My pleasure, sergeant."

"Listen, you don't mind if I have a word with Beth
here, do you?"

It was a calculated risk. Graham knew Simons
couldn't deny him — not without raising suspicion and
giving him grounds to search the rest of the house for
devotees being held against their will.

Simons had worked his face into a mask of seren-
ity, but his voice was a tad tight. "Ray, would you
show the sergeant the way, please?"

Shit. Chaperoned by the Sultan of Schmarm.

"Of course, Magus."

Caitlin and Sam were already entering the living
room through the deck entrance by the time Daisley,
with Graham and Bains in tow, made it to the far
side of the room. Graham suppressed a bitter smile.
The immaculately groomed Caitlin Bishop looked so
dweeby, so nondescript. Not even close to her shiny
TV persona. He almost felt sorry for her — almost.

254   *Donald J. Hauka*

"Beth, can I have a word with you? Outside?"

It was hard to tell whether it was shock or relief that caused Beth/Caitlin to stumble at these words, grabbing the top of the couch for support. Bains, who was closest to her, reached out and grabbed her arm, steadying her.

"Sorry," Caitlin mumbled. "Low blood sugar. Didn't eat breakfast."

"Beth, you gotta take better care of yourself," said Daisley, moving protectively to her side. "Healthy body, healthy mind. It's all one."

"Yeah, sorry," repeated Caitlin, studiously avoiding Graham's eyes.

She straightened up and made her way towards the hall leading out, head bowed. Graham and company followed her. Nobody, not even Daisley, noticed Caitlin's lapel mic stuck into the top of the couch, wiring it for sound.

Jinnah, who was hanging about the gates, wondering what the best approach to this thorny problem of being a personal saviour to Caitlin was, heard the sound of the front door opening like a prisoner on death row waiting for that last-minute telegram. His relief at seeing Caitlin was only slightly mitigated by the sight of Graham and Bains flanking her with Sam trailing behind — and Daisley shutting the door on them. He had the decency to affect a disinterested pose, leaning against the wrought iron bars, lighting up a much-needed cigarette.

She Demons   255

"Well, Hakeem. Any other reporters hiding in the weeds? One more and we can have a full-fledged press conference."

Jinnah looked pointedly at Sam.

Caitlin put her hand on his arm. "It's okay, Hakeem. Sam's with me. She knows about my camera."

"Really, Caitlin, resorting to spying. At least I stayed outside while the police were doing their business."

"Get serious, Jinnah! My camera's in there! Simons will find it."

Jinnah noted that when provoked even the mousy Caitlin looked remarkably like her on-air personality.

"So he finds it, big deal! You were so awed over meeting the Magus, you wanted to take some home movies."

"In HD?"

"So, you were really, really awed —"

"Look, what the hell does it matter? C'mon, Bains."

Jinnah was shocked to see Graham head back to the unmarked police car. He put a hand on Graham's shoulder. "Where the hell are you going, Craig?"

"Back to the office to do some useful work, Hakeem. There's nothing more to do here."

This pronouncement fell into a well of professional silence. Graham's agitated attitude and Bains's hard, cold detachment did not auger well.

"For God's sake, Craig —"

"Jinnah, the search turned up squat. No grow op in the basement. Not so much as a hemp seed on the premises. And from what I can tell, the financial records are immaculate. Simons is clean. I got bupkis.

256 *Donald J. Hauka*

And a helluva lot of explaining to do to Superintendent Butcher. Let's go."

Jinnah was so gobsmacked that he uttered not a word as Graham and Bains got into their car and roared off. He turned to Caitlin, wondering what her reaction would be. Grief? Ah, he would have to handle her gently, tenderly, perhaps console her … he was unprepared for the fierce smile Caitlin gave him as she took his arm and guided him out of the gate and towards the van.

"Hakeem, the story ain't over yet."

"What do you mean?" Jinnah frowned, the chance of consoling a distraught Caitlin Bishop with a hug (or better yet, a back massage) fading at light speed.

Kevin was waiting for them as they reached the van. His awkward expressions of concern were brushed away by Caitlin, who turned to Jinnah, remarkably free of any need for consolation. "I stuck my remote mic into the top of Simons's couch. It could prove useful."

"Useful?" cried Jinnah, not liking the direction Caitlin was headed. "What do you mean, useful?"

"I mean useful when we go back in there and get it, useful."

"Go back in?" said Jinnah, uncomfortably aware of how high his voice had involuntarily climbed.

"Yeah, in there," said Caitlin. "You have objections?"

Jinnah's mind was compiling an encyclopedia of good reasons (many of them under the letter "J" for Jordan) when Kevin chipped in. "Didn't you say being in there was a reporter's dream, Jinnah?"

She Demons 257

"Dreams? This is real life," said Jinnah, his voice a full octave higher. "I am not the stuff that dreams are made of. I'm hard reality."

"More like soft jelly," said Kevin.

"Listen, asshole —"

A murmur from the van froze everyone.

"That's coming from the mansion," said Caitlin.

It was a close race back inside the van, but Jinnah, despite suffering from retroactive mumps and testicle shrinkage, beat even Caitlin.

"What the hell have you been up to, Ray?"

"Just fulfilling your vision, Magus."

"My vision doesn't include cops with search warrants! It doesn't include having our financial records under a police microscope. I know I haven't done anything to trigger this. So I ask again: what the hell have you been up to?"

Jinnah glanced over to Caitlin. In the confines of the van they were staring at a black screen, faithfully recording the inside of Caitlin's purse, while listening to an animated conversation cum knock-down argument between Simons and Daisley. Even to an inexperienced ear, Simons sounded desperate, Daisley petulant, their public veneer stripped away by the illusion of privacy. But some of Caitlin's attention was taken up with the sound levels — were they broadcast quality? What sort of still could she use to hold up an extended piece? How much lawyering would it take to get it on-air?

"I have been loyal to your vision, Magus. I have kept it clear in my mind. But your vision has become increasingly fogged by alcohol, sex, and drugs —"

"Get off it, Ray —"

"No! It's me who's been running everything, keeping the good works going —"

"You? Like I don't —"

"You used to be our source, our centre, Magus. But unless you get back onside, there's no future for the organization...."

"Jesus," said Caitlin. "Is Ray staging a mutiny?"

All eyes were on Sam, whose own orbs were unnaturally wide. Before she could provide any insight they started hearing other sounds — sounds in an uneven stereo that was coming from both within and without the mansion. The sounds were of the righteous calling on the sinners to repent. There was no mistaking their origin.

"Ah!" crowed Jinnah "Reverend Hobbes is doing his best Seventh Cavalry imitation!"

"What does that asshole want now?" they heard Daisley say.

"Shut up, Ray. He's a guest," Simons replied.

Jinnah regretted that Caitlin's camera was locked in Simons's study. If the look on Daisley's face was anything like the expressions Hakeem saw around him in the van, it would have been a Kodak moment worth preserving (and perhaps worthy of the front page).

"A guest? Are you crazy?"

"No Ray, I'm taking a page from that diet guru — it's time to end the madness."

"Lionel, talk to me —"

She Demons 259

The conversation faded as Simons and Daisley moved out of the room. The volume of live sound coming from the front lawn was escalating. Jinnah was still trying to process Simons's theological backflip — the Reverend Hobbes, a guest? — when Caitlin slapped Kevin on the back. "C'mon, big guy."

In seconds they had all spilled out of the van. The long line of God Squad regulars and other protestors was still snaking through the front gate just down the road. Kevin had his camera on his shoulder. Caitlin was on his left. Jinnah grudgingly took up a position on the right. With Sam in the middle they'd form a flying wedge, cutting through the crowd to get to the heart of the action: the front door. Jinnah glanced over at Sam. Poor creature. She was still in shock. Perhaps she needed a hug?

"Okay, let's roll."

With Kevin at the point, they made their way at a brisk trot down the sloping sidewalk, passing chanting, singing demonstrators. The trick in a flying wedge is not to stop or slow down until you reach your position, and then to form a tiny island that cannot be moved no matter what. Jinnah had been part of countless such media battering rams, but this one was seemed woefully undermanned for the task. Then again, most flying wedges didn't have the formidable presence of Caitlin Bishop.

"Coming through, pardon me, get outta the way. 'Scuse us — watch it…."

Jinnah was impressed at the speed with which they cut through the crowd. It was, God be praised, not too thick — not yet. He glimpsed familiar faces from the demo at the outreach office, including the Bible-waving Goliath (who mercifully did not seem to even notice their presence as they swooped past). He became aware of singing — high, wavering notes of a tune.

Jesus loves you, this you know,
For the Bible tells you so,
Lionel Simons, you belong,
You are weak, but God is strong ...

Suddenly they were at the front steps. Sam was clinging to Caitlin, Kevin had planted himself firmly on the top step, and Jinnah tried his best to hold his place in the jostling, singing crowd. Just ahead of them, they had a perfect profile of Reverend Peter Hobbes hammering on Lionel Simons's front door. If they survived, Caitlin would have a helluva piece for the evening news.

"Lionel Simons! Come forth!" bellowed Hobbes. "Your redeemer summons you!"

If Lionel Simons has an ounce of sense, he'll call the cops, thought Jinnah. I wouldn't open the Jinnah-mahal to this lot. But the door swung slowly open and a disdainful cheer went up as the Rave Messiah appeared in the portal. Jinnah noted that Daisley was right behind him.

"Lionel Simons, the day of judgment is at hand."

The crowd was surging around them, not actually trying to break through the circle of media, but upset that they couldn't see this historic moment. One spindly, middle-aged man peevishly asked Kevin to move because he wanted a better view.

She Demons 261

"Watch it on the Early News," Kevin barked, immovable.

Simons stepped forward and took Hobbes's hands. "Peter. A pleasure to see you. Look, come on inside and let's talk. It's time to end all this silliness, don't you think?"

Jinnah was close enough to study Hobbes's face. Was that real surprise or just an act for the faithful? Impossible to tell.

"Brethren!" cried Hobbes. "I would have you remain here and pray while I speak with Lionel Simons. Pray for me and for Lionel!"

Ray Daisley looks like he is trying to shit a peach pit without squealing, thought Jinnah. He doesn't like this....

Daisley liked what happened next even less. Simons had manoeuvred Hobbes between himself and Ray. The Reverend entered the mansion unmolested. But when Daisley went to follow, Simons barred his way. "I won't be needing you for this one, Ray," he said.

"But, Magus —"

"In fact, I think you've been working way too hard. Why don't you take some time off, hmm? Sort of like Jassy."

Holy shit! Daisley's being fired right here in front of us! Neither Simons nor Hobbes had acknowledged the media's presence. But they were certainly playing to the camera.

"You can't mean it, Magus!"

"Goodbye, Ray."

262 *Donald J. Hauka*

Simons closed the door. Confronted by a sea of praying, chanting, and singing born-agains, Daisley, his face a mask of fury, pushed his way through them and disappeared around the corner. Jinnah briefly considered going after him, but that would mean breaking the ranks of the protective triangle. Besides, he saw the Goliath standing right by the corner, waving his Bible in the air like a flag and shouting what sounded like gibberish. No doubt Ray was taking the powerboat as part of his severance package. Jinnah wished him luck. How was the poor bastard going to get a job? Resume: right-hand man to former rock star Rave Messiah. Can rent grow op houses discreetly.

Jinnah was calculating how long they'd have to be camped on the steps when Caitlin tugged on Kevin's sleeve. "Kay. Back to the van."

"You're kidding!" cried Jinnah. "The story's here!"

"Wrong, Jinnah. Now come on."

Jinnah had no chance to argue. With the precision of the Household Cavalry, the wedge spun around and, with Kevin in the lead, plunged through the praying protesters. Sam, who had hidden behind Caitlin during the scene at the door, was so close behind that she stepped on the back of the pit bull's heels. The two had obviously bonded in one of those feminine ways that Jinnah found so mysterious. Or perhaps it was like one of those baby ducks who imprints on the first adult creature it happens upon after birth, for Sam was going though something that had to be just as traumatic.

They made it back to the van in one piece. Jinnah indulged his nicotine habit. Sam looked like she was

She Demons 263

about cry. Kevin was already busy changing tapes.

It was time for the great Jinnah-ji to assert some control over the situation. "Well, Caitlin, surely we don't camp here until they come out, hmm?"

"Of course we do, Jinnah. You forget about my mic."

"When did illegal surveillance take the place of honest journalism?"

"We should be able to hear everything...."

But once they were inside the van it was painfully apparent that Hobbes and Simons were meeting in the office, not the living room. Caitlin cursed in the good old-fashioned West Coast logger tradition. Jinnah noted it fell quite short of the more descriptive invective of the Indian subcontinent or even Africa. But it did bring Sam to life.

"Take it easy, Beth," she said softly.

"Sorry," said Caitlin. "But what the fuck are going to do now?"

"Simple," smiled Jinnah. "We're going to go back into the mansion."

"Like Simons is going to let us in the front door."

"There's always the back door," said Jinnah, his eyes fixed on Sam. "And I'm pretty sure at least one of us has a key to it."

"Let you in the back door?" said Sam, her voice devoid of both emotion and understanding."

"No one will know, I promise," Jinnah said, his voice sliding down alarmingly close to his Pepé Le Pew tone.

"But ... why?"

"Why? You have been listening, haven't you?" cried Jinnah.

"Look, Sam," Caitlin jumped in, cutting Hakeem off. "You want to catch whoever killed Thad, don't you?"

"'Course I do," said Sam, tearing up.

"Whoever that person is, they deserve to face justice, right?"

Sam nodded, lips quivering.

"No matter who it is, right?"

Another nod.

"Even if that killer turns out to be Lionel Simons?" said Caitlin softly.

Sam hesitated. Jinnah put his hand lightly on her forearm.

"Take us inside the mansion, Sam. We'll get Caitlin's bag and we'll be one step closer to catching Thad's killer."

Sam looked down at Jinnah's hand on her arm, then over to Caitlin's face. She sat up straight and pulled her keys out of her pocket.

"Let's go," she said.

And Jinnah noted that this strawberry angel had some steel in her soul.

"And he said, when you pray, pray like this: Our Father, who art in heaven, hallowed be thy name …"

Peter Hobbes kept his hope in check. Long experience with the theatric antics that Lionel Simons was

She Demons 265

capable of told him this could all be an elaborate gag designed to make him look foolish. But the Rave Messiah looked like he was deadly earnest as he stood before his nemesis in the meditation room, eyes closed, hands clasped in prayer, and recited words that the Reverend had never heard pour from Simons's mouth.

"For thine is the kingdom, the power and the glory, forever and ever, amen."

"Amen," Hobbes intoned, shifting uncomfortably on the ergonomically correct prayer chair Simons had provided him with.

Simons opened his eyes. There was a look in them that Hobbes had never seen before, and he was having a terrible time trying to put a name on it.

"Peter, I have been doing a great deal of thinking lately, and I have come to a surprising conclusion."

Hobbes's betrayed nothing. His tone was flat and even. "And what is this surprising conclusion, Lionel?"

"That I have been wrong. I have been wrong all along about the raves, about Millennial Magic, about the way I have lived my life."

Simons was so sincere, so obviously in agony, that Hobbes could not hide his surprise. And now he did recognize the look in his adversary's eyes — plain, old-fashioned fear. He was speechless as Simons sank to his knees.

"I repent of my sins. Forgive me, Peter. Pray with me a while."

Incredulous, Hobbes found himself on his own knees, his arms a comforting circle around Simons's shoulders, as the former Rave Messiah sobbed like a child.

* * *

"Just stay put, okay? I'll check out the office."

Jinnah and Caitlin nodded. They were in the deserted living room, where Caitlin had retrieved her lapel mic. Hakeem was impressed by Sam's sudden resolution. Once the young woman decided to do something, she did it without hesitation. Bossy too. He put that down to her close association with Jassy.

"Think she'll come back with the bag or the hired muscle?" Jinnah whispered as Sam disappeared down the hallway.

"Shut up or the hired muscle will get here on their own," hissed Caitlin.

Jinnah shut up, content that he was the victim of conspiracy of strong women. They obviously ran with wolves, these females. He would have to be on his guard. Outwardly calm, on the inside his heart was pounding, his nerves were shrieking for a cigarette, and an unmanly sheen of sweat was beginning to form on his ever so slightly receding hairline. Worse still, his inherent instincts were tingling. Something was up, something more than their covert operation to recover Caitlin's bag. What the hell were Simons and Hobbes doing? Why had Lionel invited his most dogged adversary into his inner sanctum and dismissed Daisley, his most trusted acolyte? He was so deep into the problem that he jumped right out of his skin when Sam poked her head around the corner and whispered hoarsely: "All clear. Let's go."

She Demons 267

Jinnah shot a glanced over to Caitlin, who knew exactly what he meant.

"Anything out front, Kevin?" she whispered into her lapel mic.

Neither Jinnah nor Sam could hear the reply, but the shake of the head from Caitlin was all they needed to see to slowly, carefully, pick their way out of the living room and down the hall into the heart of Lionel Simons's empire.

Kevin actually missed the historic moment when the Reverend Peter Hobbes emerged from Lionel Simons's mansion waving a piece of paper over his head in the religious equivalent of "Peace in Our Time." Like many cameramen, he was an artist at heart. He had been bored and started shooting cutaways of the crowd, even interviewing a few members of the God Squad, trying to get something, anything, just in case Caitlin came up empty. But mere moments after telling her that nothing was happening out front, Kevin was several metres from the front steps and facing the driveway — not the house — when the buzz behind his back alerted him to something significant developing in the doorway. He whirled about and through his viewfinder saw Hobbes holding the single sheet of foolscap aloft, like a banner. The crowd was surging forward and Kevin had to use all his muscle and elbow power to regain his position. The resulting video was somewhat shaky and uneven, but the sound was loud and clear.

268   *Donald J. Hauka*

"The Lord has delivered the unbeliever into our hands, brethren!" shouted Hobbes, triumphant. "I have here a handwritten note from Lionel Simons repenting his sins!"

Much of what Hobbes said next was drowned out by the shouts and cries of surprised ecstasy from the crowd. "Hallelujahs!" rang out, mingled with a healthy dose of "Praise the Lord!" and "Amen!" coming in a close third.

"Furthermore, Brother Simons has committed to turning his entire cult operation over to our church to cleanse and administer!"

This prompted a positive firestorm of evangelical ejaculations. The Bible-waving Goliath fell to his knees and wept, tears streaming down his face and onto the leather cover of his well-worn New Testament. As one, the crowd burst into song.

We've got a great big wonderful God,
A great big wonderful God …

Hobbes was moving through the crowd now, away from the mansion, and it was clear the demo on Simons's lawn was over. Kevin was tempted to try Caitlin's cellphone — surely she must have her bag back by now? — but refrained. She had made it clear he was not to risk contact with her while she was inside. If she needed anything, she would use the lapel mic. Typical, he thought. You can never find your meat puppet when you really need her….

She Demons   269

* * *

Inside the mansion, the meat puppet in question was frantically fast-forwarding through her DVD recorder while Jinnah and Sam waited with scarce-concealed impatience and fear, counting each moment spent in Simons's study in grams of heart tissue lost and eternities rather than the fractions of seconds Caitlin was dealing in as she looked for something — anything — useable.

"Shit!" she said. "Shit, shit, shit, shit!"

"Shush!" said Jinnah and Sam in stereo.

"I've got squat for the six o'clock show," said Caitlin somewhat less loudly.

"Don't despair, Caitlin," Jinnah whispered. "News God moves in mysterious ways His wonders to perform."

News God was terribly swift, for Jinnah had just finished speaking when they heard a loud crash. The trio froze.

"What the fuck was that?" hissed Caitlin.

Jinnah realized that both Sam and Caitlin were staring at him, wide-eyed and expectant. Instinctively, he knew what they wanted. He, the man, would have to stick his nose out of the room and investigate. These women may run with wolves, but they are unwilling to walk with suspected murderers. He overcame a momentary spasm of congenital cowardice and moved towards the study door.

"Stay put. I'll check it out."

He was disappointed that Caitlin didn't insist on going ahead or, even better, going *instead* of him. But he stuck his nose around the corner of the doorjamb and looked up and down the hallway. Nothing. Cautiously, he moved out into the deserted passageway and listened, straining to hear the slightest sound. But his ears were flooded by the raging torrent of his own blood and pumping heart. The crash had come from the far end of the house, in the direction of the pool. Pulse racing, inherent instincts screaming, Jinnah slowly edged his way down the hall towards the outer doors that led to the watery shrine. He paused, looking up and down. Still nothing.

The glass sliding door to the deck was wide open. He risked a poolside peep. One of the plaster of Paris statues of an obscure deity had fallen from its pedestal and smashed on the cement. That explained the crash. It didn't explain the next image Jinnah took in. There was something floating in the pool. Something human. Something facedown.

Jinnah didn't realize he was dragging the person in the pool to the shallow steps, having plunged right into the water without thought or hesitation, until he turned the form over and saw the face of Lionel Simons staring lifelessly up at him. For it was at that moment that Sam, who had followed him at a discreet distance, started to scream, bringing Jinnah back from the timeless realm to cold, wet reality.

Chapter Seven

"So Simons was dead when you found him?"

Graham's question was underscored by the loud zip! of the body bag being closed. The forensic boys had removed Simons's corpse, preliminary COD: drowning. The blow to the Magus's head was perhaps a contributing factor. Jinnah shivered. He was wet, cold, and as far as he could tell his Gucci loafers were ruined. The best he could manage was a shaky nod. Behind him, a sedated Sam was in the care of Victim Services. Caitlin was hovering, uncomfortable with the dual role of reporter and witness, and positively homicidal that Kevin hadn't been allowed into the crime scene.

"So someone struggled with Lionel poolside, knocking over this statue. Bashed him on the head. He either drowns or is drowned."

"Was drowned, Craig," shivered Jinnah. "Not enough time to drown accidentally between the time we heard the crash and I pulled him out of the pool. He had to have been held under."

"By who? Ray Daisley?"

Jinnah shook his head. "He'd gone."

"Then who?"

"Peter Hobbes? He was the last person with Simons —"

Constable Bains appeared in his maddeningly silent way behind Graham. "There was a window broken at the back entrance — forced entry," he said, eying Jinnah without love.

Graham looked at Hakeem, an eyebrow raised quizzically.

"Sam let us in," he said. "She has keys."

"Then who broke in, Hakeem?"

"I think I can answer that, sir, if you'll step this way," said Bains.

Graham motioned Jinnah to follow. Caitlin was immediately at their side.

"I'm entitled!" she cried. "I stuck my neck out for this story —"

Graham grabbed a stray uniform by the arm and steered him between Caitlin and himself.

"Sorry, Beth. This nice policeman is going to take your statement."

"I got rights! This is favouritism! This is about that warrant story, isn't it? I'll —"

"You'll try to explain to this constable your exact whereabouts at the time of Lionel Simons's death," said Graham brutally. "That ought to help rule you out as a suspect."

She Demons 273

"A suspect?" shouted Caitlin. "I was in the study with Sam and Jinnah —"

"Tell it to the constable."

Caitlin's protests faded as Bains led them to a different wing of the mansion.

The room Jinnah stepped into was devoid of Buddhas, divas, bodhisattvas, and even Yakshas. The God of this realm was the hidden, all-seeing eye of the security centre. A row of monitors was built into a control counsel. Jinnah kicked himself for not assuming that Simons would have his mansion wired. Bains hit the rewind on the rear entrance view. Jinnah could see himself, Sam, and Caitlin entering as the jerky footage flicked past.

"See. I told you we used keys," he said, somewhat peevishly.

"Yeah, yeah, whatever."

But Jinnah's inherent instincts were ringing a triple alarm. He knew with sudden clarity that the broken window was of singular importance.

"Craig, look, I'm telling you — the person who broke that window must be the killer! It all fits —"

"There's something else, sir."

Bains addressed himself to Graham, as usual. Jinnah subsided, his instincts suddenly overwhelmed by an inexplicable feeling of dread (and that he should have kept his mouth shut). The sergeant nodded and they watched as the video raced backwards. Suddenly, a figure emerged from the rear window, climbed down the wall, and caught a rock that flew out of the window, repairing the glass as it went. As she turned her face to the left, Bains hit the freeze button. The young woman's face was perfectly recognizable. Jinnah closed his eyes. Name of God....

"Well, Jinnah," said Graham. "Your Jassy Singh certainly does get around. What are the odds that she did the employer who'd just fired her?"

Jinnah stared at the classic profile, beautiful even in the grainy, grey security camera tape. He didn't know which made him feel worse. How the hell had he missed her in the mansion? Or how the hell was he ever going to find her now?

A considerable amount of time elapsed before Jinnah was allowed to leave the mansion. He had resented Graham's unspoken suspicion of him as a potential subject ("How did you get along with Lionel Simons, Hakeem? He did sue you several times, didn't he?"), and Caitlin's pathetic attempts to pries information out of him ("You said yourself we were in this together, Hakeem...."). Craig had even given him the old "don't leave town" speech. Now, safely inside the SGLM, parked in the middle ground of Second Beach beside English Bay, he had several crucial phone calls to make. He started with the most important one of all. But Jassy wasn't answering her cellphone.

"Son of a bitch!" spat Jinnah.

He fumbled to light another cigarette while hitting the speed-dial. He had to find her, had to....

"*Tribune* newsroom, Ronald Sanderson —"

She Demons 275

"Ronald!" Jinnah rode right over his colleague. "Are there any messages for me?"

"Hello to you too, Hakeem," Ronald's voice was wounded. "Whiteman wants to talk to you —"

"I mean real messages. Preferably from Jassy Singh."

"Let me check with Crystal...."

Jinnah struggled to inhale an entire cigarette with a single breath, feeling the searing blue smoke soothe his ravaged lungs, quicken his pulse, and assist his frenetic thought process. But he knew what Sanderson's answer would be even before he came back on the line after a few seconds and gave him the bad news.

"Nothing from Jassy Singh. Hakeem, seriously — I think Whiteman's going to have an aneurysm if you don't at least tell Frosty where you are —"

Conscious of the time — there wasn't a lot left until deadline — Jinnah weighed the pros and cons of his next move, calculated the odds of it leading to outright dismissal as opposed to a lengthy, unpaid suspension and how that might affect his pension as opposed to the possible payoff. He took one last, lung-splitting drag on his dart before giving Sanderson his marching orders.

"Tell Frosty to hold the front page. I'll be there before deadline with the line story. Meantime, get a photog down to Lionel Simons's mansion — Clint Eastward if he's not doing a dog picture, right?"

"Hakeem, what on earth ... why the hell should I ... what story?"

"Ronald, Ronald, you must learn to relax," Jinnah chided his friend. "We must keep cool during the crisis.

276   *Donald J. Hauka*

There will be plenty of time to panic later. For now, all you need to do is tell Frosty that Lionel Simons has been murdered."

"What? How do you know?"

"Because I was there, Ronald," said Jinnah pleasantly, and hung up.

He ignored the insistent ringing of his cellphone as he gunned the SGLM's engine and roared off towards the east. There was only one place left to go now, one loose end to tie up. Jinnah would rather have knocked on a thousand doors of silence, even faced Thad Golway's parents again, rather than do what he had to do now. But News God was a jealous god, and he demanded sacrifice from his devotees. So it was that Hakeem Jinnah steeled himself for a long-overdue visit.

"I am so sorry, Mr. Jinnah. Jassy has not spoken with us these past four years."

Jinnah nodded and sipped his tea. Mr. Singh was seated across from him at the dining room table, beside his wife, who looked like she could have made a fortune in Bollywood playing the role of the stern, traditional mother. He had been welcomed into the East Vancouver house by Jassy's parents with an unnerving combination of courtesy and coldness. Mr. Singh, who had a blue turban and a flowing beard, had been full of traditional Sikh hospitality, inviting him in, offering him tea and sweets. Mrs. Singh had been as cold as her ice white sari, averting her eyes and replying in monosyllables to

She Demons   277

his greetings. They had exchanged pleasantries about Diwali, about Manjit's work at the temple (of course they knew her), and about the weather before Jinnah felt secure enough to broach the topic of the Singh's errant daughter. He had a sick feeling in his stomach at Mr. Singh's pronouncement, but he persevered.

"Ah, a shame," he said in Punjabi, the tongue they had been conversing in since Mr. Singh had answered the door. "I have an important message for her from a friend."

Jinnah waited, heart in his mouth. Parents often covered for their children when they were in trouble. If Jassy had nowhere else to go, surely she would have thrown herself on the mercy of her mother and father, no matter what had happened in the past? And if she had done that after so many years of defiance, wouldn't it be her parents' duty to protect their daughter, especially from the man who had helped cause their estrangement? All his senses were straining, trying to detect the slightest symptom of disingenuousness.

"That is a very great shame, sir," said Mr. Singh, his head wagging back and forth. "As I said, our daughter has not spoken with us these past years."

Jinnah could not detect any dissemblance in Mr. Singh. All his years of experience told him that this was the truth. Still, perhaps he was one step ahead of Jassy? It didn't hurt to prepare the ground.

"That must be a great sorrow, Mr. Singh," he said slowly. "But you must pardon me if I ask, is this because you refused to talk to her, once you knew she had joined the MiMis?"

278 *Donald J. Hauka*

Mrs. Singh's eyes flashed, but Mr. Singh put a hand on his wife's wrist.

"I understand what you are saying, Mr. Jinnah. And I know you must regret the small role you played in the estrangement of our daughter. But once we are past our anger, once we remember our duty, God obliges us to forgive, even as He forgives us, you see. We forgave Jassy years ago. We tried to contact her at that place where she worked," Mr. Singh could not bring himself to say "Millennial Magic," nor could he utter the name of Lionel Simons, "but she would not return our calls. We went to that place, she would not see us, and the man there asked us to leave. Believe me, Mr. Jinnah, we pray for our daughter every day that she might find the true path once more. But even if she does not, we forgive her, and we love her."

"Mr. Singh, you are a man who speaks the truth and so I must tell you the truth of the matter. Jassy is in trouble. She is suspected of murder."

Mr. Singh's mouth made a tight, puckered "O" and he nodded slowly. Mrs. Singh's features were set, and Jinnah saw where Jassy got her chiselled looks and poker face.

"Who is she suspected of murdering, sir?"

"Lionel Simons himself, Mr. Singh."

Mr. Singh closed his eyes and his lips worked silently. Jinnah could just make out the words from the *Guru Grant Sahib* — the Sikh holy scripture.

"Man does not decide who lives on this earth and who goes away. The decision of life and death is made by God."

She Demons 279

Jinnah swallowed hard. It seemed an eternity before Mr. Singh opened his eyes.

"And your message?" said Mr. Singh softly.

"That I do not believe she did this thing. That she is being framed by the real killer — the same killer who murdered Thad Golway. But to prove it, she must contact me. She must trust me. If, God willing, Jassy were to contact you, could you pass this message on to her, hmm?"

Mr. Singh had the face of a Sikh warrior. Despite the grey in the beard and the lines around his eyes, Jinnah could well imagine his forebearers fighting Jinnah's ancestors on the dusty plains of Punjab for the supremacy of the subcontinent, and he did not wonder that his forefathers had done so poorly against this fierce people. But Mr. Singh was no statue, and his face collapsed into his hands as he wept silently, the tears streaming through his fingers, mingling with his tea. It was left to the indomitable Mrs. Singh to end the interview.

"We are very sorry, Mr. Jinnah," she said, voice trembling only slightly. "We would like to help, but we have no idea where Jassy is. The child is lost to us."

With a sharp pang, Saleem came unbidden to Jinnah's mind. "I know how you feel, Mrs. Singh," he said gently.

And with that, Jinnah took his leave, reflecting that the water of the well of emptiness was, in this case, especially bitter.

* * *

Nicole "Frosty" Frost closed her bloodshot eyes, forced herself to count to ten, then opened them again. Over Jinnah's left shoulder, to her very minor satisfaction, there was another paragraph at the bottom of the line story Hakeem had promised to deliver. That left about ten more to go, with deadline just five minutes away and the editor-in-chief breathing down her neck. It would be a near thing. She considered how much time she would save asking the hard questions now as opposed to four minutes from now, when it might be too late. Well, Jinnah was good at multi-tasking — when he felt like it.

"You realize, of course, that no matter how deathless your prose, Whiteman will never forgive you for not having your video camera at the scene of the crime."

"The right word is worth a thousand pictures, Frosty," snapped Jinnah without missing a keystroke. "It's not as if Caitlin had anything spectacular on the six o'clock news, for God's sake."

"But she had some images," insisted Frosty. "Enough to prop up the story."

"So Ian Hadley's happy — good for him —"

"Keep typing!"

"Did Caitlin fish Lionel Simons out of the pool? And did she see the video showing Jassy Singh breaking into the mansion?"

Frosty shifted uncomfortably. She was thinking about Hakeem's lede. Everything he'd written so far stood up. But there was a fine line between writing a "prime suspect" story and convicting someone in advance. And Jinnah was definitely pushing that line.

She Demons 281

"What makes you so sure Jassy Singh murdered Lionel Simons?"

"Have I said that?" said Jinnah, fingers still pounding away.

"Near as, damn it —"

"Have I not been Jassy's most fierce advocate? Have I not defended her at every step of the way?" demanded Jinnah.

"Yes — a bit of a gamble, if you ask me."

"Well," said Jinnah. "A true gambler knows when to hold 'em, knows when to fold 'em. And I'm folding 'em."

He typed "30" and hit the send key. Frosty glanced at the clock. Two minutes to spare. If Whiteman didn't insist on a lawyer, they'd make it.

"Remember, Frosty — you can't libel a dead man," Jinnah reminded his senior assistant city editor.

"It's not the stiff I'm worried about, Jinnah — it's your murderous grow op queen."

Jinnah's mouth formed that enigmatic, serpentine smile that Frosty found very hard to read at the best of times, and this was not the best of times.

"News God helps those who help themselves, Frosty. See you at the club?"

Frosty nodded. She was still tinkering with the headline. "Dead in Rave Pool" wasn't bad. Nor was the subhead: "Did burned devotee wreak watery revenge?" She could get that past the news desk if she put her foot down. For Jinnah was not the only devotee to News God in the *Tribune* newsroom.

"Well, it makes things neater, simpler, don't you think?"

"How can you possibly say that, Ray?"

"No middleman to handle or go around. We deal direct."

"And no holy man to use as a shield, either."

Daisley smiled. He put his muddy boots up on the battered desk that adorned his office in the Wilderness Camp and adjusted the phone more comfortably between neck and shoulder. On the wall was the regulation picture of Lionel Simons, looking mystic and loveable at the same time.

"Wrong. Now Jassy's offed him, Lionel's gonna be bigger in death than he ever was in life —"

"Oh, come on!" said the voice on the other end of the line.

"Seriously. Martyrs and murdered maguses attract new converts and cash by the truckload."

"You're sure?"

"Does the name Jesus ring any bells? Or John Lennon, for that matter —"

"But what about the heat? Wouldn't it be best to lay low for a bit?"

"The heat are looking for Jassy as we speak. They've even interviewed the Reverend Peter Hobbes, poor schmuck. Now's the time to act — take the partnership to the next level."

There was silence at the other end of the line. In spite of himself, Daisley held his breath. He'd taken a

She Demons 283

big risk going straight to the top of the organization with his pitch, but he knew instinctively it was the only way. Go big or go home. After a very long few seconds, he was vindicated.

"Okay. How do you suggest we proceed from here?"

"Come up to the school and we'll discuss it face to face."

"When?"

"The sooner the better."

"Okay. Let me make a couple of calls and I'll get back to you."

"Beautiful. Trust me, this is going to be a blast. We're gonna own the whole coast in a couple of months."

"Oh, I trust you, Ray. After all, we have been partners for quite a few years now."

"Great. Get back to me today if you can."

"Goodbye, Ray."

And with that, Ray Daisley hung up on the boss of the Yakshas organization.

"Irresponsible. Harmful to the investigation. A clear breach of the rules of evidence. Unethical. Yellow journalism at its worst."

Jinnah sat calmly as Graham vented at him. He noticed how Craig's hands trembled slightly as he held up the front page of the *Tribune*. "Dead in Rave Pool" screamed across the top in seventy-two point type. But Graham's fingers were drumming on the subhead implicating Jassy.

"And aside from that, you like the story, hmm?" said Jinnah. "Anyone would think you were the girl's defence lawyer, the way you carry on."

"You've practically convicted her, Hakeem!"

Graham threw the paper down on the desk between them with unbridled disgust. They were in his office. He had the moral and legal advantage and he had made sure his diatribe had lasted long enough for Jinnah to start feeling the agony of nicotine withdrawal — a considerable edge in any dealings with the chain-smoking scribe. Yet Jinnah sat there, cool and collected and even capable of wit. It didn't add up. He should be squirming or bellowing at him with false indignation masking his fear of being cut off from his sources. Instead, here he was calmly reciting the evidence against Jassy.

"My friend, we both know the security video shows Jassy breaking in. Her prints are all over the house. You yourself agreed she has motive —"

"Yeah, but —"

"Objection overruled. Further, Hobbes left the house before Simons was killed. So did Daisley. The only logical conclusion is that Jassy Singh murdered her Magus. Unless you're seriously considering charging Caitlin or Sam."

"What if I charge you instead?"

"Craig, Craig — to any reasonable person in possession of the facts as they stand, Jassy Singh is the murderer."

Graham was about to threaten Jinnah along the lines of prejudicing a potential jury and giving Jassy a

She Demons 285

chance to have a mistrial declared when Jinnah's serpentine smile stopped him dead. The penny dropped.

"You don't believe that for a second, do you?" he demanded. "You ran this story to smoke her out."

Jinnah fought hard to suppress a laugh.

"Sergeant Graham! Are you suggesting that I would hype a story that I didn't believe just to provoke a poor, scared young woman into coming forward?"

"Cut the crap, Hakeem."

Jinnah smiled at the policeman for a moment, struggling for words to give him just enough plausible deniability. "Let's just say I like bets where the odds favour the house, hmm?"

Graham briefly turned the possibilities over in his mind. Some were very promising, others terrible to contemplate. He had to decide whether to play ball or not. The problem with Jinnah was that meant almost everything came out of left field. It was risky. But what choice did he have?

"Okay, but if you see her, you hand her over to me — at once. No deals. Got it?"

"Of course, Craig, Anything else would be irresponsible, harmful to the investigation. A clear breach of the rules of —"

"Yeah, yeah. Piss off, Hakeem."

"And I love you too, Craig."

With that, Jinnah jumped to his feet, grabbed Graham's face between his hands, and gave him a big, wet kiss on the forehead. He was gone before Graham could wipe his brow clean.

"Jinnah!"

286 *Donald J. Hauka*

Graham could hear the sound of Jinnah's deep, rolling laugh receding down the hallway. He collapsed into his chair. He wished he could share Jinnah's optimism that his shameless gamble would pay off. The *Tribune* front page stared out at him from his desk, and he felt his stomach convulse and liquefy. The policeman winced and popped another couple of Tums. It looked like another liquid lunch today — of the Maalox variety.

A lunch of a wholly different kind was being served that noon hour at the Moss Street Temple. The vegetarian food being served at the langar was, as usual, delicious. But despite the high calibre of the balti, roti, and chutney, Saleem was having a hard time stomaching things.

"No burgers, huh?" he said sullenly.

"You know there aren't any," said Manjit brightly. "Vegetarian food only, so everyone feels welcome, no matter what their dietary habits."

Saleem frowned. He hadn't been to the langar in years and he was uncomfortable. To cover his embarrassment, he helped himself to some fresh naan. Beside him, Chung Wei was staring at a heating pan full of okra curry with deep suspicion.

"Don't you have any noodles, man?" he whined.

"That's good with rice," muttered Saleem. "Not too hot."

Chung was one of several new friends Manjit had encouraged Saleem to bring along to the langar. Her

She Demons

son had met them at the MiMi drop-in centre and they fit the cult's demographics to a T — young, visible minority, largely first generation, absent or overworked parents. The carrot had been free food and an afternoon off school. Saleem had assumed they were going to the Golden Arches. Instead, they were underneath the golden domes of the temple. Satisfied that her young charges would not starve (although most of them had opted for safe, carbo-loading choices like Saleem), she guided the pack of teens to a corner that afforded a good view of the long lines of people eating.

"So," Manjit said once they were all settled. "Saleem tells me that you all wish to change the world — how marvelous!"

Saleem shot his mother one of those "Don't!" looks, which Manjit cheerfully ignored.

"The world needs changing," said Chung, his mouth half full of naan. "We're gonna tear it down with love. Gonna build it up with power."

"It sounds like an awful lot of work," said Manjit.

"What Chung means is we want to change the world our own way, mom," Saleem cut in. "Use our rules, not the system's."

"And this path to change — this love power. How does it work?"

"Gotta love your neighbour. Be colourblind. Gotta climb together or the corps and the cops will keep us in the gutter."

"Ah! Thank you, Chung. When do you expect to reach this perfect world state of yours?"

"Mom —"

"Gonna take a whole lotta love. Not happenin' overnight."

"Is it not happening right now?" asked Manjit. "I mean, look around. Who do you see in here eating with you?"

"It's a Sikh temple, man," said Chung. "It's a Sikh lunch."

"Take a good look," urged Manjit. "How many people in here would you say are Sikhs, hmm?"

Saleem followed Chung's eyes, expecting to see lines of familiar brown faces, like he had during the Diwali celebrations. He was startled to see many white, yellow, black, brown, and red faces. People of all races and ages were eating together. Many looked poor or homeless. The striking similarity between the crowd at the langar and the MiMi's outreach centre could not be ignored, even by Saleem's stubborn, teenaged brain.

"We have a saying: 'the light of God is in all hearts.' This sounds something like this love power you are talking about, doesn't it?"

"What are you trying say?" said Chung, still staring at the rainbow of faces before him. "Put it straight."

"To put it straight, Chung, when choosing your path in life, there is no need to reinvent the wheel. I think all traditions depend on this love power of yours: Sikh, Taoist, Christian, Buddhist, Jewish, Zoroastrian, or Rastafarian. After all, if there is a path leading in the right direction, the one you wish to go in, would you spurn it simply because your parents or grandparents have walked it before you? Perhaps you, unlike them, will get to the end."

She Demons 289

Saleem, Chung, and the others were silent. Good, thought Manjit. They're thinking. And hopefully not about how they want to go to Tim Horton's after this. She waited until she was certain the moment of insight had faded.

"Come, Saleem," she said, slapping her son on the shoulders and handing him her plate. "After the ecstasy, the dishes."

Saleem looked up sharply, opened his mouth, took one look at his mother's eyes and promptly shut it. There was a peculiar light in them that brooked no argument. It was then he realized for the first time that there was a fierce aspect to love power, and that his mother was quite the adept.

As far as basement sanctuaries went, it wasn't bad. No natural light at all, but the walls had been painted a cheery yellow to simulate the sun. Not that you could see much of the walls, what with all the crosses, pictures of Jesus, and descending doves covering them. Add to that pictures of those who had been sheltered from authority in the past — faces brown, yellow, white, black, red. A veritable refugee rainbow. The furniture was definitely second-hand, but still comfortable in a mismatched, beaten up sort of way. Still, while it was as scrupulously clean and shiny as its age would allow, not all the paint and polish in the world could mask the faint odour of decay mingled with a trace of mildew. It permeated everything, even the reading material on the long, brown bookcases that were voluminous in nature and limited in scope. It was composed almost entirely of modern translations of the Old and New Testaments, inspirational tomes of troubled teens who had miraculously been born-again after experiencing their own equivalent of Emmaus, and apocalyptic literature describing the agony of others who had refused to hear the word of God and, as a result, had been left behind during the Rapture. The decidedly antiquated television offered little relief from this steady evangelical diet, for it was programmed to deliver only those channels that reflected the Word. Revival shows were mixed liberally with documentaries proving the historical accuracy of the Bible and painfully earnest talk shows with folks who had preached the gospel in Godless lands like South America, Russia, China, or New York City.

So it was with a sense of relief as well as surprise that Jassy heard her cellphone ring, startling her out of an uneasy slumber. These sensations were replaced almost immediately by cold fear when she saw the number on the call display.

"What's wrong, Andy?" she asked.

"How did you know —"

"This is the number of the gas bar and store nearest the Wilderness Camp," said Jassy, barrelling right through Andy's hurt and confused tone. "Think I wouldn't recognize it?"

"How do you know anything's wrong?" he said, a bit petulant now.

"Because I've used that phone myself. Are you okay?"

She Demons 291

"Yes — no! Jas, the papers are saying the Magus is dead."

"It's true," said Jassy, fighting to control herself.

"They say that you did it."

"What?" shrieked Jassy, losing any semblance of control. "Who says that?

"The *Tribune*. It's on the front page —"

"That bastard!" screamed Jassy.

"Did you do it, Jassy?"

Jassy wasn't sure which was more surreal — holding a conversation with little Andy Gill about the Magus's murder (something she could not even conceive of just hours ago) or her former acolyte asking her point-blank if she'd done it. But of course, she knew who was to blame for this — her nemesis.

"Who are you going to believe — me or that lying bastard Jinnah?"

"Oh, thank God!"

The relief in Andy's voice pierced Jassy's heart like a ceremonial dagger. His voice was, if possible, even more desperate now. "Jassy, I need help! I want out —"

"Andy, hang in there —"

"Come get me. Please, Jassy —"

Andy's voice was drowned by a sort of muffled roar in the background. Jassy pressed her cellphone tight against her ear. "Andy? Andy?"

Andy was speechless, but the muffled roar resolved itself into a loud, hard male voice. One that Jassy recognized,

"What the hell do you think you're doing? Come here!" bellowed Arnie Krootz.

"I gotta go," said Andy faintly.

"Andy! Andy!"

All Jassy heard before the phone went dead was the sound of the receiver banging against the counter as it dangled on its cord. She stared at her cellphone for a moment, numb, unwilling to process what she'd just heard. Then, in an instant, she was at the door to her room, hammering on it with her strong, brown fists, screaming. "Bring me the fucking paper! Get me the fucking paper right now, goddamn it!"

And, after a while, her guardians did bring her a copy of that day's *Tribune*, but only after saying several prayers for Jassy's immortal soul.

Chapter Eight

At that moment Jinnah's own immortal soul was in imminent danger in the *Tribune* newsroom. It was in good company, along with his professional career, his business aspirations, and whatever sense of dignity and probity he had heretofore managed to maintain while dealing with his supplier. The profanity, delivered in choicest Swahili, shocked no one within earshot of city desk, but at the other end of the line, the supplier's face was flushed with anger.

"And that goes double for your mother!" Jinnah finished up in English and slammed the phone down.

"Son of a bitch," he added thoughtfully, taking a pull on his coffee and struggling out of his coat — he'd only just dragged himself into the newsroom.

"What's the matter, sport?" asked Frosty, vastly amused despite throbbing frontal lobes. "Your house of dolls crumbling?

"You would think the sonofabitch would consider having fished a dead cult leader out of a pool as grounds for an extension on my credit line," growled Jinnah, furious. "Heartless bastard."

"What you need is an extension on your line of credibility. Whiteman was still carrying on in the morning news meeting about you failing to have your video camera on you when you did your little synchronized swimming routine with the cultic corpse. Dereliction of duty, he called it."

Before Jinnah could tell Frosty what he thought of Whiteman using a few choice Anglo-Saxon adjectives and verbs, Ronald Sanderson burst into the newsroom, breathless with excitement and spilling coffee all over his right hand in his haste to impart something momentous.

"There you are, Hakeem!" he crowed. "Have I got news for you!"

"Not another little cat caught up a tree, Ronald!" cried Jinnah. "Or is there an especially fierce form of fungus attacking the rose gardens of Victoria?"

A few deskers cocked an expectant ear, hoping for another Sanderson-Jinnah tilt to relieve the monotony, but they were disappointed. Instead of taking offence, Sanderson plowed straight ahead.

"No, but a particular powerboat has just been reported beached and abandoned in West Vancouver," said Sanderson with relish. "And it was not more than a kilometre away from Lionel Simons's mansion."

Whatever witticism Jinnah had been preparing died in his throat as his brain instantly absorbed

She Demons 295

the implications of this new information. They were huge, potentially critical for Jassy, Jinnah, and for Graham. But while Jinnah's inherent instincts told him Sanderson's news was accurate, unquestionable, professional pride dictated a display of doubt.

"And how did you happen upon this very minor piece of information, Ronald?" he asked disdainfully. "From a fellow reporter, no doubt? Or while out walking your organic yogourt eating poodle?"

"By doing your cop checks, actually, Hakeem," said Sanderson smugly. "In fact, you and I are the only reporters in the world who know about it at this moment."

Although he was grateful, Jinnah was far from impressed. He instantly guessed how his colleague had unearthed this juicy morsel.

"Oh, ho! And was the file clerk in West Vancouver who called this one in named Parjit, by any chance?"

"I called her first —" protested Sanderson.

"Of course you did, Ronald — she's a very attractive young woman," Jinnah cut in ruthlessly. "A living, breathing Babji Doll."

"Hakeem —"

The deskers were all listening now, many of them quite unabashedly. Odds were being calculated. Money would soon be changing hands....

"Was your interest purely professional, I wonder? What sort of inducements did you have to offer her, hmm?"

"I don't know what you're suggesting, Hakeem."

"Marriage, of course, Ronald. She's a very traditional girl —"

"I promised her a coffee, not a lifetime commitment!"

Jinnah was gratified to see Sanderson's cheeks glowing a fiery red. This was the sign of victory. It was also the signal for Frosty to intervene. "Instead of shooting your mouth off at the messenger, don't you think you'd better follow this lead, Sherlock?"

"What's the rush?" demanded Jinnah, who had been enjoying himself. "The soon to be married Mr. Sanderson assures me we are the only ones who know."

Sanderson coughed rather self-consciously and lowered his head. "Ah, Hakeem, there is a price for this exclusivity."

Accounts that had been about to be settled were suddenly frozen as both Jinnah and Frosty stared at Sanderson, taken aback.

"You're converting for the ceremony?" ventured Jinnah, not at all liking his colleague's tone or demeanor.

"Ah, not as such," said Sanderson. "The truth is, Parjit agreed to keep silent only after I promised her one of your Babji dolls."

Frosty closed her eyes. Oh, God! My cerebral membrane will never stand the temper tantrum we are about to witness. Please, News God, let him be speechless long enough for me to make a hasty exit....

To her amazement, all Frosty heard was silence, then a dry, soft chuckle. She opened her eyes to see Jinnah slowly reaching for one of his jealously guarded inventory.

She Demons 297

"Ronald, Ronald," he said, smiling. "For Parjit, I can do no less. This is for her."

Sanderson's eyes lit up as Jinnah placed the obvious object of desire into his hands. Ronald was still admiring the doll when Jinnah pressed a second one upon him.

"And this is for you, my friend, for all your help," he said softly. "In fact, Ronald, take them all. I'm not meant to be a vendor of rare collectables, hmm?"

"You can't be serious," gasped Sanderson, clutching his two Babji dolls tight to his chest, afraid of being the butt of yet another monstrous Jinnah joke.

"No, I am dead serious," insisted Jinnah. "And don't worry about that sonofabitch supplier. I'll take care of him."

"Hakeem, I can't tell you how truly grateful I am —"

"Then don't — I may change my mind," said Jinnah, already feeling the pangs of regretting his largess.

Jinnah wasn't the only one feeling regrets and pangs. He had just cost a number of deskers large sums, although some debts remained outstanding as accusations that Jinnah had thrown the match intentionally stirred on the far rim.

"Jesus," said Frosty. "News God certainly moves in mysterious ways. Are you sure you feel okay?"

"No," whined Jinnah, taking off his glasses and rubbing his eyes. "I feel dreadful. I am certain I am suffering from post traumatic stress disorder —"

Jinnah was saved from further self diagnosis by

the ring of his phone. He noted the number on the call display with satisfaction as he picked up the receiver.

"You fucking asshole! You lying, cheating, back-stabbing bastard!"

"My, what a witty tongue we have today, Jassy," chuckled Jinnah. "What can I do for you?"

"Besides a front page retraction and your public suicide?"

"Besides that, yes?"

"We need to talk."

Jinnah suppressed the leap of joy that filled his heart. His ploy had worked. Of course, he had known it would, but he muttered a silent prayer of thanks to News God before replying: "Name the place."

"First, no cops. No wires, no GPS tracking devices, zilch. Or you don't see me again. And that means no Andy Gill. Understand?"

"I understand and what's more, I agree," said Jinnah, reaching for a notepad. "And for the record, you also insist positively that I bring no videotaping or digital imaging devices whatever, right?"

"Huh? Well, duh!" said Jassy, momentarily thrown. "Of course."

"Now where do you want me to meet you, hmm?"

Jassy told him, named a time, and Jinnah hung up. He pulled on his jacket and with notepad in hand, made for the door.

"Mind telling me where you're going?" called Frosty.

"To the underworld," he said cryptically.

"Jinnah! Your camera —"

She Demons 299

"Can't, Frosty — condition of the interview. God knows, I tried —"

And with that, he was gone.

"Shocking, really — altogether shocking."

"I quite agree, Reverend. Shocking."

In truth, Jinnah didn't know which was more shocking: Peter Hobbes calling the death of his age-old adversary Simons a tragedy or the look of the Reverend himself. He seemed crushed, deflated — the old fire behind his eyes had gone out as he led Jinnah through the church hall, a modest, sparsely furnished building that looked antiquated compared to the MiMi's outreach centre. Hobbes seemed to be trying to fill the empty, gymnasium-like space with words that came tumbling out of him with little regard to Jinnah's replies.

"Must have been a terrible shock for you, hauling him out of the pool like that."

"To tell you the truth, Reverend, I didn't feel a thing at the time. Running on adrenaline, hmm? It was only afterwards that I started shaking."

"So often the way — so often the way," muttered Hobbes as they descended a flight of narrow, uneven wooden stairs to the basement. "So soon after his conversion."

Jinnah paused on the bottom step as Hobbes stood in front of the door, fumbling with his keys, apologizing for his poor eyesight and poorer memory, like St. Peter having an off day. His fingers ran over the metal tokens

300   *Donald J. Hauka*

like rosary beads and he uttered a little invocation for each — storeroom, sanctuary, main door. His vagueness and his sadness unnerved Jinnah, who wished like hell he'd taken a tranquillizer before coming here. He'd decided against it, knowing he'd have to be at his best during the confrontation that was now just seconds away, but how was he to be at his best with the Reverend Hobbes weirding him out like this, for God's sake? Suddenly, Hobbes turned and glared at Jinnah, a gleam of the old fire flickering in his ecclesiastical eye.

"I am convinced that death took him in a state of grace, Mr. Jinnah," he said. "Lionel Simons is sitting before the throne of God now — just like the thief on the cross."

Jinnah did not know what to say to this. He merely nodded and wondered if Simons's ideas of heaven had been anything like Hobbes's "throne of God" concept. Then he added: "Is that the right key, Reverend?"

Hobbes gave a little start, as if he'd completely forgotten his reason for being here. In a larger sense, this was likely true, Jinnah reflected. For without Lionel Simons to demonize, what was Peter Hobbes to do?

"Now be gentle, Mr. Jinnah," Hobbes said, turning the key in the lock. "The patient is fragile."

"Oh, don't worry, Reverend," Jinnah purred. "I'll be as gentle as a lamb."

Hobbes opened the door and stood aside to allow Jinnah to squeeze past him through the narrow gate.

"Your visitor is here, dear!" he called, then, to Jinnah: "I'll give you two your privacy. Back to my prayers."

She Demons   301

Jinnah stepped inside the room and heard the door click behind him with the finality of a prison cell. His eyes took in the room in an instant — the books, the pictures. Sitting in the middle of it all on the floor in the lotus position, eyes closed, was Jassy Singh, as serene and unmovable as a pagan idol.

"Nice hidey-hole, Jass," said Jinnah, looking for somewhere to sit — somewhere close to the door, just in case.

"I figured this would be the last place they would look," said Jassy calmly without opening her eyes. "Now that I'm their prime suspect. Thanks to you."

"Ah, about that!" said Jinnah, choosing a plain wooden chair for its arm's length proximity to the door and its usefulness as a defensive weapon. "I assume you've read my story?"

Jassy's eyes flashed open, but their angry gleam was almost instantly replaced with a serene look.

"How many times do you need to ruin my so-called life, Jinnah?" she asked softly.

Jinnah knew this was the key moment. His entire attitude would help decide Jassy's next move. He had considered the seductive "full Jinnah" and rejected it as tacky. He had thought about the sickly sweet penitent attitude, throwing herself on her mercy and decided it to too risky. He stuck to what his inherent instincts told him had the best shot — brutal, naked honesty. After all, given Jassy's history, that was the percentage play.

"Jassy, I simply reported what the cops think. They think you killed Lionel Simons. But I don't."

302   *Donald J. Hauka*

Jassy's eyes lost the serene look and widened. She nimbly moved out of the lotus position and knelt, hands on hips.

"Then why —"

"I was gambling that I would make you mad enough to contact me, and it paid off," said Jinnah, riding over her. "It was a cheap trick, but there's a murderer out there to catch. He's already killed Thad Golway and Lionel Simons. Andy Gill may be his next victim. So I need you to tell me where he is. Now."

Despite his outward calm, inwardly Jinnah's intestines were tied in more knots than a Boy Scout jamboree. Gordian wasn't in it. Everything was now riding on Jassy's response. If he'd picked the wrong approach, he could kiss her co-operation (and any chance of seeing Andy Gill alive again) goodbye. For a long moment, Jassy's silent gaze burrowed through Jinnah, burning a hole through what passed for his conscience.

Finally, she spoke. "I buy that. Fits your devious profile."

Jinnah wasn't so relieved that he wasn't vaguely hurt by the phrase "devious profile." But he decided to let it slide for the greater good. "So, are you going to take me to Andy?"

Jassy slowly stood up, arms now wrapped around herself, eyes downcast. Jinnah's instincts quivered. Was he about to get another story, or the straight goods?

"Jinnah, there's a whole other side of the organization that you know nothing about."

"I'll take that as a yes," said Jinnah, realizing that he has just taken his first real breath in some time. "Would

She Demons

303

this side have something to do with the prophets?"

Jassy nodded.

"They're chosen from the best of the devotees. Thad was one. They go through special spiritual and physical training at a place called the Wilderness Camp."

Jinnah's mind was racing, making connections, certain that now he was hearing the truth. He was not so naïve to assume this information wouldn't come at some price, but until it was named, he would get all the pearls he could.

"So Andy was tapped to be a Prophet right away, hmm?" he said. "And just who runs this part of the MiMi empire? Ray Daisley?"

Again, Jassy nodded.

"Lionel never went up there. Left it all to Ray. So, when Thad died and we found all those grow ops ... well, it makes sense, doesn't it?"

Jinnah's turn to nod. "You think the prophets are really drug mules, hauling B.C. bud south of the border and heroin north of it, hmm? That would explain a lot, yes?"

"Yes. But as for Ray killing the Magus...."

Jassy's voice trailed off. Jinnah decided to take a chance. He slowly stood up and left the safety of the chair behind. He took three steps over to Jassy, then knelt in front of her.

"Jassy, some new information has come to light, hmm? Ray's boat was found beached just around the point from the mansion."

Finally, Jassy's eyes grew wide with genuine astonishment and the flame of passion that Jinnah had grown so fond of leapt in them. All pretense of imitating the goddess Kali flew out the window and she was Jassy Singh, the wild pony, throwing her mane as she cried: "That bastard! The murdering bastard!"

Jinnah placed his hands gently on her shoulders. "Yes. There was just enough time for Daisley to beach the boat, run to the mansion, and drown Lionel Simons in his own pool, then escape unseen. He knew where all the security cameras were and he knew how to get out without even Hobbes and his crew spotting him. I was there when Simons fired Daisley on the steps of the mansion, Jassy. With so much drug money at stake, could he afford to let Lionel live?"

Jinnah was almost gratified to see Jassy's lips tremble, her eyes tear up. "But have you told the cops?"

Jinnah shook his head. "Jassy, we have no proof, just a theory. You can give me that proof. Give me Andy Gill. And we can end this."

Jassy turned away, tearing herself from Jinnah's embrace. She stood facing the wall of refugees, hands on her head. "Shit, Jinnah. It's not as simple as all that."

"What could be simpler?" cried Jinnah. "You tell me where this Wilderness Camp is, the cops go in and scoop Andy —"

Jassy whirled around as fast as a jinni and grabbed Jinnah by the collar of his gaudy, polyester shirt. "No cops!" she hissed. "No cops!"

"Why on earth not?" said Jinnah, wondering if her nails would pull the delicate polyester threads.

"Does the name Waco mean anything to you? It's an armed camp. You don't just waltz in there with a warrant

She Demons

and expect them to come out with their hands up."

"So they get a special warrant and go in with an ERT team —"

"Jesus, Jinnah! You think you'll see Andy alive after that?"

"This is a genuine imitation Armani shirt," said Jinnah plaintively. "Would you mind, hmm?"

Jassy took her hands off Hakeem and stepped back, breathing heavily. He had no doubt he was seeing the genuine Jassy Singh now and not some reasonable facsimile of a pagan idol.

"If you want to see Andy alive again, you have to do it my way. Once we get Andy out, you can sic your pal Graham and his dogs on Daisley all you want. But Andy and I have to be outta there and free to walk. Deal?"

Jinnah heard Graham's word echoing in his ears: "The second you find Jassy Singh, you turn her over to me, no questions asked. Understand?" He heard his own agreement. Now, this she-devil wanted him to break faith with his friend and take him into the wilderness where, God knows, she might betray him, all might be lost, and a killer might escape justice. And while logic and loyalty dictated one course of action, Jinnah's own peculiar sense of honour and instinct dictated another. But he wasn't going to through logic blindly to the winds.

"If it's such an armed camp, how are we gonna get Andy outta there, hmm?" he demanded.

Jassy's crooked smile lit up her face. For she too had inherent instincts and she knew she had won.

"I have a plan," she said.

*   *   *

The woods were far from lovely, but they were at least dark and deep. Not to mention damp. Jinnah thanked Allah for their protection and for Jassy insisting he wear a pair of hiking boots, hastily purchased at the Sears in North Vancouver on the way up the Sea to Sky Highway. His imitation Armani shirt was by now totally defiled by moss, lichen, and mud and he wondered if he could expense its replacement to the *Trib*. Surely Whiteman would agree, especially since Jinnah was holding (somewhat unsteadily) in his hand the digital video camera he had been issued, but had never used until now. Jassy had shown him the rudiments of turning it on, how to record and hit the stop button, and how to turn it off. If things didn't get more complicated than that, he would be in great shape. Hakeem pointed the lens jerkily down the tree-clad slope at the Wilderness Camp below them. The great gates swung into focus. They were simply chain-link with a token strand of barbed wire at the top to keep the triflers out. It was hardly designed, Jinnah noted, to keep anyone in.

"You see the layout, okay?"

Jinnah nearly jumped out of his skin. Jassy's voice in his ear was, in his unmedicated opinion, unnecessarily loud.

"Of course I do, for God's sake!" squeaked Jinnah, frantically trying to pan back, go wide, zoom up, or whatever the hell it was he was supposed to do to get a broader view.

She Demons

"River beside the gate. Main road out watched 24/7."

The point was well-taken by Jinnah, who didn't need to zoom in to see the two hulking prophets lounging near the open gateway. They owed their unobserved arrival to Jassy, who had known the secret logging road on the other side of a deep ravine traversed by a rickety rope bridge (the crossing of which had, quite frankly, freaked Jinnah out). Thanks to her, they had made it thus far undetected. The plan called for that to end shortly, however, and Jinnah wanted to make sure he had a record of what transpired, even if (*especially* if) they didn't make it out.

"What you're saying," he repeated slowly, doing his best Caitlin imitation for the microphone. "Is to the left of the main gate is the administration building — that log structure over there. To the right are the barracks, exercise ground, and ... Mother of God, what the hell is that?"

"It's called The Wall," said Jassy. "It's your ticket out, remember that."

"I'm actually trying to forget," muttered Jinnah. "Yes, of course," he said, louder, for the microphone's benefit.

Jassy was silent for a moment, contemplating the gate and what possibilities lay beyond it. It occurred to Jinnah to turn the uneven lens of his camera on her. He got about three seconds of her thoughtful profile before she whirled on him.

"What the hell do you think you're doing?" she demanded.

"Just want to record the moment," said Jinnah, abashed. "Jassy Kaur Singh, how do you feel right now, about to go down and confront the demons of your youth?"

Hakeem's words were awkward. He had heard TV reporters like Caitlin use them a thousand times. But it seemed very out of place here. So did Jassy's smile, for Jinnah had anticipated a scowl.

"The demon of my youth holds the lens that will record a confrontation with the angels of my older years. Which shows how strange it is when the wheel turns. Please, bear witness now, and no more questions. You know what to do?"

Jinnah nodded. "In and out fast — in a blaze of glory."

"Good. See ya."

With that, Jassy stood up and launched herself down the slope of cedar seedlings, grass, and fireweed's fossilized blooms, running red and yellow about her feet like flames as she walked, unafraid, towards the gates of her personal hell. Jinnah's own hell was in trying to follow her movements at all, let alone smoothly, through the viewfinder. He had always considered camera operators a lower form of life, but now was discovering a new respect for shooters like Kevin. Which was small consolation when he lost Jassy entirely just as she neared the gates of the compound. Cursing, he fumbled about, looked up and saw through his smudged glasses that she had already been intercepted, then wildly flung the camera lens back in the right general direction. Inadvertently, he simultaneously hit the

She Demons 309

zoom control and so was quite surprised to see both Arnie and Ray Daisley up close rather roughly escorting their former employee into the compound. Jinnah was impressed at the picture quality. Daisley's face was quite clear and recognizable. Right down to the recent scratch marks on his face....

Jinnah was not so busy congratulating himself on his new-found camera skills that he forgot about the plan. Noting that Jassy had been taken (as predicted) into the administration building, he shut the camera off, placed it in his bag, and set off down the hill muttering the verses of Hafiz in his best Persian. "You have been invited to meet the Friend. No one can resist a divine invitation ..." Oh God, oh God, oh God! His breathing was short and sharp. Not now — no asthma attack now! No time to take his puffer out, no time to pop a soothing tranquillizer. He must do this with his own strength and in his right mind. God, what if they have simply executed Jassy out of hand? What if Andy is already dead? What if I am caught? My God these hiking boots are the ugliest, most unfashionable footwear I have ever worn....

With a start, Jinnah realized his self-absorbed anxiety had carried him all the way to the now unguarded gate. Jassy had drawn everyone to her and, as she had known, the rest of the disciples and prophets were busy with spiritual practice in their barracks at this time. Scarcely believing his good fortune, Jinnah made his way to the third weather-beaten log structure at the rear of the yard. With a trembling hand, he tried the door. Unlocked. He pushed it open silently.

310

Donald J. Hauka

A long, dark corridor greeted him. Well, at least there was no light at the end to walk towards like in those near-death experiences — Jinnah took this as an excellent sign and crept as quietly and quickly down the dark passageway as he could. He was certain that the ragged gasps escaping his lungs and the pounding of his heart must be audible in the administration building (or in downtown Squamish, for that matter) and his pulsing veins and sweating pores were making far too much noise for his liking, but somehow he made it to the doorway at the far end undetected. Now for one of the most dangerous phases of the operation, for there was no telling what was behind the door of the "Punishment Room." Jassy was almost certain that Andy would be in there, having been segregated from his peers to reflect upon his weaknesses, but there was also the chance that one of the prophets was in there with him as a "spiritual advisor." Jinnah had vacillated between conning the guardian and simply kicking him in the balls until Jassy had pointed out the Prophet could just as easily be a woman ("Not in the books I've read!" he'd growled). It was now up to Providence. With a final strangled, rasping prayer, he opened the door and slipped inside.

It was the eyes that immediately caught his attention. Large, brown, they might have belonged to some nocturnal creature, blinking uncomprehendingly at the intruder in its space. From this central point, Jinnah's mind took in the rest of the details in a second in concentric rings of consciousness. First, Andy Gill's startled face (instantly recognizable from the photos,

She Demons

mouth already forming a perfect "O" as the first of his many questions prepared to give voice), then the rest of his lanky, muscular form kneeling in the centre of the room. The cell was devoid of other occupants and fairly nondescript: bed to one side, table and chair to the other. The most important item that registered with Jinnah was that the wastepaper basket in the corner was made (God be praised) of metal.

"Andy, I'm a friend of Jassy's," he hissed, running right over Andy's half born "Who … ?" and crouching down beside the boy. "We've come to get you out of here."

Andy, still bewildered, allowed Jinnah to help him to his feet. "How do you —"

"I'm a reporter," said Jinnah, anticipating Andy's next question. "I met Jassy a long time ago when she first joined the MiMis. Now let's get going."

Jinnah moved over to the wastepaper basket. Finding it distressingly empty, he hauled a sheaf of notepaper from his coat pocket and tossed it in. Then he brought out a silver hip flask.

"Uh, isn't it a bit early for a drink, even for a reporter?"

Jinnah didn't know whether or not to be glad that Andy's mental acuity had returned or insulted at the suggestion that he would need a shot at such an hour of the day. There was no time for either sentiment.

"This is firewater of a different sort," he said, sprinkling the contents of the flask onto the papers. Instantly, the unmistakable smell of gasoline filled the tiny room. Andy's eyes grew even wider — something

312 *Donald J. Hauka*

Jinnah had thought scarcely possible — as he pocketed the flask and pulled out his lighter.

"What are you doing?" he squeaked.

"We're going out in a blaze of glory, my friend," said Jinnah with a confidence he did not feel. "I do hope you can run for your life, hmm?"

So saying, Jinnah lit a small taper, took a judicious step back, and set the contents of the wastepaper basket alight. The explosion of flame and smoke was most gratifying and as he hustled Andy out of the room, Jinnah noted with satisfaction that the flames were already starting to devour the flimsy table and licking greedily up towards the drapes. The stench of an accelerant-aided fire moved ahead of them down the corridor and by the time they were out of the barracks door, the compound was stirring like a vast hive.

"This way," gasped Jinnah, grabbing Andy's arm and hauling him behind the barracks, out of view of the main compound.

The fire had already been noticed, was already drawing attention. They ran, half crouched, along the line of barracks, then past the administration building, moving further and further away from the locus of attention. Their progress reminded Jinnah of one of those Second World War POW camp escape movies. But they weren't dealing with Nazis, just MiMis, and so far the cult's response was not in the grand, Teutonic tradition. Coming around the far side, Jinnah cautiously stuck his head around the corner. As he and Jassy had hoped, everyone was occupied. There was no one at the front gate. All they had to do was sprint to

She Demons 313

it, open it up, and race up the hill for the first phase of the operation to be a complete success.

"Come on then," said Jinnah. "We go out the front door."

"Where's Jassy?" demanded Andy.

"She'll hook up with us later. Let's go!"

Jinnah led the way, no crouching now. He ran as fast as his nicotine-deprived, smoke-ravaged lungs would allow, Andy right behind him, to the metal gate that spelled freedom. He threw his weight on the iron bars and immediately regretted it. The bars remained fixed rigidly in place while his ribs bounced and bruised on impact. He bounded off with a painful gasp. Recovering, he pushed with all his might. No give.

"Gates are locked," said Andy. "Routine emergency procedure."

"Sonofabitch!" spat Jinnah, massaging his aching ribcage. "Now what?"

"I know a back door," said Andy. "Follow me."

Jinnah, who knew all too well that the back door was, would rather have been placed on a spit and roasted slowly than face the agony that awaited him, but Andy didn't hang around to be argued with. He headed to the outdoor school section of the compound, where a spur of the Coast Mountain peak that towered over them formed The Wall. Their ticket to freedom — if they lived. He paused at the base of the sheer rock face.

"Come on! I'll show you the easy path!" cried Andy.

"Is there an elevator or perhaps a handicap access of some kind?" asked Jinnah hopefully.

314   *Donald J. Hauka*

Andy was scaling the obstacle as nimbly as a mountain goat. Jinnah was in danger of being left behind, which would likely be fatal.

Daisley and Arnie had arrived at the scene of the fire, where prophets and disciples were busily employing the camp's rudimentary firefighting equipment to good effect. Arnie was shouting orders and giving directions, but Daisley was looking around the compound. Jinnah's inherent instincts told him that Ray smelled a rat and that Hakeem had better get his whiskers up The Wall, fast. Andy was already halfway up. Jinnah followed. Hafiz's verses filled his head, calming the gnawing fear in his stomach.

"We can come to God dressed for dancing or be carried on a stretcher to God's ward," he muttered, launching himself upwards.

Less than five feet up it seemed like he was headed for the stretcher when he lost his footing and, with a squawk, hung suspended between heaven and earth, panting, hot, and bruised, and contemplated giving up. At that moment, Jinnah glanced behind him and saw Daisley turn his gaze upon The Wall. Their eyes locked. Ray shouted something. Arnie whirled around, took in the situation at a glance, and sprinted his oversized muscles straight towards Jinnah.

That was all the motivation Jinnah needed to overcome his twin terrors of heights and physical exercise. His booted feet scrambled for a foothold and found one while his hands groped The Wall above for something to carry him up.

"Go left! That's the beginner's route!"

She Demons 315

Andy's shout came from well above Jinnah's head and, glancing up, Hakeem saw that the boy he was supposed to be rescuing was almost at the top. Frantically, he fumbled and clawed his way up and to the left, gaining height slowly, slowly, like some great, awkward bird. Nearly ten feet up....

"Gotcha you bastard!"

Jinnah's bowels had already dissolved into a gelatinous mass by the time Arnie's hand, extended to its full range by a mighty leap against The Wall, brushed against the bottom of his boot. They very nearly exited his body at the contact and he redoubled his efforts, fairly flying up the cliff face like a full-fledged prophet. Below him, Arnie's failed leap had caused him to miss his footing and he went down in a heap at the base of The Wall.

"Catch them!" screamed Daisley, coming up from behind. "Don't let them get away!"

Jinnah was so busy looking down that he didn't notice he'd actually made it to the top, which was a shame, for as his hand groped blindly for the next hold it found nothing but air. Overbalanced, he lurched forward then toppled backwards. The sensation was sickening, especially since the movement brought him perilously close to Arnie, who was scaling The Wall like a chamois. Just as it seemed he would fall to the ground, Jinnah felt a hand on his collar, checking his drop. With a single heave, Andy hauled him halfway up the ledge of the precipice. Jinnah managed to wriggle and flail his way over the top just as Arnie stuck his head above the uneven, rocky event horizon.

"Gill —"

Arnie's command was cut short by a muffled cry of pain as Andy gave him a vicious kick to the face. The muscular mountain man tumbled backwards, glancing off The Wall before landing on top of a startled Daisley, who was too slow to dodge in time. The two men formed a bruised, bloodied, thrashing heap, surrounded by a stunned and silent semicircle of MiMis.

"Don't just stand there! Go on! Get those two!" shouted Daisley, rising painfully to his feet.

The prophets and the disciples set off in pursuit and, after a moment, Arnie joined them. And even though the younger MiMis had had a pretty good head start, he soon outstripped them, bent as he was on being the first to get his hands on Andy Gill. And Hakeem Jinnah....

In the forest beyond The Wall, Andy and Jinnah were making the best of their lead. Adrenaline and the thought of a vengeful Arnie catching up with them did much to compensate for Jinnah's utter lack of conditioning. That and not wanting to look like a complete loser in front of Andy.

For his part, Andy used his thorough knowledge of the terrain to good effect as they raced through the trees. "Where we headed?" he asked, glancing back at Jinnah, barely even breathing heavily.

If only his father could see him now, thought Jinnah fleetingly.

"Rope ... rope bridge. Ravine!" panted Jinnah.

"This way, then!"

Andy veered sharply to the left. Out of the tangle of blackberry bushes, Oregon grape, and other

She Demons

317

undergrowth, a narrow path down a steep slope miraculously appeared. To Jinnah, this seemed a divine sign that they should stop for a minute so he could catch his breath or, even better, smoke a quick cigarette, but the sound of pursuit not far behind spurred him on. Coming around a curve, he stumbled and nearly sprawled, but Andy caught him.

"Sonofabitch!"

Jinnah was staring out over a deep ravine. Its slopes were clad in a carpet of green salal bushes and a swift, rocky stream ran far, far below them. With the golden sunshine filtered through the canopy of cedar and Douglas fir, it was an almost mystical sight. To Jinnah, it was a vision of paradise, for across the gorge there was a slender rope bridge — the same one he had crossed with Jassy's help not an hour earlier, but not with such urgent haste.

Andy gave Jinnah a look. "Across here?"

It was not so much a question of direction as it was an expression of incredulity. If he hadn't been so exhausted, terrified, and nicotine deprived, Jinnah might have been offended. As it was, he barely had the strength to nod and wave Andy on. But the boy stayed quite close to him this time, never more than a metre or so ahead as they swayed wildly back and forth on the rickety structure — which was just as well since Hakeem lost his footing several times in his haste. They reached the other side with a final, desperate lunge on Jinnah's part and he lay there for a moment, gasping like a fish, eyes closed, trying to judge how far away Arnie's bone-crushing biceps were.

318   *Donald J. Hauka*

Andy's voice, calm and assured, recalled him to life. "Still got that lighter?"

Now Jinnah really was offended. If there was one piece of equipment he guarded with his life, it was his lighter. He fumbled in his jacket pockets and, with trembling fingers, managed to pass the object to Andy without dropping it.

"Come on! Burn, baby, burn!"

Jinnah shifted himself to a sitting position and watched, gasping, as Andy applied the lighter's considerable flame to the slender hemp rope holding the bridge in place. From the thrashing and shouting on the far side of the ravine, it was going to be a near thing. Blue, pungent smoke rose snakelike into the air. A strand snapped. Then another.

"Almost home free!" Jinnah croaked.

They heard the metallic click before the voice behind them froze both their blood and their movements. The hairs on the back of Jinnah's neck were almost too tired to stand up on end.

"Put the lighter down and step away from the bridge, please, Mr. Gill. Jinnah, just stay as you are."

The voice was familiar, but lacked a certain warmth and persuasiveness that Jinnah remembered from times that had been, comparatively speaking, happier. He did risk turning his head around to confirm his suspicions, even as Andy let the lighter, now extinguished, drop. He was rewarded by the sight of Mary Demolay in full combat fatigues, carrying what Jinnah's training told him was an assault rifle. She was surrounded by Kali and several other goons. Very deferential goons. And

She Demons   319

suddenly, Jinnah knew for certain, although almost certainly too late, that Mary Demolay was far from just a legal mouthpiece for the Yakshas. She was their chief she-demon.

"Come on. It's safe to come over!"

From his position, lying flat on his belly, head down on the damp, musty forest floor by the edge of the ravine, Jinnah did not have the best view of events as they unfolded and, with a Yaksha goon standing over him with a gun pointed squarely into his suddenly sweat-drenched back, he did not have much inclination to try to improve his sightlines. But he dared to twist his neck very slightly, bringing his left eye above the leaves, moss, and loam, giving him a somewhat lopsided angle that was sufficient to see Daisley and Arnie scramble across the creaking, swaying bridge. Beside him, Andy too was prone, face down, as rigid as a board. He didn't move a muscle — not even when a distinct snap brought Jinnah's head involuntarily up.

"Stay still."

The Yakshas goon's voice was perfectly calm and perfectly quiet, but then, he had his gun to use as an exclamation point and the very slight pressure of its muzzle on the back of Jinnah's head was enough to prompt Hakeem to bury his face in the good earth. But his swift glance had revealed that not all was well with Arnie and Daisley's passage across the damaged rope span and that the fibres were snapping under their weight. Jinnah willed the remaining strands to snap, sending the MiMi pair hurtling into the abyss below, and his mental exertions were almost answered. Just as Arnie was reaching the other side, a loud popping noise and a fusillade of startled exclamations told him that the bridge had finally given way. It had lasted just long enough, unfortunately. Daisley was saved from a nasty fall by Demolay, who grabbed his arm and hauled him to safety even as it seemed certain he wouldn't make it. Ray was bent over, panting and shaking. Arnie went over to Andy and gave the teen a vicious kick in the ribs. Andy gave a slight grunt, but otherwise remained still. Jinnah had to check himself and follow Andy's example, although every particle of his being wanted to reach out and slug the overly muscled MiMi mountain man.

"Enough!" snapped Demolay. "Plenty of time for that later."

"I thought ... I thought," Daisley panted. "We were gonna meet ... at the school."

"Oh, we're going back to the Wilderness School, Ray. But I don't think we need a meeting, as such. Do you?"

Even though he could see nothing but forest floor, Jinnah could imagine the look of puzzlement on Daisley's face and the cold, evil smile on Demolay's lips. The Yakshas chief demon's tone was enough to send shivers down Hakeem's spine without the benefit of any visual information. Holy shit! She's not going to —

"We have a deal, Mary —"

"Deal's off, Ray. Just too messy. Too complicated."

"Too much money, you mean."

She Demons 321

"That too."

"You lying bitch —"

"Ah, ah, ah, Ray. It's a woman's prerogative to change her mind. Tie them up."

"Simpler to off them here. Good disposal. Just need their heads."

Jinnah's congenital cowardice instantly reasserted itself as he recognized the voice of his good friend, Quickset Kali. Fantastic. What a way for his career to end. Poster boy for a crime cartel — worse, he'd be head of advertising, so to speak. The thought that Arnie and Daisley would be going head to head with him was little comfort. He was in the hands of a demented she-demon, on her forested turf, helpless. He and Andy needed a miracle to get out of this one. And there was no promise of deliverance in Demolay's next words.

"No head taking. We stick to the plan."

"Oh? You have a plan?" said Daisley ironically.

"Of course, Ray. It involves the MiMis, distraught over the death of your leader, taking a page out of the Solar Temple cult's scriptures and checking out in spectacular fashion. Now march."

Chapter Nine

The collapse of the rope bridge forced them to hike the long way around. Arnie and Daisley had their hands tied behind their backs, but Jinnah and Andy were unbound. Obviously, Demolay didn't consider them threatening. Fighting his spine's proclivity to dissolve into jelly and his conviction that he was going to die of an aneurysm before he could be murdered, Hakeem tried desperately to think, to find some way out of this one. At the very least, he hoped he would not die in ignorance. Demolay was right in front of him as they stumbled along the narrow, winding path through the dense woods. Behind him was Quickset.

If I dare to ask a question, the bastard will probably shoot me, Jinnah thought. What the hell? He's going to shoot me sooner or later. At least this way he'll have the trouble of carrying my lifeless, bullet-riddled body out of the bush. It also occurred to Jinnah that

She Demons 323

his camera might still be recording in his bag. The visuals would stink, but the audio might be pure gold....

"There is still one thing that puzzles me, Mary," he croaked, expecting at each syllable to feel Kali's bullets bursting into his back.

Demolay turned her head, amused smile on her face. "Just one, Jinnah? You're cleverer than I thought."

Jinnah's back muscles stopped convulsing slightly. Ah! The she-demon was in a generous mood. Eager to show how smart she was. And Kali hadn't shot him — yet. He swallowed dryly and, ignoring Demolay's insult, persisted.

"Well, a couple of things, then. Why did you manipulate me into goading Graham to raid the mansion? And just why did Thad Golway have to die?"

"You just hate a mystery, don't you, Jinnah? Can't stand the idea of going to your grave without knowing all the facts for a story you'll never write."

Oh shit. Don't clam up now. Say something to keep her talking, Hakeem. "Death is the final mystery, Mary. The only one that matters, hmm? You're the mistress of life and death right now. Just as you were when Thad was murdered. You didn't actually wield the knife, but it was your decision, wasn't it? As head she-demon?"

"You're right — I am the mistress of life and death, just like Shiva. And like the god, I don't make these decisions on a whim. I never have a life taken without a larger purpose, Jinnah — a higher cause. In this case, Thad's death was the keystone in pulling down the MiMis."

324 *Donald J. Hauka*

"Okay, now I really don't understand," said Jinnah, masking the insincerity in his voice.

"Think about it. Thad's friends ran off with a crucial shipment we'd been counting on. We couldn't find them, so we killed Thad. But his death also sowed fear and distrust throughout Simons's cult. I let that fear do the rest of the work."

"But the mansion raid," Jinnah insisted. "What was the use of that? The cops never found anything!"

"I knew the police wouldn't find anything!" laughed Demolay. "They didn't have to. The raid was to break the final bonds between Daisley and Simons. When Lionel so helpfully fired Daisley, Ray snapped and killed him, leaving the entire organization open to a friendly takeover."

"Friendly? What's your idea of a hostile takeover?"

"You don't want to know."

Jinnah had, despite everything, quite forgotten that he was on a death march through the woods, the helpless captive of a murderous gang of forest demons. His sense of justice and morality had been offended. He could not keep the note of exasperation out of his voice. "What about all that legal crap you gave me at the border, hmm? And threatening to sue me for libel? 'Oh, we've never been convicted of any criminal offence!' The biggest load of bullshit I've ever heard —"

A very slight pressure in his back from the muzzle of Kali's gun stopped Jinnah in full rant and he remembered his situation.

"You know the game, Jinnah," said Demolay. "The public face and the private face. You were right

She Demons 325

about us all along. But you have helped us to expand north of the border into B.C. Don't be too sad — you destroyed Lionel Simons's cult in the process. You'd always dreamed of doing that hadn't you?"

Jinnah was tempted to reply, but with the memory of Kali's gun barrel still burning in his back, he kept mum. She was right, though. He *had* always dreamed of being the reporter who brought down the Rave Messiah. Demolay had known that. Counted on it. Manipulated him by dangling various visions of paradise before his eyes. The same way she had manipulated Daisley and all the others. Sonofabitch....

"Listen, last question," Jinnah gasped as they climbed a particularly steep slope. "Who actually killed Thad Golway? My friend Quickset here?"

"Kali?" Demolay laughed. "God, no! He'd never lower himself by killing a lowly drug mule. I save him for very important jobs. No, Jinnah, for that one, I contracted out to our northern partner."

"You mean Daisley?"

"Of course."

The final piece of the mystery clicked neatly into place. The face on Thad's murderer in Jinnah's vision was no longer shadowy and indistinct. It had come quite clearly into focus. Jinnah could see Daisley bundling Thad into his car after the argument with Simons. How had the smaller Ray handled the superbly conditioned youth he'd trained? Based on the toxicology, he probably managed to somehow give his victim a dose of heroin big enough to ensure a coma. The rest — killing, beheading, carving — would have been easy after that.

Setting the corpse under the tree would have required a bit of heavy lifting, true, but it was just possible that Arnie had helped. Jinnah had hoped as recently as an hour ago that something like this would all come out at a first-degree murder trial. Now it appeared that Daisley and Arnie were about to learn the true meaning of that old biblical saw, "an eye for an eye." Which wouldn't have bothered Jinnah so much if he and Andy weren't the "tooth for a tooth" part of the equation. He thought frantically for a way out, but he thought it was highly unlikely that he and Andy would be excused from the mass slaughter on religious grounds.

"Okay, hold up."

They had reached the head of the trail and through the thinning brush, Jinnah glimpsed the Wilderness Camp. Demolay, her goons, and prisoners were still in the cover of the trees. Kali came up behind his boss.

"You sure about this?"

Demolay gave Quickset an "oh, please!" look.

"Kali, you already scoped it out and told me the only MiMis in there are blissed-out prophets too busy stuffing themselves with brownies to keep a proper watch, and a few trainees who are scared of their own shadows. We have the only two real threats tied up and covered."

"Yeah, but —"

"Are you saying that you and the boys and your assault rifles can't take on a handful of unarmed stoners?" Demolay's tone was fretted with pink slip overtones.

Quickset took about a millisecond to figure out what sort of severance package he could expect and,

She Demons 327

being fond of his cranial and facial features, attempted a nonchalant shrug. "Okay, just thought I'd save you the trouble. Faking these cult mass suicides is a lot of disgusting grunt work, y'know."

"I'm sure you're up to it. Now move."

"Okay. Hostage shield formation."

Kali roughly herded everyone into position. Daisley, Arnie, Andy, and Jinnah were forced to form a line in front. Behind each was a Yaksha, pushing the muzzles of their firearms into the back of their hostage's head with varying degrees of pressure. Demolay had Ray, Kali had Arnie, and Jinnah and Andy each had a beefy Yaksha goon to themselves. Deadly dance partners, thought Jinnah. That would have been a great turn of phrase in his story.

"Move out!"

Jinnah stumbled forward on gelatinous knees and realized he was gasping for breath. Sonofabitch! What a stupid goddamn way to go....

"Listen, Mary," he panted, trying not to whine. "Have you thought this thing through, hmm?"

"Oh yes, Jinnah — very thoroughly. Right down to the part where Ray here gives the assembled MiMis a last, stirring address about the need for them to make the ultimate sacrifice in memory of their Magus —"

"The hell I will!"

"You will, Ray. Co-operate and I give you the gift of a swift and painless death. Fuck with me and I'll have Kali here carve your face while you're still alive. We call it a 'Living Marble' job."

"You sick bitch!"

328   *Donald J. Hauka*

"You sick bastard. Was Thad dead before you sliced him?"

Daisley shut his mouth. This wasn't the sort of response Jinnah had been hoping for so he tried to reassert some control over the conversation. "Listen, my friend. You will never get away with it, hmm? The cops will see through this hoax eventually and then —"

"By then we'll be so well-established up here they won't be able to do anything about it," laughed Demolay. "Besides, how hard do you really think they'll try to find out who dunnit? From a police perspective, we're just doing their job for them — and a damn sight more effectively than the courts."

The small portion of Jinnah's logical brain that was still functioning had to admit that Demolay was probably right. The larger portion of his brain devoted to panic was urging his faltering powers of persuasion to do something, anything! The gates of the camp loomed before them like the jaws of hell, a plume of smoke from the still-smouldering barracks above them. Jinnah could foresee the whole thing, the entire lethal scenario played out before him. The entry into the camp. The rounding up of the disciples and prophets. They'd be lined up for execution. A ludicrous image of the MiMis in neat rows, all in the lotus position, flashed through his mind.

God, what had Hafiz to say about this? From somewhere out of the depths, a verse popped to the surface of his thought. "I am a tethered falcon, with great wings and sharp talons poised, every sinew taut,

She Demons 329

like a sacred bow, though held in check by a miraculous, divine golden cord."

"What's that, Jinnah?"

Holy shit! Jinnah realized he must have spoken the lines aloud. He didn't much feel like a falcon and the only talons he possessed were words. So far, they had done precious little good. But he made one last attempt. At least he could try to save Andy. He owed Sandhu and Mr. Puri that much.

"Look, I can see why you want Daisley and Arnie out of the picture, but why do innocent kids have to die? The disciples and prophets are no threat to you."

"A cadre of super-fit mountaineers who know all our drop points and secret trails not a threat? Come on, Jinnah —"

"For God's sake, Mary —"

They were at the gates now. Mary motioned for them to stop. She turned to Jinnah.

"Well now, Hakeem, tell you what. There's no particular need for you to join in the festivities. I can always use a good P.R. man in the media. Someone to give the organization the benefit of the doubt."

"Be your media mouthpiece? You're kidding!"

Jinnah regretted the words the second they came out of his mouth, but it was too late. Demolay shrugged. "Suit yourself, Hakeem. At least you'll get the front page one last time."

Shit, shit, shit! He should have at least pretended to entertain the idea, if only to buy some time for Andy, for himself. They were entering the gate now in a V-formation (eerily like Caitlin's flying wedge),

330   *Donald J. Hauka*

Daisley and Arnie on the left, Jinnah and Andy on the right with their captors behind them. Some part of Jinnah's consciousness registered the fact that the gate was completely unguarded and that, far from alarms being sounded, loud music was being played. Dance music that Kali had to shout over as they moved briskly towards the middle of the compound.

"All right, you fucking stoners! Drop the reefers and pizza and put your hands up, like, right now, dudes!"

Jinnah had been clinging to the faint hope that some of the prophets who had followed Daisley and Arnie into the woods had seen what had happened and returned to the camp to warn their fellow MiMis and prepare an ambush. The evidence suggested they'd taken one look and fled into the mountains. For Hakeem was crushed to see that Kali's assessment of the cult's elite outdoor couriers had been all too accurate. As far as he could tell, the entire camp was gathered near The Wall, eating, dancing, playing hacky sack, and lighting up. Activities that had come to a stumbling and confused halt as the MiMis realized this wasn't some weird drug-induced vision or whack practical joke.

One of the prophets (who, to Jinnah's eyes, looked like a poster boy for the Hemp Shop with his tie-dye T-shirt, goatee, and ripped khaki shorts) stepped forward, a piece of pizza still in his hand. "What the fuck, man —"

"Cool it, Joel!" hissed a disciple.

Kali shoved Arnie forward and raised his assault rifle so that even the most bleary-eyed MiMi could see the gun barrel at their Wilderness Master's head.

She Demons 331

"I said hands up or I blow your sensei's brains out. Comprende?"

Joel raised his hands slowly over his head, still clutching his piece of pizza. The other MiMis followed suit and Kali grunted, a thin smile playing on his face.

"Now close up! Form a circle. Now!"

As the confused cultists shuffled into a ragged circle, Demolay elbowed the Yaksha goon guarding Andy.

"Take Mr. Popularity here and deal with the phone in the admin building. Fast."

The goon nudged Andy with his gun and they moved off at a brisk trot towards the log building that held the camp's office. The only lifeline out was the single phone line on Ray's desk. No cell service, no Internet in this remote region. You'd need a satellite phone to call for help, but Jinnah knew there wasn't one in the camp. In a minute they'd be beyond all aid, unless something miraculous happened.

"Okay, Ray. Time for you to round up any stragglers."

"For Christ's sake, Mary!"

Demolay reached out and gently caressed Daisley's cheek. Ray squirmed as if her fingers were red hot branding irons.

"Deal's a deal, Ray. Unless you want Kali to start cutting right now."

To Jinnah's eyes, Daisley had that crushed, whipped look of a man who could not believe he'd fallen off fortune's wheel so fast. His head drooped as the second Yaksha goon marched him at gunpoint past the MiMis who just minutes before had obeyed his every

332   *Donald J. Hauka*

command, held him in esteem second only to the Magus
— and maybe Arnie. Now they watched, mute, unmoving, as their fallen hero slunk past. Wasn't anyone going
to show some spine? Didn't these bastards know what
was going to happen? Or had prolonged exposure to
B.C. bud fried their brains irreparably?

Demolay's voice in his ear jarred him from his
recriminatory ruminations. "Okay, people! I want
everyone to sit down. Nice and slow."

Jinnah realized with a start that Demolay was
now right behind him, taking the place of the gunman who'd led Ray away. Hakeem watched as the
MiMis followed orders, sinking slowly to the ground
almost in unison near the base of The Wall, like a
grotesque ballet. This could not be happening! There
must be something he could do! But with Demolay's
gun in his back, what? Even if he martyred himself by
turning on the she-devil, he doubted if any of these
blissed-out bastards would take the opportunity to
attack the Yakshas. Especially with Quickset glaring
at them. Hell, even Arnie was simply standing there,
slumped, unmoving. If only Andy was here, Jinnah
might just try it. But Andy was in the admin building, probably yanking the one phone line out of the
wall at gun point. He'd be back in a few seconds. In
a minute or two, Daisley and his goon guard would
be returning with any stragglers in tow and the real
fun would begin. Depending on how long a speech
Demolay had written for Daisley (and Jinnah suspected it was closer to the Gettysburg Address than
War and Peace), he figured he had about five minutes

She Demons 333

to live. Depending on whom Demolay wanted dead first....

"All clear, boss."

Jinnah saw Daisley and his keeper come around the corner from the still-smoldering barracks that had so recently held Andy. That meant everyone in the camp was trapped and there was no hope — none at all.

"Okay. Just about showtime, Ray. Hope you're in fine voice."

"Fuck you, Mary."

"Perhaps in a future incarnation, Ray. Jesus, where is that asshole?"

"Still in the admin office," said Kali, uneasy. "Want I should check it out?"

"No. Take care of Daisley while Stan goes."

Daisley's guard gave his charge a quite unnecessary shove with his rifle and Kali welcomed him with a cuff as he staggered towards him. It wasn't much of a distraction, but Arnie made the most of it, launching himself headfirst into Stan's belly, laying the goon out flat, then whirling about with a roundhouse kick that Kali took in the head and crumpled. Arnie might have taken out Demolay as well, but while Jinnah instinctively dropped to the ground to get out of the way, Daisley didn't. Demolay grabbed Ray by his collar and threw him in Arnie's direction. The Wilderness Master's leaping kick felled his own boss and Ray went down, gasping. The interval gave Demolay enough time to adroitly turn her rifle around and swing it like a club across the side of Arnie's head. He fell like the proverbial ton of bricks and landed on top of Jinnah, who was winded by the impact. Demolay stood open and exposed, with no hostage and no back up. Now, Jinnah prayed. Now! Find your spines! But the MiMis did not spontaneously rise up and Demolay regained control of the situation in an instant. Brandishing her rifle at the dumbfounded cultists, she fired a burst over their heads.

"Don't even think it!" she cried.

That seemed a bit redundant to Jinnah's mind, for even under the oppressive weight of Arnie's huge form, he could see that a steady diet of B.C. bud had definitely slowed their reaction time. The pizza-munching prophet Joel had barely managed to come to an upright position before it was too late. As for the rest of them, they sat there, stunned. Jinnah closed his eyes. Arnie had fired his shot in the hole and failed. The rest would soon be silence....

"Kali! Get up. Where the hell is that asshole? Turn that fucking music off!"

Joel dutifully turned off the ghetto blaster and Jinnah's ears stopped bleeding. For the first time, Demolay sounded slightly unnerved. Kali struggled up to his knees and recovered his firearm. Stan was already up, his breath coming in short gasps.

"Get your ass over to the admin building! Stat!"

Stan grimaced and started for the building to the left.

Demolay described an arc with her assault rifle. "If one of you so much as farts, you're dead. Understand?"

"Oh, we understand where you're coming from, bitch queen."

This simple sentence from Joel the Pizza Prophet prompted Jinnah to open his eyes in amazement and

She Demons 335

shift Arnie's oppressive bulk off his person. Things happened so fast after that Jinnah had a hard time following them. Before Demolay could react, there was a shriek from the direction of the admin building. At first, Hakeem assumed Andy was being tormented back into place by his captor with the help of the other Yaksha goon. But a quick glance showed that Stan had not made ten feet towards the log structure before stopping in his tracks. Issuing from it was the other Yaksha guard. At least, Jinnah assumed it was him, for the figure that ran and staggered towards them in erratic semicircles was completely naked and raving mad.

"The apocalypse! Brown curtains! Demons, demons!" he shrieked.

Stan started towards his stricken companion even as Kali dove for his AK-47. At that precise moment, a movement to Jinnah's right caught his eye. Forms were flying down from the top of The Wall. Demolay and Kali fired at them even as Hakeem became aware of an unearthly, animal-like screaming. Then there was a bursting sound and a white cloud enveloped them, raining down from the now-sagging forms suspended from the ropes. The MiMis had flattened themselves out of harm's way, lost in the clouds.

Before the swirling cloud cut off his vision, Jinnah's instincts told him to look back towards the admin building. In a flash, he saw the two running forms of the Yaksha goons go down, stricken, it appeared, by long, brown cobras. They proved to be dirty, worn climbing ropes, whipped with ferocious energy at neck height, but to Jinnah, they were miraculous, divine golden cords. Figures were now running through the compound as Demolay and Kali choked in the white haze. Pizza Prophet piled into Kali as he clawed at his eyes and hacked out his lungs. By now Jinnah was on his hands and knees, groping about in the cloud, barely able to breath, but somehow cognizant of the dozen prophets swinging down from The Wall into the compound, trussing up the fallen goons and racing toward the centre of the circle of darkness where he crouched at the feet of Demolay. His mind was too numb to take it all in, his eyes stinging and blinking back tears, but something in his inherent instincts told him he was close to rescue — agonizingly close. If only someone could disarm Demolay....

Too late. Before Jinnah could crawl to safety, he felt the foot of the chief she-demon on his back, followed by the now all too familiar sensation of her gun muzzle at the back of his head. He was sent sprawling on his belly and he heard Mary's voice carry above the confused sounds of the struggle. "Freeze! One move and the reporter dies!"

Even given his circumstances, Jinnah could not help but think that Demolay had uttered a death sentence for them both. He could not imagine this crowd shouting anything but "Make our day, Mary!" It was no threat at all. God, if in your infinite compassion you can get me through this — send me a ministering angel —

Jinnah's prayers were answered not so much by a sacred bow as a sickening blow to the back of Demolay's head. The she-demon pitched face forward, firearm flying, and once again Hakeem felt a hefty human form

She Demons 337

landing on his back. He had just enough time to idly wonder if he would live to need a chiropractor before, through the haze of choking white dust, backlit by the sun, a female figure loomed over him, assault rifle in hand. To Jinnah, it was an angelic vision. She seemed more beautiful than any woman he had ever seen — save Manjit. The vision even spoke unto him just before he passed out. "The police are on their way, Mr. Jinnah," said Jassy Kaur Singh proudly.

"All right, Bains! Get them in the wagon. And tell that chopper pilot to shut his goddamn engines off, like, yesterday or I'll have his licence. Ms. Bishop, will you please tell your cameraman to back off or I'll have his balls for breakfast."

The old Caitlin Bishop would have taken offence at this, since both blasts were aimed directly at her. It was her helicopter (or at least, the station's) that had its rotors slowly whirling in anticipation of whisking her off to Pemberton, where they could do a live satellite hit to complement the rather spectacular footage Kevin had shot, including the close-ups he was getting at this moment of Daisley, Arnie, Demolay, and her Yakshas crew — all wearing cuffs — being bundled into a police van. The new Caitlin Bishop merely smiled and thought how good Graham looked with the wind in his hair, directing operations at the centre of the hive of activity that was the crime scene. He looked years younger, in fact. But then, solving two murders and crushing two drug cartels in the same afternoon would be enough to make any law enforcement officer's day.

"Okay, Kev — we have enough!"

Kevin whirled around belligerently, but a look from Caitlin was enough for him to put his camera down and pretend to check his levels. Satisfied, Graham gave Caitlin a thumbs-up.

"Sergeant? A moment of your time? Off camera?"

Graham had better things to do right now than to have an off the record chat with the prima donna pit bull who had made his life misery. But since she was the only TV reporter at the scene — the only reporter period, save for Jinnah — he decided a little media management might be in order. He nodded and motioned to the side of the smoking barracks. Around them, officers swarmed, taking soil samples, casting footprints, snapping photos, and videotaping everything. They were about as alone as they were going to get. Graham was so preoccupied with logistics and so busy trying to guess what angle Caitlin was going to try to weasel out of him that he almost missed what she said.

"I'm sorry, Ms. Bishop — what was that?"

"I said thank you."

Graham was now genuinely puzzled. This was not the Caitlin Bishop he knew.

"For helping me out in Simons's mansion," Caitlin explained, pouring her words into Craig's silence. "You could have exposed me, but you didn't. I appreciate that."

Part of Graham wondered if this was Caitlin's way

She Demons 339

of buttering him up before going for his jugular, but the rest of him was convinced by her sincerity. Almost....

"Yeah, well, you're welcome," he said awkwardly. "I, ah, suppose that's why you sat on your story about Thad being a police informer?"

Caitlin smiled to ease the painful truth. "Not really. I did that for Jinnah. He told me there was a larger truth."

Graham grinned. "Well, thanks anyhow. You have the bigger truth now."

"And a better story. Now, off the record, what really happened here?"

Graham's grin blossomed into the first full-fledged smile he'd cracked since getting the call to go down to The Corner what seemed like an eternity ago. This was the Caitlin Bishop he knew after all. Sort of....

"Slow down. You fed the Yaksha bastard magic mushrooms and what? Acid?"

"That and ecstasy, if you can believe it," said Jassy.

"And a hit of mescaline too, don't forget," added Andy.

Jinnah shook his head and wrote it down, scarcely believing that he was in a position to do so. Or that Jassy Singh was actually granting him an interview of her own free will.

"Okay, so you surprised Andy's guard in the office, whacked him on the head, forced him to strip naked at gunpoint and then force-fed him this hallucinogenic

340   *Donald J. Hauka*

cocktail. You waited until he was totally flipped out before sending him out as a decoy. Brilliant. But whose idea was it to rig the bags of heroin to the climbing ropes at the top of The Wall?"

"That was Jassy too!" cried Andy. "Jassy came up with the whole plan! The tripwire ropes, the prophets hiding at the top of The Wall — everything!"

"And the ear-splitting music covering the noise of the preparations at the top of The Wall? Incredible! But how the hell did you convince the prophets to let you go in the first place, hmm?"

"I told Joel and the others they'd left guarding me that Daisley had killed both Thad and the Magus, and was tied up with this American drug cartel, and that if they were smart they'd get their asses outta here. They wouldn't believe me until a couple of prophets who had followed Arnie and Ray into the woods came back and told us what had happened at the bridge. They started listening after that."

"But how did you sucker them so thoroughly? Why did you let them into the compound? You must have known they meant to kill you!"

"I took a page out of the Yaksha's book, Jinnah. I presented them with a vision that they wanted to see. They wanted to see docile, doped up disciples who were easily cowed. So that's what I showed them — an illusion."

Jinnah shook his head in admiration. Kali had been right — Demolay should never have left her forest fastness to challenge Jassy on her home turf.

"So, you two have agreed to help the police with

She Demons 341

their inquiries?"

Jassy and Andy nodded.

"And after that?"

Jassy put a sisterly arm around Andy. "We are going home to our families, Jinnah," she said.

"And in future, I expect you to fight for your charter rights!"

"Charter rights mean squat when the cops seize something as evidence, Whiteman! I was out in the middle of nowhere. It's not as if I had a lawyer. I can't pull a restraining order out of my ass, for God's sake!"

It was late, past deadline, but most had stayed well past the end of their shift to witness this moment. The betting line was six to four that Jinnah would at least be suspended — ten to one that Whiteman would fire him. The reporter and the editor had been going at it hammer and tongs at the city desk every since the front page had been put to bed. Frosty, caught in the crossfire, was holding her throbbing head in her hands, wishing fervently they would just shut the hell up so she could slide across the street for a drink. But Whiteman, who had seen Caitlin's "exclusive report" from the Wilderness Camp, showed little sign of letting go of this particular peccadillo.

"The police had no right to seize that camera! I suspect you didn't argue very hard when they did."

"There wasn't anything on it, for the love of God!" cried Jinnah. "A few jiggly images of Jassy going into

342   *Donald J. Hauka*

the camp, then I put it in my bag and forgot about it."

"You admit that it still recorded audio! Everything that was said! Perfect for the paper's website —"

"If you want to get Demolay and Daisley and their gang off for publicizing evidence, sure! Go ahead, put Demolay's confession on the worldwide web. See how long it takes the Yakshas's lawyers to file for a mistrial. Sonofabitch!"

"Jinnah —"

"Boss," Frosty cut in. "I have a few questions for the chase edition, if you don't mind."

Cut off in mid-tirade, Whiteman's lips quivered for a second, ready to burst. But in an instant he had calmed himself. He looked at Frosty coolly and said, "Carry on, Ms. Frost."

Turning on his heel, Whiteman was aware that every eye in the newsroom was on his back as he walked slowly towards his corner office. He could feel the hostility directed his way, burning into a spot right between his shoulders.

He allowed himself a small smile before pausing at his door, turning, and addressing the whole of his staff. "Good work today, Jinnah. There's an open tab at the club until closing time."

Whiteman closed his door, secure in the knowledge that while Jinnah may be the hero of the moment, he was still the Lord of the *Tribune*. And that an angry and insulted Jinnah would not rest on his laurels. Or ask for a vacation. He had just enough time to work on tomorrow's promotion before sauntering over to the club to toast Hakeem's success. I wonder what sort of a follow the sonofabitch comes up with. Doubtless something about the family — after all, the funeral was tomorrow....

"Two counts of first-degree murder, multiple counts of conspiracy to commit murder, multiple counts of forcible confinement, conspiracy to traffic in narcotics — Jesus, is that all? They'll be out of jail in no time!"

"Not a chance. Andy and Jassy will be testifying for the Crown. I hear that Arnie may cut a deal too. And if Daisley doesn't sing like a canary just to sink Demolay, well, I have sadly misjudged the man's lack of character."

"Deadly dance partners — how do you dream up this shit?"

Frosty and Jinnah were alone at city desk. The mention of free booze at the club had emptied the newsroom. Jinnah knew that Frosty would follow them soon. But he also knew there was something she was dying to ask him first, privately.

"I found it curious that you didn't name either Jassy or Andy. And I didn't see their faces in any of Caitlin's footage, either."

"Neither did Whiteman. I think that's what he's actually pissed about. Not that stupid digital camera."

"Are you gonna answer me or do I have to take your byline off the second edition?"

"Frosty, Frosty — they are lost children who have been found. Give them their homecoming in peace, hmm?"

"How long is this joyous homecoming going to last? They'll both be in Witness Protection before you can say 'Yaksha hit team.' Probably getting their names changed already."

"Not before they reacquaint themselves with their parents," said Jinnah. "I suspect the Yakshas will be busy amongst themselves for a while, finding a new boss she-devil. Nature abhors a vacuum. The interim belongs to the children."

"That oughtta wrap it up nice and tight," growled Frosty, hitting the send key. "No loose ends for a change."

"Oh, there's a few, actually," said Jinnah. "But not for publication, hmm?"

The Moss Street Temple was ablaze with light. Jinnah, dressed in his finest, basked in the special glow that surrounded Manjit. Beside them, Saleem looked about in wonder at the crowd: young and old, dressed in a mix of traditional and modern clothes, moving like a human river through the doors for the morning service of Diwali, the festival of lights.

"So good of you to come, Hakeem," Manjit whispered to him for the tenth time. "And look at your son! It's as if he'd never seen Diwali before."

Before Jinnah could spoil the moment by observing that it likely was the first time Saleem had seen Diwali or attended to the celebrations without having his goddamn nose in his goddamn Nintendo DS or

She Demons 345

some other goddamn electronic device, he and Manjit were greeted by a beautiful young woman wearing a fabulous white sari.

"Sat Sri Akal, Jinnah-ji," said the angelic figure, salaaming. "Greetings, Mrs. Jinnah. And you too, Saleem."

It took Jinnah a second to recognize Jassy Singh. And to record her parent's presence right behind her. Mr. Singh's eyes were full of tears.

"Thank you, Mr. Jinnah for giving our daughter back to us!" he cried. "Gone for so many years. Now she is home."

A pang shot through Jinnah as he looked into the eyes of Jassy and her parents. It wouldn't be a long reunion. Witness Protection would see to that. He groped for words to say.

"It's only fitting," he finally replied. "The time was right, Mr. Singh. Diwali is a celebration of reunion and freedom after a long captivity, is it not?"

Jassy gave Jinnah a hug. Hakeem felt his cheeks burning.

"Will you come inside with us, Jinnah?"

"I must respectfully decline," said Hakeem, carefully avoiding Manjit's eye. "I have performed my duty to the living. Now it is time to deal with the dead."

Jinnah shook Mr. Singh's hand, bowed before Mrs. Singh, and, blowing his wife a farewell kiss, pushed his way through against the current of humanity and out of the temple, leaving Manjit to explain that Jinnah, as usual, had business to attend to.

* * *

Holy Rosary Cathedral is perhaps Vancouver's most beautiful Catholic church. On those rare West Coast days when the sun shines through its stained glass windows, it is a space that can transport the believer into another world. On this day, however, the world was too much with the sacred structure and the pews were packed as Thad Golway was laid to rest a week after his death. The number of mourners was swelled by the presence of the media (all desperately chasing Jinnah and Caitlin's stories and hoping to pick up a few crumbs) as well as the police, led by Graham, who sat rather ostentatiously right up front between the two reporters of the hour, Hakeem Jinnah and Caitlin Bishop. Normally, Jinnah sat at the back so he could survey the crowd and make a quick exit, if necessary. But he had pulled a few strings to secure seats right behind the Golways. Just behind Hakeem sat the Reverend Hobbes, looking stoic and stricken and very alone without his God Squad. Hakeem was no stranger to Christian churches — he'd covered many a funeral in his time — but this was the first one where he had actually stopped writing his next story in his head long enough to pay attention to the service. Thad's coffin, covered in flowers, was at the very front of the church. In the pulpit, framed by the stained glass windows, a white-haired priest was giving the reading.

"Then the King shall say; 'I was hungry, and you gave me food; I was thirsty and you gave me drink.'"

Jinnah instantly recognized the verse. Gospel of Matthew, Chapter 25. He'd heard it at more than a

She Demons 347

few funerals during his career. But this time, the words lifted off the page and seemed to fill the air....

"And the righteous will answer him: 'Lord, when did we see thee hungry and feed thee, or thirsty and give thee drink?'"

Jinnah thought of The Corner. The MiMi's outreach centre. The langar at the temple. And of Lionel Simons. And he felt the tears well in his eyes.

"... when did we see thee sick and in prison and visit thee?"

The rest of the service passed as if in a dream as Jinnah felt the grief, horror, and joy of the last week wash over him like an uncontrollable tide. His eyes were blurry and his glasses foggy as he stood with the rest to watch the pallbearers, led by Mr. and Mrs. Golway, hoist Thad's coffin and carry it slowly down the aisle. Stumbling, he followed as they filed out behind the coffin and he found Graham had a hold on his elbow.

"Steady, Hakeem," he whispered.

Jinnah wiped his eyes as discreetly as he could as he moved along in the flow of mourners, passing pew after pew, recognizing colleagues, cops, the curious. And in the very back, he was moved to see Sam and several of the squeegee kids from The Corner. Then he was out the door and he saw to his horror that the Golways were at the head of the steps, shaking hands with everyone as they filed out, paying their respects. He found himself shaking Mr. Golway's hand and without words, the grieving father told Hakeem with his eyes that it was all right, nothing to forgive now, it's done. Mrs. Golway hugged him.

348 *Donald J. Hauka*

"Go with God, Mr. Jinnah," she whispered.

Jinnah nodded and, blinking back tears, somehow managed to make it to one of the stone pillars at the top of the stairs. From this vantage point, he watched as first Caitlin then Graham shook the Golways' hands. After a moment's hesitation, Graham put an arm around Caitlin's shoulders and steered her towards Hakeem.

"Jinnah, you look like you need a drink," smiled Caitlin.

"I'm dying for a cigarette," said Jinnah. "Jesus, what's with me? Crying like a baby, for God's sake!"

"You've fallen into the story, Hakeem. We all do, once in a while — we're only human, after all," said Caitlin softly.

"We've all been through a little bit of hell in the past week, buddy," added Graham. "Especially you."

"A week in hell? A small sacrifice, my friend," Jinnah said, taking a deep breath and pulling himself together. "There are those who spend a lifetime in the flames."

At that moment, the squeegee kids reached the Golways. Without hesitation, the couple shook hands, smiling at these, Thad's friends. And Jinnah, the toughest sonofabitch cop reporter in the city, had to fight the tears back again as the Priest's final words echoed in his head.

"And the King will answer them: 'Truly, I say unto you, as you did it to one of the least of these my brethren, you did it to me.'"

"Absolutely goddamn right," muttered Jinnah. "Absolutely right!"

Frosty's comment about loose ends had been increasingly bothering Jinnah as the funeral service

She Demons 349

progressed. He had thought that the usual story he filed around the ritual of death would tie things up nicely. But he had been wrong and the nagging feeling that there were still threads dangling from the narrative had grown to a full-fledged conviction. Lionel Simons had told Jinnah that the heavenly kingdom was spread upon the earth and now Hakeem realized that this kingdom included the garbage and the flowers of The Corner. But the people, the general public, did not see it. Who was to be their eyes? Jinnah saw clearly that there was a crime in progress down on The Corner. Not the individual muggings, drug deals, and thefts, but one long, slow mass murder. Well, he was a crime reporter, wasn't he? It was his business to tell stories, not just chase the front page headline. There was a new gospel to be preached from Main and Terminal. Jinnah had finally found the loose ends. He moved away from Graham and Caitlin towards the squeegee kids.

"Hey! Jinnah! Where the hell are you going?"

Jinnah, feeling totally restored, tossed back his head, pulled out his smokes and lit up. "I have a few packs of cigarettes to give out to my friends from The Corner," he said, words framed by blue smoke that floated like incense up to heaven.

Acknowledgements

Story based on the screenplay by Donald J. Hauka and Michael McKinley.

Also by Donald J. Hauka

Mr Jinnah: Securities
978-0-88882-231-4
$10.99

Hakeem Jinnah enjoys an ordinary life of working the *Vancouver Tribune*'s crime beat, flirting with women, seeking interested investors in a mail-order-bride scheme, and driving around in his satellite-guided Love Machine. But when he and another *Tribune* reporter begin competing to cover the story of a shady stock promoter's death, he finds himself embroiled in a murder investigation.

This entertaining and suspenseful debut introduces us to an unforgettable lead character. Mr. Jinnah, a politically incorrect but resourceful reporter, proves to be a wily and relentless investigator. Hindered in his pursuits by the police department, Mr. Jinnah searches out the truth in an increasingly bizarre investigation. Meanwhile, he and his cousin seek their fortune in a scheme to marry Russian peasant women to wealthy Chinese men.

More Great Castle Street Mysteries from Dundurn

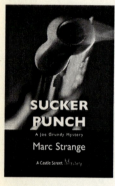

Sucker Punch
Marc Strange
978-1-55002-702-0
$11.99

Joe Grundy is an ex-heavyweight boxer whose main claim to fame was that he got knocked out by champ Evander Holyfield. Now he's chief of security for a posh old hotel, the Lord Douglas, in downtown Vancouver, and life is pretty good. But then a young neo-hippie inherits more than half a billion dollars and decides to give it all away. As soon as the kid checks into the Lord Douglas with the intention of holding a press conference to announce the scheme, Joe knows big trouble is headed his way, especially when the kid winds up dead.

Grundy sets out to discover who murdered the would-be philanthropist only to collide with suspects and sucker punches around every corner. Joe had some pretty tough battles during his days in the ring, but this time the stakes are higher, the opponents are lethal, and the final count could be fatal.

Blood and Groom
Jill Edmondson
978-1-55488-430-8
$11.99

Someone in Toronto has murdered nearly bankrupt art dealer Christine Arvisais's groom-to-be. Former rock band singer and neophyte private investigator Sascha Jackson lands the case because she's all Christine can afford. The high society gal was jilted at the altar and she's the prime suspect, not to mention Sascha's first major client.

In order to trap the murderer, Sascha enlists her ex-boyfriend and former band mate to pose as her fiancé, but will her ruse make her ex the next victim on the hit list and lead to her own untimely demise?

Available at your favourite bookseller.

What did you think of this book?
Visit *www.dundurn.com*
for reviews, videos, updates, and more!

Marquis Book Printing Inc.

Québec, Canada
2010